Utopian Pasts and Futures in the Contemporary American Novel

Hell aus dem dunklen Vergangnen
Leuchtet die Zukunft hervor.

From the first verse of
Brüder, zur Sonne, zur Freiheit
(Hermann Scherchen, 1918)

For Anselma, Anton, and Marlene

Utopian Pasts and Futures in the Contemporary American Novel

Tim Lanzendörfer

EDINBURGH
University Press

Edinburgh University Press is one of the leading university presses in the UK. We publish academic books and journals in our selected subject areas across the humanities and social sciences, combining cutting-edge scholarship with high editorial and production values to produce academic works of lasting importance. For more information visit our website: edinburghuniversitypress.com

Edinburgh University Press Ltd
The Tun – Holyrood Road
12(2f) Jackson's Entry
Edinburgh EH8 8PJ

Typeset in 10.5/13 Adobe Sabon by
IDSUK (DataConnection) Ltd, and
printed and bound in Great Britain.

A CIP record for this book is available from the British Library

ISBN 978 1 3995 1914 4 (hardback)
ISBN 978 1 3995 1916 8 (webready PDF)
ISBN 978 1 3995 1917 5 (epub)

Contents

Acknowledgements

I began writing this book late in 2012, after the re-election of Barack Obama: a less thrilling occasion than his 2008 victory, but still a moment imbued with a certain limited sense of hopefulness, if a negative one, stressing the possibility that no matter how small the advances, it would be hard to dial them back. No expectations of a utopia to come but still a sense that progress was possible. Its first draft was done in the summer of 2018, a year and a half after the inauguration of Donald J. Trump, after Brexit, after the rise of right-wing populism across much of Europe, when hope was far from every rational mind. It began to wind its way into publication in early 2020—in the middle of a global pandemic whose final consequences are impossible to sketch and may range from a revolutionary communalism in which our being thrown back on ourselves identifies for us the importance of the social, or alternatively propels more right-wing takeovers. Its final draft was completed in March 2022, in the middle of Russia's invasion of Ukraine, a war made in commitment to restituting a past, rather than shaping from its darkness a future. In other words, still a time to hope.

This is far and away the most difficult study I have written; whether it succeeds at what it sets out to do, I cannot be the judge. But I need to acknowledge a variety of debts incurred in its writing: members of seminars taught using material from the book at the University of California, Davis, in the fall of 2016, and in the spring and fall of 2017 at Johannes Gutenberg University, Mainz, Germany. General thanks are due to my former colleagues at the Obama Institute for Transnational American Studies at Mainz University, who read a draft of the Introduction and of the first chapter in the summer of 2017, and in particular Dr. Nele Sawallisch, who also read a draft of Chapter 6 attentively. Audiences of conference talks on the topics of Chapters 1 and 2 at the University of Lincoln, UK, and the University of Brighton, UK, were helpful in sharpening these chapters' arguments. I am grateful to Sabina Vogel for a crucial thing. Thanks are due to Schott Music for permission to use the epigraph to this book. Finally, I want to thank the anonymous readers for Edinburgh University Press for their insightful and rewarding comments, and the editorial staff at EUP for being a constant support in getting this book to print.

My most important debts, as always, are to my family. This book is dedicated to them, my wife Anselma, my son Anton, and my daughter Marlene.

Introduction

Speculative Historism, Visible Historical Futures

In Shalom Auslander's novel *Hope: A Tragedy*, Solomon Kugel and his family move to the village of Stockton, a town "famous for nothing" and "unencumbered by history." The Kugels have "chosen Stockton because history had not" (2012, 14), seeking escape from their past. Stockton promises the Kugels a "new start" (15). A bad smell in their new house turns out to come from octogenarian Anne Frank, who has spent the past sixty-five years hiding in the attic, working on a novel. Anne proves an obnoxious squatter, unable to accept being the poster child of Holocaust memory. At the novel's end, Solomon saves Anne from a fire in which he himself perishes while Anne goes on to haunt a different family moving to Stockton in order not to have to think about anything but her own personal future, and to write a novel that no one will ever read.

Chris Bachelder's 2006 novel *U.S.!* also enacts the return of history in the body of a writer. Upton Sinclair is literally resurrected repeatedly by left-wing activists and repeatedly assassinated by those out for fame and fortune. Sinclair's brand of Socialist agenda seems to have lost both mass appeal and the ability to mobilize social change, but even so, Sinclair keeps writing, keeps lecturing, keeps sending letters of protest. In its engagement with embodied history, *U.S.!* formally enacts a withering and broad critique of American life. It uses Sinclair's presence to portray an America that has abandoned Leftist politics. Sinclair's resurrections set this society in relief, declaiming a progressive stance by implicit contrast. And in *U.S.!* novels, at least tentatively, effect change: at least one conversion to the Socialist cause.

"[T]he content of a given historical moment enables or limits its representational form, or better still, its narrative possibilities" (Jameson 2013, 264). I depart from this observation to analyze a major phenomenon in the contemporary American novel, the use of elements from popular, speculative genres to reactivate the political potential of history in contemporary literature. *Hope* and *U.S.!* stand as markers of two different contemporary approaches to history in fiction. *Hope* is a historical novel in the narrow, quasi-realist sense, a simple alternative history. "Why not a famous survivor in Stockton," Solomon asks after his first encounter with Anne, "[i]t wasn't impossible" (35). *U.S.!*, by contrast, from the first page avows that it is speculative: Sinclair was dead and now lives again. The shift of perspective enabled by the explicit avowal of speculative narrative structures permits history to function again as a source for alternative and utopian visions of the future and marshals the potential for thinking thoughts that are seemingly unthinkable today, of potentially radical political, social, and economic change.

Hope's is alternative history, in as much as Anne Frank did not live out World War II, but minimally so, and it does not breach the basic realist ontology of the historical novel. An octogenarian, the math of Anne's survival works out; and as she cannot prove her survival, cannot prove that she is, in fact, Anne Frank, she remains dead to everybody else—indeed, it remains possible to the end to doubt that she really is Anne Frank. *Hope*'s limits will help us understand what is at stake in what I call speculative historism. It connects a number of issues that will remain relevant to this book: the Kugels' desire to escape history and their belief that such a thing is possible, the apparent failure of this ultimately reactionary desire, and its titular conclusion that hope is tragic, are all tied to its quasi-realist narrative form. In that form, the intrusion of a historical figure into the present points to the limitations of its realistic narrative. It links the desire to escape history—rather than make use of history—with a refusal to commit to speculation formally.

The Kugels aim to escape their personal history, the near-death of the youngest member, Solomon's son, which drives the family to seek out Stockton as a place without history, as though they could there escape the specter of death. Anne Frank, sitting in her attic, is driven by the realization that her sole achievement, as far as history is concerned, is having written a diary and then having been murdered. As she realizes, her death is vital in this context. She has spent sixty years writing a novel to prove that it was "the quality of her prose" (215) that made her diary enduring. She is not just an avatar of the inescapability of history that *Hope: A Tragedy* emphasizes; she is also an avatar for *Hope*'s own sense that the writing of fiction cannot be socially effective any more than history can have a positive effect on the present. Anne's novelistic quest to write enduring prose is as doomed as the desire to escape history, whose traumatic effects keep pulling the Kugel family down and apart. History in *Hope* is narrow and personal. Anne's very survival ensures that her historical legacy becomes obscured: the novel presents her as an obnoxious, delusional, spiteful old hag, whose literary ambitions end up producing reams of unpublished and unpublishable fiction, precisely in an effort to leave history behind. "I'm sick of that Holocaust shit. I'm going back to my novel, Mr. Kugel, I'm a writer, not some goddamned essayist" (333). If her diary was a powerful reminder of the dangers of fascism, Anne's new project goes no deeper than to prove to the world that she is a writer: to sell again "thirty-two million copies" (214) of a book. She is uninterested in literary agency, in writing about history, or in making a political point.

Hope constantly reinforces the sense of futility which this project engenders: as Solomon notes, "I don't think people read so much anymore" (217). A similar idea is voiced in *U.S.!*: "Nobody reads" (57), as an exasperated resurrectionist of Sinclair's notes. But Sinclair, accused by reviewers of not understanding that "art and polemic" do not mix, still keeps turning out his ill-selling, poorly written novels. His personal persistence pays off symbolically when his writing recruits a precocious young boy to the Socialist cause, and the constant circle of assassinations and resurrections gets broken. The novel ends on hope, suggesting the importance of Sinclair's constant resurrections, the writing of politically engaged fiction, and, in effect, the importance of drawing upon history to gain a sense of utopian promise for the future. *U.S.!* produces a sense that literature can actively shape contemporary politics, and that contemporary problems are intimately connected with historical trajectories, capable of solution but only through the mobilization of a utopian imagination. Both novels are satires; in both, history intrudes in the form of living individuals to interact with the present, historically important figures, of "historical names" (Jameson 2013, 291). But *Hope* and *U.S.!* require us to read their central writer-figures as representing different beliefs in the efficacy of the novel form to engage with social reality and different conceptions of history. It is no coincidence that these different views are realized by these novels in two formally distinct ways. *U.S.!* draws its capacity to imagine a hopeful future precisely from its speculative nature, its fantasy conceit that Upton Sinclair and the Socialist tradition for which he is made to stand can be interminably resurrected. *U.S.!* connects two apparent impossibilities: those imposed on literary form by a realistic mode of representation (you cannot have a literary novel with fantastic elements) and those imposed by the limits of a larger capitalist realism on the imagination of political and social alternatives to the existing order (you cannot have a different politico-economic system). *Hope: A Tragedy*'s explicit insistence on its own realist possibility is symptomatic: stuck in the double rut of contemporary realisms, both its literary and capitalist manifestations, it cannot but truck on. Thus, in its epilogue, Anne sits again in an attic above another young couple's house, probably still writing a novel, because history is "too damned much to bear" (340). The eponymous tragedy of *Hope* is that there is no hope: no sense of a future in which things are better, no sense in how the Kugels' unique encounter with history can contribute to such a better future.

The novels of speculative historism, including those discussed below, follow *U.S.!*'s pattern of tying speculative conceits to historical consciousness. Speculative historism is understood here as a literary form registering the cultural and social developments after the turn of the last century, a form of literary intervention mobilizing the potential of literature to imagine hopeful and notably different futures. Tying into a larger "rebirth of history" (Badiou 2012), the form stands on a historical trajectory from the ostensible "end of history" (Fukuyama 1992) as well as the rise and fall of postmodernism. Speculative historism not only conjoins the genres of historical-realist literary and speculative fiction, to use shorthand, in the manner of the oft-cited "genre turn" (see Rosen 2018). If this were all it did, we might reasonably claim for it little more than a status as a new publishing phenomenon. What distinguishes it is the production of what Jacques Rancière calls a "heterology," in which "the meaningful fabric of the sensible is disturbed: a spectacle does not fit within the sensible framework defined by a network of meanings, an expression does not find its place in the system of visible coordinate where it appears" (2006, 63). Rancière argues that "[s]uitable political art would ensure, at one and the same time, the production of a double effect: the readability of a political signification and a sensible or perceptual shock caused, conversely, by the uncanny, by that which resists signification" (2006, 63). This suggests immediately why speculative historism must be connected to a desire for political change even on purely formal grounds. To be speculative, to break the boundaries of realist fiction, shifts the framework of a realist network of meanings.

I am interested in the broadest conception of the question: "What kind of history can the contemporary historical novel be expected to 'make appear'?" (Jameson 2013, 263). And what kind of hope can a contemporary utopian novel make visible? My texts are "contemporary novels which are profoundly historical" (Jameson 2013, 264), but refuse the realism of the historical novel. To be "profoundly historical" is to have an awareness of history's force on the contemporary (Lukács 1983); it means to be fully within the historical moment, and to realize that nothing happens out of time and context-less (Huehls 2018). Even this minimal intervention is already meaningful, given this contemporary's place at the end of the various beliefs in an endless present.

Speculative historism may be merely the most radical expression of such historicity: it understands history as a necessary ground for an engagement with the present, notwithstanding doubts about the possibility of ever getting at the "actual" history.

From the End of History to the Return of History (by Way of Postmodernism)

Writing in 1992, Francis Fukuyama famously argued that we were at the end of History, having witnessed the triumph of liberal democracy, and with it, of neoliberal capitalism, the "economic manifestation" (44) of that system. "Today," he notes, "we have trouble imagining a world that is radically better than our own, or a future that is not essentially democratic and capitalist" (46). Fukuyama offered an influential narrative for an age of "endisms" (Sim 1999, 12): "[D]espite our objections to it on various grounds, usually ideological, everyone largely accepted that he was right" (Thompson 2013, 2); "widely derided," Fukuyama's diagnosis was "accepted, even assumed, at the level of the cultural unconscious" (Fisher 2009, 6).

"Endist thinking fits in very neatly with the cultural movement known as postmodernism" (Sim 1999, 14). Despite disagreements as to the exact nature of the end of history and its precise form, "the implicit or explicit presence of such expectations for the future has been the bond that gave a measure of coherence to the many varieties of postmodernism" (Breisach 2003, 11). Jean-François Lyotard had earlier defined postmodernism as "incredulity toward metanarratives" (1984, xxiv): an end to all kinds of totalizing narratives, beginning with the general idea of historical progress and ending in the truth claims of scientific knowledge. Lyotard also speaks of History: the notion that there is a greater, explanatory philosophy at work towards an "ethico-political end" (xxiv), a "grand narrative" with emancipatory power trending towards an ultimate and ulterior goal. "The grand narrative has lost its credibility, regardless of what mode of unification it uses, regardless of whether it is a speculative narrative or a narrative of emancipation," which he directly links to the consequence of the "redeployment of advanced liberal capitalism, [. . .] a renewal that has eliminated the communist alternative and valorized the individual enjoyment of goods and services" (37–38). The demise of the Eastern bloc signaled the demise of one of the most powerful metanarratives, Marxism: "[Marx's] grand narrative has been tried and found severely wanting, and we have in consequence nothing more to hope from it" (Sim 1999, 23). The coincidence of "nothing more to hope" and the ineffable accession of liberal democratic capitalism as argued by Fukuyama is telling. Fukuyama's notion of the end of history affirmed precisely the kind of metanarrative of progress that Lyotard denied—but the consequences were the same as far as their proclamations against the emancipatory narratives of Marxism were concerned, and in their shared disregard for the hopeful narratives of utopian imaginations of the future (see also Jacoby 2000).

Fukuyama's argument highlighted the now-global reach of the capitalist market system, the "closing of the global frontier of capitalism" (Wallerstein 1998, 93). Hand in hand with the triumph of the idea of the end of history went a similarly pervasive belief: that, as the saying goes, it was easier to imagine the end of the world than it was to imagine an end to capitalism. The ascent of postmodernism and the end of history were thus linked to the death of utopia conceived as a radical vision for a hopeful future, a future increasingly impossible to imagine.

The end of history thesis and the state of postmodernity are both tied to the literary imagination of the past. As Peter Boxall points out, to "locate oneself 'after' postmodernism is to orient oneself in relation to a phenomenon whose cultural power has rested to a considerable degree on its cancelling of the distinction between before and after" (2013, 58). Fredric Jameson writes, "It is safest to grasp the concept of the postmodern as an attempt to think the present historically in an age that has forgotten how to think historically in the first place" (1991, ix). Postmodernism's answers are "historical fantasies" (368), shorn of any relation to a historical referent and solely concerned with the representation of "our ideas and stereotypes of the past" (25). History, with a capital H, vanishes behind its pop images. In its place we get what Linda Hutcheon calls "historiographic metafiction," which "while teasing us with the existence of the past as real, also suggests that there is no direct access to that real which would be unmediated by the structures of our various discourses about it" (1988, 146). History's end, that is, is not just a political fact at the end of the Cold War, it is also a narrative necessity: while you can meditate on the writing of history, you cannot ever access history anymore (though cf. Parrish 2008; Cohen 2009; Löffler 2015). There is an important correlation between how liberal democratic, capitalist triumph at the end of the Cold War is understood and the "waning of our historicity, of our lived possibility of experiencing history in some active way" (Jameson 1991, 21) as a more general diagnosis of the postmodern moment, as "the cultural logic of late capitalism," a totalizing socioeconomic mode. Such a reading turns to the challenges to the economic hegemony of neoliberal capitalism that came to the fore with the Great Recession of 2008. If postmodernism is truly buried, then it is buried by economic shifts (see Nealon 2012). This is crucial in conceiving of a reason for the return of the historical imagination in the contemporary moment, which has seen challenges not just to liberal democracy but more notably to neoliberal capitalism's triumphant narrative.

The failure of this narrative propels the quest for other utopias, utopias not coincidentally difficult to come by in postmodernism. "There is little of the Utopian in the postmodern" (1988, 215), Linda Hutcheon points out, a judgment that is widely shared (see Brooks and Toth 2007, 2; Tally 2013, 3). This belief cannot be understood without reference to the systemic determinants under which it takes place. For adherents of the end of history thesis, utopia necessarily lost its force: after all, utopia was already here, or at least an already more hopeful future, "the easing of the sense that a terminally bad time [. . .] might be just around the corner" (Cohen 2009, 192). Postmodernism could hardly imagine a better future in its perpetual present. To the contrary, as Mathias Nilges points out, it has "become the dominant language of contemporary capitalism" (2021, 194). Both of these variants of imagining oneself in a good place have no use, and no access, to genuinely hopeful thinking, specifically as a function of their approach to history.

Inverting this argument, then, one of the ways in which the novels I discuss are after postmodernism is exactly their interest in hopeful futures. History engages hopeful thinking by destabilizing our expectations of a "future that is the same as our present" (Jameson 2009, 415). It shows us a past in which the expectations for that past's future are noticeably different from our present, or else by pointing to the often miniscule and contingent, certainly not inevitable, events that shaped that past into our future. It is "the past that furnishes us with the resources of hope, not just the speculative possibility of a rather more gratifying future" (Eagleton 2015, 32). The utopian function of history is thus, paradoxically, not the affirmation of the necessity of a particular historical trajectory but rather the foregrounding of contingency. In the disavowal of one *grand récit*—the notion that history must repeat itself if played out again, because it is structurally determined, because it inevitably leads to one end, and one end only—lies the possibility of resuscitating another, an emancipatory story in which *Hoffnung* may yet persevere.

Speculative Historism and the Contemporary Moment

Speculative historism is the form of that story: a story readable only in conjunction with its moment. As Fredric Jameson has argued, "the emergence of a full-blown new genre or subgenre constitutes an indubitable fact, a symptom of some more general historical displacement" (2015b). But what is speculative historism's form? "Speculative" obviously picks up from discussions of speculative fiction, and if I have not defined the precise nature of the "speculative," that is because I am interested in use and interpretation, for which distinctions between non-realist modes are unhelpful. Critics have increasingly agreed on the possibility of all kinds of non-realist modes to offer alternative visions whose political potential lies in the particular content they offer, not in the modes themselves (see, for instance, Suvin 2000; Miéville 2002; Jameson 2005). "Speculative" is the catch-all term for the non-realist—in other words, the term is used here to highlight what the differentiable modes of non-realist narrative share, rather than puzzling out where they differ, largely because they differ little in the ability to offer utopian visions of the future. The choice of term also permits me to include texts that badly fit categories, where traditional taxonomies fail. The major formal connection between the texts I discuss in this book then is essentially a negative one: none of them are realist in the conventional sense, they all present in narrative something that is, "in reality," impossible. Speculative historism challenges and interferes in the particular kind of reality that is constructed by contemporary capitalist realism, that realism which does not even permit the mere imagination of alternatives to its societal status quo (see Fisher 2009; Shonkwiler and La Berge 2014). Speculative historism formally and thematically disavows both the aspiration of mimetic representation and the sociopolitical insistence on a system without alternatives. It replaces these with literary-formal and thematic innovation that declares the need to rethink the possibility of hopeful futures in both the literary and the political realm.

"Speculative" here has useful echoes that might be kept in mind besides its sense of generic inclusivity. It suggests links to discussion of the interrelation between literary form and speculation in finance, which themselves raise questions of "the insufficiencies of both postmodern and realist strategies" of representation (Shonkwiler 2017, xi). These questions have often been read somewhat narrowly, identifying speculative fiction with science fiction (see most of the essays in Carroll and McClanahan 2015 and Higgins and O'Connell 2019). Here, as in the use of historism, my terms aim to be more inclusive. "Historism" somewhat facetiously picks up and shifts the ideas of "speculative realism" (Saldívar 2013) and "speculative formalism" (Eyers 2017). Indeed, Ramón Saldívar's concept addresses many of the issues I explore in detail, especially the importance of the specifically historical embeddedness of texts, and his idea of "historical fantasy" names something close to speculative historism but insists on this form's ethnic specificity. Other strands of utopian criticism such as Afrofuturism (Bould and Shavers 2007; Womack 2013; Zamalin 2019; Lavender and Yaszek 2020) or indeed queer futurity (Muñoz 2009; Jones 2013) are helpful modes of thinking about the capacity of literature to imagine the future. Yet they tend to reduce future thinking to science fictional thinking, and to sectionalize it through recourse to identitarian configurations. I identify a broader, wider attempt at forging alliances by ways of a more expansive literary–genre amalgamation across identitarian and class boundaries. This book's mode of engagement—close reading in considerable depth—means that it will only be able to argue exemplarily, but it nonetheless claims to detect a meaningful formal constellation in contemporary fiction.

I take speculative historism to enact formally the contemporary political moment in which (still) we appear to stand at a threshold of possibilities. It is the "immediate crisis of our time that began in 2006" (Harvey 2011, 78) that propels the potential dissolution of postmodernist historical logics, the end of history thesis, and unrepentant faith in the global economic system at the same time, propels the dissolution of capitalist realism, in fact. In this term, the condition of cultural work and the economic coincide. The "corrosion of the social imagination," as Jodi Dean has it (in Fisher and Dean 2014, 28), is one of capitalist realism's major achievements: it trades heavily on the idea that it is without alternative. But "when capitalist realism as a general ideological formation fails" (Fisher in Fisher and Dean 2014, 26), the possible modes of representation change along with it. Capitalist realism and the system which brought it forth as a literary formation shared in their "repudiation of any utopianism" (Fisher in Fisher and Dean 2014, 34). Conversely, the increasingly critical view of the capitalist economic system after the Great Recession is suggestive of the increasing failure of capitalist realism's claim to hegemony and the opening of possibility in social space. The failure of capitalist realism as an ideological formation, as "the only [thinkable] viable political-economic system" (Fisher in Fisher and Dean 2014, 26), is also the moment of the end of the end of history, where the sense of the need for a valid systemic alternative has again begun to grow. In Alain Badiou's formulation, the contemporary moment is a "*time of riots*, a rebirth of History, as opposed to the pure and simple repetition of the worst," and simultaneously the "rebirth of the Idea" (2012, 5–6, original emphasis).

I second Andrew Hoberek's wager that the Great Recession "will ultimately prove the most significant event[] in early twenty-first-century literary history" (2017, 237). But I would also stress that literature is not "after" these events, though it may be the events that make literature's timeliness readable. Rather than privileging the economic or political realm by suggesting that literature can only react to its developments, I hold with the possibility of tracing in literature original developments, of moments which anticipate reactions to developments which the "real world" will yet have to go through: registrations of the smaller shocks preceding the quake. The post-millennial return to the mobilization of history for the imagination of various hopeful futures did not depend on an earth-shattering and foreseeable crash of the economy, but rather was already ongoing, and in this sense becomes genuinely symptomatic (see also Shapiro and Lazarus 2018, 8). It is wider than the riots, understood as singular moments and events. Behind the rebirth of history stands a renewed, communal challenge to the existing system. History in Badiou's capitalized sense is "the emergence of a capacity, at once destructive and creative, whose aim is to make a genuine exit from the established order" (2012, 20). It is the matrix of this established order that forms the framework for my investigation. I certainly do not suggest that all current engagements with history in the contemporary novel seek a "genuine exit" from that order, but some texts do, and are intimately concerned with the ways history may function as prefigurations of a utopian future.

I derive from Alain Badiou and Jacques Rancière a sense of a renewed importance of history, the belief in the literary text as a site where it is possible to remain faithful to the idea, and an argument for the vitality of an exploration of literary form as the symptomatic mediation of such events and ideas. At the heart of my argument rests a claim to the power of literature: the power to keep alive, or return to life, the belief in a better future, which it is impossible to think ahistorically. Badiou's philosophical terminology—communism, history and the "historical," the inexistent, the visible ("what is merely visible should not be considered genuinely given" (2012, 98))—can be made useful to reading speculative historical fiction. For Badiou, the reborn "Idea" is "an egalitarian, rational figure of collective organization for which the name is 'communism'" (9), "a society that is radically different because subtracted from the sway of Capital, normed by equality and governed by the free association of those who constitute it" (64). Communism is a situation in which "action can be driven by the conviction that another political, collective and social world is possible, a world in no way founded on private property and profit" (Badiou 2013, 14–15). "[T]he event," then, "the historical riot, is a break in time—a break in which the inexistent appears" (70). Badiou argues that we are in an "intervallic period" which, "running from 1980 to 2011 (and beyond?)" (40), is marked by the dominant insistence that "things have resumed their *natural* course" (39). If the demise of alternative visions for the future signaled the end of history, the revival of the alternative vision, of the Idea, signals the potential rebirth of History, understood as "the emergence of a capacity, at once destructive and creative, whose aim is to make a genuine exit from the established order" (15). Badiou's point is that riots which we witness in the contemporary political arena signal the "possibility of a new situation in the history of politics" (27), and this is what makes them "historical." They open to "visibility" the mass of people whose plight has gone unnoticed in the post-Cold War normalization of capitalism, reaffirm the potential resurrection of the greater Idea in and through the individual event, and point towards the possibility of returning to "the idea of History its full meaning, charged as it is with sustaining and validating radical political options" (36).

Event and Idea are key terms in Badiou's lexicon, and are related to two others: Truth and Fidelity. (A note on capitalization: "fidelity," "truth," and indeed "idea" are not much of a problem in the following. Event, however is somewhat awkward. I'll therefore capitalize Badiouan Events. Secondary sources do not always follow this practice, however, and I have chosen not to emend them.) In Badiou's thinking the Event involves "the creation of a possibility"; the name of this possibility is Idea, "that which, regarding a given question, proposes the perspective of a new possibility." As Badiou summarizes, an "Idea is associated with an event because the event is the creation of a possibility and the Idea is the general name of this new possibility" (2013a, 14). Fidelity names something like staying true to the possibility the Event creates, which is also always taking up an engagement. Through fidelity, expressed in the realms of love, science, politics, or art (Badiou's "truth-procedures"), Truth—the ultimate expression of the possibility contained in the Event, or in Badiou's words, the "the generic set of the evental consequences" (70)—is constructed. Truth, Badiou argues, is "an undertaking," a way of collectively organizing our view of the world. But it is also "concrete," as he has it: "it is what we make of" love, politics, literature, and so on. Truth, finally, "makes it possible for the subject to exist" (145), the subject which "consists, precisely, of this new orientation of experience rendered possible by an inaugural event" (49).

Badiou's thinking references the "present politico-aesthetic situation" (2013a, 78), a term which already suggests his belief in the necessity to read political and aesthetic concerns in tandem. Badiou sees the ideas of a possible "end of art" and the "end of history" as related, and suggests that "[w]e're in an artistic situation that's altogether confused and uncertain because we are in an interval period when art's forces will have to be reconstituted in an infinitely more affirmative modality—one that's infinitely more bound to real processes and political proposals" (77). What is involved here is, crucially, the possibility of a "new Idea of what a given art is" (74), one whose shifts are produced by individual artistic events; in turn, the "artistic event is signalled by the advent of new forms" (69). Thus, in the contemporary situation, Badiou sees the most promise in "experiments [which] attempt to catch hold of shreds of the real by the formal means available and to affirm, within the formal resources of art, something regarding the contemporary world" (77).

Events become evental only ever retrospectively. That is to say, the fidelity to the idea that they create is what makes them Events in the first place. In the words of Jean-Jacques Lecercle, "when an event occurs, since it is indiscernible, evanescent and unnameable, it can only be grasped in the future anterior, *it will* have occurred, and it will be grasped retroactively through a process of enquiry" (2010, 168, original emphasis). This dialectic of temporal registers is suggestively linked to historical fiction already, narratives which narrate events that already have occurred, but which, at the same time, only will have been written in the future, from the narrative's perspective. Such narratives then function generally analogously to the way events become Events, in as much as the events narrated were not, at the time of their occurring, part of a narrative, especially when the process of their literary mediation is itself foregrounded explicitly. The utopian potential of past events, then, lies in the ability to be reframed as Event, and thus as a source for a new truth about the world.

In the cosmos of truth-procedures, all of which follow Badiou's progression from the Event to the subject, literature appears to stand out: "literature seeks to capture an event which has not occurred in its own field, it has a representative rather than a presentative form" (Lecercle 2010, 138). Literature may pick up on Events which "properly" belong to other truth-procedures, of which the most important for my purposes here, unsurprisingly, will be politics. Literary texts may not only "be the site of an event" (158) but also offer a "staging of its consequences" as well as the "general conditions of all events," not as mere representation, but as a pursuit in its own right of the truth of these Events. Lecercle raises this point in the context of fantastic fiction (and recognizes, as do I, the "deviations from the straight and narrow path of Badiou's theory of the event" (165)). In a fantastic text, "[s]omething emerges [. . .] that makes manifest the void on which it is based, something impossible, an embodied paradox, an unnameable element" which is "the incarnation and the trace of an event, the event, whether it be creation, metamorphosis or quasi miraculous emergence, that gave birth to it" (164). I suggest that both versions of the literary registration of the Event are usefully brought to bear—"put to work" (166)—on speculative historism. The Event figures in these texts as a literary staging of a historical—political—

Event. Read like this, *U.S.!* can be read as itself producing fidelity to the idea which the Event of the emergence of a Socialist consciousness in the early twentieth century germinated, a means by which history becomes relevant again for the contemporary moment by figuring it, retrospectively, as a "source" for an Event. And these Events are often staged as themselves fantastical, in Lecercle's terms, whether they are Junot Díaz's "fukú" or Joyce Carol Oates's "Crosswicks Curse." Badiou's categories, then, of Event, idea, fidelity, and truth serve as a means of making sense of the relation these texts sketch between their historical imaginaries and the contemporary moment, a way of naming the way in which history becomes (again) meaningful for a contemporary situation.

Badiou himself refers to the ultimate consequence of the production of Truth as a postfactum "reconstruction of the visible" (2013a, 71). Jacques Rancière and Fredric Jameson offer complementary views. Speculative historism can be understood on the one hand as the formal realization of what Badiou sees as making visible the "existence of the inexistent" (2013a, 56) by representing the realistically unrepresentable. Literature, as Badiou has argued, "can name a real to which politics remains closed" (qtd. in Apter and Bosteels 2014, ix). What is politics, though? For Rancière, it is

> the cluster of perceptions and practices that shape this common world. Politics is first of all a way of framing, among sensory data, a specific sphere of experience. It is a partition of the sensible, of the visible and the sayable, which allows (or does not allow) some specific data to appear; which allows or does not allow some specific subjects to designate them and speak about them. It is a specific intertwining of ways of being, ways of doing, and ways of speaking. (2010, 152)

To reframe the sensible, to make visible the invisible, is politics; literature is part of the system in which the sensory data of lived experience is framed, it is, in this sense, always and already political. This is clearly not unrelated to the Badiouan notion of the event; shifts in politics in this sense become possible when there is, as Badiou notes, "a minimal sense of rupture [. . .]. You have to have the conviction that something needs to be done that escapes the law of the world" (2013a, 3). Such a rupture would be what Badiou calls an Event, "something that brings to light a possibility that was invisible or even unthinkable" (2013a, 9). For Rancière, the question of form necessarily intrudes here. Different forms of literature make different things visible differently (2006, 13). Literature itself is, to Rancière, "a certain way of intervening in the sharing of the perceptible that defines the world we live in: the way in which the world is visible for us, and in which what is visible can be put into words, and the capacities and incapacities that reveal themselves accordingly" (2011, 7). This relationship between form and politics, Rancière notes, is a matter of choice: and, he suggests, the choice of "plastic or narrative devices can be identified with an exemplary political awareness of the contradictions inherent in a social and economic order" (2006, 61). The grounds to read politics and literature together is that they both "construct 'fictions', that is to say material rearrangements of signs and images, relationships between what is seen and what is said, between what is done and what can be done" (2006, 35).

Badiou and Rancière provide the theoretical backdrop to what follows: their thinking about how literature, politics, and the contemporary interrelate, as I will show below, is deeply apropos of the work that speculative historism does even as it offers suggestive frameworks for reading it. What I want to do in the last few pages of this Introduction is offer a working through of this reading framework, which I dub "utopian hermeneutics."

Utopian Hermeneutics, or: Reading for Hope

Reading the figurations of history in the contemporary novel is necessary work. The utopian imagination inheres as much in the works themselves as in our reading—our interpretation—of them, if indeed Ernst Bloch is right that "the quality of our cultural heritage and its meaning are determined by our ability to estimate what is valuable and Utopian in works of art" (Zipes 1988, xxxvi). From capitalist realism we have come to the contemporary moment, in which the rebirth of history coincides with an increasing sense of the coming end of postmodernism as a cultural dominant and of the need for a utopian imagination in the face of structural crises in the neoliberal capitalist system. And this need for a utopian imagination is firmly tied in the contemporary to the speculative historist form, and our ways of reading it, in particular of reading it for utopia.

I consciously use "utopia" and "hope" more or less interchangeably in what follows, understanding that they span a spectrum of responses to the contemporary that we must read jointly. For Bloch, hope is "the imagination and the thoughts of future intention," which become utopian when they are perceived as "*directing acts of a cognitive kind.*" It is, as it were, *rational* hope, "in the newly tenable sense of the forward dream, of anticipation in general" (1995, 1:12, original emphasis). Speculative historism harbors an inherent utopian impulse. When it imagines hopeful futures, it does so in a world in which the utopian impulse is constitutive of human existence. Rather than establishing only *if* such an impulse is operative in any particular text, I aim to reconstruct *how* it is operative, and what it means. In literature, as Darko Suvin defines it, utopia

> is the verbal construction of a particular quasi-human community, where sociopolitical institutions, norms, and individual relationships are organized according to a more perfect principle than in the author's community, this construction being based on estrangement arising out of an alternative historical hypothesis. (2010, 30)

Utopia in literature is always *something*, or rather *a* thing, a concrete version of a better community, realized in its particulars. Suvin's utopia is always *concrete*, "a real possible future" (Levitas 2010, 15). This is one meaning of Suvin's "alternative *historical* hypothesis" (my emphasis): against the wishful, and ungrounded, abstract utopia, the concrete utopia realizes that "although the future is open, in that there is a range of real possibilities, it is not unconstrained" (Levitas 2010, 15). Speculative historist texts' grounding in a historical past bespeaks their realization that to merely imagine a better future, without adequately grounding it in a historical logic, is futile. "Historical" here suggestively encompasses both the sheer fact that there is historical content of some kind and the meaning of the historical content as such, which is to require us to understand past, present, and future as contingent. Finally, Suvin's invocation of estrangement sets us firmly in speculative territory. Suvin here invokes his own argument, taken from Brecht's *Verfremdungseffekt* and the Russian formalists' notion of *ostranenie*, that science fiction is the "*literature of cognitive estrangement*" (Suvin 1977, 4, original emphasis), but meaningfully abandons the idea of cognition, by which Suvin explicitly differentiated science fiction from fantasy and myth. Estrangement serves to set a recognizable "reality" against something unfamiliar, what Suvin dubs a "novum," a concrete instantiation of the "new," here understood as exactly an "alternative historical hypothesis." It may be clearer now why I want to retain both the systematizable idea of utopia as well as the broader sense of hope. Much can be hopeful, and indeed, utopia is merely a concretization of hope writ small; but hope does not fully suffice to explain the formal procedure which speculative historism provides in the way that utopia does. Suvin's own understanding of utopia is indebted to Bloch, from the notion of the "cognitive" which echoes through both thinkers' arguments, to the concept of the "novum" by which both designate the concrete new that shifts the visibility of the possible, to the idea that this novum can be simply a future set firmly in an alternative historical hypothesis.

None of the texts I discuss are utopian narratives in the sense of the tradition from More to Bellamy to LeGuin. Given where we are coming from—a place where utopia as such was deemed impossible—it would be surprising to see these texts engage in the immediate construction of utopian communities. This is why I invoke hermeneutics. The texts propose the possibility of a better world as a readable possibility, an interpretative possibility. To think of my engagement with these texts in terms of a utopian hermeneutics (cf. Muñoz 2009, 19–32), a reading *for* utopia, thus helpfully brackets a variety of positions on contemporary literature. By shifting the question of where utopia resides to the side of interpretation, any worry about whether you can still write utopian fiction in the present comes to be immediately less important. Reading, interpretation, and hermeneutic attention can still draw hope from a text.

Reading is contested ground today. Critics have sought to decenter hermeneutic reading in favor of various postcritical stances (see Best and Marcus 2009; Di Leo 2014; Felski 2015; Levine 2015; Moi 2017; Anker and Felski 2017; Anderson, Felski, and Moi 2019; Felski 2022; cf. Lanzendörfer and Nilges 2019; Nilges and Lanzendörfer 2023; Robbins 2022; Tally 2022). Postcritique embodies the very set of concerns that I have identified above with our immediate past of Fukuyama and postmodernism. As Stephen Best and Sharon Marcus admit, their argument for surface against symptomatic reading is in part due to being "skeptical about the very possibility of radical freedom and dubious that literature or its criticism can explain our oppression or provide the keys to our liberation" (2009, 2). Surface reading "hopes to freeze time" (Lesjak 2014, 27) in its disavowal of context (see Felski 2011), and freezing time amounts to an eternal present, ahistorical and futureless. In postcritique's embeddedness in the present private moment of reading, in its attention to momentary affective responses and in its desire to displace the already-historical because ultimately materialist conception of literature as symptomatic, it is more in line with the postmodern, posthistorical, postutopian commitments I have sketched above. The disavowal of hermeneutics in postcritique corresponds with a disavowal of utopian hope.

As Carolyn Lesjak points out, when you shift away from symptomatic reading and models of depth to surface reading and postcritique, the "hermeneutics of suspicion is replaced by a suspicion of hermeneutics, a disavowing of interpretation itself" (2014, 26). What is at stake in postcritique is the foundation of this study, which does insist on interpretation. I want to see where bridges can be built. I take up postcritique's call to take texts "seriously in their own terms" (Felski 2015, 6). Utopian hermeneutics of the sort I am advocating here takes the utopian impulse of the texts I discuss seriously, especially that of texts fully inscribed into the realm of "genre fiction." To take texts seriously is a precondition for reading them as utopian in the first place. To take genre fiction seriously as a locus for utopian thinking in contemporary writing permits us, given genre fiction's spaces of reception, to understand how widely the renewal of utopian engagement has permeated literature. As Phillip Wegner points out, "to read for Utopia involves developing both a more attentive practice of reading [. . .] and openness to a wider array of narratives" (2020, 17). Texts such as *Ready Player One*, which, especially after Steven Spielberg's feature film, was panned for its grave flaws, are part of such an opening, part of a recognition that the utopian imagination need not be fully realized to be perceivable, and to be meaningful to a novel which might casually have been said to have no meaning at all.

All the same, to read for utopia in the sense in which both Ernst Bloch and more recently Ruth Levitas have used the term cannot be done without reference to the socioeconomic and sociopolitical situation of its production: "In practice, utopia as a hermeneutic method returns us time and again to the social" (Levitas 2010, 16). Peter Thompson has suggested this most clearly for the contemporary moment:

> We are in a Gramscian interregnum in which the old world of the absolute hegemony of capitalism and its ideology is dying, but a new world, or even the semblance of a new world, has not yet emerged to replace it. What is important with Bloch's work now has therefore changed since the first conception of this book. Whereas once it was conceived as a counterblast to the shimmering illusions of the bright satanic mills, now it has become a way of maintaining the "principle of hope" against a growing darkness and uncertainty. (2013, 2)

If the utopian is the "overtaking [of] the natural course of events" (Bloch 1995, 1:12), we may see here speculative historism's capacity of resistance, its destabilizing of the assumption that things will simply go on as they are—or get worse, as Thompson suggests.

The ways in which this utopian potential is mobilized are multifarious and complex. My aim here to take seriously the limited utopian impulse of some of the texts I discuss below is in line with Fredric Jameson's old point. A "Marxist negative hermeneutic, a Marxist practice of ideological analysis proper" must in the practical work of reading and interpretation be exercised simultaneously with a Marxist positive hermeneutic, or a "decipherment of the Utopian impulses of these same still ideological texts" (1983, 286). Such a reading method still exercises an interpretative reading for meaning, and it is already tied to ostensibly more affirmative modes of reading. As José Esteban Muñoz notes, "Utopian readings are aligned with what [Eve Kosofsky] Sedgwick would call reparative hermeneutic" (2009, 12). It is still "decipherment" (Jameson 1983, 288): the "Utopian impulse calls for a hermeneutic: for the detective work of a decipherment and a reading of Utopian clues and traces" (Jameson 2009, 415). Such a hermeneutic is necessarily extensive and pays thorough attention to the text. Ideally, it requires knowledge of and access to the texts under discussion, a communion over the actual text, presence in "the same plane as readers," so as to produce the conditions for "the 'minimal communism' of real and productive dialogue" over the "totality of the text" (Wegner 2020, 47). This book, then, is avowedly for readers of its primary texts, enjoins readers to also read those texts (rather than just this book), even as I believe the texts are also exemplary of the crucial strands of speculative historical literary engagement. The utopianism of utopian hermeneutics entails not just claims to fiction's utopian potentials, but also the hope present in the act of shared discussion of these claims' merits. Utopian hermeneutics foregrounds the principles of hope operative in the texts I discuss, and the need for extensive, attentive, close reading. It presents a dialectical relationship between text and criticism, as it is the utopian hermeneutics that produce the text as speculative historism at the same time as the texts' formal features justifiably allow us to read them through the lens of a utopian hermeneutics. Such a utopian hermeneutics, then, is itself a making visible in the Rancièrian sense, a means of reframing what it is we see when we look at these literary texts. It is, in that sense, also avowedly political: you cannot read this way without yourself looking for a better future world.

The Structure of this Book

A number of threads run through this book. One is the importance of the 1980s as both a point of origin for the contemporary neoliberal economic paradigm and its problems, and by extension its potential role in envisaging a useful past. Another is an engagement with Socialism, in various forms, as an overt other and a realm of possibility in the contemporary moment, rescued from obscurity by repeated reference to its past promise, and often embodied, as in the way both *The Accursed* (Chapter 2) and *U.S.!* (Chapter 3) employ the figure of Upton Sinclair. A third is the variety of different intended audiences, identified with different modes of reading and often understood to be quite separate. The final thread is the underlying question of the entire engagement with speculative historism, which is the development of a form adequate to describe the contemporary moment's resurgent interest in thinking, to pick up from Darko Suvin, "more perfect" futures.

Against this backdrop, each chapter addresses specific cases of contemporary speculative historism in depth, and twice, reading two books against one another, while seeking to advance the general arc of my argument for the development of speculative historism. This arc's trajectory begins and ends with texts which are, only very slightly speculative: Ken Kalfus's *Equilateral* (Chapter 1) and Colson Whitehead's *The Underground Railroad* (Chapter 6), both of which provide narratives hinging on grandiose construction projects of tentative realism. In Kalfus's text, it is the possible existence of Martians which marks it as more than just a historical novel; in Whitehead's, it is the confusion of temporal moments and the inscription into a variety of registers of speculative fiction including the grand underground construction project of an actual railroad. I speak of an arc between them advisedly here, for the study does move in something like a parabola: the books it discusses first become more overtly speculative and utopian, indeed more fundamentally critical of the contemporary (Chapters 1 through 3) and then turn back to books where speculation is more tentative and less overtly utopian (Chapters 4 through 6). That arc also traces (not perfectly in lockstep) a move to more overtly generic and popular texts, only then to return to more overtly literary ones.

The point of the trajectory is to understand speculative historical form and genericity as linked to public receptivity and the literary field, to understand narrative forms and utopian arguments of "genre" texts as linked increasingly firmly with those of the "literary." To do so is to ultimately read them as becoming "the same," but not without understanding how they also have remained—and potentially continue to remain—distinct. To do so is also to see the ways in which different texts have negotiated conceptions of speculative historism as a form. Speculative historism operates formally, then, but also within the logics of the literary field, two dimensions my account of the mode aims to reproduce. At the same time, by the final chapter, the idea of the literary–genre–literary parabola, its utility in naming what is practically happening in speculative historism, may itself be questioned. Rather than moving from one mode to another, up and down a sliding scale of literariness, we should be able to recognize these texts as being shortchanged by any desire to link them to hierarchies of value founded on genre. Genre comes to be decentered in this narrative: what is foregrounded, instead, is these texts' shared engagement with the construction of utopian pasts and futures. In the final analysis, the heuristic of the parabola may vanish behind the idea of different texts' negotiation of a form commensurate to a shifting sociopolitical moment: speculative historism itself may come to be foregrounded in its negotiation of a form that not just narrates but produces hope.

Chapter 1

At the Edges of Realism: Ken Kaltus's *Equilateral*

In Ken Kalfus's 2013 *Equilateral*, set in 1894/95, a huge project is underway to excavate an equilateral triangle in the sands of the Great Western Desert at the Egyptian–Libyan border, each side of which is a trench measuring 306 miles long and five miles wide. The trenches will be coated in pitch and then filled with petrol, which, lit, will be used to make contact with an advanced civilization on Mars. The novel's protagonist is the (fictional) astronomer Sanford Thayer, a disciple of the (historical) Italian astronomer Giovanni Schiaparelli, who, observing Mars in 1877, saw its surface covered with what he called "canali," rendered in English as canals. Cut in what appeared to be great circular routes around the planet, these canals seem to connect the polar regions of Mars with its equatorial deserts. Astronomers observe, around those canals, a "seasonal thickening and darkening of the lands adjacent" (15), suggesting the growth of vegetation. The conclusion is that there exists a civilization in decline on an increasingly desertifying planet Mars, a civilization more advanced than Earth's. In their desperate quest to find enough water on their planet, the Martians have advanced far beyond humanity. Thayer's plan is to make contact with that civilization, for all the benefits such contact will bring.

The Equilateral project brings together the money and power of six European countries, the United States, Egypt, and the Ottoman Sublime Porte. It is better funded than the Suez Canal, and has mobilized nearly a million men. It is "the greatest international peacetime undertaking in the history of man" (13). Yet the motivations for this shared endeavor could not be more different. For Thayer, they are idealistic. He calls Mars "this planet of heroes, pale and fragile" (24). To achieve what it has achieved, Thayer believes, Mars must be advanced both in terms of technology as well as in terms of social organization. In the wake of its catastrophic desertification, Thayer believes that Mars's internal strife has been replaced by a planetary struggle for survival: "The contest has become a supremely civilized one. It depends on worldwide cooperation, the rational organization of the classes of labor, individual altruism, the promotion of the sciences, and the elevation of irrigation science as the highest art" (24). Meanwhile, the so-called Mars Concession, the conglomerate of commercial interests that actually finances the excavation project, is interested largely in trade: it seeks Mars's markets and its technologies for its own monetary gain.

Central to the novel is the question of the ontological status of that Martian civilization. None of its characters doubt the validity of the observations made, and the entire effort, with its immense mobilization of money, men, material, and imagination, hinges upon the existence of the Martians. But the novel remains highly ambiguous on whether or not they actually do exist, ending on a moment that serves to highlight ontological uncertainty. *Equilateral* is centrally about the imagination of the future, and it connects the possibility of a utopian future to the possibility of both seeing and imagining an alternative, outside position: in its case on a different planet. Set before the beginning of the twentieth century, its historical perspective permits the imagination of a completely different trajectory to historical events. Mars's civilization, and that civilization's discovery of a common danger that exceeds and ultimately successfully causes its inhabitants' "destructive impulses [to be] subsumed" (24) under the imperatives of collective survival, function as an outside position to the existing economic and political systems on Earth. They are capable, at least in Sanford Thayer's imagination, to work as a catalyst for the development of a similarly utopian system on Earth.

I will focus on two major aspects of *Equilateral*'s presentation of this issue: first, the ways the novel makes use of the idea of vision, understood both as the act of seeing and as the act of imagining beyond the seen. The novel's discussion of the links between seeing and imagining are not just necessary to unravel to understand its own stance, but usefully prefigure the discussions of later chapters and the way in which literature itself opens new ideas to view. Then, I will note how *Equilateral* works as a critique of one of the most pervasive narratives of cultural development today: the idea of transnationalism, with its at least implicitly emancipatory gesture of global interconnection and understanding a utopian ideal that is not a challenge to neoliberal capitalism but a necessary consequence of it. Kalfus's novel gestures towards the hope for a better future while suggesting that such hope may be misplaced within systems that will merely perpetuate the existing. *Equilateral*'s critical yet hopeful vision depends on its speculative historism. Its historical setting permits it to set the clock back to a time when it was still possible to imagine an outside, and its speculative ontology permits this outside to look radically different.

"Everything worth seeing lies at the edge of visibility": Mars, Martians, and the Imagination of Utopia

Equilateral's fantastic rests on readers' knowledge that no Martian civilization exists. But this is based on empirical knowledge: we know it does not, but we only know this historically, we only know this *now*. The characters have no doubt about the existence of Martians; to them, the novel's events are not fantastic. It is this tension the novels holds throughout, between readers' position in history and the novel's placement of its narrative before the shattering realization that the outside position signified by Martian civilization does not exist. The novel's speculative historism depends on this connection between the time of reading and the historical setting, on the recognition that it is *now* fantasy to imagine Mars as the promised land, but that in the not too distant past—before the catastrophes of the twentieth century—such an imagination, and all the utopianism which it entailed, was possible.

Mars figured prominently in the scientific explorations of astronomers in the late 1800s and early 1900s, but also in the popular imagination: ever since Schiaparelli's publication of a map tracing the various lines which he had seen on the planet, astronomers had built an image of Mars in the mirror of Earth. They saw in their telescopes geographic features which they read in analogy to those they knew on Earth. By 1894, Percival Lowell, the American astronomer after whom the character of Sanford Thayer seems partially modeled, argued that the "canali" of Schiaparelli's map were evidence of intelligent life on Mars. The indications of geographic manipulations visible even from Earth were that these inhabitants had created a major, technologically advanced civilization: contact with them, as Lowell and others thought, might usher in great progress on Earth as well (see Lane 2010, 1–21). If it could potentially become the source of technological advances, at the same time, the red planet also figured as a projection space for different conceptions of societal development. Lowell believed that the inclement conditions of life on Mars would necessarily have produced a society that managed to leave behind strife and war and, blessed with advanced technology, found itself in full social harmony—a harmony of necessity, forced upon them by the growing desertification of their planet. "As an evolutionary wonderland of advanced technology and peaceful social relations," K. Maria D. Lane notes, "Lowell's Mars stood as an example and beacon for the Western world [. . .] the red planet must be an utopia of sorts" (178).

Lowell's exuberance, set against a range of critics arguing essentially the opposite, highlights the "deep implication in philosophical debates" (Lane 2010, 185) which Martian civilization had. For the characters in *Equilateral*, Mars functions as a screen on which they can project their various expectations, desires, and hopes for the future. To Sanford Thayer, the purpose of the project of contacting Mars is twofold: as a matter of purely practical benefit, contact and communication with Mars will help counteract what he believes is the necessary evolution of planet Earth. Thayer thinks that "it's in the nature of planets to lose their water as they age" (70), yet this is a problem that Mars appears to have solved through its canals: this is their "promise and dread" (21). If the fate of planets is a steady decrease of their water supply, Mars's dryness also suggests its age. Its age suggests the necessary progressiveness of its civilization: it harbors a civilization which "must be superior in technology, morals, and interplanetary manners" (41) thanks to the workings of a progressive cultural evolution. In this argument, Thayer echoes Lowell.

It is this progressive cultural evolution that is at the heart of Thayer's second, more utopian purpose in making contact with a Martian civilization. Because of its age and what Thayer believes is the ultimate logic of evolutionary theory, Mars must be "home to a race in which the forces of natural selection have enjoyed further millennia to secure positive social traits" (72). It must have produced a society which "will be the force that makes us truly civilized, truly kind to each other, wise, prudent, responsible to the natural world, courageous in facing our global challenges, and paradoxically, truly human" (73). In many ways, finding possible content for these vague phrases is the development which Thayer undergoes (the phrasing "global challenges" seems anachronistic, but points to the way in which history functions to illuminate the present in *Equilateral*). This development is anchored both by his quest for Mars and his present in the Egyptian desert, events which help him develop precisely those hopes for which Mars is to be the fulfillment.

For Thayer, the experience of controlling the equilateral project is a steady conflict between his ideals and the project's necessities, his own initial social and moral beliefs and those which he develops. There are also the views offered him by his Western advisors, his amanuensis Adele Keaton and chief engineer Wilson Ballard, and those implicit but increasingly weighty through Thayer's contacts with his Egyptian servant girl and caretaker Bint, with whom he will have a child. Ballard represents most clearly the practical and self-assured side of the venture, with an unabashedly imperialist perspective. Thayer believes Ballard to see the Equilateral as "no more than another engineering project." The engineer is solid and staid, and unmoved by the "grandeur" of either the project or its aims (47). Ballard regards the local workforce as dispensable. He despises the Arabs with whom he works and against whose rebellions he acts, but remains cool and dependable: a solver of problems without regard for morals, and only a hint of disquiet at the "immaterial theory and desire" which underlies the entire project. After Thayer has regaled Ballard with the history of the equilateral triangle and its role as "the basis for all human art and construction," Ballard replies, "'Bloody difficult to dig, though'" (127). Similarly, Keaton is a calm and collected presence; she is "fully trusted as the single individual capable of keeping the entire scope of the undertaking, theoretical and practical, within her field of view" (20). She takes over the management of the project full-time when Thayer falls ill. Her unrequited love for the astronomer drives her, but she develops doubts in the course of the novel. Where Thayer remains convinced that Mars harbors an advanced civilization, Keaton's increasing inability to see the developments which Thayer (and Bint) regularly identify among the canals of the red planet makes her more and more uneasy—Keaton becomes, in the course of the novel, a quiet, but distraught disbeliever in Thayer's conclusions.

Thayer represents the imaginative force of the entire venture beyond the mere intricacies of logistics, politics, money, and workforce, beyond the realism of the everyday. To him, Mars "permits us a vision of our own future, existential and moral" (72). At least at first, however, the particular way in which Thayer imagines this future is hardly emancipatory. Thayer's politics is imperialist; but through his various interactions with the other characters, Thayer gradually develops a more nuanced understanding of the possibilities of the equilateral project as well as its necessary limits. Witnessing the execution of several mutineers, Thayer muses on the Martians' reaction to the scaffold, noting that given their necessarily advanced society, "they'll likely find it barbaric" (89); but such early scruples are easily overcome. While the construction of the project is at stake, while contact with the Martian civilization has not yet been established, Mars's imaginary past can still figure as a justification for Thayer's ruthless pursuit of his project, even to the extent of confirming his Spencerian world-view:

> The canal builders, in the course of their history, must have also contended with brutes who would have scuttled their race's progress. The construction of the water transport system on which life on the Red Planet depends would have required fierce determination. It would not

> have been put off by bourgeois morality. Rebellions would have been subdued, perhaps with force. Vast wars would have roiled the globe's surface. They would have included the mechanized butchery that has accompanied our own military strife, augmented by more advanced and more gruesome weaponry. So Mars will not judge us harshly. The planet's history will show that conflict was ended only through the application of the universal laws of evolution and natural selection, when the superior and inferior specimens of the Martian race diverged into separate species, as is inevitable on Earth. A race of savants and a race of slaves, with breakable necks or not. (93)

Despite the momentary quelling of his own impulse not to follow the tenets of Anglo-Saxon imperialist discourse, Thayer is increasingly disquieted by the possible reactions of the Martians to the violence the human race is capable of (96–98). Keaton seems to be the source of Thayer's own initial social conservativism, and the often racially charged and coded choices Thayer makes for the sake of the project. Faced with another delay, Keaton suggests appealing to human "competitiveness, instilled into man by his species' fight for survival. Every individual, even the lowliest Arab, needs to come out ahead of his neighbor" (113). Thayer adopts this proposal, and addresses himself to the Arab workers, tasking his listeners to pass on his message to their work companies. However:

> Given the peculiar ideas embedded within his rhetoric—for example, about how competition allows a man to find his place in the social order, as if God were unable to locate it for him—the speech will be misheard and distorted, bent to the cultural and religious mores of its audience. [. . .] By the time the message reaches the farthest segments of the Equilateral, it will bear no relationship to what was said [. . .]. (115)

Thayer, racked by his malarial fever, begins to realize much of this. He finds himself suddenly unconvinced by Keaton's underlying premise, by the claims to universality that she has made for evolutionary theory. Thayer's own thinking about the possibilities of imagining Mars shifts and becomes more questioning, more ready to imagine Mars as the locus of radical difference:

> If evolution is not a universal process, if competition is not a universal principle, if Mars is not subject to Darwinism, the planet's economy may have developed according to entirely different natural laws. How does Mars apportion its commodities and goods? What is the role of capital? Of labor? How is personal status attained? By what means are

> social hierarchies erected? Does Mars enjoy a gentler sex that raises its young and performs the traditional female duties? If not, then . . . (116, original ellipsis)

Thayer's shift into Marxist vocabulary is as striking as the implications of his ellipsis: Mars may challenge the naturalization of fundamental assumptions about social life on Earth and its future trajectory. Thayer's thoughts range across a spectrum of questions, not of answers: they open the possibility for thinking (implicitly) Socialism, of doubting the value of capitalism, of making personal status independent of upbringing and wealth, of seeing social hierarchies established on the basis of personal behavior (or altogether abolished), of an equitable distribution of gender roles, all without explicitly naming any of these alternatives. "If not, then . . ." is powerful: it hints at the consequences of abandoning the point of view of the imperialist Western world. What is more, the kind of Darwinism which underlies the what-if is not biological Darwinism, but the "universal" Darwinism which permits the extension of Darwinian or pseudo-Darwinian thinking into non-biological realms. The problems which Thayer's ruminations pose are not confined to Mars: if evolution is not a universal process on Mars, it is not a universal process, *period.* This insight undermines the entire world-view to which Thayer and the other characters adhere. Most notably, if competition is not a universal principle, then the entire edifice of capitalism on which Earthian society rests (then as now) is built not on immutable truth, but on contingent development. It is to see that the foundational logic of the system under which he operates may not necessarily be true.

Equilateral is a meditation on the strength and power of the imagination; the entire narrative is dependent on the human ability to imagine what is not, or may not be, or may not yet be, "really" there. The fantastic heart of *Equilateral* is its constitutive uncertainty about whether there is life on Mars. Thayer, Ballard, and even Keaton remain (largely) committed to their belief in a Martian civilization. But the novel plays with this belief and complicates it: it continually leaves open the possibility that all of the ostensible observations are merely collective delusions, wishful seeing of what is not really there. It ties together the possibility of a reality in which there are no canals with the characters' willingness to *see* such canals, and to make their decisions accordingly.

This willingness to "see" recalls the concern of both Alain Badiou and Jacques Rancière with the "visible": "[p]olitics, before all else, is an intervention in the visible and the sayable" (Rancière 2010, 37). To make "what was unseen visible" becomes the epitome of the political act: "it places one world in another" (Rancière 2010, 38). This discourse of the visible permeates *Equilateral* and becomes the major pivot around which the actuality of its extraterrestrial contact narrative as well as its politics rotate. This becomes especially noticeable in a scene in which Thayer, Keaton, and Thayer's servant Bint gather around the telescope to observe Mars once more. Thayer's effort to find signs of civilization, as usual, is initially unsuccessful: "Patience is required. The eye must accustom itself" (60). As it does so, Thayer becomes more aware of what it is possible to see on the surface: "before he's fully conscious of it, he discerns something stirring on the surface of the planet; no, it's beneath the surface, bubbling up. Vague ripples. Shadows. Shadows of shadows. They're there and then they're gone and then they're back, more emphatically" (61). As Thayer devotes himself with almost meditative patience to seeing new developments on the surface of Mars, he finally begins to make out features. Yet the language in which these discoveries are couched leaves clear their tentative nature: "'Something's there, I think,'" Thayer says. A line "appears to emanate from Agyre, at the edge of the dead sea—perhaps the vanguard of a waterway project," but only really readable as such "in the light of France-Lanord's [another astronomer's] sketches" (62). Astronomers' dim observations return in other astronomers' equally dim confirmations. The assorted changes to the landform that are related to the Martian excavation efforts are plentiful; new canals crop up with astonishing frequency in observations that are not readily repeatable (32). But "[n]ot a single canal has ever been distinguished in a photograph" (63). In contrasting the empirical reality of the photograph with the interpretatively open observations of the astronomers, *Equilateral* takes a stance on the power of the narrative imagination and hermeneutics: without a shred of "hard" evidence, Thayer has been able to convince and cajole the world into sponsoring his excavation project.

Thayer turns this impossibility to grasp the truth of Mars's civilizational status objectively into a major epistemological truth. Having done his observations, seen the things he was meant to see, Thayer asks Bint to take her own look at the red planet. "'Look well, Bint,'" Thayer encourages her. "'Everything worth seeing lies at the edge of visibility [. . .]. Every discovery lies within the standard error of measurement. The most important truths about the cosmos can hardly be separated from illusion'" (63). Bint, as Keaton notes, cannot be expected to understand Thayer, as she speaks no English; yet when she looks through the telescope herself, she apparently sees what Thayer sees. She draws onto her hand what Thayer and Keaton take to be the representation of precisely the features which they had seen before. This, as Keaton realizes, is extraordinary: "The first time laypeople observe the planet through a telescope they rarely see any landforms at all, not even icecaps" (65).

The novel points out the simple problem: the layperson's difficulty in seeing what Thayer, Keaton, and the other astronomers see "makes it difficult to convince skeptics of the canals' reality: '*I didn't see them, so they can't be there!*'" (65, original emphasis). The invisible becomes the impossible, the sensible determines the real; and to return to Rancière, the "one world" which the act of making visible "places [. . .] in another" here comes to signify the conjunction of two worlds, Mars and Earth, and the placing of the utopian world of Thayer's Mars in the reality of today. *Equilateral* in this sense re-presents a possible history of Mars. As Mark Fisher points out, "[n]o cultural object can retain its power when there are no longer new eyes to see it" (2009, 4). Fisher aims at the dialectical relationship between the established and the new generally: "the exhaustion of the future does not even leave us with the past" (3). In *Equilateral*, there is a direct relationship between a disavowal of seeing an object, a disavowal of accepting its existence on the basis of one's own individual sensory data, and a disavowal of the utopian consequences that develop imaginatively and interpretatively from the object's existence. If you cannot see the canals, you need not think about what they potentially mean; not seeing is disbelieving, and disbelieving is acceptance of (capitalist) realism.

Seeing, as the novel makes clear, is a process intimately connected with the imagination. Thayer, for example, knows

> [t]he corresponding visual weaknesses and strengths of his colleagues: whose eyes are capable of resolving close double stars but are unable to recognize faint shadings or patterns on a planetary surface; whose eyes are easily blinded by a disk's full illumination; *whose optic nerves are connected to brains of plodding imagination.* (178–79, my emphasis)

Seeing Mars's canals depends in no small part on the imagination, on a willingness to see them: it is doubly visionary. Bint, like Thayer, seems to see the developments that other astronomers have reported as taking place; Keaton fails to do so. The experience of having Bint see the canals on Mars on her first try, while she herself cannot, makes Keaton doubt, makes "a disquiet [tug] at her. Something she can't quite make out" (65). Not only does the idea of "making something out" suggest, once more, the issue of visibility; but here the process by which Keaton is replaced in the imaginative appraisal of the things to be seen in Thayer's telescope by Bint suggests precisely the necessity of periodically having new eyes see what the old cannot.

The novel keeps insisting on the conjunction between seeing and the willingness to see, between the visible and the imagined. Ultimately, the

Equilateral is completed; it is lit—during an attack by Mahdi rebels—slightly too early, slightly before the time at which Mars would be able to see it best, and before North Africa has turned to face the red planet, making its flash vanish into space, but it stays lit, and hopes can yet be entertained that Mars might react. Months later, when Earth and Mars are once more at the point of greatest proximity, Thayer sees something: an equilateral triangle, "conveniently situated to be observed from Earth" (180). This triangle, too, Bint appears to see, and draws onto her palm. Again, Keaton does not see it. She does not admit this failure: she "suspects that her inability to distinguish the Mars Equilateral lies within herself, and that this failure reflects a weakness more profound than a defect in her eyesight" (181–82). Indeed, this is very much the thrust of the novel, which has fused the two meanings of vision—seeing and imagining—in the person of Thayer. Keaton, now unable to see the Equilateral on Mars, is also unable to keep imagining the existence of Martians and all that is attendant upon this imagination.

The novel's ambivalent conclusion plays with this centrally important notion of seeing. With a Martian fleet presumably on the way, the Mars Concession's most eminent men congregate at the Equilateral, the obvious point for a Martian landing. Yet as time passes, and nobody can detect the Martian ships in their course from the red planet to Earth, people become increasingly unsure. Thayer's answer is disdainful: "'They can't see them! [. . .] The ships from Mars won't be any brighter than the twelfth magnitude until they're almost upon us. None of these instruments, not even Verzola's, will pick them up, certainly not with his vision. The man needs glasses. [. . .] And they won't show up on any plates either. They shouldn't waste their film'" (199). When the moment passes for which Thayer has calculated the Martians' arrival, the assembled dignitaries at the Equilateral grow uneasy but, significantly, do not leave immediately. They leave, rather, when Mars's journey around the sun takes it (as seen from Earth) into the solar glare, and it becomes lost from view. It is the sudden invisibility of the red planet that shifts the mood entirely, and doubled invisibility that the novel enacts here: "At daybreak, as blown sand starts to obscure the Equilateral, the British prime minister and the French president depart for Alexandria in separate caravans" (204). If Mars is invisible, now the Equilateral itself becomes lost in a sand storm, one that will last through the final moments of the novel; and the departure of the heads of state and government, emphatically in separate vehicles, becomes symbolic of the dissolution of international cooperation that the Equilateral project had engendered. The novel extends the symbolic obscuration of vision throughout these final pages: when Ballard goes to see Thayer, confined now to the infirmary, he looks in on Bint, in the final stages of her pregnancy. She is attended by Bedouin women in full robes, so that Ballard "can't see the girl" (204). He goes on to visit Thayer and realizes, with a start, that Thayer's illness has cost him his eyesight (205). And here, with Mars out of sight, the Equilateral hidden, Bint hidden behind a wall of local women, and Thayer blind, the novel concludes on a profoundly ambiguous note:

> A foreign howl, a prolonged wail, slices through the sickroom. It reverberates against the walls and shivers the windows. Ballard looks up abruptly, gazing through the open door into the hallway.
>
> Thayer falls silent. The cry, the first time this voice has been heard in this world, has penetrated down, down, down to him. [. . .]
>
> "They've arrived," he whispers, barely audible, and barely in the room. "They're here."
>
> Miss Keaton drops her head and stares into her lap.
>
> Ballard continues to look away, into the hallway. In the corridor the nurses hold their breaths. Carts brake on the plaza before the customs hall. The fellahin put down their packs and look up. A caravan driver raises a bony hand and a long, outstretched finger to order a halt. He listens. Men in offices lift their pencils from their documents and allow them to stay in place, hovering. Diplomats pause in their negotiations. No one speaks as they wait for the next signal, the inevitable call of life; intelligent, companionable, needful, rampant life. (206–7)

The novel demands two understandings of this scene. Thayer may be right: the Martians may have arrived, the Equilateral project may have been successfully concluded, the possibilities envisaged by Thayer and the Equilateral Concession may all become true. Or Thayer may be wrong: what we hear is not the wail of spaceship engines descending or the language of a landed Martian, but merely the first cry of his and Bint's child. There is room for either reading and for doubt about both: would a baby's first cry shiver the windows and cause the entire encampment to halt in its business? Perhaps not. Yet would not a baby's cry be more likely understood as "the first time this voice has been heard in this world" than a descending ship, or even the greetings of a landed Martian? Perhaps so.

The final scene may become more intelligible by recourse to Slavoj Žižek's reading of the fictional Event as an immanent event, one which needs no recourse to its relation to the outside (2014b, 203). It remains, to be sure, an Event in potentiality only, unresolved even on the novel's own terms. A Martian landing would be a "true" Event: the signal of a change "of the very frame through which we perceive the world and engage in it" (Žižek 2014a, 10). Instead of hypothesizing on the organization of Martian civilization, it would now be possible to experience it, and to understand the absolute possibility of different social organizations. But if this final "call for life" is merely Bint and Thayer's newborn baby? This would not spell the end to the possibility of Martian civilization, but it would signally reduce it. It would raise other—still progressive—issues (perhaps a stable relationship between East and West on Earth is possible). But I would suggest that all the readings possible in *Equilateral*'s ambiguous ending in fact are not to be resolved: Thayer's blindness itself suggests that the resolution of the external events one way or the other becomes unnecessary, embodying both the potential that vision is no longer necessary and that it is no longer possible.

Thayer's development, his increasing readiness to imagine Martian society as radically different, crucially does not depend on any actual encounter with this society: rather, it is a purely mental development, and his blindness marks this dimension. Thayer recognizes the limitations of his own thinking: seeing the world in evolutionary terms, he is unable at first to think beyond these limits. Mars's civilization will merely confirm the triumph of Anglo-Saxonism and the division of the world into rulers and servants. This is hardly an emancipatory stance to take. It is replaced by his increasingly progressive belief that the Martians may in fact operate under completely different social structures. What Thayer undertakes is an act of thinking, in Badiou's terms: "the construction of an idea that, according to opinion, is inconceivable, or can only appear as 'idealism'" (Reinhard 2013, xviii). Thayer's thinking is much in advance of the capitalist system which makes available the money for the construction of the Equilateral: it is radically opposed to it, envisaging an inconceivable society where "selflessness is imbued deeply within [. . .] character" (72). Thayer wavers uneasily, especially when the completion of his project is at stake. But ruminating upon the conditions of Martian existence has allowed Thayer to develop inconceivable ideas about the development of society on Earth. Thayer's vision of contact with Mars involves avoiding the declension narrative that he has produced for Mars, in which violent strife must precede the coming together in necessary harmony—this is the suggestion which controls Thayer's belief in the possibility to "learn" (72, 106, 184) from Mars. The novel connects the inconceivable idea that all is not strife with the act of seeing, so that seeing becomes doubly encoded and mutually reinforcing, endowed by the double sense of vision as a creative, forward-looking act and the mere recognition of the visible. Thayer's vision of the future and his seeing of Mars's canals are inextricably intertwined, and become reinforced by the fact that Bint, too, sees: sees in this double

Rancièrian sense. Seeing, vision, and visibility are the central metaphors for *Equilateral*'s readability as at heart utopian: they encode the necessity of the imagination and its ability to move, merely on the strength of interpretation, vast amounts of labor force and money, to go beyond the material and to envisage the future in terms of a radically different social system. By the end of the novel, this has become an internalized process: it is emphatically not required to see the future inscribed on the Martian surface, but the processes which this act of seeing has engendered in Thayer can now be fully internalized. This is also why a resolution of the ambivalent ending is structurally unnecessary: either way of resolving the question retains a utopian stance towards the future, either in the prospect of Martian contact or in the relationship between Bint and Thayer, and all that it implies. In this gesture, *Equilateral* prefigures what will return over and over in the discussions below, that the utopian moment does not inhere in utopian fulfillment, but in the opening of utopian possibility, and sometimes even in the opening of the possibility of beginning again after failure.

The relationship between Bint and Thayer brings me to my second point. Against Thayer's growing idealism, the novel sets the mundane conditions for the completion of his visionary project: the very movement of labor and money, the everyday acts of management, which make it possible in the first place to build the Equilateral and thus to make the necessary contact with Mars. In outlining the economic and political conditions of the project, *Equilateral* provides a critique of the idea of transnationalism, suggesting the limits to transnationalism as a contemporary utopian ideal.

"Mankind's solidarity": The Conditions for Transnational Utopia

Kalfus's novel interprets transnationalism in two ways. The first is the conjunction of the Equilateral project's aims, its location, its practical execution, and its imaginative power. The project "is" transnational in the sense that it aims literally beyond the concern of nations, outside the planet proper. It is located across the boundaries of Libya and Egypt; it is executed by a corporation—the Mars Concession—which consists of an international assemblage of financiers and controlling interests; it is imaginatively aimed at sublating the nation into a unified Earthian community capable of solving the problems of humanity. To this last point, add the imaginative power of the idea of Mars itself across national boundaries as represented by the novel's insistence on the different nationalities of the astronomers who confirm the reports of developing canals, from Giovanni Schiaparelli himself (an Italian) to Thayer and the French astronomers Camille Flammarion and Hector France-Lanord (16). In all of these aspects, the novel establishes an underlying interest in transnationality.

The second way in which the novel "is" transnational is much more personal: Thayer and Bint's increasingly intimate relationship, an intimacy both physical and psychological. It is a celebration of the possibility to communicate across conventional boundaries, of which some are in the first place transnational (class, religion, and education) and some are transcended in due course (the very fact that Bint is of a different nation than Thayer). The difficulties encountered in communicating between cultures and languages mirrors the imagined future relation between Earth and Mars, on the one hand; on the other, their overcoming of these difficulties highlights the finally personal grounds on which the novel believes transnationalism must be based. Bint and Thayer's relationship culminates in the ultimate human connection, a child, which at the same time as it represents the coming together of two disparate ways of life also gestures towards the future itself.

The novel's ambiguous ending connects these two strands: in letting us read the ending as either describing the culmination of the Equilateral project's effort to make contact with Mars or as the birth of Bint and Thayer's baby, it refuses to decide between two ways of seeing transnationalism's potential; in refusing closure, it also refuses to endorse even the very possibility of utopian transnationalism. In this sense, *Equilateral* performs a critique of transnationalism: it probes the possible grounds of a genuine transnationalism and suggests the difficulties of both the commercial-globalized and individuated approaches to transnationalism. *Equilateral* is concerned with transnationalism as a way of rethinking the world and its limits within its own socioeconomic preconditions. Transnationalism frequently takes on utopian dimensions, suggesting a possible future in which the problems inherent in the nation-state system may be replaced: if transnationalism is "a world that is in the process of becoming" (Bieger, Saldívar, and Völz 2013, viii), such becoming is already dimly hopeful. Hopefulness about the consequences of transnationalism as a global practice of living is echoed by Steven Vertovec's conclusion that a "more cosmopolitan future is one possible outcome of the current global transformation," which here means the neoliberal processes of globalization in the wake of the end of the Cold War. If Vertovec clearly acknowledges the possibility of other outcomes, "[a]t present this seems a future towards which numerous processes of global interconnection [. . .] are moving" (2009, 163). *Equilateral* critiques the predominant strains of contemporary thinking about the transnational condition: will we be truly transnational when we are reaching out, as a planet, to the stars? Or must we understand the personal relationships between people of vastly different backgrounds across national boundaries as the best expression of the hopeful future that awaits us when we have become transnational? What, in other words, needs to happen before we can truly be transnational, or think transnationally?

The novel's emphasis falls on the first idea of transnationalism: the Equilateral project's goal of establishing "interplanetary communication" (120), something which Thayer at least reads conclusively as a project which will unite the planet. The assumption of a unified Mars pervades the entire book, and the novel's characters have already accepted that they represent the "planet" (12) Earth, rather than the nations of Earth. Here, the novel situates its first critique of transnationalism, by establishing the conditions which need to be met in order to achieve interplanetary communication.

The possibility of realizing the Equilateral is deeply interwoven with material concerns. Behind the project stands the Mars Concession with its mercenary aims. As the novel establishes early on, the project is the Concession's, with Thayer merely the "public face" (7) with little ultimate power. The Concession is described in strikingly transnational terms:

> As of this date the Mars Concession has been capitalized at sixteen million pounds sterling, twice as much as Suez, funded by massive state expenditure and private investment, not least the collection of small coins from the schoolchildren of six nations, their ha'pennies, sous, and pfennigs inserted into the slots of thousands of little tin boxes emblazoned with Giovanni Schiaparelli's most revealing map. It has drawn extravagantly from the coffers of several European and American banks. It may draw from them again. Demanding cooperation among rival governments and financial enterprises from one end of the world to the other, the Equilateral is the greatest international peacetime undertaking in the history of man. It has spawned new legislation, new protocols, and new treaties. In the marshaling of human resources *regardless of national origin*, it suggests the only possible future for human life on Earth . . . (13, my emphasis; original ellipsis)

Set against the specter of life on Mars, the problems of the "trivial little globe" (16) of Earth seem to take a backseat.

The conflict between Thayer's idealist vision and the much different motives of the Mars Concession becomes nowhere clearer than in the immediate aftermath of the successful completion of the Equilateral.

The novel emphasizes the realities of the merely globalized commercial project: the first building to be erected at the triangle's apex is a customs house (191). The Concession excludes Thayer from the expected welcoming party; the utopian dream of contact with a world in which social life functions differently collapses around him. As the Concession's head, the surnameless Sir Harry, tells a shocked Keaton:

> "The interests of the Concession are strictly commercial. [. . . T]he Concession has been granted a monopoly on trade with Mars. The Concession will hold the terrestrial patent for Martian inventions. Now that our enterprise has fully assumed its mercantile aspect, men of business will have to take center stage [. . .] The investors expect to profit." (195)

The novel holds the Concession's orientation towards profit in tension with the fact that if the Concession's motives are less than idealistic, its actions do not preclude the possibility that the utopian ideas which Thayer has for contact with Mars may yet come to fruition. But Sir Harry's frank admission serves the novel to highlight the conditions under which transnationalism may come to be: it can sustain its idealistic core only where commercial and idealist impulses coincide.

The connection that *Equilateral* draws between the consummation of the utopian project of interplanetary communication and the Mars Concession's economic plans suggests the interconnections the novel recognizes between globalization and a broader transnationalism. Globalization is "filled with glorious hope" (Wallerstein 2004, ix), constituted by "the opening of all frontiers to the free flow of goods and capital" (86), a field of tension, in other words, in which the triumph of capitalist enterprise is connected with the triumph of the value systems of the capitalist West: already a utopia of sorts. Globalization is the economic and commercial undergirding of the larger, more diffuse idea of transnationalism. The novel thus connects utopia, transnationalism, and globalization, and understands them as necessarily interrelated. "Utopia [. . .] connotes the desire to transgress borders and to encounter other lands and peoples, to connect together otherwise disparate places and identities across the globe. In this way, utopia and globalization are born together" (Hayden 2009, 51). This holds also for transnationalism, which elides the economic preconditions it depends on. Globalization "'appeared as response to the trauma of the twentieth century, in a moment of hope when it seemed, not for the first time, that the possibility for a worldwide civil society was finally at hand" (Alexander 2009, 33); this is its utopian aspect. At the same time, globalization results in a world with no outside (see Dath and Kirchner 2012, 18); this is its contradiction, because capitalist enterprise in fact requires demand from outside of the capitalist system (Harvey 2011, 108).

In *Equilateral*, Mars is the new final frontier to be opened. For the time being, the project's promise has successfully papered over the many differences which competition between the great powers produces. The novel's setting in 1894/95 here comes through most powerfully. Wars loom on the horizon of *Equilateral*'s future, both immediate colonial crises and the twentieth century's world wars. From the very beginning, the kind of international cooperation geared towards transnational goals which the project represents is counteracted by the political problems on the ground. Egypt itself is "a land where political power rests on semiviscous sands" (49)—nominally Ottoman, but really British-occupied, its southern border threatened by the Sudanese Mahdi, and desired also by the French (Omdurman and Fashoda both lie in the immediate future). These conflicts remain unresolved: for a brief moment, the expectation of an imminent Martian landing not just reveals the commercial goals of the Concession, but also brings together the European prime ministers and the Khedive himself, ambassadors and industrialists, "the greatest convocation of temporal power since the Congress of Vienna" (197). But when the Martians do not arrive on time, concerns shift once more to the great power politics of the age:

> As the days pass in unremitting sun, the statesmen of Europe meet to exchange views on terrestrial concerns, especially unrest in the Transvaal and loans to China. Certain levers of power are softly pressed. Borders in the Balkans are quietly redrawn. Populations are shifted. Sums are debited and credited to the accounts of distant banks. A royal engagement is arranged; so is an assassination. (200)

As the novel puts it, "[t]here's only so much time that the prime minister of Britain can spend with the president of France before troubles arise somewhere in Africa" (202). With no Martians arriving, no vision available that would direct the imperialist energies outside the planet, the utopian promise of Mars collapses in all its dimensions—the British prime minister and French president depart, significantly, in "separate caravans" (204). The novel thus suggests the power of the outside position offered by Mars: bringing together the world's powers, it promises avoiding looming conflicts, but this is a function of its economic potential. What has driven the international project of the Concession is the logic of capitalist accumulation: its transnational goal of a market outside the planet becomes readable as a mere extension of the system of imperialist expansion on which the wealth of the Concession's major investors is already based. The apparent failure of establishing contact with Mars, conversely, collapses the promise of peace, and ushers in the reality of the twentieth century as we know it.

The novel discusses transnational connections on a more personal level, too, as noted, in the relationship between Sanford Thayer and his servant, Bint. Transcending national and cultural boundaries and emphatically about the problematic of cultural and linguistic communications, it represents the transnational ideal of cosmopolitanism (Vertovec 2009, 69–70; Appiah 2006; see also Lanzendörfer 2019). In conceiving a child together, the two symbolically connect East and West, imperialist oppressor and oppressed, and suggest an alternative dimension of transnational hope for the novel: the surmounting of various forms of identitarian difference in personal relationships across borders. Yet here as before, *Equilateral* offers a critique.

Communication is the crucial issue here, both between the culturally and linguistically diverse people that encounter each other in the Saharan desert and with Mars. Communication with Mars, of course, is the very quest for which the entire Equilateral project is built. Around this narrative hub spin smaller stories of communication, each querying the conditions for transnationalism. Among these aspects of communications are some that are directly related to the different aims of Thayer and the Concession; they are questions of translation, both linguistic and conceptual, of the project's aims and its more practical everyday demands, to the local political, social, and economic contexts. The increasing understanding between Thayer and Bint is vital, but what is at issue goes beyond them: their difficulties are merely symptomatic of a more general failure of communication between East and West, and their ultimate form of wordless understanding perhaps more particularly open to interpretation.

Bint's role in the narrative progressively becomes clearer, as she increasingly takes over Adele Keaton's role as Thayer's chief supporter in the camp. Keaton's position within the novel is at the junction between Ballard's practical engineering and Thayer's speculative star-gazing. She, as noted, keeps both sides of the project in view. The preeminent realist of the novel, she is a scientist at heart, happy with "the rigors of measurement and logic" (26), deeply imbued with the morals and conventions of her age: classist and imperialist, she pays Bint little regard until, in terms of her relationship with Thayer, it is too late. The novel's tendency to narrate from the focalizing perspective of the characters, but to do so in barely marked shifts, hinders appreciation of Keaton's ultimate stance, but in her actions towards Bint, she largely dismisses the younger woman's ability to fathom anything that is going on. Beyond that, too, her view of Mars is radically Spencerian in outlook:

> The inexorable drive for survival must have demanded beings endowed with godlike capabilities and judgment. And through natural selection and nonbiological processes, through brutality and education, through calculated humiliations and measures of grace, by pitting every individual against the other to determine who was more suited to their purposes, the engineers would have forged a separate, servile race that has put its servility to productive use, for the salvation of the planet they share with their masters. That's what it's taken to carve their lines into the fourth planet's hard red rock. (111)

This, the novel might as well say, is what Keaton believes, and continues to believe. When Thayer comes to wonder whether Darwinism is truly a universal force, this comes on the heels of a contest which Keaton has suggested to spur their workers to quicker labor: "The premise of Miss Keaton's argument is that competition is ingrained in man's universal character because it's encoded in creation through natural selection" (116). In practice, this argument fails: the workers work haphazardly, cutting corners, so that the Equilateral becomes an "irregular polygon" (136), its upper section slightly angled inwards. Given the previous insistence that nothing must interfere with the construction of a regular triangle, this new form is a radical departure from the plans. Ballard intervenes, offering his own practical take on Martian civilization and suggesting that if the Martians are able to make out the slight irregularity in the triangle, they would still be willing to forgive the slight mishap and chalk it up to mankind's immaturity, and Keaton bows to the need to accept the situation. But for her, the project that the Western Concession is trying to carve into the Egyptian desert is, and has always been, essentially idealist: the Equilateral's "tangible, physical reality *is* the Platonic" (134). Inscribing this ideal into the world, as it turns out, is a complex and difficult proposition, hindered by a mutual lack of understanding.

One of the most telling of these examples of communicative failure also illustrates the novel's ambivalence towards the kind of idealized understanding that, at other times, Thayer and Bint seem to have. In the aftermath of Thayer's decision to hang a troublemaker, Bint speaks to him in eloquent Arabic:

> "And when you put men to death, you place the Equilateral in moral jeopardy! It no longer serves the people. It serves . . ." She pauses before she decides on the next words. "The Devil!"

> [. . .] Thayer almost grins at Bint's attempt at speech, none of which he can follow.
>
> "I believed once that the Equilateral was the gift of God, directly from the mind of God," she says hesitantly. Her eyes are moist. She moans softly before she continues: "I believe that no longer. It is the work of man, with all the compromises and imperfections of man. But I have confidence that the Equilateral can still be completed. It may yet find favor in God's eyes, if we complete it according to His law."
>
> Thayer is puzzled by the Arab girl's attempt at complex expression, which comes out as a series of freakish grunts and cries. He says, "I don't understand you at all." (106)

For Bint, the Equilateral has taken on a greater purpose: a religious significance that is as idealistic as Thayer's own vision of the project, a project unifying its makers behind a transcendent goal. Bint shares his vision, telling him, "If you die here, the project fails. We will never speak with Mars. We will never learn from them." But Thayer, behind the language barrier, can merely inquire, "Pardon?" (106). The possibility of deeper understanding is compromised by the lack of an ability to communicate, a lack that neither side strives very much to overcome.

Late in the novel the Egyptian Khedive situates transnationalism again politically. Present at the camp that is urgently awaiting the arrival of the Martians, he "[o]n the one hand [. . .] appears to imagine that social intercourse with Egypt will be Mars' primary objective; at the same time he urges his fellow dignitaries to remain at Point A to demonstrate mankind's solidarity." Martian society will have passed the state of warring nation states, and they will accordingly be expecting to speak to a similarly denationalized Earth: "'The visitors from Mars will care little to distinguish either between the Frenchman and the German or the Egyptian and the Englishman,' he says, raising hackles up and down the palace's plushly carpeted, electrically lit corridors" (202). The Khedive's suggestion is self-serving as well as radical. The consequence of Mars's postnational state is, he suggests, a similar decline in the importance of nationality on Earth. The transnational project of the Equilateral thus contributes to the dismantling of the nation-state system still cherished by the imperialist powers that have financed the project. For the Khedive, the Equilateral project becomes a means of political agency: he plays off the imperialist powers against each other. Insidiously, the demonstration of mankind's solidarity that the Khedive here demands serves eminently practical political goals of (national) emancipation, a national egalitarianism that is both clearly a prerequisite for the kind of utopian transnationalism that the novel critiques and a difficult ideal against which the economic and political interests of the imperialist powers militate.

The contingency of nationhood and the system of nation states remains contested in the novel because of its ambiguous ending, which finally does not reveal if Mars genuinely has left behind the concept of nations. Even so, the personal relationship between Thayer and Bint symbolically enacts the possibilities of transnational understanding in the necessary presence of nation states. It marks the possibility of a meaningful connection unmarked by the obvious differences between languages, cultures, ethnicities, and almost literally any marker of identity. Their relationship is marred by fundamental misunderstandings. Late in the novel, we discover that "Bint" is not a name, but the Arabic word for "girl"—Bint herself has been replaced with a different girl (157). Thayer demands Bint—whose actual name is Alya (meaning, perhaps significantly, heaven or divinity)—back, and signally conflates her return with the larger project of the Equilateral:

> "You fancy her, Effendi?"
>
> "I've been ill," Thayer murmurs. "The Equilateral must be finished . . ." (158, original ellipsis)

The Equilateral becomes symbolically elevated here from a technical project to a beacon of a generalized hope, something the novel also implies when, in the aftermath of Thayer's demand to have Bint back, it lets him stumble "in his personal, internal fever" through the camp, and notes that he can "no longer separate the specific from the general" (158). Thayer's relationship with Bint, his quest for contact with Mars, all speak the same language of a desire to transcend the conventional boundaries of the "specific," as it were, the identitarian, the national, the narrow, in favor of the general: the things which, in all dimensions from the interpersonal to the interplanetary, are united.

The narrative symbolically enacts this union in the horrible events during which the Equilateral is lit. As Mahdi rebels ignite the pitch-covered excavation without warning, both Thayer and Bint become temporarily engulfed in in a fireball:

> Immersed in light, they were nuzzled and licked by the flames and were rocked by its updrafts. They held tight. They sucked in the sweet, rarified air and found something cool and emollient in the core of the holocaust. After the fire extinguished itself and the settlement fell quiet, save for the strangled cries of the dying, the astronomer and the girl rose from the vitrified sand stripped of every article of clothing, their skin glowing pink. The scouring fire had reduced them to a state of nature. Even though they were unharmed, their figures were markedly altered. Their skulls were smoothly bald and every hair, every eyebrow, every cilium,

> and each pubic tuft were removed from their bodies. Not a single strand will grow back. They observed their hairlessness with wonder, as if truly seeing each other for the first time. (174)

Thayer and Bint are symbolically, fantastically reborn in the fire, and deprived of markers of ethnicity: both equally pink and hairless, stripped of their clothing, reduced to a "state of nature." That this rebirth occurs at the moment of the consummation of the Equilateral project is no coincidence. What the Equilateral does for the greater transnational dimension of the novel, the personal relationship between Thayer and Bint marks for the lower-key transnationalism of interpersonal relations. Removing all the conventional markers of difference, the novel suggests the conditions for thinking genuine transnational relationships, the recognition of a human commonality underneath these markers. But the moment is passing: Keaton takes control of the situation and reinstitutes the old hierarchy between master and servant; the class differences between Thayer and Bint remain. Their personal connection now makes them stand apart from the rest of the society gathered around the Equilateral: dressed similarly, their "robes and common baldness set[s] them apart" (175). They communicate, haltingly, without language; again, as before, Bint is capable of seeing the things Thayer detects through his telescope. Yet the novel recognizes the difficulties of this relationship. Returning from a stay in London, Ballard regards Bint's pregnancy as "the most striking measure of Thayer's decline" (192); their relationship peters out. Thayer, increasingly confined to bed by his worsening illness, feverish and comatose, cannot act at all, and, as noted, the novel ends when, perhaps, Bint gives birth to Thayer's child. Where the relationship goes, and what it does, the novel ultimately does not answer.

Rather than being in any way for or against the transnational idea, *Equilateral* deconstructs the conditions under which transnational, utopian perspectives become available and transnational projects can be undertaken. It highlights the tensions that almost necessarily will underlie such projects, even in their most innocent forms. It is no coincidence that Thayer's efforts at communication with Mars speak the language of pure form. The Equilateral is the ideal, making its marring at the hands of the workers symbolic of the problems that idealism—utopianism—encounters in the real world. Yet the ostensible universals that Thayer sees at work in the Equilateral are quickly put aside. Even mathematics is not innocent in *Equilateral*: in his early musings on the possible fate of Earth, Thayer draws a connection between mathematics and cultural virility, suggesting that "civilized man [. . .] may forget the sciences and arts that he invented, just as the Arab lost his mastery of mathematics and astronomy" (72). Mathematics, like every other aspect connected to the Equilateral venture, is both a sign and a tool of imperialist power.

Conclusion: Equilateral and Speculative Historism

Equilateral enacts the antinomies of global capitalism and of transnational thinking at the beginning of the twenty-first century in fantastic form. Slavoj Žižek has suggested that the principal problem of that moment lies in the impossibility of finding a sociopolitical order commensurate with the reach of global neoliberal capitalism. It is precisely the globality of the economic system that creates the political backlash of regional, social, ethnic, and religious identities which make it impossible to obtain on the base of the global economic system a similarly global polity. Militating against the repressive economic order, categories of difference (such as ethnic and religious identities) become politically stronger (see Žižek 2014b, 160–61). In terms of the novel, even as the combined economic strength of the West sees its culmination in the construction of the Equilateral, the realities of the locale in which this occurs intervene. The Equilateral, the Mahdi's followers have decided, "stands contrary to Mohammedan principles"—yet because this point is made through what must be Ballard's focalization, we also get the addendum "whatever they may be" (160). The novel recognizes the way in which the Equilateral project causes a backlash not necessarily on its own terms: its significance becomes refracted through the lens of local identities and more complicated precisely because of the interaction between those identities and the blithe dismissal of them by the Western powers. "Whatever they may be" speaks both to this Western dismissal as well as to the displacement of the cause of the rebellion. The rebels do not know what these principles really are and how they relate to the Equilateral, but to claim this relation between their religious principles and the Equilateral's necessary destruction permits them to react not against the overbearing force of Western colonial capitalism, but rather against its symbolic enactment, the Equilateral. The novel thus highlights the ways in which especially Thayer's ideas lack universality even on Earth. The "blatant acts of insurrection leveled directly at the Equilateral; as well as strife traveling circuitously from abstruse causes toward obscure ends" (101) become readable here as the violent reaction against the symbol of globalization that the Equilateral also is, a process *Equilateral* asks us to think historically. Globalization enabled the "final shattering of the ties that bind us to the realities of the nineteenth century" (Wegner 2011, 121), and this suggests the importance of the novel's setting. The final decade of the nineteenth century becomes an end point both in the chronological as well as in a more metaphorical sense, a final moment of hope before setting the trajectory of our present.

The novel's emplacement in history is as crucial as its ultimately speculative notion of Martian life, enabling us to read it against the contemporary moment precisely through its speculative historism, its combination of a speculative element (Martians) with its concrete placement in a historical context. As Thayer notes, "this moment in our planetary history *demands* the Equilateral" (70, original emphasis). If Thayer bases this claim on his perception of an evolutionary downward spiral in store for Earth, counteractable only by recourse to Mars's successful management of the same trajectory, from today's vantage point, the argument becomes more concrete. The utopian possibility of recognizing planetary commonalities and instituting a global community is set against the historical trajectory of the twentieth century. Thayer is unwittingly correct: the Equilateral promises a way to avoid the disasters of the twentieth century.

It is necessary that Thayer believes that he "has *seen* this planet of heroes, pale and fragile, trembling in his eyepiece" (24, my emphasis); from this literally visionary belief stems not only the entire Equilateral project, but all its potential outcomes, including those which are most utopian. Certainly, if Martian civilization exists, if it has made contact at the end, then all the questions which Thayer has asked himself remain: what would we do upon encountering a civilization with radically different social structures? The novel does not answer the question. This is more than a mere refusal to spell out a satisfactory conclusion: *Equilateral*'s own utopian potentially stems from recognizing that the actual facts about Martian civilization may be less important than their imagination, hopeful possibilities more important than ostensible facts.

The possible landing of Martians becomes less important than the immanence of the Event in the novel itself. We can locate "within [the novel] itself a multitude of signs which point toward the authentic Event" (*Žižek* 2014b, 203) which does not require narration. The point of the ambivalent ending is that "they've arrived" and "they're here" can be read absent of any necessary connection with the Martians. Perhaps the Martians have arrived; but what has certainly arrived is Thayer's awareness of the political alternatives which he envisioned Mars to stand for. Thayer's utopian imagination already has had a major impact on Earth, it has "spawned new legislation, new protocols, and new treaties" (13), it has already produced the greatest international project in history, it has given a collective goal to the entire planet—

all without needing Martian life to be real. If these achievements are independent of the existence of Martians, they hinge powerfully on the speculative form of the novel. Its speculativeness permits the venture to appear as more than merely quixotic. It turns a narrative which could easily devolve into a story of necessary failure (there are no Martians, therefore there are no outside positions, therefore conclusions drawn from envisaging this impossible outside are themselves impossible) into one in which possibilities remain open.

Equilateral stages two things: the possibility of hopeful futures and the conditions for thinking the particular utopian idea of a transnational world. The realities of the project cannot be ignored. As Bint notes to Thayer, "[i]t is the work of man, with all the compromises and imperfections of man" (106). In this sense, the novel denies an easily positive evaluation of transnational existence without noting carefully its underlying "compromises and imperfections." In *Equilateral*, these stand out more radically, perhaps, than they do for transnational thought today. But the novel's point remains clear nonetheless: beneath the Equilateral project's goal of interplanetary communications, its transnational conception as a common project of mankind, lie the hard realities of commercial interest, imperial oppression and exploitation, and a mere temporary respite from the nationalist agendas that each of the individual partners in the venture retains.

The novel does not for a moment pretend that the actual process of interplanetary communications, its central transnational undertaking, can take place without the mobilization of the resources of the system under which it takes place: this would have been altogether utopian (in the derogatory sense!). Its critique of transnationalism highlights the need to be clear-eyed about the practical preconditions under which, in 1894/95 as now, transnational endeavors both public and private can take place, and that they, in and of themselves, need not necessarily be hopeful at all. At the same time, the novel leaves open the possibility that such a thing as transnationalism can be consummated (literally): after all, Bint and Thayer do conceive a child together, and its future, just like the future of mankind, is left open at the end of the novel. *Equilateral* thus does not construct a concrete utopia, but it suggests, speculatively, the possibilities stemming from envisaging hopeful futures.

Chapter 2

The Prismatic Lens of Genre: Joyce Carol Oates's *The Accursed*

Equilateral looks resolutely forward and is little interested in the historical developments that led to the particular situation in which its narrative is set. Joyce Carol Oates's *The Accursed* (2013), set only a little later in 1905–6, offers a different view of speculative historism: it draws its hopeful future in large parts from an overcoming of the past to envision a different and better future. Largely set in Princeton, New Jersey, it involves an assemblage of historical figures (among others Woodrow Wilson, president of Princeton University; Upton Sinclair, fresh from the writing of his soon-to-be bestseller *The Jungle*; Socialist icon and novelist Jack London; as well as cameo appearances by Grover Cleveland and Mark Twain) and an even larger group of fictional ones, most notably the Slade family, especially patriarch Winslow Slade. The narrative's speculative aspects center on the Slades, with the so-called Crosswicks Curse, named after the Slade family mansion, the central speculative motif of the novel: a series of fantastic events, of deaths, disappearances, and monstrous appearances, engulfing the Slade family and their friends.

The novel's plot is best given in broad strokes here. In the summer of 1905, a series of mysterious events occurs in Princeton. Grover Cleveland nearly falls to his death on seeing the ghost of his dead daughter. A mysterious stranger named Axson Mayte arrives in town, ostensibly an associate of Winslow Slade's. Women find themselves mysteriously drawn to Mayte; he bewitches Winslow's granddaughter Annabel Slade into absconding from her wedding to Dabney Bayard. Annabel's brother Josiah tries to find her, but fails, because, as we discover upon Annabel's return several months later, Mayte is a supernatural figure, perhaps a demon of sorts, and the Count and master of a parallel world called the Bog Kingdom, where he has impregnated Annabel. Annabel (apparently) dies giving birth to what may be a snake; her death leaves her brother and family distraught. And the curse does not lift: having expended his Mayte-persona, the Count of the Bog Kingdom (whom I will call Mayte throughout) returns in different guises, as does his sister, the Countess Camille. As Count English von Gneist and possibly as Jack London, he is implicated in the death of several upper-class Princetonians. The novel's focus in the wake of Annabel's death gives it room to acknowledge the breadth of the curse's effect, and its insidious complexity. Pearce van Dyck, a professor at Princeton, becomes obsessed with unraveling the workings of the Curse through the use of the method of ratiocination, which he adopts from Sherlock Holmes, slowly succumbing to the mad notion that Holmes is a real figure. Then, a surprise midnight visitor to van Dyck turns out to be none other than Sherlock Holmes himself. He tells him that the child his wife, Johanna, is bearing is not really his, but the spawn of a demon loose in Princeton. Pearce must kill it to defeat evil. Before van Dyck can kill his son, he is caught, and accidentally killed himself, by Josiah Slade, a former student of his. The fate of the Slade family remains at the heart of the tale. Oriana, Josiah and Annabel's cousin, is found dead as though she had fallen off a roof, killed (perhaps) by ghosts. Todd Slade, another cousin, is found, apparently turned to stone, in the Princeton cemetery; in fact, he has managed to cross the strange boundary between the Bog Kingdom and the real world and will later play checkers with Mayte for his life, defeating him, killing Mayte, and ending the Bog Kingdom. Josiah, trying to escape voices in his head and ghostly visits from his sister, goes on an Antarctic expedition, where he finally succumbs to the voices and jumps into the icy sea—though he is recovered, he appears dead. Finally, Winslow Slade dies, of a heart attack brought about (maybe) by more of the ghostly-demonic snakes, while publicly preaching a sermon admitting to his horrific past deeds. The things which happen to the younger members of the Slade family become readable (ambiguously) as the consequences of his murder and rape of a young Black woman fifty years before the events of the novel, in which he was assisted and encouraged by another avatar of Mayte's, long covered up and only now revealed.

These speculative events are woven into an otherwise realistic narrative whose major plot points are frequently political. Wilson's struggle for progressive reform at Princeton University is an issue throughout (although the novel removes the confrontation from 1908–9 to the years 1905–6 (Cooper 2009, 102–19)). The novel introduces us to the struggles of Upton Sinclair and his larger place within the American Socialist movement; Josiah Slade becomes an ardent follower of Sinclair's. Notably, the backdrop to the entire novel, repeatedly intruding into the narrative, consists of the deep divisions in fin-de-siècle American society; its party-political depravity; the legacy of slavery; the oppression of

Black Americans, of women, of immigrants; the power of the conservative impulse; and the opportunities and dangers of contrary movements from anarchism to Socialism.

Oates's novel enacts a hopeful vision of the future predicated on overcoming the past, a relationship it allegorizes through the connection between Winslow Slade as the representative of the old United States and the supernatural events of the Curse. The novel ties the supernatural and the realistic through the connection between Winslow Slade and Axson Mayte: Slade personifies the status quo of societal power, Mayte the force by which this status quo is achieved. Mayte's defeat spells also the doom of Winslow Slade and what he stands for. The novel seems to indicate here that it is easier to overcome the past in the imaginary realms of the supernatural, where simple rules apply and we do not have to worry about the complex relationships of power in the real world. Like slaying the dragon, Todd Slade's defeat of Mayte, which takes the whole supernatural edifice down, argues the need to break free of the past imaginatively, and at the same time points to the possibilities inherent in a younger generation willing to break free from the fetters of the old (cf. Ghosal 2020). Nancy Watanabe has suggested that Oates "evokes pathways within [the] complicated and sticky web of American cultural and historical development," but that for Oates, "salvation of the soul, not economically fueled class struggle, is the main issue" (1998, 14). But reading Oates's fiction as predominantly oriented towards the moral and ethical cannot fully contend with *The Accursed*, which does, in fact, foreground more fundamentally political, indeed in parts outright Socialist, issues, issues it locates temporarily in several historical moments.

Oates has always seemed to move between high-literary naturalism and the penny-dreadfulesque Harlequin romance (McGurl 2009, 42). In the 1980s, she wrote a quartet of novels (Cologne-Brookes 2014, 303; 2005, 127) in her "Gothic Saga," including *The Accursed*. These texts interweave "the so-called real world, the world of history, and the world of the imagination" (Cologne-Brookes 2005, 101). Inscribing herself in the Gothic tradition, Oates transposes "realistic social and historical as well as psychological and emotional experiences" (Manske 1992, 138) into a form that opens a broader vista of possibilities (though cf. McLennan 2020). As Oates notes, reimagining the forms of our perceptions "forces us inevitably to a radical re-visioning of the world" (1985, 514). Gavin Cologne-Brookes believes that Oates's Gothic novels "mark the point at which Oates suddenly seemed far more interested in looking outward at American history and culture than any deeper into the kinds of philosophical abstractions that compete for attention in her earlier novels" (2005, 90). For Oates, the "escape into the imagination is also an immersion in history" and, perforce, an avowal of "public commitment" (107). Her Gothic novels are a way to "rewrite herself and her experiences in historical context" (132), thus explaining her return to realist fiction afterwards. I would like to offer a different reading, one which reads *The Accursed* and its speculative historism less within the context of Oates's personal career and more against its particular historical moments: the moment of its narrative in 1905–6, the moment of its writing in the 1980s, and the moment of publication.

First, I will address the issue of the novel's historical imagination. *The Accursed* is avowedly metahistorical, concerned not just with the impact of history, but with the writing of history. Its narrator, M.W. van Dyck II, a self-declared amateur historian, insists repeatedly on the factuality of his narrative, especially on the factuality of its supernatural elements. Through the narrator's insistence on introducing speculative elements into his otherwise realistic historical narrative, the novel lays claim to a broadened vision of what history entails, and suggests the need to make metaphorically visible what has remained unseen. Second, I will address the connection between the novel's speculative elements—the Crosswicks Curse itself and its various manifestations—and its conception of a break with history, culminating in the death of Winslow Slade. Finally, I will point out how the novel connects all of these issues—the hopeful possibilities enacted by a new view of history and a break with the past—with a curious and not altogether unambiguous utopian Socialism throughout, from Upton Sinclair's experiences in Princeton through the Slade grandchildren's final decision to renounce their heritage and join Sinclair at his utopian community of Helicon Home Colony.

"The mimesis of a 'fable'": History and Narrative

As the author of the text that the novel pretends to be, a history of the Crosswicks Curse also called *The Accursed*, the narrator M.W. van Dyck's concern to be seen as an accurate and objective observer and interpreter of events drives him to a variety of interjections concerning the interferences between historical narrativization and actual historical fact. Van Dyck admits to two related objectives in his writing of what he calls the "history of the tragic events" (132). On the one hand, his book is an effort to provide a counter-narrative to existing histories of the Crosswicks Curse, a counter-narrative that connects to writing a speculative history, fully admitting to and integrating the kinds of fantastic events that his predecessors have elided. On the other, he seeks to "expose to a new century of readers some of the revelations" (1) which he has obtained from access to the various documents that give an insight into the true nature of the Crosswicks Curse. This new century—our century—is the ultimate horizon of van Dyck's explorations of history. From the outset his story is in good part an instrument in its resistance to traditional historiography, which translates to a resistance on the level of Oates's novel to realist storytelling. Both of these levels are, in their own way, critical to *The Accursed*. "One resists the truth of a given history not only by labeling it as false but also by writing, or enacting, a counterhistory in narrative form" (Parrish 2008, 2): history requires retelling if it is meant to be changed. *The Accursed* performs this task of retelling on two levels. First, on the level of van Dyck's narrative, which enacts a counter-history to the (fictional) histories of the Crosswicks Curse that refuse to acknowledge the supernatural. Second, and more complicatedly, on the level of Oates's novel, which provides a counter-history of the first decade of the twentieth century in which the various contractions of time and space that the novel performs narratively unite diverse elements of progressive politics and set them against a powerful and supernatural past. Navigating the often treacherous shoals of this past is van Dyck's most difficult, and therefore frequently vocalized, task.

Van Dyck himself straddles the entirety of the vast divide between the narrative time of the novel and the time of the completion of his own narrative, in 1984. Born at the height of the Curse in 1905, van Dyck is a curious mixture of uptight late-Victorian propriety redolent of his upbringing in early twentieth-century Princeton society, and an underlying grudging appreciation for the progressive futures envisaged by his characters. He is loath to penetrate too deeply into his protagonists' private lives and writes at a critical and often almost sardonical distance from them. Introducing Sinclair as he is passing by Annabel Slade's disastrous wedding, the narrator lets drop that Sinclair "naturally associated [with the name Slade] the extremities of capitalist exploitation of the masses" (141). He channels Sinclair's "frustration in trying to convert the downtrodden who clutched to their hearts the delusions of the ruling class as if such delusions could be their own" (146), and ends a long monologue of Upton's on the future of the Socialist revolution on his wife's simple plea that she only wants to go home (244). There is a sense of benevolent irony towards Sinclair, but outright judgments are left to "the reader" (145). Sinclair, in van Dyck's narration, is deeply earnest in his convictions, but the target of soft humor for it; Woodrow Wilson, likewise, is presented as a man of principles, but these get as much space as his digestive problems, his tendency to solipsism, his obsession with status, his Presbyterian uptightness, and his awkward familial relations. Van Dyck seems to develop a more generally progressive attitude as his narrative goes on, but never manages to state outright his own positions.

Van Dyck desires to have his narrative understood as unbiased and objective, as a "fact-based chronicle" (257); but the process of the narrativization of history is key to him, and suggestive for the work of speculative historism. Early on, he offers a "Historian's Confession" in which he notes the difficulty of being "confined to a linear chronology" (133) that only inadequately renders the simultaneity of events. When, at the end of the novel, Todd Slade's game of checkers in the Bog Kingdom coincides with Winslow Slade's final confession and death, and simultaneously the various presumed-dead younger members of the Slade family awake, van Dyck again cautions that "this chapter occurs simultaneously with the preceding" (623). He notes that the causal links between the Count's defeat in the Bog Kingdom and Slade's death remain opaque: "the historian must throw up his hands and trust to his material to communicate a tale, and a meaning, beyond his own ability to fathom" (624). The "historian's dilemma" is that "we can record, we can assemble facts meticulously and faithfully, but only to a degree can we interpret. And we cannot *create*" (180, original emphasis). He recognizes and insists that history is a narrative—"fact-based" but going beyond mere reportage. As he acknowledges of his own text, it "moves forward in the mimesis of a 'fable'" (132). "Fable" is an interesting choice we may take to highlight the text's allegorical nature and its inculcation of a lesson to van Dyck's readers; but quite as interesting is his insistence on the term mimesis. *Mimesis*, in the Aristotelian tradition, is set against *poesis*—representation is set against creation. It is also a particular kind of representation, namely "the representation of reality" (Auerbach 1953); at the very least, it is "associated with realism" (Jameson 1991, 195). Van Dyck might be referring to his own text as being merely the *mimesis* of a fable, a third-order representation of what fables actually are, and be nodding once more towards the constructedness of his narrative. However, he could also be suggesting that his own story, slightly paradoxically, is a particular *kind* of mimesis, the particular kind of representation of reality a fable constructs. If so, we should probably focus not so much on the details of the fable-form, but rather on the fable's greater willingness to be open to the fantastic. In a reading in which mimesis is invested in realism, the fable-like narrative which van Dyck constructs for us in his novel becomes a new form of realism—perhaps a necessary choice for a counter-narrative to the kinds of pedestrian history written by his predecessors.

Van Dyck frequently foregrounds various other problems of historical narrativization, highlighting the difficult negotiations speculative historism undertakes. The novel opens on an "author's" note, written by van Dyck, prefacing the history of the Crosswicks Curse that the novel pretends to be. From the very beginning, the novel complicates the relationship between fact and fiction, between history and the (speculative) imagination, by simultaneously insisting that it is both history and a novel. If speculative fiction is presented as history on one level, it is also history presented as a speculative narrative—a play with different levels of narrative that complicates its own relationship to historical truth. As van Dyck notes, "there may be multiple, and competing, histories." The history of the events in Princeton that van Dyck is writing is already in one sense fictitious. In his "chronicle of the mysterious, seemingly interlinked events occurring in, and in the vicinity of, Princeton, New Jersey, in the approximate years 1900–1910, 'histories' have been condensed, for the purposes of aesthetic unity, to a period of approximately fourteen months in 1905–1906" (1). Aesthetic form apparently takes precedence over historical accuracy; but this point gets lost almost immediately, when the narrator-author speaks of "those fourteen months of ever-increasing and totally mysterious disaster" (3). The narrator here already naturalizes his own construction: the condensed version becomes the real history of Princeton's Crosswicks Curse.

Van Dyck's history emphasizes the difficulty of historical writing only as a practice, not as a philosophical and epistemological problem. If it is metafictional, it is also insistent on the possibility of truth. This is the upshot of van Dyck's insistence that the historian can and should be faithful to the facts and that he cannot create. History exists independent of its narrativization and independent of the historian's verification of the underlying facts that form history: "what of the past can be verified exactly, even if we were eyewitnesses" (256–57). Van Dyck debates the wisdom of using some of the most "shocking and questionable" materials. Perhaps most telling in this context is his worry about using "materials pertaining to Winslow Slade," which he is so "doubtful about" that he "sometimes wake[s] in the night wondering if I should destroy it at once." The material is worrying to van Dyck at least in part because it contradicts the publicly available materials, and because it "cannot be verified, and cannot fail to disturb." Since "*The Accursed* is intended as a work of inquiring moral complexity, and not a 'sensationalist' rehashing of an old, dread scandal far better left to molder in the grave" (259, original emphasis), van Dyck implies, it might perhaps be better to not use this material. But it is these sources, "kept under lock and key in my Ebony-Lacquered Box where no one save this historian has access to it" (626) that supply the key epilogue to the novel, the final sermon of Winslow Slade in which he admits to his rape and murder of a young Black woman sometime before the Civil War. Van Dyck recognizes the need to let these materials speak for themselves, and also (finally) the need to leave a mistaken sense of propriety on the sidelines in favor of a full presentation of the historical record (cf. Beville 2009, 7–8, though).

Van Dyck's argument conflates the (morally) shocking and unverifiable nature of his (supernatural) materials and the problem that they cannot be verified and are therefore questionable, the normative claims about what society will accept and what can be factually established. This is a mutually reinforcing duality, in which the refusal to say what cannot be verified from within the prevailing societal norms strengthens a sense of moral propriety that, in turn, informs the decision to withhold the now both morally and factually dubious information. This constitutes the literary equivalent of what Graham Harman has called the "learned habitual gestures that have come to seem like natural extensions of ourselves," in this case of a deferral to public morality. As Harman notes, until we "endure a break down of the usual situation in which perceptions and meanings simply lie before us as obvious facts," we are forced to utter ultimately "empty words" (2012, 258) about our lives. This notion of the "empty word" comes up in mutated form in discussion about the "unspeakable." If van Dyck acknowledges that he "is in fact ignorant of what the 'unspeakable' might be" (476), this is perhaps protesting too much. Throughout the narrative, the "unspeakable" describes various things: racial miscegenation; the rape and murder which precedes the lynching of a young Black couple; a vampire's homosexual rape and subsequent murder; and ultimately, the lingering cause of the curse, Winslow Slade's own rape and murder of a young Black woman. The narrative interweaves concerns for sexual propriety, racism, and the supernatural in the "unspeakable." To go beyond these societally conditioned choices about the possibility and desirability of representation by refusing to withhold the sermon in which Wilson Slade finally reveals all the details of his past is the chief development which van Dyck goes through as a narrator.

It is also, however, only a logical consequence of the kind of narrative that van Dyck has produced up to this point, all of which is essentially concerned with speaking about what should not be, or could not be, spoken about. All of the materials in his exclusive possession are distinguished by their forthrightness about the supernatural events which their authors have witnessed: memoirs, secret diaries, coded diaries, and scrapbooks, among several others, all of which include overtly supernatural events. These are the central issue through which van Dyck distinguishes his own history of the Curse from those of his predecessors, yet it is almost casually announced, and never understood at all as a possible ontological problem. His introduction sets out the terms of his engagement with the Curse. His book is a revisionist narrative, contrasting his own efforts at rendering the reality of the Curse with those of his "fellow historians" (9) and engaging and criticizing that previous work as short-sighted because it has ignored the reality of those supernatural events. Previous books have been "misleading, obfuscatory, and timid" (256): unwilling to face up to the necessary conclusion that the events of the Curse are supernatural, that they are all the consequence of a "single Evil" (3) that ties together the various manifestations occurring in Princeton. Van Dyck's insistence on his various sources recalls Jacques Rancière's notion that the writer of literature is "the archeologist or geologist who gets the mute witnesses of common history to speak" whereby "literature imposes its new power, [which] is not at all based, as is commonly claimed, on reproducing facts in all their reality." Rather, it is "based on deploying a new regime of appropriateness between the significance of words and the visibility of things" (2011, 15). In the case of the literary work done by the van Dyck narrative in Oates's novel, this new "visibility of things" depends on narrating the events of the Curse with a full awareness of the need to also narrate the fantastic events that decisively distinguish it from others. In so doing, *The Accursed* lays out the stakes of speculative historism more generally.

Gothic Speculation and the Fetters of History

Jacques Rancière has argued that "banal things must be given back their suprasensible, fantasmagorical aspect for us to see the secret writing of the functioning of society appear there" (2011, 22). Van Dyck's insistence on including in his history precisely those fantasmagorical aspects of Princeton history produces a narrative that does exactly that: it gives back to history those aspects which conventional narratives elide. It is ultimately the power of Todd Slade's imagination that permits the lifting of the Curse; lifting the Curse permits the potentially progressive developments to take place for which Upton Sinclair and Woodrow Wilson stand.

The Accursed starts with a conversation between Woodrow Wilson and his kinsman Yeager Ruggles about a lynching: a young Black man and his pregnant sister have been murdered by a Ku Klux Klan-led mob. Ruggles wants Wilson to speak out publicly against the murder and to lend the weight of his office and his personal credibility to the struggle. When Wilson refuses, Ruggles reveals that he is partially of Black heritage, a revelation that shocks Wilson. As Ruggles departs, Wilson collapses on the floor. Coming to, he finds himself reflecting on the encounter in starkly conservative terms. He muses on the need to protect his wife and daughters from knowledge of the lynching, on the defeat of the Confederacy as the origin of mob violence against Black people and as the "defeat of—a way of civilization that was superior to its conquerors." Finally, he feels

> a shuddering voluptuous surrender to—he knew not what.
> *The Bog Kingdom. Bidding him enter! Ah, enter!*
> *There, all wishes are fulfilled. The more forbidden, the more delicious.*
> (21, original emphasis)

The short encounter between Ruggles and Wilson and its immediate aftermath lays out the stakes of the novel. For Ruggles, the struggle against lynching is a communal one, in which he "and others like me in this accursed United States of America are so very *concerned*" (19, original emphasis)—a communal concern that goes beyond those sharing Ruggles's mixed heritage and reaches into society at large. Ruggles's claim that the entire U.S. is "accursed" prompts us to read the Crosswicks Curse as symbolical of a larger struggle also encoded through the speculative moment of Wilson's being called to the Bog Kingdom. Wilson falls back, despite his belief in his own rectitude ("He was a *Democrat*. In every public utterance, he spoke of *equality*" (18, original emphasis)), into less-than progressive thoughts tied to the seductive call of the Bog Kingdom. This is a connection the novel will expand, associating first the Bog Kingdom with Winslow Slade and then Slade and the Kingdom with an American past that needs to be overcome in order for a truly progressive future to be possible, even as that past remains seductive—both in literal and in metaphorical senses.

Ruggles already takes a first step in the strong and important link between Slade and the Bog Kingdom: he requests that Wilson ask Slade to preach a sermon on the lynching. Wilson goes to speak with Slade, introducing the central if not always foregrounded figure of the narrative. The extent of Slade's role in the narrative does not become fully apparent until the epilogue entitled "The Covenant," in which Slade explains his past. Even this epilogue, which represents Slade's own view of events, requires reading through the rest of the narrative. Slade's interpretation of events does not hold much water; the story itself, on the other hand, comes together in it.

When his granddaughter Oriana dies, about halfway through the narrative, Slade, at her graveside, commits himself to a story, an ultimately realistic narrative of his past that, while it reveals parts of his behavior, couches it in psychological and personal terms. In this initial graveside confession, Slade explains that, while studying at Princeton seminary in March 1855, he found himself suddenly driven from the library in which he was studying by the appearance of a "flame [that] leapt up [from his hands] to his exposed eyes, and entered his brain." He unhesitatingly gives this a natural explanation: "he understood that the flame was some sort of optical illusion, some pathology of the optic nerve exacerbated by overwork and by his recent illness" (443). Consequently, he wanders the New Jersey countryside, finally ending up at a pub, where a strange man picks him up and brings him to a crude cabin, in which he finds a "young woman, more precisely a girl," of "mixed race, Winslow thought; not 'colored'—not 'black'—or obviously 'Negroid'—but of some mixture of these, with European ancestry" (445). This young girl, named Pearl, in Slade's retelling seduces him; the man and a companion rob him, and Slade finally staggers home mortified, only to discover that Pearl is later found killed. The man who has dragged Slade to her, Henry Selincourt, is accused of the murder, and hanged. And this might have been the end of the story. Slade's story, although initially shocking, leaves the audience assembled at Oriana's graveside in deep consternation, but immediately willing to forgive; Slade's confession, however, does not lift the curse, as his listeners hope. In the book's epilogue, his final sermon, we obtain Slade's real interpretation of the events, and also the truth of his past behavior. Slade renders events as his personal divine punishment, and the supernatural creatures that are behind them as angels, out doing the work of the Lord. As he finally admits, he killed Pearl himself, in the manner of a "true demon not baptized as a Slade," and then dragged her body into a forest and swamp-land that bears a striking resemblance to the Bog Kingdom, and where he believes he is being spoken to by God. (The epilogue is all caps in the original; I will quote this without throughout.) The divine voice places his sin in the larger context of the Slade family's historic misdeeds:

> what bit of naughtiness have you performed in secret as all of the Slades performed in secret from your days of slave-holding until now your great fortune which is the Lord's blessing harvested from the bent and broken backs of factory workers, mill-workers, dumb and stammering immigrants missing fingers, toes, eyes. (652)

Like the ominous voice he hears, Slade ties the severity of his misdeed to the fact that the woman he killed was "a descendant of those brought from Africa in chains" (654). As he leaves the swamp, Slade is told that his "God" makes a covenant with him: leaving him to do as he pleases for fifty years, but then sending his "angels of wrath" (655).

Slade returns to life in Princeton, but his path has been unalterably changed. From his encounter with God/Mayte in the forest, he draws the inevitable conclusion that "the Lord God is a jealous God," and that "meekness, servility, unbridled fear and trembling be the lot of mankind" (658). His own behavior therefore sees him publicly exalt the righteous behavior of a good Christian on the pulpit, all the while he acts differently. He does not speak up when the stranger who picks him up at the pub is hanged for the murder of Pearl. He preaches forgiveness while conducting heresy trials; preaches resignation in the face of racial oppression and class inequality, even though he realizes that action is needed (662); admits to becoming New Jersey governor through ballot-stuffing (663); and acts to sow destruction in putting down strikes (664). When he finally retires, he is exhausted by his life. He feels he "no longer had the power to perpetuate evil" (666). His due punishment, he feels, is now God's wrath visited upon his grandchildren—the Curse manifesting itself—and he bows to the inevitable confession that "I, Winslow Slade, am guilty as well of all of the manifestations of the Crosswicks Curse [. . .]. For the angel-demons were by way of me, and could not have unleashed such misery upon you save by way of me" (667). Thus concludes Slade's sermon: he feels he has done God's service, is now being visited by God's righteous wrath, and dies, on the pulpit, even as in the Bog Kingdom, his grandson kills Mayte and lifts the curse. Both the history of the Slade family as Winslow Slade lays it out in his sermon and the narrative of events at Princeton in 1905–6 as *The Accursed* presents it are structured by a supernatural agent. The crucial difference between Slade's initial testimony and the final sermon in the epilogue is the public acceptance of a supernatural explanation.

At the heart of *The Accursed* lies a Gothic motif. As Catherine Spooner explains,

> Gothic texts deal with a variety of themes [. . .]: the legacies of the past and its burdens on the present; the radically provisional or divided nature of the self; the construction of peoples or individuals as monstrous or "other"; the preoccupation with bodies that are modified, grotesque or diseased. (2007, 8)

The legacies and burdens of the past engage Oates's novel on several levels: in the Slades' family history; in the political and social legacies of the past; and in the past as reported history which has so far obscured the view of the real historical events in Princeton, as van

Dyck's narrative lays them out. In *The Accursed*, the Gothic motif serves to highlight the need to re-evaluate the past in order to understand the present; it becomes interwoven with the essentially forward-looking idea of speculation. In calling this form of narrative "Gothic speculation," I highlight the multidimensional nature of the crucial poetic choices in the novel, its multileveled grounding in the past and in history, its equally decisive turn away from the pasts it narrates and the histories it deconstructs, and the expansion of the form of Gothic fiction which it produces by using it to usher in a progressive vision. Gothic fictions, as L. Andrew Cooper has noted, "give form to social phenomena" (2010, 19). In the case of Oates's novel, the Gothic elements also offer suggestions for possible ways forward, often beyond the traditional concerns of the Gothic. In his preface to *The Castle of Otranto*, Horace Walpole criticizes the fictional author of his found narrative for offering merely the apparently simple Old Testament moral that "*the sins of the fathers are visited on their children to the third and fourth generation*" (1769, viii, original emphasis). *The Accursed*, even as it narrates the story of a family in which the third generation suffers from the sins of its grandfather, also listens to Walpole's complaint. It goes far beyond this simple moral and suggests that overcoming the sins of the fathers requires a break with the past, a break which *The Accursed* (the novel) mediates through the fantastic.

The novel's initial scene between Yeager Ruggles and Woodrow Wilson lays out all of these issues. The inclusion at this early stage of Winslow Slade precisely as a moral instance becomes retroactively readable both as a wrong move and as signifying the impossibility of obtaining the kind of progressive vision that Ruggles desires, whilst the old structures of moral leadership are in place. The library in Crosswicks Manse in which Wilson and Slade meet is symbolic of these issues. On the library's great fireplace's mantel, amidst a library of the great classics and pictures of the "distinguished Slade ancestors" (26), the motto "HIC HABITAT FELICITAS" ("here happiness abides") is carved—this is the very fireplace through which, later on, Todd Slade will find his way to the Bog Kingdom. Everything here looks into the past, Winslow Slade included. And here, too, the symbolic release of the Curse is enacted. Wilson picks up a jade snuffbox, an "engaging object, though hardly beautiful, covered in a patina of decades, its lid engraved with a miniature yet meticulously wrought serpent that, coiled, looked as if it were about to leap out at the observer" (40). The serpent, too, becomes readable later, when snakes become one of the most notable forms in which the Curse manifests itself, and in its echo of similar descriptions of Axson Mayte himself. Towards the end of the meeting between Wilson and Slade, the box falls onto the table while the two men tussle, and breaks open: "a cloud of aged snuff was released, of such surprising potency both men began to sneeze; very much as if a malevolent spirit had escaped from the little box" (44). The novel's version of Pandora's box indeed stands at the outset of the various supernatural events which now begin to populate the narrative.

The first and most important manifestation of these is the appearance of Axson Mayte himself, who is introduced, seen by Annabel Slade, as someone "who'd wandered out of Dr. Slade's shadowed library" and now stands, in "formal, just slightly old-fashioned clothes, like clothes Winslow Slade had worn decades ago" (55), in the garden of Crosswicks Manse. Annabel is quite struck by him: she sees a man "in his early thirties perhaps," of "more than medium height" and with a "noble, well-shaped head, and very dark, silken, tight-curled hair" (59). Mayte's appeal to Annabel is mysterious; it becomes more mysterious when the same Mayte is encountered, walking with Wilson, by Josiah Slade, and described as "a singularly ugly man [. . .] with a flaccid skin, fish-belly-white, and close-set eyes of some intense though unnatural-seeming color like bronze; and a reptilian manner about the lips" (88). Mayte's appearance is as malleable as his dress: when Josiah spots him, he wears a costume "suitable for a Princeton undergraduate," specifically one belonging to the very eating-clubs that Wilson's campaign for a more progressive education seeks to disestablish (89). Few people who meet Mayte share in Josiah's reflexive loathing. The only person who does is, significantly, Upton Sinclair. Seeing Mayte and Annabel together, Sinclair wonders "how so lovely a young woman [. . .] should have been aligned with a gentleman so singularly repulsive!—[. . .] squat-bodied, flaccid-faced, and with a face like a toad's" (144).

Josiah and Sinclair are by far the most progressive figures in Oates's novel, and both see through Mayte's facade, genuinely *see* Mayte—not as supernatural, but as something different from the attractive upper-class gentleman that he is taken for in Princeton high society. Fredric Jameson has suggested that "[t]he modern gothic [. . .] depends absolutely in its central operations on the construction of evil," and that evil "is here, however, the emptiest form of sheer Otherness" (1991, 290). Axson Mayte, notably, is clearly evil—there is probably no better word for it—but he is not sheer, empty Otherness: in fact, for some members of Princeton society, he is not any Otherness at all. In the reactions to Mayte, fundamental positions about society are mediated. When Josiah, Wilson, and Mayte part ways, Josiah finds himself deeply troubled, and decides not to walk, but rather to take the town's segregated trolley bus. Josiah, reflexively, takes a seat among the Black men and women at the back of the trolley, "hoping to relax among them, as he could not relax elsewhere; and trying to take no note that, with his arrival in their midst, the men had abruptly ceased talking" (91). Josiah becomes aware of his class and race status; much of the narrative will be devoted to his own journey in drawing political conclusions from this.

Gothic narratives are ultimately class fantasies, as Fredric Jameson has argued: if Oates's beyond-Gothic narrative has already complicated the notion of the Gothic's relation to otherness, its relation to class fantasy shifts gears from traditional forms to the progressively speculative that I argue is its chief contribution. In lieu of the "privilege and shelter" of the Gothic (Jameson 1991, 289), the hermeticism of which is broken by the danger of envious forces but does not produce anything but personalized anxiety, *The Accursed*'s Gothic threat—the sins of the fathers, out to be visited upon the children—enables the exposure of the fantasies of the ruling class. It does not force this exposure. Josiah makes the necessary deduction and throws himself into the Socialist cause, ready to forego both money and privilege in the search for a more hopeful future, but much of his family and the other upper-class families does not. The various personas which Axson Mayte and his sister take on reflect the deep class divisions under which Princeton society—and American society at large—labors. Mayte himself poses, perhaps merely, as a well-to-do Virginia lawyer and associate in the Presbyterian Church of Winslow Slade. But even in the next encounter, he has upped his social rank, when Josiah, searching for Mayte and his sister after their departure from her wedding, encounters Mayte and his sister in different guises in an inn: there, they are François and Camille D'Apthorp, apparent French aristocrats. A similar class-consciousness is present in Mayte's later return as the Count English von Gneist, and his sister Camille's insistence to Woodrow Wilson that she is really the Countess de Barhegen. Each of these personas plays off of, or aims to play off of, Princeton society's "snobbishness."

Crucially, Mayte in this reading also is precisely not the embodiment of otherness, but rather the embodiment of that society, of the really existing social contradictions in Princeton and the U.S. That the events and concerns current in Princeton are merely in smaller scope concerns for the entire United States is a point repeatedly made. Mayte's easy acceptance into Princeton society suggests the nature of this society and its values. Mayte certainly is, to pick up on Fredric Jameson's term again, "evil" (1991, 289)—a term which Jameson himself puts in quotation marks to signify the banality of such designations and the problematic of the Gothic as he conceives it—but he is not an individual evil. He is the evil of the societal system which

Princeton society is based on and which Winslow Slade represents most profoundly.

The novel highlights the close relation between Slade, the Curse, and the supernatural evil of which Axson Mayte is the personification, in what is its most sustained engagement with the reality of the speculative: Todd Slade's arrival in the Bog Kingdom, his game of checkers with the Count—Axson Mayte—and the eventual defeat of Mayte and the destruction of the Kingdom, which coincides with the death of Winslow Slade and the resurrection of the Slade grandchildren. At the time of his own departure into the Bog Kingdom, Todd is the sole remaining Slade grandchild at Crosswicks. Annabel is apparently dead in childbirth, Todd's sister Oriana ostensibly dead of exposure, and Josiah hardly at home anymore, about to depart on an Antarctic expedition. Lonely and reclusive, Todd has for some time been hearing and seeing Annabel and Oriana. Now, a year into the curse's presence in Princeton, he disappears. At least subconsciously, he realizes the truth: neither Annabel nor Oriana is dead; he merely needs to find them to bring them back. His journeys take him to Winslow Slade's library, where he discovers one of the mysterious whisperings that follow him around, "hic habitat felicitas," engraved on the fireplace. Searching around in the fireplace, he discovers a loose brick, and finds after some removing of masonry a passage, through which he moves and "disappear[s] from his grandfather's study as, indeed, from our world" (486).

When the narrative returns to Todd Slade's adventures, it does so again through a metahistorical preface. Van Dyck notes that while "[h]istorians are in general agreement that June 4, 1906, marks the date of the 'exorcism' of the Curse on the Princeton community, being *coincidentally* the date of the death of Winslow Slade [. . .] none has yet attempted to link the events in any convincing manner." Once more, it is "evidence [. . .] to which I alone am privy" that permits van Dyck to offer a counter-narrative, a counter-narrative which is complicated by the problems which chronological linearity imposes on the events which, as he notes, "are occurring *simultaneously*," one in the fantastical and otherworldly Bog Kingdom, the other on the pulpit of Slade's First Presbyterian Church (600, original emphases).

Slade's sermon is a desperate confession, but more importantly it is a crucial misreading of his and his fellow parishioners' actual situation. This is set into sharp relief by the events in the Bog Kingdom, which offer a radically different view, precisely the kind of counter-history which sets *The Accursed* off from the histories van Dyck criticizes. There is little enough ambiguity in van Dyck's own reconstruction of events. It is Todd Slade's arrival in the Bog Kingdom that "would precipitate the deaths of his family's enemies" (602)—rather than echoing Winslow Slade's belief in the divine nature of his curse, van Dyck sets out the need to understand the relationship between the Slade family, the Curse, and the Bog Kingdom.

Todd's arrival in the Bog Kingdom is "a novelty, and something of a shock" (602): children do not, apparently, exist there. The Kingdom is ruled not merely by the Count/Mayte and Countess, but also by an oppressive ennui, "the inevitable curse of a seasonless and timeless land" (a land of eternal presence, we might say), and for a while, Todd Slade provides distraction. He discovers that it is a custom in the Kingdom to be able to challenge the Count/Mayte to a game of draughts for the rulership of the Kingdom; the risk is, however, that the loser also loses his life. Todd is initially chary of attempting to overthrow Mayte, but eventually realizes that this is his only chance of escape. The game is rigged. Mayte will cheat whenever possible, at the slightest distraction of Todd's from the board; the lord of the Bog Kingdom therefore does not really fear Todd when he issues the challenge. The game devolves into a contest of wills in which Todd, finally, succeeds. Mayte is defeated; his sister notes, "It is over. The game—our game—the Bog Castle—the Kingdom" (621). Indeed, Todd has to commit the final act in taking Mayte's life by severing his head, and then

> the shadowy hall with its gaping witnesses vanishes—and the Bog Castle vanishes—and the Bog Kingdom vanishes through its vast waste stretches; and Todd Slade wakes, his young heart hammering with life [. . .]. He knows only in that wondrous instant that the Curse has lifted, and he is alive—again alive. (621)

The novel is not exactly subtle in suggesting the meaning of Todd Slade's game, his victory, and the larger implications of both the events in the Bog Kingdom itself and the identity of Todd Slade. In a lengthy narrative aside before he even decides to play, we find out that he has "committed to memory a passage from Anaximander: *It is necessary that things should pass away, into that from which they are born. For things must pay one another the penalty, and the compensation, for their injustice, according to the ordinance of Time*"; and also a line from Heraclitus: "*Time is a child playing draughts, the kingship is in the hands of a child*" (609, original emphases). The last half-sentence is also echoed by both Mayte and the Countess after Mayte's defeat (621). Todd, the child, is Time, the assayer of penalties for the injustices committed by Mayte—and, of course, of Winslow Slade, whose death he precipitates in his defeat of Mayte. The symbolism of the younger generation not merely overcoming but actively stopping their fathers, of not merely being haunted by their sins but of handing out the penalties and ordaining the compensations for them, is overt. As Mayte points out to his sister in accepting Todd's challenge over her objections that Todd is merely a child: "'is a "child" not *one who will replace us?*'" For Mayte, as the narrator points out, there "was something treacherous, something uncontrollable, indeed something *unnatural* in the very concept of a child," because a child "will alter by degrees" (611, original emphases). In denouncing change and growth—progress—and in highlighting the danger of a younger generation replacing the older, Mayte highlights how the Curse's protagonists see the status quo as desirable, even in the face of their ennui, even if this status quo is not desirable for any other reason than being the status quo. It is not that the Bog Kingdom's status is immutable: any of the creatures sharing the kingdom with Mayte and his sister might challenge him; they do not do so because they have "become cowards," a consequence of a lack of "fresh blood" (611) in the Kingdom. Todd Slade provides the fresh blood: a possibility of change that stems from his ability to see differently.

The Gothic is "pervasive precisely because it is so apposite to the representation of contemporary concerns" and provides a "language and a lexicon through which anxieties both personal and collective can be narrativized" (Spooner 2007, 8–9). Such narrativization is a necessary first step in the process of overcoming anxieties, but is hardly enough. Indeed, in many ways Oates's novel deliberately exceeds traditional Gothic motifs in the process of producing a speculative narrative that not merely locally serves to symbolize the overcoming of private and collective angsts, but even serves to argue for the need to render this in speculative historism. If the Gothic allows for a broad range of positions, if "[i]t can be progressive or conservative" in equal measure (Spooner 2007, 156), *The Accursed* situates itself firmly on the side of a progressive possibility it produces both in its narrative, for its characters, and outside of it, by offering a re-reading of history and the historical possibilities inherent in envisaging a better future.

"Isn't the artist by nature a revolutionary?": The (Literary) Politics of *The Accursed*

The destruction of the supernatural Kingdom and its inhabitants which the novel so closely ties to the reactionary positions which Winslow Slade stands for already suggests a new situation for the twentieth century, and sketches a truth about the contemporary moments of the narrator's writing and the novel's publication. The novel is interested in resurrecting a particular kind of narrative of truth—even of Truth. The central agents of this narrative are Josiah Slade, whose slow but steady turn away from upper-class Princetonian society to the egalitarian Socialism of Upton Sinclair signals the revelatory power of the Curse and the possibilities opened by its demise, and Upton Sinclair, whose seriousness of purpose stands in contrast to the intellectually vacuous, easily led, and socially unconcerned upper class upon whom the Curse is visited and who themselves are implicated in it.

Gavin Cologne-Brookes has suggested in relation to Oates's first Gothic novel, *Bellefleur*, that "[f]or all its Gothicism, it is about nineteenth-century capitalism" (2014, 308). *The Accursed* is about what will become of this nineteenth-century capitalism in the twentieth century, and what can become of it beyond. This is the effect produced by the inclusion in the narrative of Upton Sinclair, fresh off his groundbreaking and accusatory muck-raking novel *The Jungle*. *The Accursed* does not aspire to the journalistic naturalism of Sinclair's novel, but that is because it is not exactly interested so much in the plight of the early twentieth-century worker under laissez-faire capitalism as it is in the allegorical and metaphorical potential which the association with the Event signaled by *The Jungle* brings.

The novel's plot and characters, its narrative form, and indeed its publication history interact complicatedly in producing this sense of an Event to whose Idea it is possible, indeed necessary, to remain faithful. Certainly the most obvious dimension here is the narrative one itself: Upton Sinclair's struggle to advance the Socialist cause, his involvement with Jack London, the supernatural events which are part of this plot; Josiah's growing interest in Socialist politics and his and Annabel's becoming members of Sinclair's Helicon Home Colony in the end. The novel deserves attention also for the way it structurally reinforces its narrative thrust. We need to take account of its narrative perspective, which takes in almost the full span of the twentieth century from M.W. van Dyck's place in the early 1980s. This clear temporality is crucial to the novel's politics, for, as Jean-Jacques Lecercle points out, "an event [. . .] can only be grasped in the future anterior, *it will* have occurred, and it will be grasped retroactively through a process of enquiry" (2010, 168, original emphasis). In other words, to recognize the events of *The Accursed* as an Event requires the retrospective narrative position, and indeed more than the comparatively facile generalized third-person, past-tense form of the historical novel. Publication history matters here, too. I am reading the novel as part of a set of contemporary texts responding to contemporary concerns, since it was published in 2013; but the first draft was finished in 1984. The significance of this point may be best seen by recourse to reading this as a necessary repetition (see Wegner 2009). These three issues are also already arrayed in their necessary logic: it is only because of the particular lower-case event(s) that *The Accursed* narratively discusses that the novel's narrative perspective and publication history can become readable as acts of "remaining faithful to a past event" (Badiou 2013a, 13). This offers us the possibility of a strong reading of *The Accursed*'s belated publication as evincing a curious fidelity to a political position that still seemed possible in the 1980s, and was considered impossible or unnecessary until *The Accursed* finally saw publication nearly thirty years later.

We must begin, then, with an analysis of the role of Upton Sinclair in the novel. For the narrator, van Dyck, Sinclair is, and remains, a curiously ambivalent character. This begins at Sinclair's first introduction as he passes the church in which Annabel Slade's wedding is just occurring, and about which Sinclair knows only the name of the bride, "*Slade*, with which the young Socialist naturally associated the extremities of capitalist exploitation of the masses" (141, original emphasis). To the narrator, Sinclair's association between the Slade family and their class status seems a tad too pat, but only perhaps—it is this uncertainty about van Dyck's estimation of Sinclair that prevents the novel from being, as it were, a didactic, Sinclarian text. The scene lays out the two main strands of Sinclair's story: his unwavering pursuit of a Socialist agenda in his engaged writing, and his personal marital troubles. Sinclair, married with a child, wavers on the value of this "*bourgeois* social institution": he "dearly loved his wife; yet, he knew that such love is hobbling, and enervating; and not worthy of the Socialist ideal." There is trouble with his wife Meta, and has been "for the past several weeks" (142, original emphasis). Meta is a constant source of anxiety for Sinclair, as she is to herself—torn between her own Socialism, motherhood, and the dissatisfying life she lives with Sinclair, she becomes suicidal before she encounters, and apparently has a dalliance with, Axson Mayte. Before the narrative can fully pursue this strand of Sinclair's life, however, it switches to the consequences which the troubles in his private life have for his Socialist engagement, and interweaves the private and political. His life appears to him "like the progress of Socialism in the capitalist societies of Europe and America, precarious and somewhat haphazard, unpredictable as a vast game of chance" (143). Broader social struggles obtrude:

> It was evident that reform was needed on every side, from the shame of child-labor in factories throughout, to the debased and dehumanizing conditions of the Southern Negroes, whose lives were hardly improved

> from the slavery of their grandparents. Yet, how should he and his fellow Socialists confront such a massive entity? *Had he the requisite courage?* (143, original emphasis)

As he is musing on these issues, he passes the church in which Annabel Slade is just then getting abducted by Axson Mayte. Lost in his contemplation of his problematic marriage, Sinclair is struck by the "singularly repulsive" (144) visage of Axson Mayte. Sinclair, as noted, is among the select few who can see through Mayte's glamour: if neither Josiah nor Sinclair manages to make the immediate fantastical deduction that would also reveal Mayte's true nature, there is a clear sense here that Mayte's ability to deceive is bound to a particular class-consciousness.

Sinclair's second major appearance occurs only towards the end of the novel, after Todd Slade's departure for the Bog Kingdom. By this time, Sinclair has been angling to get Jack London to become head of the Intercollegiate Socialist Society. London, Sinclair, and Josiah Slade meet at dinner in New York. The New York episodes that follow are significant for the novel in providing a counter-space to Princeton, especially for Josiah, who moves there in the aftermath of his cousin Todd's "death." For Josiah, cosmopolitan New York is a revelation. His sudden contact with "German, Polish, Hungarian, Jewish, Ukrainian, Italian, and Greek" and his increasing participation in various Socialist activities open vistas unavailable in Princeton; his involvement in Socialist thought is directly linked to his early turn away from his family. After Annabel's death, he admits to Winslow Slade that he finds the Bible can no longer answer his questions (289). In New York, the migrant population and the "rough vitality, vulgarity, and foreignness" of the city serve to draw him away from the "enchanted island" (291) of Princeton. In New York's bookstores, Josiah finds the Socialist magazine *Appeal to Reason*, with its serialized version of Sinclair's *The Jungle*. Josiah's reading of *The Jungle* precipitates quarrels with his father. Here again, the novel explicitly equates the older generation at Princeton with a conservative stance. As Josiah insists on reading from *The Jungle*, his father counters, "'Josiah, enough. Those are Socialists and Anarchists—they are not to be trusted! Free Thinkers, Suffragettes, Atheists—those who would overturn our civilization, and set it to the torch. You will not upset your mother and your grandfather and me, at such a time in our lives.'" To which Josiah, in a measure of his increasingly radical stance, replies, "'What better time, Father? If the world is in upheaval, what are we to do but heave ourselves up with it?'" (435). New York and its access to both a different kind of social life as well as a different political stance becomes a vital alternative to the stifling life in Princeton under the Curse. Leaving Princeton is a necessity for Josiah: while at home, he is increasingly pursued by the various emanations of the Curse, visions of Annabel beckoning him to join him in death. Josiah's full-time departure to live in New York, late in the novel, is thus a matter of resistance; his own promise to himself, as van Dyck reports it, is that while the Curse might destroy Josiah, it would not do so by his own hand (522).

It is against this background that Josiah and Sinclair's encounter with Jack London must be read. For both, London is a hero: the "boy socialist" whose early literary and political career make him seem like the ideal candidate to lead American Socialism forward. But these notions fall to pieces when London is actually encountered. A blowhard, anti-Semite, Social Darwinist adulterer, London and his companion, Miss Charmian, "ever more repelled" Sinclair. London, as it turns out, gives only lip-service to the deeper core of Socialism: in lieu of a brotherhood of man, London insists on a "natural aristocracy" (524) and on the "primeval spirit" (525) of the "Nordic Soul" (526). Sinclair sees a "sort of prankish demonism" (525) in London's eyes as he speaks. The meeting concludes with a short fight between Josiah and London, who believes Josiah has been flirting with Charmian. London is struck down and Josiah flees the scene, shocked by what he has been witnessing.

Josiah, like Sinclair, is appalled by London's demeanor, and they also share an interpretation of it. Conditioned by their Princeton experiences, both entertain the possibility that London is "*yet another demon*" (520, original emphasis). London seems too far removed from the figure they had thought he would be. It was "tempting to think that the enemies of Socialism had somehow conspired with a malevolent force, to prevent a Socialist hero, and sabotage the Revolution . . ." (516). The novel does not authorize the reading of London as an incarnation of Axson Mayte, but that is unnecessary. The connection which Sinclair and Josiah draw hinges on London's behavior and his position vis-à-vis progressive politics. In Sinclair and Josiah's understanding, being a demon has already become not an ontological state but a set of behaviors and positions—the same logic, essentially, which the reader is now free to read into the entire manifestation of the Curse. Whether or not Mayte-as-London is actively sabotaging the Socialist cause, as Sinclair dimly believes, the things London stands for (and which are deeply similar to the kinds of behavior through which the Curse has expressed itself in Princeton) all *do* militate against the Socialist cause. The true demon of *The Accursed* then is an anti-progressive, reactionary politics, whose various manifestations abound in the novel. Josiah's self-description as a "'belated but energetic convert' to the cause of socialism" (518) reinforces the sense of a developmental trajectory to the character. Beginning as the well-to-do scion of the most renowned of upper-class Princeton families, Josiah's encounters with the Curse have driven him from Princeton to New York; now, in the face of the disappointment with London, he joins the Antarctic expedition during which he will briefly die.

The net effect of the encounter with London is to offer a necessary corrective to both Josiah's and Sinclair's sense of what their Socialist alternative requires: individual leadership. London, it turns out, cannot be the leader they are looking for, and so they cease to look for a leader, but rather act themselves. Two things are put forward as helpful here: reading and understanding the right books, or experiencing the problems of society for yourself. It is in this light, too, that we may read the narrator, van Dyck's, own philosophy of history and the power of novels, suggested in a footnote. As Sinclair enters Princeton University's library, he is reported to have "no doubt that books might change the world," and of having as his model Harriet Beecher Stowe, "whose Uncle Tom's Cabin was popularly credited with having precipitated the Civil War!" Van Dyck notes that this is a popular misconception:

> Thus the reader is made to think that a single individual, in this case a female novelist, might help direct the course of history for the better. Thus the reader is made to smile, as one might smile seeing an affable dog staggering upright on his hind legs. The historian is one who must expose and correct such misconceptions, in the service of authenticity. (153)

Van Dyck's note reacts against simplistic, great-men philosophies of history, and against the belief that singular events, rather than systemically produced Events, may be said to produce historical change. But the insistence on the "female" novelist suggests a comment on Oates herself and the writing of *The Accursed*. As a tongue-in-cheek comment on her own aspirations, van Dyck's note thus interweaves the efforts of past and present, of writing *The Jungle* and writing *The Accursed*. No single individual may change the world—but books may (a motif we will come back to in Chapter 3). When, at the end of this passage, the novel notes that "Upton was a gentle person, and had never 'cursed' in his life. But, he was determined to learn" (154), the further play on the novel's title suggests the way in which Sinclair's writing may lay a finger on the nature of the systemic ills of his time. If this, by van Dyck's account, is not enough to "direct the course of history for the better," neither is it all that *The Accursed* ultimately enacts. Rather, it is one moment of many that together may have a progressive effect: Sinclair's writing of *The Jungle*; the novel's effects as narrated within *The Accursed*; the repetition of these acts in van Dyck's 1980 narrative;

and finally, the repetition of these acts in the 2013 publication of the novel. *The Accursed* becomes the "fictional account of the advent of an event, of the traces that it leaves, of the procedure of truth that it initiates, and of the process of subjectivation that ensues" (Lecercle 2010, 173). In *The Accursed*, it is especially Josiah and Annabel Slade on whom this process of subjectivation is enacted. The novel renders its readers into subjects as well; and, as Badiou notes, "political subjects"—such as Josiah and Annabel, but also we readers—"are always between two events" (2013a, 13). *The Accursed*'s representation of the first of these events, the coming into consciousness of a systemic alternative to the various regressive positions which are symbolized by the Crosswicks Curse, is merely the first iteration of a series of events in between which political subjectivity resides.

Against these developments we can read the conclusion of the novel, about which the narrator notes that "it is necessary to suggest an immediate future beyond" (646), a future provided only in rough sketches. Josiah and Annabel Slade become members of Sinclair's utopian project, the Helicon Home Colony, in New Jersey, and are joined by Yeager Ruggles, who brings with him "particularly 'radical and revolutionary' ideas ranging from union organizing to farming, worker-owned factories to 'race-free' education and housing; ideas, *unfortunately*, far ahead of their time" (646, my emphasis). The interpolation of "unfortunately" is the narrator's, and counteracts the sense of ironic detachment which van Dyck affects throughout much of the narrative. Investing "virtually all of their trust-fund money" (647), Josiah and Annabel enact their turn away from the Princetonian past of the Curse. The final scene, as the narrator introduces it, is a wedding ceremony in which Annabel Slade marries Yeager Ruggles—given Ruggles's mixed-race ancestry, a strongly symbolic move.

At the heart of *The Accursed* is a historically informed argument about class, one which reads in Josiah and Annabel's surrender of their inherited wealth and turn to Sinclair's utopian community a bourgeoning class-consciousness—not necessarily in the Lukácsian sense, as the ability to "organise the whole society in accordance with [its] interests" (Lukács 1983, 52), but rather in the sense of Rancière's notion of the distribution of the sensible. Josiah and Annabel, "all unconsciously and helplessly, as they are *Slades*" (94, original emphasis), are not just snobs (the context of the quote), but also—in the novel's metonymic class argument—caught in the system. At least, that is, until they struggle to free themselves from it after having been in direct contact with the ravages that the class system of their time produces. The novel's final lines (save the appendix) are Sinclair's: "'Comrades! It is the dawn of a new day!

Revolution now!'" (648, original emphasis); but they echo the sense of progress which the narrative has enacted. The Curse and all it stands for has been exorcized; a new way of organizing communal life has begun; the revolution so desperately looked for is truly now. The sole remaining question may be, which "now"?

Conclusion: The Return of the 1980s and the Truths of History

The Accursed was initially drafted, as *The Crosswicks Horror*, in 1981, after the publication of *Bellefleur* and contemporaneously with *A Bloodsmoor Romance* as well as Oates's "political novel, *Angel of Light*" (Oates 2007b, 399). Its publication fell victim to what appears from Oates's diary to be largely a financial decision. Even at the time, however, Oates conceived it as having "allegorical purposes" (421): as she notes, it is among other things at least an "allegory" of "class struggle" (429). Indeed, this Marxist or Socialist motif should perhaps not come as a surprise; in her diaries, she wrote of *Bellefleur* in February 1980, "[i]t comes to me that one of the secret themes of *Bellefleur* is something very simple: class warfare" (Oates 1980, 355). And she goes so far as to suggest that "*Bellefleur*, and many of the other novels [are] . . . in part . . . in secret . . . Marxist parables" (356, original ellipses), while disclaiming that she herself is a Marxist. Indeed, the point here is not that Oates herself is or has been a Socialist; rather, that her novel becomes readable politically through placing it against the backdrop of its contemporary contexts, in this case, of both the time of writing, in the early 1980s, and of the time of publication, in the 2010s. Such a reading must itself be necessarily speculative and symptomatic. The 1980s figure prominently as a returning trope in much contemporary fiction (as they do throughout this book), and they do so precisely because of the paradigm shift through which what Alain Badiou calls the "'red years'" (2012, 14) beginning in 1960 were replaced by the neoliberal consensus of privatization and desocialization. What Oates calls "class warfare" simultaneously comes to the front and becomes relegated to the backwaters: in simple terms, class warfare seems (remember Fukuyama) to come to an end in the success of a neoliberal consensus that leaves no room for utopian imaginations. If all history is the history of class struggle, then no history anymore is also no class struggle anymore. There is maybe no necessary but clearly a suggestive connection between the moments of drafting the five Gothic novels and their publication in the early 1980s, and the moment of 2013 (with the exception of 1998's *My Heart Laid Bare*). That *The Accursed* was drafted in 1981 does clearly not mean we cannot read its narrative against the background of the particular political and economic constellation facing it in 2013. Rather, it makes it necessary to speak about *both* 1981 and 2013. When Oates writes in the 1985 afterword to *Mysteries of Winterthurn* that she considers the subjects of her Gothic novels to be "uniquely American and *of our time*" (1985, 373, my emphasis), this claim to topicality extends to *our* time as well now. The issues which the novel broaches, in their radical conclusion at Helicon Home Colony, seem now to be possible again.

Brenda Daly has contended that Oates's "ambitious project" over all her writing is the "examination of American society, past and present, especially in terms of the distribution of power" (1996, x); *The Accursed*'s unique position as a 1981 novel set in 1906, narrated in 1984 and published only in 2013 enables it to offer a multidimensional survey of these concerns. Just as Badiou's "return of history" indicates the way in which we may read our own time as one that is after an almost automatic assumption of neoliberal hegemony, so the non-publication of *The Accursed* in the 1980s may be read as a symptomatic acceptance of the impossibility of imagining in print the kind of progressive-socialist narrative that *The Accursed* enacts. In a slight chronological modification of Phillip Wegner's thesis that the fall of the Berlin Wall and 9/11 bounded the distinct period of the 1990s as events recognizable only in their own repetitiousness (2009, 24), *The Accursed* also nods to repetitive events bounding a period. Here, the publication of the novel in 2013 repeats the project it was written as in 1981, and the act of narration in 1984 repeats the Event of the Socialist alternative of 1906. Each of these doubles repeats the other, too, suggesting Oates's novel's incidental periodization of a contemporary class struggle viable as a motif in 1981, and then increasingly impossible until it returns in 2013.

The novel's relationship with the narrativization of history then is not particularly postmodern, and despite the outward trappings, neither is its relation to genre. In her afterword to the *Mysteries of Winterthurn*, Oates explains the thinking that underlies her Gothic saga:

> Why "genre," one might ask? Does a serious writer dare concern herself with "genre"? Why, in imagining a quintet of novels to encompass some eight decades of American history (beginning in the turbulent 1850s in *Bloodsmoor*, ending in 1932 with the election of FDR in "*My Heart Laid Bare*"), and to require some 2600 pages of prose—why choose such severe restraints, such deliberately confining structures? But the formal discipline of "genre"—that it forces us inevitably to a radical re-visioning of the world and of the craft of fiction—was the reason

> I found the project so intriguing. To choose idiosyncratic but not distracting "narrators" to recite the histories; to organize the voluminous materials in patterns alien to my customary way of thinking and writing; to "see" the world in terms of heredity and family destiny and the vicissitudes of Time (for all five novels are secretly fables of the American family); to explore historically authentic crimes against women, children, and the poor; to create, and to identify with, heroes and heroines whose existence would be problematic in the clinical, unkind, and one might almost say, fluorescent-lit atmosphere of present-day fiction—these factors proved irresistible. The opportunity might not be granted me again, I thought, to create a highly complex structure in which individual novels (themselves complex in design, made up of "books") functioned as chapters or units in an immense design: America as viewed through the prismatic lens of its most popular genres. (1985)

Oates understands genre as already formally involved with a "radical re-visioning of the world": she produces a speculative form that already takes up opportunities whose realizations are at work in all the texts I discuss. The "prismatic lens" of genre fiction permits the particular attention to "crimes against women, children, and the poor" unavailable in the increasingly common, capitalist realism of the 1980s, and then the 1990s and 2000s.

If the power of genre is to make available points of view from which a radical revisioning of American history is possible, it may bear summarizing what this revisioning amounts to in *The Accursed*. On the one hand, certainly, we have the emancipatory conclusion to the larger narrative; in Winslow Slade's death, we find many of the political concerns of the novel brought to a close. The death of the patriarch concludes symbolically the entire patriarchal system and its effects, racism, misogyny, and class privilege. In several ways, Slade's own final refusal to accept the reality of events, and effort to make them part of a world-view that has shaped his life for decades, mark also the necessary failure of his generation to accept the new, something also hinted at strongly in making Todd Slade responsible for the downfall of the Bog Kingdom.

Saved from the Crosswicks Curse and restituted to their families, Annabel and Josiah Slade do not linger in Princeton. Instead, they move to Upton Sinclair's utopian community Helicon Home Colony. The novel certainly could end here, but it does not. The narrator instead takes care to inform us that notwithstanding their investments, the Helicon Home Colony failed, burning down in 1907 and being subsequently disbanded. It is an odd choice for a narrative that has focused so strongly on its emancipatory politics. Yet perhaps curiously, this apparently unhappy ending to Sinclair's utopian project need not be read negatively (Oates's narrator does not do so himself). The "productive use" of past instances of radical political stances lies not in celebrating them for the "triumphant reassemblage as a radical precursor tradition" (Jameson 1991, 209) but rather precisely in the recognition of their failure. History, as Jameson reminds us, progresses by failure rather than by success.

Thus we must read Annabel and Josiah's move to Helicon in at least two ways. It is at once a recognition of the radically new circumstances in which they find themselves as well as symbolic of the larger circumstances of the new century. Their and the colony's failure is an admission not of the futility of utopian projects, but, in simple terms, of the need to keep on trying. "Even when they failed, utopian communities radically altered people and perceptions"; "[o]ut of defeat emerges [sic] ideas, changed people, and new movements" (Jacoby 2005, 5). What "needs to be salvaged" from the past in reaction to the present apparent lack of viable alternatives are precisely the "catastrophic attempts at living differently" (Williams 2011, loc. 618). Terry Eagleton more broadly suggests that "the most authentic kind of hope is whatever can be salvaged, stripped of guarantees, from a general dissolution" (2015, 114). Oates's ending looks forward to the new century with a spirit of hope rekindled, rekindled all the more powerfully in point of fact for realizing the immensity of the historical events that are yet to come, and the devastation that they will wreak.

Chapter 3

A Less Oblique Mode of Political Art: Chris Bachelder's *U.S.!* and Jason Heller's *Taft 2012*

The Accursed ends with the future laid out before an Upton Sinclair at the height of his fame and in the middle of an actual utopian experiment in Socialist living. Chris Bachelder's 2006 novel *U.S.!* begins on the backseat of a car which the unnamed narrator of the opening episode shares with Sinclair. Sinclair is dead: that is, he is still dead, but expected to recover momentarily, as he has done countless times in the past: "it just sort of happens naturally" (4). Indeed, Sinclair wakes from death, spitting out clods of earth, "the last best hope of the American left" (6). This opening sequence is set in the winter of 1980: Ronald Reagan has won the presidential election. Against this backdrop, Sinclair's waking question rings deeply hollow: "Are we Socialist yet?" (7). Yet it is this question and its corollaries: will we ever be? Shouldn't we be? How will we become? that underly Bachelder's narrative. "What do you want with me? Why have you brought me back?" Sinclair asks; the answer, inevitably, will be "[t]hings aren't fair is why" (10). And the reply, delivered here by a smiling Sinclair, is as inevitable: "That idea is quite likely to get us killed" (11).

On its first pages, Bachelder's novel reveals both its central conceit and its central political argument; more than that, it interweaves them so as to make them inseparable. The speculative motif of a resurrection that has happened over and over in the past and is set to continue indefinitely into the future opens to view the state both of society and of specifically Leftist politics in the United States. The rather episodic looks at Sinclair's earlier and later resurrections are an "actual history of the brief rises and long, tumbling falls of the American Left" (Cohen 2012, 210). The novel presents this history with sarcastic verve and formal ingenuity. The first half is a kaleidoscopic journey through the absurdities of a world in which assassinating Upton Sinclair has become a popular pastime of sorts. From transcripts of calls to the Upton Sinclair tip hotline (at 1-800-US-Watch) its panorama extends to song lyrics, to letters Sinclair writes to his son (who is also "the last folksinger"), to journal entries, to memos exchanged within a video game company that is developing a game whose goal is shooting "recently resurrected leftists" (38), to a syllabus for a college course taught by Sinclair, Amazon.com reviews, eBay auction descriptions, and an article on the Museum of Upton Sinclair Assassination. Interspersed throughout are short texts narrating episodes from Sinclair's various returns, in which we see him visit a conspiratorial Socialist rally (while commenting on an unpublished utopian science fiction novel), write books in a far-away cabin (and there narrowly and rather ineptly evade another assassination attempt), and meet (and completely fail to connect to) E.L. Doctorow.

The second half of the book is much more straightforward. In the town of Greenville, Alabama, the quasi-folkloristic local Anti-Socialist League is planning its annual Fourth of July Book Burning. The precocious son of the League's current president volunteers to organize the event, ordering 500 copies of Sinclair's new novel. The order leads Sinclair to believe that there is an imminent Socialist revolution in Greenville, so he goes to join the Fourth of July celebrations. Sinclair's probable presence in Greenville draws a number of Sinclair assassins, including his most successful, Gerald Huntley already retired, and his would-be successor, Francis Billings. Sinclair discovers that there is no imminent Socialist uprising; the assassins fail; Huntley decides not to assassinate Sinclair; and Stephen Rudkin, the kid who had bought Sinclair's books to burn, settles down to read one and becomes, at least for the duration of the novel, a devoted Socialist.

The novel ends in a short postscript of just two pages, encompassing the final song written by Sinclair's now also assassinated son, a song that ends on the hopeful injunction to "[d]ream the dream that never fades" (302). In the kind of ironic complication that the novel delights in throughout, it makes Greenville out to be precisely the Socialist model town that Sinclair discovers it most assuredly is not.

Any reading of Bachelder's novel must necessarily integrate an interpretation of its central speculative conceit, its larger sense of literary form, and the novel's insistence on both the general hostility to Socialism as well as Socialism's enduring call for radical change. *U.S.!* is a novel about the political capacity of literature, about the need to envisage hopeful futures no matter what the current situation is, and a novel that sees this hopeful future reflected emphatically in the political proposals of Socialism. These separate strands are held together precisely by Upton Sinclair's constant resurrection: the narrative's insistence on resurrection in lieu of, for example, immortality is a crucial literary strategy. The novel is speculative through the resurrection of Sinclair; it is historical through its resurrection specifically of Sinclair, who stands as an avatar of the American Left's origins. In part, Sinclair comes to stand as synecdoche for the narrative of the Left's rise and fall which Samuel Cohen has identified. Bachelder's novel raises a vision of the future dependent on the recognition that the kind of endist narratives which suggest final conclusions (such as Sinclair's death) may be questioned, that hope really does spring eternal. It taps into a reservoir of historical events and subject positions that suggest the possibility and the necessity to remain faithful to the (Socialist) idea no matter what intervenes. Sinclair's resurrections afford him what Jameson calls "the possibility of reentering the stream of history and development over and over again," and thus to interact with the "incomparably longer temporal rhythms of history itself," rather than the individual human life span (2005, 7). As a speculative device, resurrection permits *U.S.!* to suggest the prematurity of claims for the demise of Socialism as well as the necessity to hold on to it as an idea.

U.S.! is also a complexly literary novel—far more so than Kalfus's or Oates's novels, I would argue. Lee Konstantinou has called *U.S.!* a "work of metafiction" (2014, 455), but *U.S.!* is only very tentatively interested in its own status as narrative or fiction, or the status of fiction writing as such. It is, to be sure, a text crafted with attention to its own textuality, but not wholly about this textual production. If it is metafictional, it is political metafiction, "rethinking and reworking [. . .] the forms and contents" of political fiction (rather than history (Hutcheon 1988, 5)) and of the social novel's social-political content. Konstantinou's suggestion that the novel is best understood in its relationship to postmodernism and the recognition that it shares certain ulterior motives with postmodernist writing while seeking new forms of "injecting news, politics, and critique into the novel" (2014, 461) points usefully to continuities with some forms of postmodern thought. But this does not exhaust the reach of *U.S.!*'s formal choices as a means of political performance. In *U.S.!*, criticism and remembrance of the past coincide forcefully precisely because of Sinclair's constant revival, supplying the criteria for being prepared for an event in Badiou's sense (2013a, 13–14) and thus opening to view the possibility for rethinking the contemporary laws of the world. It is not that Sinclair appears in this as a paragon of hope and Socialist virtue, or as a shining knight of Socialism's cause. "Bachelder does not necessarily disagree with [a] fictional reviewer's aesthetic assessment of Sinclair" as "a poor writer, an egomaniac, a gullible freak, and a bad father" (Konstantinou 2014, 463). *U.S.!* depicts Sinclair as earnest, but also ridiculous. The novel as a whole clearly juxtaposes the necessity of ironizing and criticizing Sinclair and Socialist idealism with the need to take seriously both Sinclair's message and the possibility that someone has been truly converted. Even in its ironic distance it presents Sinclair and Socialism as the only possible even if flawed hopes in a society that it ironizes and criticizes even more strongly. The novel recognizes implicitly that "political subjects are always between two events. They are never simply confronted with the opposition between the event and the situation but are in a situation upon which events of the recent or distant past still have an impact" (Badiou 2013a, 13). Both Sinclair in the novel and the readers of the novel are political subjects in this sense. Both of them carry and are made to carry the idea of Socialism and the utopian hopes that come with it. Understanding the work which *U.S.!* does thus develops my argument from the previous chapters in a text that is more forcefully political, more fully speculative, and more overtly literary than Oates's or Kalfus's novels.

In what follows, I will first analyze the particular politics which Bachelder's novel produces, and seek to relate this politics to the moment of its publication in 2006. Second, I will seek to elaborate on the way Bachelder's novel tackles the problem of the contemporary social novel—the kind of novel which Upton Sinclair himself engaged in writing. *U.S.!* reforms the social novel for a contemporary moment in which the Sinclarian, didactic, realist novel cannot adequately function anymore; but it does so even as it seems to reaffirm this kind of novel's power in its own narrative. This dialectic serves to emphasize the peculiar kind of work literary writing can perform. Finally, I will relate *U.S.!* to Jason Heller's *Taft 2012*, which brings former U.S. President William Howard Taft into the twenty-first century, there to run in the 2012 presidential elections. Heller's formally similar novel offers a considerably different perspective on what hopes the present requires; but more than that, it serves to juxtapose the kind of literary novel which *U.S.!* certainly aspires to be with a far more readily generic, popular version of a similar argument. The two novels serve to establish a more general sense of the narrative encoding of hopeful futures through the bodily return of history into the present; but they do so within the constraints of their generic operations.

The Steady Beat of the Left: The Politics of *U.S.!*

To observe that *U.S.!* is a political novel at least in a broad conception of the term is largely banal, given its subject and protagonist. That this constitutes a problem is more evident when we realize that while politics permeates the fabric of the novel in a larger, vague sense, in a more narrow one—read and understood as party politics—politics is an overtly sidelined aspect of life in the novel's world. Politics in this sense does not happen at all: there are no elections and no engagement in the political arena, no sense of what the state of politics is in the worlds into which Sinclair is resurrected. For any reading of the politics of *U.S.!* to succeed then, we must grasp politics as a theory and a concept, without losing track of the importance of the novel's representation of the state of politics.

When I speak of the politics of *U.S.!* I mean the term to be understood in the dual sense permitted by the novel: the political positions and actions which are represented in narrative form and a broader sense of politics as one of Alain Badiou's "truth procedures," one way—perhaps a privileged way—of making a "possibility" appear (2013a, 10). The novel's engagement with politics is conditioned both by its sense of what is pervasive and regressive about the political situation it narrates, as well as the understanding that it still, actively, is concerned with possible literary conceptions of the "political event." *U.S.!* mediates such events: in the efforts to bring the resurrected Sinclair into contact with people interested in hearing his message, and in the Greenville book burning: not as the certainty of change, but as the possibility of a beginning.

Politics, Badiou suggests, is "the organized collective action which in conformity with some principles, aims to unfold in the real the consequences of this new possibility" (2005, 12) to reimagine human relations. The particular sense with which Badiou imbues the political thus runs into conflict with a more colloquial sense of politics also found in the novel, the struggle between parties or ideologies and the identification of individuals with them. Politics, then, occurs on two levels in *U.S.!*: as the representation of the state of politics in the various moments the novel narrates, and as the inherently progressive, hopeful vision of politics which stems from Badiou's philosophy. This dual perspective permits us to realize the way in which the novel itself sees the duality of politics work. It does not condemn the idea of political action so much as it highlights the deficits in exercising it. It does not see no escape and no future, but rather highlights how in any meaningful sense of the term politics, no politics is operative in *U.S.!*. No true subject position remains in a world in which no fidelity to an evental truth persists. This status quo gets broken, or at least questioned, both by the novel's form, which indicates the fidelity to the ideas contained within it, and by its narrative, the events in Greenville through which shines forth a glimmer of a new subjectivity in Stephen's new-found fidelity to the idea transported in Sinclair's novel. Upton Sinclair in this reading of *U.S.!* through Badiou becomes overtly an avatar of a fidelity to the truth contained in the event of the birth of a Socialist political stance.

The novel sets these two senses of politics in opposition, to draw out a meaningful sense of what prospects for the future are at hand. Formally, the novel starts out with the somewhat deprived version of political consciousness that circumscribes its sense of a dearth of real politics. Much of its initial section shows glimpses of how politics has been emptied of meaning, and political engagement replaced by a fundamental indifference. In this section of the novel, form exceeds the central question of its speculative historism. It is not reducible to Sinclair's status as a counterfactual character of sorts. The first section presents a series of collected artifacts, all of which offer readers glimpses into the historico-fictive facts of Sinclair's life. But these artifacts do more than offer the kind of documentary insight which the collage technique can provide: by the very choice of collage-texts, *U.S.!* suggests the depoliticization and the structural poverty of the political sphere in which the novel takes place. *U.S.!* represents a United States which is fundamentally apathetic to the substance of disagreement in the political realm.

Examples of this indifference abound. A rock band naming itself "Ezra Pound Postcard," a reference to the last words Sinclair utters during one of his assassinations and to Sinclair's receipt, during his 1934 gubernatorial run, of abusive missives from the poet, disclaims that this has any political meaning. "We're not a political band,' the front man insists (114). The architect of the Museum of Upton Sinclair Assassination acknowledges that she

> didn't approach MUSA as a political project. I was commissioned to design a museum, just as I am commissioned to build a research park or a corporate high-rise. [. . .] I suppose there are politics involved there, but none that really concern me as a working artist. (169)

What is important here is the architect's vague supposing that "there are politics involved there," a point raised a number of times in other contexts. That a museum is just like a research park or a corporate high-rise is obviously symptomatic, but more importantly, the assassination of Sinclair has itself lost political meaning. There is something vaguely political about a museum dedicated to the assassination of the most prominent Socialist in the country, but it is *only* vaguely political; what it has become is largely entertainment. Another document which the novel offers up is thus a memo sent within a video game company, commenting on an early version of "Glorious Phantoms!," a "great-looking" game with the fatal flaw of its premise: to dig up and resurrect

"Malcolm X, Sinclair Lewis, Emma Goldman, Eugene Debs, Mother Jones, Shelley, Old Joe Hill," to name a few. As the memo points out,

> the kids who play our games don't want to make the world a better place. [. . .] They are unconcerned about the distribution of wealth and access to the means of producing. They want to shoot things. This may be sad, but it's true. Listen, I'm on your side here, politically speaking. I had the Marx and Ingels [sic] Reader on my shelf in college. I recycle. I intend to vote for Gore. But we're running a business here, and we've got to run it wisely or we're going to be out on the street following around what's his name. We just can't let our politics mix with our business practices, and certainly not with our games. (39)

U.S.!'s world is without politics. Such resistance to Leftist politics as there is is rendered through recourse to the question of profitability, but by far more important is the sheer fact that resistance to Leftist politics itself is rendered in apolitical terms. The Museum of Upton Sinclair Assassination is not a place of capitalist resistance against Socialism; the crucial problem which the games company sees with "Glorious Phantoms!" is not that it celebrates Leftist politics. The novel highlights the total surrender of political engagement in the cultural realm in stressing the acceptance that the logics of games company and architect alike are not political, but economic. *U.S.!* enacts the surrender to capitalist realism, suggesting that the very idea of political engagement does not hold. In both cases, the idea that art can, and more properly should, be political is voided by a defensive recourse to such a logic.

This is certainly a representation of capitalist ideology triumphant: operative to the point where it has become second nature, a refraction of the moment of the novel's publication in 2006. But the novel's insistence on framing this not as a matter of political rejection, but rather as being "unconcerned," as having abandoned conviction more generally, is crucial. This is a position that the novel frames as having a historical place, as the particular post-Cold War situation of the early 2000s. It does so, again, through a historicization of Sinclair's relevance. It is no coincidence that the novel opens in the shadow of the election of Ronald Reagan, at the beginning of the triumphant march of neoliberalism which also coincided with the rejection of the *grand récit*. When we next meet Sinclair, he is meant to give a speech at a high school graduation in 1987—a speech about the "will to succeed," which "touches lightly on the thread of nuclear annihilation" and "uses the terms *capitalism* and *democracy* more or less interchangeably." Sinclair does not in fact deliver this speech, with its shades of Fukuyama—he instead attempts to offer an argument for Socialist cooperation and fervently hopes that "[t]his could be [. . .] the cradle of American Socialism" (22). It is a crucial phrase: it highlights the juxtaposition between Sinclair's offer and the reflexive resistance he encounters, the catcalls of "Communist!," "Godless!," and "Russia!" that his audience throws at him. Sinclair's hope, of course, is fantastic. There is no reason to assume his audience will hear him out, much less turn towards his cause, and it leaves him faintly ridiculous. But this, at least, is still a form of political opposition, in which the still-unresolved Cold War provides a backdrop to the audience's resistance to Sinclair's Socialism.

In the more contemporary moments of *U.S.!*, both the radical systemic alternative and the principled defense of the status quo are understood to be in trouble. On the side of Sinclair's opponents, this fundamental problem is symbolized by the most famous of Sinclair assassins, Gerald Huntley. When Huntley-scholar Lionel Pratt speaks of Huntley in an interview that forms one of the texts of the book's long first section, he notes that

> [y]ou can find Huntley in the prison library a lot more often than in the prison weight room. He is an avid reader and a real student of history and politics. After many hours in his company, I have come to see that he is intelligent and thoughtful. (149)

What drives Huntley is a genuine, if violently displaced, political disagreement. As Pratt notes, "Huntley sees Sinclair's politics as a grave threat to the individual and to the world" (150). But Huntley is also, by the time of the main action of novel, something of a relic of the past; his personal significance has come to exceed, and to diminish, his principled political opposition. "His fame had transcended morality or politics" (296); assassination too has turned into a spectacle; politics transmogrified so that even the ultimate act of political assassination has become little more than a spectator sport, celebrity-driven and divorced entirely from any political rationale. This is most evident in the figure of Francis Billings, "Billings the Kid," the seventeen-year-old who wants to be the most famous Sinclair assassin ever. Asked by an interviewer what he knows about Socialism, Billings replies, "'I know I hate it. That's all I need to know"; asked which of Sinclair's books he hates the most, he says, "'They all bad. I hate them all. All that socializing. I'll kill him" (229). If the audience of Sinclair's 1987 speech could, at least, still relate its opposition to Sinclair to an overarching larger ideological struggle and correct use of terminology, and find itself politically active in the colloquial sense, Billings's averseness to "socializing" points out what has gotten lost in the intervening decade or so. Any realization of the relevance of the struggle has been replaced by its mere perpetuation as a spectacle, a public entertainment of sorts in which the genuine ideological difference of an earlier age has become evacuated, if only on one side.

That this is the case only for one side—the side that has apparently won the ideological struggle—holds true even as *U.S.!* seems to highlight the increasingly quixotic nature of both Sinclair's personal persistence in the cause as well as that of those who resurrect him, the sad groups of secret admirers who meet in dark basements to hear Sinclair speak, but whom we never see in political action, who never march, or protest, campaign, or electioneer. These groups "don't think of [themselves] as part of a movement" (121), at least initially, but passively observe Sinclair's persistence in the struggle. But then something shifts. The crowd (in a segment notably narrated in the first-person plural, in which "we watched" and "acted") is suddenly confronted with Sinclair himself and finds itself transformed, "filled with a sense of possibility, of creation" (141), even after belatedly realizing that it has in fact not met Sinclair but has been watching an artfully edited documentary. As the crowd leaves the place of the screening, understanding dawns that "the hardest thing of all, will be to keep, somehow, the faith" (142). In its struggle for fidelity this crowd enacts Badiouan politics in the midst of a desert of politics; a possibility created and imagined much earlier is turned, via artistic mediation, into an affirmation of an earlier event.

U.S.! mediates politics through art and represents politics as mediated by art. Most of its engagement with art and politics suggests a fundamental indifference to the political potentials of art, indeed a refusal to see art as political in the first place. But the novel also discusses what the formal consequences of this generalized truth are. Perhaps the most overt example of this is the short interview which the artist Treadwell gives on the subject of his *Sinclair Centerfolds*. An abstract painter, Treadwell has made three "high gloss and hyperrealistic" (86) paintings of Sinclair, naked, to resemble the *Playboy* centerfold models. The paintings show him as "weak, frail, and feminine," as the introduction to the interview, an encyclopedia article, notes: an apparent setback for the cause for which Sinclair stands. As the article quotes E.L. Doctorow, "'If the Left wasn't already dead (and I suspect it was), then the Sinclair Centerfolds killed it'" (87).

The question why Doctorow holds the paintings in such disdain is, the novel makes clear, connected to the realist form:

TAPEWORM.COM:	[. . .] Why the shift to realism and representation?
TREADWAY:	All my work is representational. You can't not be representational.

TAPEWORM.COM:	Why the shift to a more overt political subject or mode?
TREADWAY:	Political? All my work has been political.
TAPEWORM.COM:	Perhaps, but not— (88–89)

There are a number of other issues at work in this section of the novel which we need to look at to situate the interview. Treadwell is a postmodernist of sorts, one who rose to fame on pastiches of Western paintings to which he has added modern technology. His performance art is alternatively read as "recognition of hope irrepressible" and a "'nasty, tragic joke'"; his paintings, "hilarious and disquieting" and "juvenile and suburban" (86). His period of work extends from 1989 to 2001 (85), a notable time period (see Wegner 2009); his work becomes representative of a more general contemporary belief in the limits of historical representation and art. But at the same time, the interview goes on to see Treadway deny the notion that realistic painting is more accurate than any other painting, noting how it still is just two-dimensional representation. There is a paradoxical structure of political art which the novel sees at work here. The ostensible realism of the Sinclair Centerfolds produced backlash because its realism appears more easily intelligible to viewers. Viewers realize the political content of these hyperrealist paintings where, at least if we are to believe Treadwell, they have missed the political importance of his earlier, abstract, postmodern work. Realism comes with a double edge here: it is more readily capable of being political, in the sense that an audience will more readily perceive its political nature, but at the same time it fails to do what it sets out to do; it strengthens the wrong side of the political struggle. On the other hand, however, the ostensibly political art which Treadway has, by his own reckoning, always produced, not only did not get understood as political, but was received with ambivalence, as either vaguely mobilizing or complete nonsense. More importantly, however, his move into realism—despite the undoubted fact that realism, too, is just a formal effect, not in any way more representational or accurate, as Treadway correctly insists—is detrimental to the cause which it apparently supports. This is the key insight of the chapter: realism of the type which Treadway in art and Sinclair in writing engage is not the obvious right choice for the temporal moment in which Treadway paints, and in which *U.S.!* gets written. Through the Treadway interview, the novel mediates the very problematic conjunction in which non-realist art forms leave an audience unable to obtain a political message, and realist art forms cannot move the cause of the Left anymore.

The relationship which *U.S.!* enacts between art and politics is a complex one which becomes more complex still when we try to account for its own position on the political power of art. On the one side stands Sinclair, with his insistence that his writing, at least, has and will make a difference (57); on the other, a more generally negative belief that art changes nothing. It is easy, of course, to be critical of any claim to art's capacity to engender a progressive politics. As Jacques Rancière points out, despite no longer actively believing in the artistic logic, we

> continue to act as if reproducing a commercial idol in resin will engender resistance against the "spectacle", and as if a series of photographs about the way colonizers represent the colonized will work to undermine the fallacies of mainstream representations of identities. (2010, 136)

What Rancière calls the "*pedagogical* model of the efficacy of art" (2010, 136, original emphasis) in part applies to *U.S.!*. It would be foolhardy to assume that its own "reproduction in resin" of what it sees as its contemporary moment's abstention from politics is effective in undermining this very abstention. *U.S.!* reflects this problem in Treadway's performance art, a Sunset Exhibition that for various reasons never really shows a sunset, highlighting the effect of pollution and urbanization on the natural environment, which, predictably, does not in fact manage to be more than merely art, does not in fact have consequences. Neither the interviewer nor Treadway faces this Rancièrian problem. Mainstream art which ignores politics, or simply adopts the ideological status quo, prevails.

The question, then, is where, in this system of art, politics, and literature, hope prevails. How does *U.S.!* see the potential of its own form, and by extension how may we see the form of speculative historism, to exceed the limits which the art it represents appears to be confounded by? To be sure, it does not have a general answer to the troubling problem of the impossibility of art to work politically, but it does have one for the form that interests it most, the social novel. Upton Sinclair figures in this political work of the particular kind of social novel that *U.S.!* sees as still important, still perhaps effective, in a dual sense. His literary and political work are inseparable, and this not merely because the work we see him undertake in the novel is largely the act of writing more and more novels. It is because Sinclair himself, as a historical figure, was inescapably both a political and a literary figure, engaged in writing about the existing state of affairs and in the political act of changing them. This key duality is a crucial element of the novel's restitution of the social novel in a new form, as speculative historism.

"Nothing is a priori impossible": *U.S.!* and the Rewriting of the Social Novel

One of the first little documents in *U.S.!* is a review of Sinclair's 107th novel, *Pharmaceutical!*. The reviewer is savage, blasting the novel as an "embarrassment" and a "formulaic, simplistic Socialist screed" (12) in the opening paragraph. After addressing himself to a short recapitulation of Sinclair's career, the reviewer expands his argument to the entirety of the Sinclarian canon: "Sinclair's novels today seem vulgar, tendentious, hysterical" (13), and stresses that this is an "aesthetic" issue:

> art and polemic do not mix, [. . .] great and lasting art has no authorial agenda. Novels are not tracts or pamphlets; they do not serve to convince the readers of anything. A novel may ask questions, but a good one never supplies an answer. (14)

The "naïveté and artistic bankruptcy of [Sinclair's] narrative mode" (15), the reviewer concludes, cripples Sinclair's fiction even without recourse to his politics. But the reviewer constantly needs to address this politics: "It isn't simply that his ideas are extreme, outdated, and irrelevant (though they are; no serious thinker today takes Socialism seriously)" (13), he avers at one point. At another, he insists that the "wonderful thing about America is that you always have a shot, while the dreadful thing about a Sinclair novel is that you don't" (15).

There is a complicated argumentative interweaving of aesthetics and narrative and literary politics in this fictional review of a fictional novel. It stresses an apparently apolitical disavowal of Sinclair's style, an insistence that the novel fails aesthetically rather than merely politically. The reviewer approvingly quotes Edith Wharton, in a letter to Sinclair about the latter's novel *Oil!*: "It seems to me an excellent story until the moment, all too soon, when it becomes a political pamphlet. I make this criticism without regard to the views which you teach, and which are detestable to me" (14). This insistence on objectivity collapses when read against the review's repeated invocation of *Pharmaceutical!*'s faulty politics. The reviewer cannot reduce his criticism to aesthetic judgment except to claim that "great and lasting art has no authorial agenda" (14). This insistence on an ahistorical, unpolitical aesthetics highlights one of the central questions of *U.S.!*: how to think about the writing of the social novel. "Sinclair [. . .] was once considered a mildly important figure in American literature and politics" (13), as the reviewer notes early on. It is this necessary interconnection which Sinclair symbolizes like few other writers that permits him to stand symbolically for this problem.

The fictional review of *Pharmaceutical!* sets out three ways of thinking about literature and politics. The first is that literature should not mingle in politics at all, that the social novel, in other words, is always already an artistic and aesthetic failure, that aesthetics (contra Rancière) has nothing to do with politics. The second is that literature has everything to do with politics, that a realist aesthetics is the way to write the social novel, and issues such as style are subordinate to the overt political message. The third is the most interesting: in the very way the review fails to make a convincing case for a complete divorce of aesthetics from politics, it suggests the possibility of a different literary aesthetics capable of holding the political up again, an aesthetics that is less pamphlet and more something else. More, in fact, *U.S.! U.S.!* holds the second and third ways in abeyance. It speaks to the impossibility of writing the social novel in Sinclair's fashion today even as it recognizes the possibility of its continuing effectiveness, while it insists on the political power of the novel.

This is a metafictional move of sorts, a debate about the form of the social novel in the very act of offering a rewriting of the social novel. But *U.S.!* engages the question of the power of literature on the level of narrative, too. If the fictional review of *Pharmaceutical!* is generally hostile only to Upton Sinclair's writing, the novel not much further onward expands this problem to the entire canon of social novels of the early decades of the twentieth century. A thoroughly disillusioned fellow traveler roughly tells Sinclair:

> The books don't matter. I'm sorry. Not The Jungle, not The Octopus. Not The Grapes of Wrath. Have you noticed? The poor are still with us. We still have tainted meat. We still have layoffs. We still have an economic system that eats people to get stronger. Nobody reads. We have hundreds of TV channels. Nobody gives a shit. This has not been a century of progress. (57)

Yet if this is so, at the novel's end, it is precisely one of Sinclair's books, its aesthetic failings notwithstanding, that does matter. His latest novel, *A Moveable Jungle!*, becomes the catalyst of Stephen Rudkin's conversion to Socialist thought. From a disavowal of the power of political literature, the novel's plot thus comes fully around to re-establishing it. Even as it undertakes its own rewriting of the social novel, then, *U.S.!* simultaneously appears to endorse the form of the social novel as it existed a hundred years earlier. *U.S.!* both reflects the writing of the social novel and actively undertakes its rewriting. In arguing that *U.S.!* rewrites the social novel, it is necessary to emphasize and unravel this complex interaction of stances towards the very idea of the social novel.

U.S.! is deeply interested in the chronology of the American social novel and its various forms. It centrally brings us to an encounter with perhaps the most notable social novelist of the late twentieth century, E.L. Doctorow, the "epic poet of the disappearance of the American radical past," as Fredric Jameson has it (1991, 24). Doctorow, as the author of *Ragtime*, also and by no means coincidentally stands at the center of the debate on the meaning of postmodernism. Jameson notes that *Ragtime*'s chief problem is that it is a "postmodern artifact" (1991, 22) deprived of its artistic power to reshape the sense of U.S. history that Linda Hutcheon ascribes it (1988, 88–101) by its partaking in a cultural system in which the "historical novel can no longer set out to represent the historical past; it can only 'represent' our ideas and stereotypes about that past (which thereby at once becomes 'pop history')" (Jameson 1991, 25). For Jameson, *Ragtime* is the poster child of an engaged Left stuck in the cultural constraints of its time—"mark and symptom" of an "aesthetic situation engendered by the disappearance of the historical referent" (1991, 25).

It is against this theoretical background that *U.S.!* situates the encounter between Doctorow, Sinclair, and itself. The section begins: "At this time in our history the writer E.L. Doctorow was still writing his novels" (103). Placing the narrative time of *U.S.!* in a then-distant future, and at the same time invoking the concept of history again, the novel goes on to talk about *Ragtime* in less-than-flattering terms that echo Jameson's critique:

> The narrative distance allowed equally for nostalgia, sentiment, reportage, and irony. This sort of larceny was very much in fashion. The book sold millions of copies and was made into a musical. Many readers today do not know if Emma Goldman was a real person or a fictional character. When asked if the events and chance encounters in the novel really happened, Doctorow answered coyly, They have now. This answer upset those on the left and the right. It seemed decadent. (104)

U.S.!'s Doctorow disavows the idea of history as anything but a story of history. He capably spouts one-liners in lieu of complex analysis in an interview (including one about "the poetics of engagement" which we will come back to) published "in a doomed literary journal with a small circulation" (104–5).

U.S.!'s E.L. Doctorow is an amalgamation of the real and the imagined: a character created from quotations from interviews with such doomed (real) journals as the *Ontario Review*, free interpretations of lines from such interviews, and complete invention. This Doctorow encounters Upton Sinclair, an encounter introduced with a recall to the introduction of Doctorow: "This was the time in our history when Sinclair was being resurrected and assassinated" (105). The line juxtaposes the two writers' different levels of commitment (writing versus sacrificing one's life), a theme which remains vital throughout. More important, however, is their discussion of the question of the social novel's form. In his critique of *Ragtime*, Jameson focuses on the language Doctorow employs, which, Jameson argues, appears to attempt to produce a past tense that separates "events from the present of enunciation and to transform the stream of time and action into so many finished, complete, and isolated punctural event objects which find themselves sundered from any present situation" (1991, 24). *U.S.!* picks up on this. Sinclair comments on his appreciation of Doctorow's style, "You write beautifully, Mr. Doctorow. I wish I could write sentences like yours. It is not my gift. I am a writer but not a poet" (Bachelder 2006, 107). Sinclair's interest in writing like Doctorow takes second place to his stinging critique of the uses to which Doctorow puts his work. Sinclair bemoans Doctorow's sense of "all history [as] just a story." He argues that "[f]acts are important. Lynchings are important. Child labor is important. You did not make this up. You made Ford a Jew-hater. [. . .] He did in fact hate Jews. [. . .] Such a fact is not created by the historian" (107–8). Sinclair avails himself of an almost Jamesonian critique of the depthlessness of Doctorow's writing. As Jameson notes, *Ragtime*'s inclusion and paralleling of historical, fictional, and intertextual figures operate to "powerfully and systematically reify all these characters and to make it impossible for us to receive their representation without the prior interception of already acquired knowledge or doxa" (1991, 24). Doctorow's misrecognition is the failure to understand the fundamental difference between actual history and historical fiction, and to produce, thereby, in lieu of a challenge to received historical narratives, easily domesticated versions of it. *U.S.!*'s Doctorow cannot acknowledge this poetics: "One might suggest a history cannot be flawed," he offers Sinclair; challenged to say whether he himself would go that far, he can only shrug. Sinclair then offers a more general appraisal of the contemporary moment: "The World Trade Center is gone and so is truth and so is history. And so is the Left. I do not think you believe what you claim to believe, young man" (Bachelder 2006, 108). Sinclair's triad—truth, history, the Left—signals his belief in the importance of the former two for the survival of the Left. Crucially, in suggesting that Doctorow's claims about the philosophical underpinnings for his formal choices are not actually something Doctorow believes in, he implies the possibility of resuscitating a novelistic form that departs from either Sinclair's or Doctorow's postmodern writing.

At the end of this section, *U.S.!* has laid out a trajectory of the social novel, at whose beginning stands Sinclair's didactic realism, whose midpoint is Steinbeck, whose somewhat problematic late version is Doctorow, and whose potentially possible contemporary form is *U.S.!* itself. Sinclair's resurrection, however, at the same time leaves his form of social fiction as a persistent presence. Indeed, at the same time that the novel narrates the success of Sinclair's latest attempt at his social novel, it also itself becomes formally less adventurous. Foregoing the collage technique of its first section, the novel now provides a straightforwardly realist (with the exception of the presence of Sinclair) narrative in which we follow three narrative strands. The first is the staging of the annual Fourth of July Book Burning in Greenville, Alabama, which a somewhat precocious twelve-year-old named Stephen Rudkin volunteers to organize. Stephen cleverly orders 500 copies of Sinclair's last novel from Sinclair's publisher. *A Moveable Jungle!* is, by all accounts, no great improvement over Sinclair's other novels; its theme is the outsourcing of labor to cheaper countries, and, like all Sinclair novels, it ends in a proscription for Socialism, thus serving as the ideal fuel for the Greenville Anti-Socialist League's annual endeavor. In the second strand, we follow the consequences of Upton Sinclair's conclusion, on receiving word of Stephen's order, that a Socialist revolution is imminent in Greenville, and his decision to travel there. The third strand is the recruitment of Sinclair assassin Gerald Huntley to shoot Sinclair in Greenville, preempting Francis Billings's own attempt to do so. As these plots play out and interconnect in Greenville, Billings fails to shoot Sinclair, Huntley refuses to do so (urging instead their mutual retirement), and Sinclair's son Albert dies (yet communicates with his father telepathically at the moment of his death). But only 499 of Sinclair's books get burned. Stephen, on the night before the great bonfire, sits down in the garage where the many copies of Sinclair's novel are stored, and begins to read. He begins the new day convinced of Sinclair's Socialist tenets: perhaps the only conversion Sinclair has achieved.

This conversion to the Socialist cause must not be divorced from the means by which it is achieved, reading Upton Sinclair's last novel. *A Moveable Jungle!*, like *U.S.!* itself, mobilizes history; its reference to Sinclair's powerful *The Jungle* must not go unnoticed (it certainly symbolically brings Sinclair's work full circle). Its title is a necessary reminder of the power of protest literature, but also, implicitly, of the historical strength of American Socialism, notwithstanding its current decline. Any claim for *U.S.!*'s utopian imaginary rests more, however, on the realization that *A Moveable Jungle!* is Sinclair's most recent book, a book that would not have been written without his repeated reanimation, and one which is therefore predicated precisely on the persistence of Sinclair himself, the Leftist activists who keep on resurrecting him, and by extension a belief in the possibility of a better, different future. Samuel Cohen has argued that "[i]f the use of the fantastic in *U.S.!* is essentially a confirmation of the lostness of its cause, the ending offers a counterargument" (2012, 216). It is essential to recognize, I think, that the ending offers this counterargument only through the novel's use of its speculative conceit: Stephen is converted not by any old Socialist screed, or even by reading Sinclair's early work, but by a work addressing a contemporary problem, written by an avatar of the historical legacy of American Socialism. *U.S.!* thus brings Sinclair back bodily not merely as a reminder of the past, but as an active agent in shaping possible futures. At the same time, Sinclair's role as an avatar for the persistence of the Badiouan idea also becomes more obvious. He keeps alive "the perspective of a new possibility" (Badiou 2013a, 14) in himself—becomes, so to speak, the "living Idea of a general alternative to the existing order" (35)—and in the iterations of an ever-similar yet thematically changing complaint about the structural inequalities of the capitalist system.

Perhaps the most challenging aspect of *U.S.!* is this, the highly entwined nature of its imagination of an efficacious social novel. There are at least three levels to this: first, the realist nature of Sinclair's novel and its success at conversion; second, the non-realistic nature of *U.S.!*, which paradoxically appears to problematize its own form as a social novel; and third, the quasi-realistic form of the narrative of the Greenville book burning.

In part, the problem here is one of expected scale and of the possible contemporary role of the social novel. When the novel first turns to Sinclair in this section, he imagines the reception of *A Moveable Jungle!* as the fulfillment of his "roadmap to international Socialism" (213). Set against this hope, of course the actual outcome of Stephen's conversion must disappoint. Lee Konstantinou has cautioned that the ultimate conclusion of *U.S.!* points towards the doubts the novel has about any changes which reading *A Moveable Jungle!* might have produced: "one boy's political awakening can hardly mollify the enduring power or appeal of the American right" (2014, 463). But this is an argument which appears to invalidate the idea of the symbolic power of art—in this case, of a novel like *U.S.!*—and its corollary is, of course, that any novel which does not narratively produce radical and systemic change cannot be said to encourage thinking such change. Konstantinou misses a significant dimension of what it means to rethink the social novel today. Clearly, *U.S.!* does not envisage the ultimate triumph of the Socialist idea: but then, such an ending would be facile in the first place. What *U.S.!* is interested in is not the mechanics of a Socialist revolution, but the persistence of the Socialist idea, and the ways in which such persistence shapes the resurgence of hope. In this, *U.S.!* is the social novel of its moment. Konstantinou points out that despite its realistic trappings in its second section, "it remains fantastic" (2014, 463) simply on account of Sinclair's presence. He does not mean this in the Todorovian fashion but to point out the narrative's fundamental incommensurability with reality—capitalist realism—and thus in a manner of speaking falls into the old trap. Without intending to be dismissive of the narrative's mode, he must necessarily be. The speculative foundation of Bachelder's narrative is reduced to a failure of ontology, and may—more powerfully than even the reading of Stephen's turn to Socialism as an aberration—permit the dismissal of Bachelder's underlying utopian argument. Bachelder, Konstantinou writes, "finds himself unable to find a way to move forward" (464). In Konstantinou's understanding, he finds himself incapable of writing a novel "composed in terms of a 'poetics of engagement'" (465), a call back to E.L. Doctorow, who used that phrase to mean "some kind of new aesthetic possible that does not undermine aesthetic rigor" (qtd. in Konstantinou 2014, 464).

This is the argument which *U.S.!*'s version of E.L. Doctorow makes in the course of the interview with the "doomed literary journal" and the later dinner with Sinclair. Yet to argue this is to miss, I think, the way in which *U.S.!* disavows Doctorow (though cf. Gula 2012). When Doctorow considers going to meet Sinclair, he reflects on the "laudable" passion of Sinclair's writing, suggesting that "[a] poetics of engagement would necessarily begin with the novelist's refusal to cede the world to politicians and comedians and cable news networks. Doctorow was worried that he would get shot or asked to provide a blurb" (105–6). Doctorow's own engagement has clear limits—immediately, he worries about being too entangled with Sinclair's writing to engage in the kind of actual engagement that Sinclair has lived his life in, but also to endorse the kind of writing Sinclair undertakes, all for fear of bodily harm. To be sure, what is at stake is poetics, the forms and styles of literary writing, rather than political action; but Doctorow's hesitation marks precisely this, and suggests the emptiness of a mere *poetics* of engagement. As Sinclair's singer-songwriter son Albert muses, getting ready to play his last show before being assassinated himself, the night of July 3rd, "[w]hat was required, he knew, was a poetics of engagement. And yet what was also required was that Journey song, you know the one" (261). The idea of the poetics of engagement has become a trite commonplace, and its pairing with "that Journey song" is instructive: Journey's most popular song, "Don't Stop Believin'" certainly suggests a deeper consideration than the somewhat sterile notion of the poetics of engagement, on the one hand, an almost affective willingness to hold on to a greater idea. Yet it may also mean, far more simply, that there is an entertainment factor, too, one which cannot be ignored in the writing of the social novel.

U.S.! rejects Doctorow's version of the social novel. But it does not fully validate Sinclair's poetics, either: it is far too caustic towards Sinclair, and far too ready to mock his inartful writing. But is *U.S.!* itself the third option here? Lee Konstantinou has argued that it is not. Recognizing that the simple political realism of Sinclair is no longer possible, Konstantinou argues that Bachelder "hopes to find a way back to partisan realism" through a Doctorowian mode of "fantasy signifiers," but that he "finds himself unable to find a way to move forward" after all: "*U.S.!* is less the sort of novel that Bachelder wishes that he could write—a novel composed in terms of a 'poetics of engagement'—than a novel outlining the difficulty of writing such a novel in the present" (2014, 464–65). This mistakes the complexity of Bachelder's argument. Perhaps the central problem in Konstantinou's reading is his insistence on what Bachelder "rejects," "wants," and "finds" (464), rather than on what the novel does. For despite Konstantinou's belief, stemming from his engagement with Bachelder's overt remarks, that *U.S.!* is, in effect, a failure—a novel about the difficulties of writing an engaged novel, rather than itself an engaged novel—such a reading misses the question of what it means to be engaged, and what the limits of a mere poetics of engagement are. The point is not "finding a way to reanimate [the real] Sinclair's literary legacy with better sentences" (462). This is in fact an already-dismissed option in the novel. The Sinclair–Doctorow dinner section's second epigraph already suggests this. A Doctorow quote, it reads, "the failure arises from diction" (102). This is an actual point Doctorow made in the same *Ontario Review* conversation the novel draws on heavily throughout. Asked by the interviewer if "you can't have a very powerful political work that is also aesthetically excellent" (Morris 1999, 64), Doctorow contends that while this is possible, it would force an acknowledgement of political ambiguities. It could not be advocatory, or overtly ideological in nature. When an author adopts the "diction of politics"—this is the diction which the epigraph refers to—literature loses its rationale, language. The novel already suggests that to envisage "better sentences" as a way of reimaging the social novel is a conceptual mistake—you can either have a Sinclarian or a Doctorowian social novel (or, as I argue here, the third form of Bachelder's novel), but you cannot have Sinclarian politics and Doctorowian style, as Sinclair himself implies when he says to Doctorow that Doctorow is "too much the artist" (106).

To argue that *U.S.!* is a failure at what it does is to ignore the possibility of a specifically contemporary social novel, one which explicitly insists on its departures from Sinclair, Steinbeck, Doctorow. An early artifact in the novel, a syllabus for a course Sinclair teaches called "Advanced Fiction Writing," outlines the limits of Sinclair's vision for fiction:

> No romance novels. No fantasy novels. No coming-of-age novels. No father–son hunting trips. No literal vampires (metaphorical bloodsucking is fine). No beach houses. No divorces or affairs. No suburban malaise. No point-of-view stunts. No fragmentation. No gentle fading of the light. No ice cubes rattling in cocktail glasses. No coitus against walls. No ambiguous narrative stances. No subtle shifts. No celebrations of chaos. No rhythmic evocations. No irrelevant beauty. (68–69)

These formal demands on one level simply mirror Sinclair's own writing. But they also highlight a more general datedness in a tradition of American realism that might take in such figures as F. Scott Fitzgerald, John Updike, or Jonathan Franzen. Sinclair's insistence on realism and narrative coherence is clearly ignored by *U.S.!* But more, in fact: it cannot possibly be expected to adhere to these restrictions. If we took for granted that Bachelder's novel aims at social revolution, then we might be more on board with Konstantinou's belief that Bachelder has failed. In the novel, Sinclair, indomitable, echoes these aspirations for his own social novels: "'This one is going to change everything'" (215), he says of *A Moveable Jungle!*. We should not confuse these aspirations with the aspirations of *U.S.!* To pick up a formulation of Carl Freedman, whatever one wants to say about *U.S.!* in contrast to *The Jungle* (for instance), of Bachelder's writing in contrast to Sinclair's, we must understand that Bachelder could not possibly be Sinclair. To ignore the historically specific authorial position of Sinclair by suggesting that *his* form of the social novel is *the* form of the social novel is unhelpful. Bachelder's novel cannot aim at social revolution because the conditions under which such revolution was imaginable as a consequence of literary writing have passed. This is no reason not to keep hope alive, or to stop believin', but it is to recognize that the form of the social novel changes with history.

U.S.! concludes with a very short (two-page) final section, another "found object," apparently a description off an auction site: the handwritten final lyrics written by Sinclair's son, the "Last Folksinger," which reference both the hope signified by the Greenville events and the connection between the work of father and son. If "emancipatory politics is possible only when some fathers and mothers and some sons and daughters are allied in an effective negation of the world as it is" (2014, 90), as Alain Badiou has it, this reconciliation in political action between father and son Sinclair is certainly significant, adding a different dimension to the same process of fidelity which Sinclair already represents. If "*this* was the time in our history when Sinclair was being resurrected and assassinated" (105, my emphasis), this suggests that this is no longer the case at the time of the novel's narration. If that line can be read as questioning the possibility of lasting fidelity, the overt connection between father and son, the apparent way in which the son's art and activism replaces and extends the father's also suggests that Sinclair is ultimately replaceable. If hope remains only hope, not realized fact, at least it may be transferred, may take on a different form—much as *U.S.!* itself is a different form of the hopeful social novel.

Whatever literary weight *U.S.!* possesses rests on its speculative historism, on the conceit of Upton Sinclair's constant resurrection and return into an increasingly apolitical shifting present. Its literary trappings are unmistakable: its readiness to shift voice, point of view, tone, and forms, and to leave ambiguous what appear to be crucial plot points, suggest its literary aspirations. In the final section of this chapter, I would like to read it against a novel that offers virtually the same conceit—the bodily return of a past political figure into the present read as being in serious disarray, to which the avatar of a better past brings hope. Jason Heller's *Taft 2012* is, in blunt terms, generic: a plot-driven, somewhat artless if earnest text. *Taft 2012* nonetheless serves me to highlight again the most important points of my overall argument: it, too, makes history available for progressive causes in the contemporary through the adoption of a speculative form.

Care for the Future Shaped by the Past: Jason Heller's *Taft 2012*

In their shared interest in both the figure of Upton Sinclair and the inevitable connections to a Socialist tradition in American life and letters which he opens up, Bachelder's and Joyce Carol Oates's novels work against the fact that the "socialist intellectual tradition has often been ignored and suppressed," as Michael Denning has it (1996, 423). This is certainly a major issue for both of these novels, and impossible not to connect to their shared formal features. But it would be too limiting and too expansive at once to claim that what I take to be a new form—speculative historism—is exclusively concerned with restituting such a *Socialist* imaginary for the present. It is, instead, a broader sense of utopian hope and possibility that we encounter in the fictions which constitute the new form—a hope whose form is part of the effort at triangulating a useful space in the contemporary literary field. My logical progression thus is from Kalfus's meditative sense of hopeful potentials outside to Oates's novel, in which Upton Sinclair as the avatar of Socialism remains a historical figure, to Bachelder's, in which he becomes a contemporary one, to Jason Heller's novel *Taft 2012* (2012). That novel takes a different historical figure into the contemporary, and broadens our vista not just politically, but also with regard to the texts we read. Heller's novel shares the speculative form of Bachelder's text. But William Howard Taft, whom Heller's novel brings to the 2012 election, is not just a fundamentally different political figure, and Heller's narrative does not just work towards different (non-Socialist) ends: it is also, in similarly simple terms, not literary. *Taft 2012* is almost ostentatiously a popular novel, a work of genre fiction. In exploring how *Taft 2012* responds to the same kinds of cultural prompts that engage the three novels I have discussed so far, I aim to take a first stab at a larger claim about the effects of reading speculative historism as a form in contemporary literary culture. The adoption of speculative elements into literary fiction requires us to read ostensibly generic fiction more carefully, and indeed more generously, as part of a larger continuum.

Taft 2012 begins under the White House lawn, where newly returned William Howard Taft, mysteriously transported from the moment of Woodrow Wilson's inauguration in 1912 to the autumn of 2011, awakes, digs himself up, and ambles away, only to be shot by the Secret Service. Recovering from the bullet, he quickly becomes the center of a political movement that sees in his old-fashioned morals and political positions a sense of a better politics. With his great-granddaughter, the Ohio independent Congresswoman Rachel Taft, he eventually agrees to run for president in 2012, at the head of what appears to be a grass-roots movement, the Taft Party. His personal platform is very basic: a focus on education and food safety, propelled in part by an encounter with products of the Fulsom food production conglomerate. When the Taft Party convention rolls around, Taft discovers that his ostensible grass-roots appeal has been driven by Gus Fulsom's money. Instead of running and becoming a stooge of the company he most despises, Taft hands the campaign over to his great-granddaughter. The outcome of the 2012 election apparently is not successful for Rachel, but a later one is; in an epilogue, she swears in her great-grandfather as Chief Justice of the U.S. Supreme Court in 2021.

This short summary may already indicate that *Taft 2012* is not an overly complex text. But it thematically and (genre-)formally coincides with *U.S.!*: it insists on the value of bringing the past into the present bodily and understands its historical personage as an avatar of past conceptions of possible politics. Like *U.S.!*, it is a collage novel of sorts, if less complexly, combining narrative, emails, tweets, notes, eBay entries, letters, TV show transcripts, and other forms to narrate Taft's short presidential campaign and the general situation within which this campaign becomes possible. But if *U.S.!* is firmly invested in a radical politics, *Taft 2012* is far more ambivalent about both its diagnosis of the present and its belief in what the past can bring to the table. In the way it represents Taft as standing for a vague, bipartisan progressivism, a political mode which triumphs chiefly as a matter of more civil discourse, rather than persuasive political arguments about pressing problems, *Taft 2012* offers a lower-keyed utopian hope for the present that sees its problems as eminently, and unequivocally, solvable, even as these problems suggest the limits of its own vision.

It is the figure of William Howard Taft that most interests me here, an odd bearer of utopian aspirations. A consummate public servant, the historical Taft's career began in the law in New York, which led into a first political appointment as governor-general of the Philippines, newly an American "possession." Afterwards, he became Secretary of War in Theodore Roosevelt's administration, and succeeded Roosevelt as president in 1908. Four years on, Roosevelt ran against Taft and Woodrow Wilson in the 1912 election, dooming Taft's re-election chances and leading to Wilson's victory. Taft became Chief Justice of the Supreme Court in the 1920s. An uncharismatic, businesslike leader, Taft never achieved his predecessor's rapport with either the populace or the press, and by 1912 had become the less progressive Republican of the two. Taft, then, a colonial administrator and increasingly lukewarm defender of the progressive ideals, cannot be expected to serve as an ideal contender for the contemporary Left's ideas—and indeed, as *Taft 2012* frames it, he is not.

The novel gives us two versions of Taft: the reflective interiority of the character himself, his own sense of what he stands for and what he wants to achieve politically, and the external projection space which enables him to run for president again in the first place. These two are, at least at times, at odds. As Taft is represented, he is perhaps much more a man who inhabits the sensibilities of the twenty-first century than one of the early twentieth, whose easy adoption of the social changes in the hundred years since his disappearance are chalked up, by himself, to the fact that he is "a Republican, a member of the party of progress" (62). Whether it is interracial relationships or the question of marihuana (62, 184), Taft's progressive take on these positions frames him as a progressive even today, and the past hundred years as a strangely inert century. Taft realizes that his identification as a "Republican and a Progressive" (103) has become a contradiction in terms. He is not without doubts about his ability to serve in the modern world, but he is, by his own reading, a principled, decent, capable, and above all open-minded man, less a politician than an impartial judge.

The novel endorses this view. Early on, a fictional editorial note from the *Washington Herald* upbraids the departing president on March 5, 1912, for his trust-busting of U.S. Steel, his "refusal to sign legislation that would have sensibly restricted immigration to the literate," and for the sky-high 1 percent business tax rate (9). This is also the general tenor of one of the repeated documents which the novel uses, the (fictional) historian Susan Weschler's Taft biography, *Taft: A Tremendous Man*. Weschler's account presents Taft (in part correctly) as reluctant and unambitious for the presidency, duty-bound, driven by an incorruptible sense of ethics. Taft's actual politics as president—which included, among other things, a reversal of Theodore Roosevelt's progressive position that he would not dismiss Black federal employees because of racist concerns—play little role in this evaluation. Indeed, as Taft becomes increasingly more popular with the U.S. public, his great-granddaughter successfully absolves him from the "more controversial things from your presidency": she suggests that his followers are "skipping" over them in their celebration of Taft because they are "a little too dated to translate well today" (114). Without giving us a hint of what those controversial decisions in fact were, the novel already writes them off as historical, in a bad way: as the kind of problem which has already been decisively overcome and now rests in memory alone.

Both Taft himself and the novel see him as a fundamentally good, well-meaning, honest, and importantly, even in twenty-first-century terms, progressive non-politician, one with whom and whose positions it is easy to sympathize. In his fundamental doubts about his ability to serve, Taft stands as an exemplarily modest, relatable figure—one which would appear to make a desirable president indeed. This is what many of his devoted followers find charming about him; but at the same time, Taft also becomes something like an empty signifier for them. What these voters are interested in are not so much the concrete politics as the "spirit of a more dignified American era" (53), with a "more sensible, more decorous class of participant" (111). The party which Taft assembles is composed of the "rabidly independent" (95), perhaps "moderate to the extreme" (100), voters which the novel sees as alienated by the increasing polarization of the political system around the 2012 election.

What these voters want, Taft is told, is "a new direction. They want a return to values and tradition. They want new leadership, one driven by reasonable common sense rather than ego or ideology" (104). They want a "president who *doesn't* lust for power" (115, original emphasis). There is a vague affective animation guiding the interest in Taft's return, then, one which is almost entirely evacuated of concrete politics and which enables the Taft Party to bridge old party lines. As a late interview indicates, the Taft Party spans former "Big Labor" (181) and Democrats, Republicans, even Libertarians (195), all of whom are more fundamentally concerned with the style of discourse than with Taft's positions. Or, at the very least, they are more interested in assuming that Taft's 1912 positions will also be his 2012 positions, which is to say they read politics ahistorically. During the Taft Party convention, delegates are quoted as deriving their support for Taft from his various actions in the early twentieth century: his refusal to use the military against the Philippine insurrection, his decision to fire a forestry official well liked by Theodore Roosevelt, or even the mere fact that he used to be a Republican. At the same time, however, the substantive issues of the day fall by the wayside. Wondering about "Taft's stand on immigration," a delegate cannot but conclude (with a mixture of hope and ignorance) that because he "was around before racism even existed," Taft will find an amicable solution to the immigration problem (222–23). Taft's own positions are similarly vague, rooted in the perceived problems of the first decade of the twenty-first century, as when he disavows the proliferation of executive orders, and vaguely progressive, as when he suggests that he is in favor of "helping the prosperity of all countries," even if it is only so that trade can be more valuable (180). Not least through Taft's own vague positioning, then, he becomes a kind of empty signifier, one on which people are capable of projecting a wide variety of political positions.

The only agenda which Taft himself affirmatively subscribes to is idiosyncratic and somewhat puzzling: his quest against the industrial food producer Fulsom Foods. In the wake of experiencing a painful encounter with its near-turkey product on his first Thanksgiving, Taft embarks on a campaign to improve American foods. There is a surprising echo of the consequences, if not the intentions, of Upton Sinclair's *The Jungle* here; there is also a glimpse at the underlying problem of *Taft 2012*'s politics. Sinclair, after all, was incensed that his novel of labor's struggle and exploitation was read by the public chiefly as an exposé of the methods of meat production in Chicago. Famously noting that "I aimed at the public's heart, and by accident I hit it in the stomach" (Sinclair 2003, xi), Sinclair found himself struggling with the popularity brought by what was read as a public health crusade. Against this, *Taft 2012* presents Taft's own efforts at reforming the food industry as the core of a program. The emphasis on industrial foods appears quixotic (despite a short nod to its entanglement with education). As Taft realizes in speaking to his party, "[h]e'd known this was going to be a hard sell in an America obsessed with terrorism and rampant unemployment and partisan squabbles" (187). In fact, this sells the absurdity of the quest short: Taft eventually discovers that his movement is largely financed by Fulsom Foods, and at the same time realizes that he himself, heavily overweight after all, would be a bad spokesperson for a campaign against the food industry in an age of images. This becomes the reason for his withdrawal from the presidential race. Having run on open dealing and fairness, this is certainly consequential; but it only highlights that no higher purpose controls Taft's political aspirations. If "reason and fairness and honesty and free thinking" are the "fundamental principles of our platform"; if he can call on his followers to "seize their towns, their states, their country by the horns—together!," the problem which the political vision of *Taft 2012* exhibits lies in the conclusion to this rallying cry. Having done that, Tafties can "make of it what they will" (244). This is the ultimate empty projection space, ready for his supporters to fill it with widely divergent ideas.

What is at issue here, then, is not so much that *Taft 2012* argues that a more polite and measured political tone, the kind described by Taft himself as "thoughtful discourse" through which he can "provide a voice for the good women and men of America who can't be heard over the din of all this twenty-first-century madness" (173), will solve all problems. The novel is more ambivalent than that. It simultaneously acknowledges the truth of the complaint in general—there are unheard voices—and ponders the more fraught issue of what an inclusion of these voices would bring. Taft is no innocent. He plays shamelessly on the Obama birther controversy, commenting, knowingly, that "in my day [Obama] barely would have been an American" (98). The novel represents Taft as a populist, one who makes use of existing dissatisfactions and channels them towards his goals; but at the same time, he cannot fully make use of them, largely because, as the novel also acknowledges, such a populist movement, unframed by ideology, will remain shapeless. This, for some time, appears the novel's redeeming quality. It acknowledges that while the kind of historical politics Taft brings to the contemporary appeals, it is also profoundly empty. As one of the Taft Party's support organizations phrases one of its core values, it is about "Care for the Future Shaped by the Past" (110, original capitals), a suitably amorphous phrasing that leaves entirely open what actual politics could emanate. Taft, that is, does not appear to be a solution, in as much as the novel avoids solutions to the problems it identifies and refuses to suggest that something positive must necessarily stem from Taft's return. This conflicted stance, however, then becomes more fundamentally revised in its insistence on concluding with the election of Rachel Taft to the presidency, suggesting that whatever the Taft Party stands for, it is enough to win the highest office in the land. Given that much of the Party's apparent message, and apparent unique selling points, revolve around a radically outdated economic policy, this is at least vaguely troubling—but not to the novel itself. *Taft 2012* insists that this is not only good enough for the Taft Party to win a presidential election, but also, certainly implicitly, that it is a good thing, that we should cheer the election of Rachel Taft and the consequent appointment to the Supreme Court of William Howard Taft as the validation of their call for a more reasonable discourse. Taft, the empty signifier, the avatar of an amorphous hopefulness for a better future, receives a happy ending, but what Rachel Taft governs like remains of no interest to the novel.

In some ways, then, *Taft 2012* enacts a specifically liberal hopefulness: a belief in the possibility that deep partisan divides may be overcome by the voice of reason. It is following this logic when it refuses to name a politics, too: because, after all, if reasonable discourse will overcome the political divides plaguing the country, then these politics themselves become less meaningful. Reason prevails, and that is the ideal state. This is *Taft 2012*'s utopian hope, a utopian hope it sees best realized through its speculative realist conceit: it believes that a plausible source for the kind of discourse that it feels will save contemporary politics can be imagined only in the depths of history, and can be transported only by an avatar, rather than a more generalized historical consciousness.

Formally, then, *U.S.!* and *Taft 2012* are very similar; but in their conception of politics, they differ. Like Upton Sinclair in *U.S.!*, Taft comes to stand for something greater than himself. But where Sinclair represents a coherent idea, Taft does not—as he himself insists. The most revealing exchange in the novel, in political terms, comes almost at the end, during Taft's farewell address to his supporters. After offering a somewhat dated, 1970s critique of consumer capitalism—"If there is a problem with America today [. . .] it is that we look for self-worth in consumption, rather than in the pursuit of personal achievement"—he suggests that pursuit of personal achievement is something to be performed "alongside others" (240). At this, a cry from the crowd: "Socialism!" Taft disagrees: it is "simple self-respect," and asks the heckler if he grasps "what socialism truly is." Taft does not in fact answer this rhetorical question, but we should not miss the disavowal for what it is: a denial that Taft is after an idea. In lieu of a political idea, Taft represents an essential humanism that is easy to subscribe to, but symptomatically difficult to translate into concrete politics. In fact, through the entire novel, Taft never proposes an action or a law, never hints at what policies a Taft administration would pursue beyond the ones it pursued in 1912—and which, as Taft himself recognizes, are difficult to translate into the contemporary.

Conclusion: Resurrection as a Formal Act

What unites *U.S.!* and *Taft 2012* is their shared interest in the speculative idea of resurrection: the bringing into the present of a historical figure, the living embodiment of a better or more hopeful past. The two novels do not simply have characters with broadly similar, speculative backstories; rather, they share narratives that address a similar problem, what the meaning of a bodily insertion of a historical figure into the present can be. Catherine Gallagher's exploration of the ontology of alternate-historical characters concerns itself with the status of characters in realist historical fiction—characters who stay in their own historical moment. Against these, Gallagher reads "the alternate-history genre, which insistently invites hypothetical thinking and solicits our participation in the creation of alternative worlds where the counterparts of historical characters are said to make world-historical changes" (2011, 333). The Hegelian category of the "world-historical" is problematically strong, but the point of Gallagher's analysis goes in a helpful direction. It sets itself against the theory that "fictional characters automatically generate possible worlds" (332) and argues that no purely fictional character can do so. It requires the historical character, and the overt signals given through him that the novel's world significantly differs from ours, to make the possibility of alternate worlds—and thus, of a radically different, or at least hopeful, future—present. In Gallagher's reading of counterfactual characters,

> making alternate worlds bound to ours by their shared human inhabitants, rather than creating characters, is the main activity of alternate histories, and so the double vision they encourage goes beyond our awareness of the two timelines across which the historical figure persists. (333)

Alternative history cannot function except through the presence of the historical figure, which alone guarantees that the alternative history is capable of being envisioned too as a form of our history, even as it alone, without a formal anchor in the present, is already available to the contemporary reader.

This is not the view which either *U.S.!* or *Taft 2012* is endorsing. Their choice to bring a historical figure into the present suggests something about the volatility of connections to the present that are available only implicitly. Not for nothing do these two texts tie their historical visions directly into the contemporary moment, unlike the texts which I have discussed so far—and, importantly, unlike *U.S.!*'s own implicit counterpoint, *Ragtime*. The contrast with *Ragtime* provides some illumination here because, as Fredric Jameson notes, it was initially conceived to start "in our present" in the writer's home. In the published form it is unmoored from the present of writer and reader, which permits the novel "to float in some new world of past historical time whose relationship to us is problematic indeed" (1991, 21–22). *Ragtime* rests on this destruction of an "organic relationship between the American history we learn from schoolbooks and the lived experience [. . .] of everyday life" (22). Deprived of a firm connection to the present, *Ragtime* enacts formally the "disappearance of the historical referent" (25) and our backwards projection onto the past of our ideas about it.

We must read the narratives of the intrusive presence of the past that I have talked about in this chapter against this, as formal moves. As Jameson has elaborated, *Ragtime* reveals "reincarnation" as "the postmodernist relationship to historical names" (2013, 292), because it offers a simultaneous sense of exact similarity with a previous figure even as it offers a radical difference: the names are the same, but the named are not. The contemporary historical novel, not postmodern anymore, may be more problematic still. In it, historical individuals become "little more than their names" (288), as Jameson contends. Such "names without events" destabilize the history they used to be a part of, an acknowledgement of an "Archive" of historical narratives none of which has the capacity of being taken "at face value" (288).

What is significant about *U.S.!* and *Taft 2012* is that they explicitly go beyond the "empty shell of mere names" (Jameson 2013, 296) in their invocation of historical individuals by the expedient of substituting resurrection for reincarnation. Instead of offering a revision of historical figures, these novels decide to investigate their meaning for the contemporary moment, to make them available not as versions of history as such, but as transhistorical entities. To be sure, they are still the transhistorical variant of versions of their historical figures. But even this minimal change insists that instead of considerations of historical truth, they become mediations of historical meaning, precisely the kind of mediation which a historical novel without such an overt connection to the present must—or certainly may easily—forego.

We may solve this dilemma by recourse to the texts themselves here, or at least by recourse to *U.S.!*. Sinclair's and Taft's resurrections are formal acts because they function differently from Gallagher's counterfactual characters, and open a different set of possibilities. The alternate worlds of *U.S.!* and *Taft 2012* are bound to us both through the historicity of their protagonists and through their presence in a largely recognizable, though admittedly satirically heightened, present. This permits them not just to reflect the fragility and the contingency of our present, as the living artifacts of historical developments that could have gone differently, but to highlight the contingency of the future, too. Their irruption into the present becomes a metaphor both for a historical continuity, in which we cannot simply let the past be past, and also for the present's own possibilities. If possibility inhered in these figures' historical time, in the very contingency of their development, why is it not available today? If our present is the result of struggles that could have ended differently, then the capitalist realism that insists on this being the only possible best state of affairs becomes more tenuous. Resurrection, as a formal move, requires the navigation of such thoughts.

If resurrection is a formal act, then it also becomes clearer that navigating this formal act in different ways, as *U.S.!* and *Taft 2012* do, is not merely a difference in narrative choices, but it is a different solution to the same problem. Nicholas Brown has argued that art's autonomy under contemporary market conditions may lie precisely in finding an appropriate solution to such problems, which are problems of genre. That solution is to satisfy the conditions of genericity, while orienting the work to a more profound project (Brown 2013, 161; 2019). *Taft 2012* and *U.S.!* reveal the way this works. To be sure, they do not, in and of themselves, form a genre—there are probably no rules yet attached that would make "resurrection novels" a genre. But they epitomically highlight the thrust of Brown's argument, and serve almost incidentally to stress the importance of autonomy for the power of politically engaged art.

Brown approvingly quotes *The Wire* writer and producer David Simon as saying, "[f]uck the average reader," in arguing that the TV show manages to navigate the requirements of the police procedural, only to then make the genre available for a genuinely autonomous, Leftist project (2013, 161). The quote highlights Simon's insistence on artistic autonomy from the very market within which the show functions, the way that the mass of commercially necessary readers need not understand its meaning. We may see here a glimpse at an argument about the relative value of *U.S.!* and *Taft 2012*, too, and the chief difference between them with respect to their different approaches to the same formal problem. *U.S.!* insists on the repetitiveness of Sinclair's death and resurrection, while *Taft 2012* makes it a singular event. *U.S.!*, in other words, is very much concerned with the continuities of radical thought in the United States, rather than with breaks—with the upturns and downswings of a social movement, rather with utopian revolution; with a sense of the combined and uneven development of progressive politics, rather than with *Taft 2012*'s sense of a better past lost and now regained through Taft's sudden return. Where *Taft 2012*, then, is essentially nostalgic, with all of nostalgia's contemporary appeal (see Chapter 4), *U.S.!* is not: it does not locate its hope quasi-historically, but ideally, transhistorically, and enacts this hope formally in the way it frames its resurrections. Within the constraints of the resurrection narrative, *U.S.!* finds a more overtly reader-unfriendly, resistant mode of art. In simple terms, *U.S.!* is challenging, while *Taft 2012* is not, in a number of stylistic, structural, and indeed argumentative ways. Taft in Heller's novel is a simple protagonist, through whose consciousness we obtain most of our information; by contrast, Sinclair's status as an avatar of the Leftist Idea never really translates into making him the protagonist of Bachelder's novel. *Taft 2012*'s happy ending contrasts sharply with the openness of *U.S.!*, but is also symptomatic of the more general thrust of the novel's interests: where *U.S.!* is heavily interested in what happens to the Socialist idea, *Taft 2012* is heavily invested in Taft himself. What he stands for remains diffuse, and its very diffuseness is the reason why it does not say, "fuck the average reader," but rather the obverse. *Taft 2012*'s politics is affirmatively aimed at an average reader, at the (perhaps hypothetical) person willing to assume that political differences may be overcome by thoughtful discussion, who can be Republican, Independent, Democrat, or perfectly disinterested in party politics, in a way that no reader of *U.S.!* can be.

The point here is not so much that one of these novels is better than the other. The point is that in their engagement with the formal conditions under which they are written, only one succeeds in becoming more than what Brown calls an "art commodity" (2013, 162), by navigating the formal constraints of the resurrection narrative in such a way as to make it speak to a greater problem than the politics of its resurrectee. What the direct comparison between those texts reveals, then, is that speculative historism as a genre, as a form, need not be always successful at producing a complex meditation on the utopian possibilities inherent in a mobilization of the past for the present. Speculative historism too is a formal problem, whose solution may offer art and avenues for political engagement—but it may also produce market conformity.

Chapter 4

Escapism, Nostalgia, and Hope: Ernest Cline's *Ready Player One*

I just suggested that a closer look at the generic and popular *Taft 2012* allows us a more ready appreciation of the broader impact of speculative historism. Now, addressing another genre text, Ernest Cline's 2011 novel *Ready Player One*—a text which also is interested in tracing the possibility of a socioeconomic change as utopia—I will highlight the importance of taking genre texts seriously. Such texts can turn up a new set of readers and address the concerns of speculative historism at a broader audience. I want to not only read *Ready Player One*, but also to set out on the final argumentative steps of this book, drawing in on speculative historism's place in the contemporary literary field.

Set in 2044, *Ready Player One* unveils a dystopian future: its protagonist, Wade Watts, lives in the "stacks" just outside Oklahoma City, low-cost suburbs made from vertically stacking trailers. Wade, a seventeen-year-old student at an online high school, spends much of his free time in the OASIS, the "Ontologically Anthropocentric Sensory Immersive Simulation" (48), a fully immersive virtual reality. The OASIS serves as Wade's, and most everyone else's, escape from a world racked by an ongoing energy crisis, in which the stretches of land between the big cities have fallen to roaming bands of outlaws, travel has become almost impossible, work is difficult to find, and futures look exceedingly bleak. Indeed, the OASIS harbors the most likely escape route for any of its millions of users: winning the Hunt for Halliday's Easter egg. James Halliday, the now-deceased developer and owner of the OASIS interface, has left his immense fortune, and control of the OASIS, to the person who manages to solve a series of online riddles, and find the egg, within the virtual reality of the OASIS. The Hunt is both the main focus of a host of individuals, like Wade, who alone or in clans, as so-called gunters, seek to win the prize, as well as the sole purpose of IOI, a sinister transnational IT service provider. IOI employs hundreds of people to win the quest and to secure the OASIS—hitherto free—

for itself. Through the course of the novel, Wade develops from a fully selfish desire to simply escape Earth in a giant spaceship to a far more radical and hopeful desire to use the wealth he stands to gain for the betterment of mankind.

This is what is at stake, then, securing control of the most important cultural and economic trophy the world has to offer. The choice is either to monetize it to the detriment of the poor masses who depend on it for education, enjoyment, social contacts, and access to more than the nearest couple of kilometers around their homes, or to secure it for all, and to ensure that what profits accrue from it actually better the world at large. As befits a genre novel, the stakes could not be higher, and the fault lines hardly starker. The quest itself appears simple enough: solve a series of riddles, each of which grants you access to a game in which you can win a "magical" key; find the gates which these keys open, and succeed at another challenge there; and at the end, collect the egg, which immediately grants you victory, riches, and control of the OASIS. Thanks to a sudden flash of inspiration, Wade discovers the first of these key–gate combinations, vaulting him from an unknown, low-level player to the forefront of the Hunt. The consequences are brutal. IOI, after failing to recruit him, attempts to murder him. Wade goes on to pursue the Hunt with the help of a group of online friends, including his love-interest, Art3mis. While they initially fall behind, through teamwork, luck, perseverance, and a superb command of the knowledge required to crack the riddles of the Hunt, Wade and his friends manage to fight their way back into the game. Most of the events of the novel take place in the OASIS, though the final hundred pages or so also include Wade's clandestine real-world infiltration of IOI and his and his friends' being safe-housed by James Halliday's business partner, Ogden Morrow. With the aid of Morrow's advanced VR gear, Wade manages to win the Hunt, and he gets together with Art3mis.

None of this, one would have to admit, is particularly surprising narrative. The book's quest structure is simple enough, and it is not particularly artful. It contains long, awkwardly expositional descriptive passages that serve to draw the background to the story in a severe case of telling rather than showing. What makes *Ready Player One* interesting is the way it situates itself between overt nostalgic longing, escapist fantasy, and utopian imagination, and the way the first two, at least, are always also readable on the metalevel, as themselves meditations on the structure of nostalgia and escapism. These issues manifest as speculative historism.

Ready Player One's speculative setting is obvious, but to read it as historical requires some explanation. The most overt way in which the novel is interested in history is also the way in which it is, or at least appears to be, nostalgic. The crucial element here is the nature of the Hunt's riddles. James Halliday, as it turns out, has based these around his reminiscences of his youth in the 1980s: contestants must have an almost encyclopedic knowledge of late 1970s and early 1980s popular culture, from music to comics to films and especially video games. For Halliday, this is clearly an expression of nostalgia for his own childhood, looking back on the 1980s as a more innocent time. The 1980s may appear to us only indifferently "historical," but from the vantage point of *Ready Player One*'s 2040s setting, they take on a different valence. *Ready Player One* reinforces its characters' nostalgia through its own immersion of the reader in this nostalgic look back. The novel appears to successfully build a political moment from an apparently anemic look back at a better, though willfully misconstrued, historical time.

Something very similar happens with the novel's representation of escapism. Here, *Ready Player One* becomes metageneric, offering a consideration of the political possibilities inherent in genre fiction. The representation of the OASIS highlights its apparently fully escapist role. It functions in part as a real-world substitute (as in the online school that Wade goes to) and an economic system-within-the-economic system (as in the various means by which jobs can be worked online, or offline riches impinge on one's status online). In this, it does not fully disconnect its users from the real world for any length of time. Yet in its enactment of magic, science fiction, and the fondest dreams of its users, it is both implicitly and explicitly a means of escape. So it would seem is the novel itself, not simply because as genre fiction it is immediately to be suspected of simply offering a couple of hours' respite from the world, but also in the form its narrative takes. Its plot, which solves not just its love plot and the immediate quest but also apparently the systemic problems that plague the time of its setting, appears fully to condone escapist reading practices, a willful immersion in a happy-ended story.

The novel thus represents what it appears to enact, and enacts what it appears to represent. From this inauspicious ground springs a utopian narrative that resuscitates both nostalgia and escapism as forces capable of engendering meaningful change. *Ready Player One* works through the transformation of escapism into activism, of retreat into fantasy into an emancipatory act. These interconnected elements combine to produce a vision of a better future, in which the nostalgic recollection of a happier past and the escapism of genre serve to counteract the systemic forces which have created the dystopian future of *Ready Player One*'s world. I want to first engage the question of nostalgia's contemporary meaning; secondly, address the question of popular form and escapism;

and thirdly, relate these points to what I take to be *Ready Player One*'s quest for a vision of radical freedom, one which takes in both the possibilities of the virtual world as well as those of the real. In shortly outlining what I take to be the theoretical confluence of its narratives of nostalgia and escapism, I also offer a recapitulation of how utopian hermeneutics figure into reading the novel.

"The Good Old Days": Nostalgia and the 1980s of Popular Fiction

Shortly after he obtains the copper key, the first of the three artifacts which open the three gates that are part of the quest, and sets off the increasingly violent phase of the Hunt, Wade travels to the location in the OASIS where the gate is hidden. The place is a small planet named Middletown, created by Halliday, "named after his hometown in Ohio. The planet was the site of a meticulous re-creation of his hometown as it was in the late 1980s. That saying about how you can never go home again? Halliday had found a way" (85). Middletown, where "Halliday had preserved his childhood forever" (103), is only the most overt example of how nostalgia suffuses the novel. In Halliday's home, Wade spots popular-cultural high points of the late 1970s and 1980s, at least for a teenager: films such as *WarGames* and *Tron*, *Dungeons & Dragons* rule books, an Atari console with game cartridges, a TRS-80 computer. Halliday's reconstruction, as Wade acknowledges, is superficially perfect; beneath its nostalgic accuracy, it leaves no room for the truth which the past hides. Looking at a family photo of the Hallidays reproduced here, Wade muses, "there was no hint that the stoic man in the brown leisure suit was an abusive alcoholic, that the smiling woman in the floral pantsuit was bipolar" (103). What is recalled at Middletown is an inoffensive, indeed maybe mediocre, ideal place whose chief claim to fame is the personal associations raised by it.

In this, it is the perfect condensation of nostalgia. "Nostalgia," as Svetlana Boym points out, "is a longing for a home that no longer exists or has never existed" (2001, xiii). Nothing in the sterile, uninhabited, computer-reproduced version of Middletown is really like the 1980s—it is a simulacrum centered on the artifacts which recall for Halliday the most positive side of his childhood; these have existed, but not in the detached way they do in this fantasy, devoid of any social concretization. Halliday's nostalgia is, in Boym's terms, "reflective," in that it is "oriented more toward an individual narrative that savors details and memorial signs, perpetually deferring homecoming" (2001, 49), but it is not ironic in the way Boym sees reflective nostalgia work. Rather, the novel takes seriously Halliday's past as a hallowed better time. These simulated memories elicit a very similar nostalgic response in Wade, for whom this "home [. . .] has never existed" at all. Middletown is the most overt display of the importance which the OASIS founder attaches to his childhood experiences and the objects he valued, and the impact this has on the world at large. *Ready Player One* narrates the creation, among other things, of "'imagined nostalgia,' nostalgia for things that never were" (Appadurai 1996, 77), at least not for those most implicated by it. The novel's introduction acquaints us with the basic fact of Halliday's, but also the rest of the world's, relation to the 1980s. "Halliday had harbored a lifelong obsession with the 1980s, the decade during which he'd been a teenager, and [the invitation to the Hunt] was crammed with obscure '80s pop culture references" (2). Having made public the nature of the Hunt, Halliday offers players access to "Anorak's Almanac"—named for his avatar—which turns out to be a thousand-page-long document of Halliday's nostalgic obsession with 1980s pop culture, crammed full of reflections on his favorite books, films, TV shows, video games, music, and so on:

> This led to a global fascination with 1980s pop culture. Fifty years after the decade had ended, the movies, music, games, and fashions of the 1980s were all the rage once again. By 2041, spiked hair and acid-washed jeans were back in style, and covers of hit '80s pop songs by contemporary bands dominated the music charts. People who had actually been teenagers in the 1980s, all now approaching old age, had the strange experience of seeing the fads and fashions of their youth embraced and studied by their grandchildren. (7–8)

Ready Player One sees Halliday's nostalgia seeping into a quasi-nostalgia on the part of the culture in which Wade lives, and the multilayered nature of nostalgia in *Ready Player One* (Halliday's; the 2040s'; the novel's; and readers') for the 1980s needs to be unraveled in order to understand nostalgia's work in the novel. Far from simply being a private obsession, the Hunt has transformed Halliday's nostalgia into a contemporary quasi-religion. Only slightly later, Wade muses about his playing of reproductions of 1980s coin-operated video games, "I didn't think of them as quaint low-res antiques. To me, they were hallowed artifacts. Pillars of the pantheon. When I played the classics, I did so with a determined sort of reverence" (13). Wade uses similar language in connection with the OASIS, too. Reflecting on what he finds out about IOI's plans for the time after obtaining control of the OASIS, he mentally accuses them of trying to "pervert and defile" (139) the OASIS.

Wade's nostalgic longing and his reverence for the means of accessing it are just two of the key issues here, however, the third being the more complex problem of what the novel invokes when it evokes the 1980s. *Ready Player One* trades heavily here on creating a sense of nostalgia for the 1980s in a reader-consumer who today is among the affluent group of around-forty-year-olds willing to glance back longingly at a simpler time, the time of their own childhoods. This is almost certainly the chief purpose of the long, loving descriptions of the various popular cultural artifacts and the long lists of films, TV shows, music groups, and video games with which the novel abounds; a very peculiar nostalgia for what are, in the final analysis, commodities. Like Halliday's memory of Middletown, the nostalgia which the novel appears to seek to engender in the reader is a commodified one, devoid of personal touches, a coldly commercial entertainment product.

It is almost inescapable in this context to link this largely commodified form of cultural nostalgia to postmodernism. For Fredric Jameson, speaking about then-contemporary filmic representations of the 1950s, nostalgia is bound up with the demise of genuine historicity, the rise of pastiche and depthless historicism, "the random cannibalization of all the styles of the past, the play of random stylistic allusion" (1991, 18). They are in a "nostalgia mode" which is a largely aesthetic approach to history, one which substitutes precision in historical representation with the "glossy qualities of the image" and the "attributes of fashion" (19), that is, by looks and feelings, which come to stand in for genuine historicity. Rather than engaging with the historic facticity of the objects under consideration, nostalgia, Jameson avers, "endows present reality and the openness of present history with the spell and distance of a glossy image," and so "emerge[s] as an elaborated symptom of the waning of our historicity, of our lived possibility of experiencing history in some active way" (21). Such a view of nostalgia is certainly negative. It is also bound up in the logic of postmodernism: the nostalgia mode stands not coincidentally at the beginning of Jameson's long exploration of the chief characteristics of the period, but rather symptomatically enacts many of its chief characteristics.

To speak of nostalgia now, then, is always to speak also about our relation to postmodernity. Arjun Appadurai notes that the "most radical postmodernists" would claim that

> pastiche and nostalgia are central modes of image production and reception. Americans themselves are hardly in the present anymore as they

> stumble into the megatechnologies of the twenty-first century garbed in the film-noir scenarios of sixties' chills, fifties' diners, forties' clothing, thirties' houses, twenties' dances, and so on ad infinitum. (1996, 30)

For Appadurai, in such cultural production "the present is represented as if it were already past" (83), an insidious version of the concept of an end of history largely figured as an infinite recursion. To use the "megatechnology" of the OASIS to reproduce the low-res, low-tech video games of yore—the notion of adding '80s Ataris and '70s movies to Appadurai's list—may certainly seem to qualify as a refusal to live one's present, now, however, understood to be a global phenomenon, rather than an American.

It would be possible to offer a number of further examples of how nostalgia, generally perceived as a problematic, indeed often negative, version of historical perspective, permeates postmodern critical thinking, from Jean-François Lyotard's apparent equivalency between "nostalgia and mockery" (1984, 74) to Paul Ricœur's insistence that nostalgia is at best a "regressive trend" (qtd. in Ashcroft 2016) to Linda Hutcheon's suggestion in her attempt to recuperate the historical vision of postmodernism that "if nostalgia connotes evasion of the present, idealization of a (fantasy) past, or a recovery of that past as edenic, then the postmodernist ironic rethinking of history is definitely not nostalgic" (1988, 39). Rather than dwell on the critique of nostalgia, though, I want to hold up the way that of late, critics have increasingly sought to recuperate nostalgia, to give it a positive critical valence, one which we must increasingly relate to the end of postmodernism. Svetlana Boym argues, for instance, that "[n]ostalgia is not always about the past; it can be retrospective but also prospective. Fantasies of the past determined by needs of the present have a direct impact on realities of the future" (2001, xvi). John Su suggests that many contemporary authors employ nostalgia's peculiar mixture of "imagination, longing, and memory in their efforts to envision resolutions to the social dilemmas of fragmentation and displacement described in their novels" (2005, 3; see also Bauman 2017). Nostalgia does indeed function in a more complicated way in *Ready Player One* than as a mere yearning for the lost. The novel negotiates the complex relationship between temporalities and modalities that Boym sketches: between pasts, presents, and futures, and between fantasy and reality; between the passive recollection of the past and the active shaping of the future; and it triangulates a version of historical awareness that draws upon the potential of nostalgia to recuperate energies for change.

It is the desperate economic situation the novel's 2040s are facing that largely propels *Ready Player One*'s nostalgic vision of the 1980s for the majority of OASIS users. As the novel at various times establishes, outside of cities, "lawless badlands [. . .] now existed" (163), "wars, rioting, famine" (195) are prevalent everywhere, ghettos have cropped up in the cities. "The once-great country into which I'd been born," Wade muses, "now resembled its former self in name only" (201). The novel offers a modicum of historicity in narrating these changes, revealing an understanding of the relations between economic growth and its immediate consequences, and so of the socioeconomic system at large: "Our global civilization," Wade narrates, "came at a huge cost" (17). Wade seems tentatively aware of the (historical) reasons for the plight which the world is in. Yet this does not translate into anything like historical awareness: after all, Wade concludes that "life is a lot tougher than it used to be, in the Good Old Days, back before you were born" (17). The pendulum shifts back from a sense of historical development to a somewhat disquieting nostalgia for a lost, great, past. What is perhaps surprising here is the way in which *Ready Player One* refuses to acknowledge the sociopolitical developments of the 1980s as at least the proximate source of the troubles which engulf its present. These include the rise of neoliberal capitalism, the slow dismantling of the minimum social security state, the end of a systemic alternative to capitalism, the globalization of the Western economic model. That is to say, it never acknowledges the 1980s politically, but only as a source of its popular cultural lore. We may certainly chalk up part of this lack to the perspective of the narrator, whose limited adolescent viewpoint is exhausted by his effort to grasp the full import of the Hunt and its many challenges. Nevertheless, the curious lack of a fully articulated historical awareness posits an interpretational challenge, given that I want to claim that *Ready Player One* has a progressive, indeed utopian, vision of socioeconomic change. As I will go on to show below, the sense of a historical awareness which permeates some of its discussion of the consequence of the exploitative nature of contemporary capitalism becomes more fully available in the novel's discussion of the OASIS's impact, of the escapist nature of the OASIS. Yet something similar is at work in its recuperation of nostalgia. Nostalgia, of course, is always ahistorical. But in this case it is precisely the lack of historical awareness that permits it to activate the 1980s for a progressive vision of the future. It activates the essentially apolitical, the popular cultural as such, to mobilize political action. The novel shows an awareness of historical trajectories, of developments which reach back into times before the birth of its major characters and indeed which encompass the whole endeavor of the OASIS. The nostalgia which the novel evokes for the 1980s is not just one for a moment where things were still, as it were, "good," notwithstanding the location on a historical trajectory and their irreducible place as the moment of departure into the world of 2044 (and by extrapolation, our own). They were also the moment where things could still potentially have gone right. Here "the space opened up by the memory of authenticity freewheels on as the very desire it stimulates for [the] impossible return"; or, in other words, the nostalgic longing for a gone past becomes itself a recall of an outside to the existing, to "the real subsumption of labor under capital" (Brown 2005, 62). This latter bit all the more so because *Ready Player One* has already highlighted the complicated conflation of work and play in the OASIS, its existence as a digital workspace and the way the OASIS must appear itself as a totality with no meaningful outside. There is a real world; but it is no alternative. Paradoxically, however, it is the nostalgic representation of the 1980s inside it that evokes the kinds of alternatives and possibilities that the OASIS itself technically disables.

This is, I would argue, one way in which it may be said to recuperate the readerly nostalgia which the novel is geared towards. The unlikely nostalgia evoked by the Hunt in the 2040s for the 1980s is a proxy for the far more likely nostalgia which adult readers of science fiction such as *Ready Player One* may have for the 1980s of their own childhoods. *Ready Player One* evokes simpler times for readers in the present, indeed celebrates them. Yet even this past may become potentially useful, and even our wallowing in its memory may be, the novel insists. If in the case of readerly nostalgia, the concrete mechanisms are more obscure (though the question of how reading a popular novel may be a politically useful act is never far from the surface), in the case of the novel's narrative they are quite clear. Not all of the nostalgias the novel deals with are finally recuperated, but the imagined nostalgia which Wade and his fellow gunters have fallen for pays off. After all, the solution of Halliday's riddles, and thus the winning of the Hunt, are entirely dependent on it. This is where the stark contrast between the impeccably trained, deeply knowledgeable, and effectively equipped IOI teams and the real gunters, Wade included, lies: IOI's wholly mercenary desire to obtain the maximum pay-off from the Hunt contrasts with the emotional attachment which the gunters have. To be sure, for long stretches, the shared and superficial interest in the 1980s, solely conditioned by the chance to win an incredible fortune, offers absolutely no kind of redemption otherwise. Rather, it appears as something of an ersatz religion, one in which a full immersion in 1980s trivia masks the fact that only one of the millions of people involved in the Hunt will be able to make ultimate use of this knowledge. But as the novel progresses, this shifts: their shared nostalgia for the 1980s, their shared identity as gunters, enables the proletarian users of the OASIS to see themselves as engaged in a common struggle with the IOI. The ultimate extent of this is to be seen towards the end of the novel: Wade describes the descent of the gunters on the scene of the novel's final showdown as an "otherworldly Woodstock" (329). Earlier, in the process of discovering the final key, it is Wade's emotional reaction to finding the guitar that houses the key, and deciding on the spur of the moment to play it, which makes him privy to the knowledge that only teamwork will open the final gate (which turns out to be the stumbling block for IOI later on). As Wade muses, the strongly streamlined IOI operation is unlikely to have invested the time in the sheer joy of making nostalgic music and thus almost certain to have missed the important note which Wade receives through his actions. It is, then, the fullest involvement with the 1980s both as a matter of scholarly knowledge as well as emotional attachment that finally permits Wade to win the quest, and gain control of the OASIS, Halliday's fortune, and the future.

The redemptiveness of the novel's 1980s nostalgia lies in its full elaboration, somewhat paradoxically: it is only in bringing it full circle, in winning the quest which has powered the OASIS's obsession with the 1980s, that its spell on the OASIS can be broken. If, as Svetlana Boym notes, the "ersatz nostalgia promoted by the entertainment industry" offers a "cure that is also a poison" to the ahistorical lives lived under postmodern regimes of time, we may now shift this around to suggest that *Ready Player One* reads 1980s nostalgia and its "souvenirization of the past" (2001, 38) as a "poison that is also a cure," a way to use the past to shape the present and the future. If nostalgia, then, is the means by which history gets incorporated into the present, the particular form which this history takes—popular speculative fiction in terms of the novel's own form, and popular culture in terms of the things the novel holds available in its nostalgic recollection—requires further elaboration. Here, too, and perhaps unexpectedly, the novel makes counterintuitive use of what appears to be a related concept—escapism—in order to formalize the mobilization of history as a broader perspective. The fact that the novel mobilizes its particular nostalgia of the 1980s is significant here. Were *Ready Player One* to evoke an imaginable nostalgic longing for, say, *Wall Street*'s Gordon Gecko and the time when men were Masters of the Universe, or for Reagan's SDI or Margaret Thatcher's "no such thing as society" comments, or for the jingoism of the Falklands War, or for privatization and deregulation, or for the rise of the finance economy, we would be hard pressed to find anything redemptive in its vision of the 1980s. Because it mobilizes, instead, the apparently apolitical, it can recuperate nostalgia as an avenue to political upheaval. What *Ready Player One*'s 1980s pop culture nostalgia does is trade off a historically conscious version of the past against an emotionally mobilizing one, suggesting that the precise material constitution of a historical moment is less important than its ideational potential. In this form, the Idea of course is not precisely Badiouan—not as such historical—but rather comes into being from the perspective of the nostalgic remembrance only evoked by the novel. But if an idea is "really the conviction that a possibility, other than what there is, can come about" (2013a, 14), as Badiou notes to Fabien Tabry, we may be within our rights to suggest the relation between the way nostalgia evokes alternatives to what is—indeed, to what was, in greater historical terms—and a further exploration of alternatives. This is what *Ready Player One* figures through the OASIS, and Halliday's Hunt. In so doing, it also elevates the very notion of escape.

"The only thing that makes our lives bearable": Popular Fiction and Escapism

The danger of stepping back into a celebration of a lost past rather than engaging with the difficulties of the present reappears in the second key category which *Ready Player One* engages: escapism. Like nostalgia, escapism appears to suggest that you can simply refuse to engage the present, and instead hide in fictional worlds where better lives exist, or else in virtual worlds which do not finally change anything about your real life. *Ready Player One* engages this trope. The novel layers versions of escapism, all refracted through the medium of popular fiction or the technologies of popular entertainment, for instance in the way the novel initially frames the Hunt itself: "Like winning the lottery, finding Halliday's Easter egg became a popular fantasy among adults and children alike" (7). In calling the quest for ultimate control of a vast fortune and the entirety of a simulated universe a "popular fantasy," the novel nods towards both its own "popular" fictionality as well as the negative coding of fantasy. From this point of departure, we must read the entirety of its engagement with escapism and popular fiction. There are at least three levels to this engagement. On the level of narrative, we see Wade's development from a user of the OASIS for escape from his dreary surroundings to the hero of his own story and the potential harbinger of a better future. On the level of commentary, Wade reflects upon the use of the OASIS by others, and thus opens to view the challenges of virtual reality, and of the kinds of lives that can be lived in it. This is also a metalevel, however, given that

Ready Player One through its narrative produces something very escapist in its own right, a science fiction story with a happy ending that permits readers to escape the constraints and anxieties of our present. Yet these three forms of escapism finally all come together in a larger claim about their ultimate usefulness. For, after all, its lesson will be that even an entirely immersive, uncritical, escapist engagement with popular art will yield, under the right circumstances, the kind of knowledge and power that enables one to seize control of the fate of the world, and thus comments on the very question of what popular fiction itself can do. What *Ready Player One* ultimately recuperates in its own form is the very act of reading escapist fiction, through the most apparently escapist device of all, the happy ending. This is possible only, however, in so far as the novel first establishes the power of escapist fantasy in its own narrative arc. That is to say, not all happy endings equally reconstitute genre fiction as progressively utopian, but those which have already tied escapism affirmatively to progressive change may, and *Ready Player One* does.

I am calling what *Ready Player One* simultaneous produces, narrates, comments upon, and finally appears to affirm as a social practice "escapism" here, notwithstanding this successful transmutation from a derided uncritical reading practice to a challenging and progressive action, precisely because of the kind of bad reputation of the term. This is what Ursula K. LeGuin alludes to when she asks, "[t]he direction of escape is toward freedom. So what is 'escapism' an accusation of?" (2017, 83). I do not deny that *Ready Player One* is escapist, in an effort to recover the novel's critical potential. I am interested in suggesting that it is precisely its escapism, and its awareness of the potential power of ostensibly escapist fantasy, that make it available for rethinking the present in progressive terms. If utopia is always already a form of escape, any recuperation of utopian thinking is also a recuperation of escapism. Or, as Paul Ricœur puts it, "[a]t a time when everything is blocked by systems which have failed but which cannot be beaten [. . .] utopia is our resource. It may be an escape, but it is also the arm of critique" (1986, 300).

It is impossible to neatly separate the novel's three escapist registers—escape into the OASIS, commentary on the OASIS as a means of escape, and the novel itself as escapist literature. Central to its discussion of escapism, obviously, is its virtual reality engine, the OASIS. Like nostalgia, virtual reality has been explored by postmodernist thinkers, notably Jean Baudrillard (1994), for whom it is the final form of postmodern hyperreality, and Fredric Jameson, whose Baudrillard-inspired notion of simulation likewise rings with concern for the subject. We should briefly note that Baudrillard, when he speaks of virtual reality, means something different from the full-on embodied experience which both VR today means and which the OASIS is imagined to be (see Poster 2001, 125), and that Jameson, too, sees simulation at work in more mundane 2D film. Yet in both cases, the processes recall the way in which the VR of the OASIS replaces the real world, certainly as the preferred place to "be," for most users. The novel finally appears to disavow the need for this VR, and its overall ambivalence about the technology suggests that it does not see VR quite in the way postmodernist theorists would have it. It suggests again the novel's distance from postmodernism, which, ultimately, returns us to the question of how the valence of genre writing has shifted, and may be regarded as registering a more fundamental sociopolitical change.

We may also get a sense of this from the way the novel is interested in providing the sort of sociopolitical and socioeconomic background to its VR engine that its engagement with the 1980s misses. The novel spends a considerable amount of time on outlining the history of the OASIS, and much of that history is valuable to understand the way in which the OASIS works in it. It is the product of a long-standing cooperation between two video game designers, Halliday and his partner Ogden Morrow, between the brilliant game designer and the business mastermind, who manage to amass a fortune from their work from the 1980s through the first decade of the 2000s. They then settle down to create their greatest success yet, the OASIS, a system which "would ultimately change the way people around the world lived, worked, and communicated"; from a simple "new kind of massively multiplayer online game, the OASIS quickly evolved into a new way of life" (56). Ogden and Halliday launch the OASIS to great fanfare, giving away the OASIS 3D operating system for free and charging only the most nominal fee for participation; what they make money off is the virtual real estate into which much of commerce moves in the wake of the OASIS's release (shades of the Metaverse). As the system gains users, and as these users find themselves increasingly enamored with the possibilities of their new virtual reality, the OASIS takes over many of the functions reserved for real-world existence:

> Before long, billions of people around the world were working and playing in the OASIS every day. Some of them met, fell in love, and got married without ever setting foot on the same continent. The lines of distinction between a person's real identity and that of their avatar began to blur.
>
> It was the dawn of a new era, one where most of the human race now spent all their free time inside a videogame. (60)

This vision resembles simple extrapolation from such then-contemporary fare as *Second Life*, where much of this already happens albeit on a smaller scale, or idealizations of the globalizing force and connectivity of the Internet, and the ultimate version of the popular science fiction trope of virtual reality like the *Star Trek* holodeck. Yet to *Ready Player One*'s credit, it quickly turns away from a simple celebration of the liberating potential of virtual reality to its real-life consequences. "The OASIS was an online utopia" (59), it insists, but its emphasis is very much on the "online," with dire consequences for offline living. The novel sees the OASIS's success both as a consequence of its technological innovativeness, that is to say, what it offers as a system, and as a consequence of a brilliant business strategy. It is not just that the OASIS is world-encompassing: "It was *free*" (59, original emphasis). What is entailed in this simple acknowledgement, both narratively and for the novel's sense of history? *Ready Player One* takes heed throughout, whenever it chances to meditate on the conditions which have produced the particular situation of 2044 in which it takes place, of what Darko Suvin has called "*history as socio-economic lawfulness*" (2000, 223, original emphasis). It recognizes implicitly the way that the nature of the OASIS and the stakes of the Hunt are predicated on the material conditions surrounding it, and the manipulation of consumers that is entailed in marketing. The OASIS's genesis in 2013 (really, December 2012 (56)) anchors the future history of *Ready Player One* squarely in its time:

> At a time of drastic social and cultural upheaval, when most of the world's population longed for an escape from reality, the OASIS provided it [. . .]. The ongoing energy crisis contributed greatly to the OASIS's runaway popularity. The skyrocketing cost of oil made airline and automobile travel too expensive for the average citizen, and the OASIS became the only getaway most people could afford. As the era of cheap, abundant energy drew to a close, poverty and unrest began to spread like a virus. (59)

In its refusal to spell out a time line for these events, *Ready Player One* must leave us with a clever sense of unease, suggesting both a progression in an increasingly dire situation as well as an already-dire situation in 2013. Its narrative of how the OASIS figures into this is as simple as it is frightening: "Every day, more and more people had reason to seek solace inside Halliday and Morrow's virtual utopia" (59). By 2044, as the novel notes, there have been over twenty years of economic recession (51), blunted only by the possibility of escaping most of it in the fantastic lands opened by the still-free OASIS.

There is, then, a complicated dialectical relationship between the possibility of escape and the need for escape sketched by the novel. Conceived as the ultimate version of the massively multiplayer online (MMO) game experience, its "'open-source reality'" (57) is immediately recognized to serve escapist ends: "You could log in and instantly escape the drudgery of your day-to-day life" (57). The reality is a bit more complex: as more day-to-day life shifts to the OASIS—from work to shopping to relationships—it becomes more than a realm of mere escape, it becomes more than just a game platform, and instead it grows to be a replacement of much of real life. In serving as a means of escape, it lets people leave behind real life in search of alternatives, but at the same time, real life follows people, with consequences for the world outside. As we discover, the successful partnership between Halliday and Morrow failed twenty years before the beginning of the novel precisely because of what the OASIS had become. As Wade quotes from Morrow's biography, it "had become a self-imposed prison for humanity [. . .]. A pleasant place for the world to hide from its problems while human civilization slowly collapses, primarily due to neglect" (120). In implicitly condoning Morrow's view, the novel suggests a public complicity in the political, economic, and ecologic deterioration which, by 2044, has created the structures within which Wade lives:

> [His] generation had never known a world without the OASIS. To us, it was much more than a game or an entertainment platform. It had been an integral part of our lives for as far back as we could remember. We'd been born into an ugly world, and the OASIS was our one happy refuge. (34)

Wade starts out very much the same, making full use of the OASIS's capacity to simulate a better reality to escape the dreary life he lives in the stacks. For Wade, in a complicated recall of Halliday's nostalgia, "the OASIS is the setting of my happiest childhood memories [. . .] I never wanted to return to the real world. Because the real world sucked" (18). People living in the reality of the 2040s are caught in the tension between these various issues. Life in the real world offers little hope, but escape into the virtual reality of the OASIS only exacerbates existing real-world problems. What we would take to be real-life issues such as work, school, or relationships have moved online themselves, and indeed in due course the OASIS becomes the battlefield on which the most decisive economic struggle (that for control of the OASIS itself) is taking place. Finally, the fact that even the escape the OASIS offers is itself limited is a stark reminder of the inequities of the real world.

Wade, accessing the OASIS via a "console," realizes that his escape is not as perfect as it could be: only "with a new state-of-the-art immersion rig, it was almost impossible to tell the OASIS from reality" (27). Wade and most of his fellow gunters, the entire mass of the online proletariat, are escaping superficially, always held back by the inadequacies of their gear, inequalities of access.

These issues notwithstanding, for much of the early part of the novel, the equivalency between being in the OASIS and having escaped the realities of everyday life outside appears to hold true for most. The existence of the OASIS dampens interest in taking care to shape the world outside again. This is most obviously the case with Wade himself, for whom the quest for Halliday's Easter egg starts from solipsism. The challenge of what to do with Halliday's inheritance comes up early on in the novel. In his first long chat with Art3mis, Wade is quizzed on what he wants to do with the "hundred and thirty billion" dollars or so that he might expect to win (to say nothing of control of the OASIS). Wade's revelatory plan is to build an interstellar spacecraft, load up all of Earth's cultural artifacts, a copy of the OASIS, and a couple of friends, and then "get the hell out of Dodge" (97–98). Wade embarks on a fantasy of literal escape, a literal fantasy of escape, one which immediately runs into the practical, and communal, perspective which Art3mis outlines: "'But you do realize that nearly half the people on this planet are starving, right?'" Art3mis juxtaposes her own plan: "tackle world hunger [. . .] fix the environment and solve the energy crisis" (98). Wade is dismissive of this plan, as he might perhaps well be; but Art3mis insists on the need to try. Wade's journey takes him from his original solipsistic and defeatist position, in which his own material betterment fully supersedes any engagement with others, to a series of increasingly more communally spirited ideas. Later on, having witnessed the consequences of the OASIS's potential takeover by IOI, Wade is already critical. Confronted with IOI's claim that they were no more or less interested in the Hunt for its own purpose than any other gamer, and that they shared "the same goal," he wonders silently, "*What goal is that?* I wanted to shout. *To ruin the OASIS forever? To pervert and defile the only thing that has ever made our lives bearable?*" (139, original emphasis). There is an implicit contrast here to his own goal for the Hunt: to leave behind, without much concern for them, almost literally all of the "us" to whom Wade now acknowledges he belongs. The increasingly violent, increasingly life-threatening opposition from IOI—the manifestation of the capitalist subsumption of all public goods for the sake of private profit—nudges him towards a more radically utopian position. The threat from IOI also begins to make clearer what kind of space the OASIS is, beyond a simple means of escape. As IOI's plans for the OASIS become clearer, revealing the danger of a corporate takeover of what is, despite its commercial uses, essentially a proto-communist space, the OASIS's other participants in the Hunt, the gunters, band together. Having cordoned off the location of the first key that Wade found, IOI is now facing an assault by "all of the large gunter clans" (161). This public uprising against overbearing corporate pressure appears only to reaffirm the basically egalitarian nature of the OASIS. The assault proves successful, taking IOI's defenses down and opening access to the key to all again. From here on out, IOI is faced not just with the casual hostility of the gunters who have previously striven alone or in groups, very much in the way Wade has, for the egg, but with their joint opposition.

Logging on to the OASIS increasingly becomes not (just) an act of escapism, but an act of resistance, certainly for the gamers we encounter as characters. "Escape" into the VR of the OASIS is not actually held against the novel's characters at all. Indeed, full immersion in the illusion becomes the solution to its troubles, as the novel makes clear at midpoint. Having obtained both fame and a modest fortune through his initial successes in the Hunt, Wade decides to put this money to use. Safely hidden from IOI thanks to a variety of fake identities, he moves into an apartment in Columbus, Ohio, rigged with precisely the state-of-the-art full immersion gear that permits the OASIS to become almost indistinguishable from real life. Wade's purpose in this is simple: "I would abandon the real world altogether until I found the egg" (166). In narrating the following weeks, the novel takes care to note ways in which this act might appear utterly selfish: early on, after querying his user interface for news, the computer replies, "Just the usual. Wars, rioting, famine. Noting that would interest you" (195), and that is true, as far as it goes. But at the same time, it is also the case that Wade's isolation from the world is a crucial preparation for the final struggle against IOI. The full-immersion gear helps him get into better shape physically and mentally; and when IOI appears to take an insurmountable lead in the Hunt, Wade makes full use of his equipment to catch up with the corporation's goons. Wade's sacrifice of life in the real world, his ensconcing in a fully equipped suite, is the prerequisite for the success that his quest finally achieves.

It is certainly possible to hear echoes in *Ready Player One* of Baudrillard's hyperreality. Hyperreality is at the same time the ultimate outgrowth of capital and its stark limit, a delimitation of the mechanisms of power. Baudrillard concludes his thoughts on the power of simulation by suggesting that "[t]his situation will no doubt end up giving rise to socialism" (1994, 26). Virtual reality can become liberatory, precisely because it unhinges the levers by which power is usually exerted. To speak of "the real world" versus "the hyperreal world" is not to take Baudrillard's argument too seriously: *Ready Player One*'s virtual reality is not the hyperreality of Baudrillard. But when Baudrillard suggests that "danger comes at [power] from simulation," and the way that in the face of this danger, "power plays at the real, plays at crisis, plays at remanufacturing artificial, social, economic, and political stakes" (22), he also suggests the way the apparently escapist virtual reality logic of the OASIS shapes a space for utopian, progressive political change. After all, the kind of revolution which *Ready Player One* enacts in its last few chapters is literally only available in a virtual reality. The same capitalist logic that has produced IOI has also produced the potential of its own downfall. Indeed, the very device which has propelled IOI's rise, the OASIS itself, also is the device which permits its destruction.

Nothing about the novel's final pages narratively suggests that the OASIS is still a place of escape. Wade soon discovers that one of his best friends online, a Japanese player going by the name of Daito, has been murdered in his Tokyo apartment by IOI agents. And even as Wade reassures Daito's online-brother Shoto that "[w]e live here, in the OASIS. For us, this is the only reality that matters" (243), *Ready Player One* increasingly shifts its narrative offline. Wade infiltrates the real-life IOI headquarters in Columbus to obtain access to the company's files; once he has achieved that goal, and sent out word of IOI's murderous ways to the world at large, he is picked up by Aech and finally flown to Ogden Morrow's house in the Pacific Northwest. All of these events belie Wade's claim that the only reality that matters is online. The final battle, of course, takes place online: it pits the united force of the OASIS's gunters against IOI's attempt to keep the location of the final gate shielded off against Wade and his friends. At this point, no one is still escaping into the OASIS to take refuge from the lives they lead offline: rather, the OASIS has become the center of the most important conflict in their lives. It is a conflict which the gunters win by application of their talents as fantasy knights, science fiction fighters, robot warriors, spaceship captains, and so on. The end of the novel, in other words, affirms the usefulness of their otherwise entirely meritless, escapist pursuits, highlighting the way these endeavors may become potent, much in the way nostalgia does.

The final question, then, is how we can relate the narrative shift of the idea of escape. It takes us from an avowed, narratively reinforced sense that participation in the OASIS is a political regressive act to the narrated truth that participation in the OASIS on the OASIS's own terms, adopting fantasy and science fiction tropes and indulging completely in the nostalgic escape to the 1980s, is the only way forward into a fairer socioeconomic future. None of this, of course, invalidates the initial observation that the novel suggests that the OASIS is a means of getting away—merely that what used to be a problem no longer is. In this shift, *Ready Player One* nearly wholly recuperates all the variants of escape that I have outlined above. No wholly offline strategy of resisting or counteracting the capitalist depredations which people escape in the OASIS is promising, but online, somewhat counterintuitively, escape itself has created the conditions to permit change to the world proper. Much as the OASIS created the conditions under which the problems offline appear to have worsened, the novel's conclusion suggests that such a pull–push can now be used in the opposite direction. The struggle online will decisively shape the struggle offline. IOI's CEO, after all, gets arrested almost immediately for his crimes, the company itself appears to be on the verge of dissolution, and the wealth and capabilities of the OASIS lie in the hands of a new generation, one which is conscious of its position in the system and apparently willing to do something about it.

Ready Player One and the Quest for Radical Freedom

Ready Player One is after a fundamentally radical vision of freedom, of radical freedom even. It is a radical vision in as much as it arguably slams the brake on the very developments in the contemporary which it places center stage, and which have frequently been read as part and parcel of the contemporary impossibility to think utopia. Here, "'future shock'" (Žižek 2014a, 65) denotes the impossibility to stay abreast of technological developments, to integrate them into one's world-view, and by extension to control them, including controlling them to progressive or utopian purposes. As Slavoj Žižek explains, "Things simply move too fast; before one can accustom oneself to an invention, it is already supplanted by a new one, so that one more and more lacks the most elementary 'cognitive mapping' needed to grasp these developments" (2014a, 65). The technological imperative of contemporary capitalism reinforces its economic and political logics, each subscribing to the notion that no change is possible, but with a twist: change is becoming so rapid that it is impossible to make it meaningful, to make it part of larger narrative of what possibilities are (now) open that formerly were not. There are two levels to this. "Cognitive mapping" identifies a fairly basal conception of the social space, of what happens in it and how and why; but it also leads us to Jameson's use of the term, modified to identify the way in which literature can come to map what he calls "global social totality" (2005, 31) in form, content, and aesthetics. Neither version of Žižek's claim is ultimately true. *Ready Player One* suggests itself as a cognitive map of the present moment in Jameson's terms, as an aesthetic and formal registration of significant shifts from the 1980s through the imagined future of the 2040s; at the same time, it narrates a story in which the logic of Žižek's claim no longer holds true. This latter moment in almost meta-utopian fashion eliminates future shock as the driver of an anti-utopian logic. It does so by picking up on the kind of technological progress which Žižek identifies, presenting it as the wonderland of the OASIS, where everything is possible and thus no stable moment can be found, but also rendering this technological advance as an almost-stasis, in which no meaningful, larger technological change has apparently occurred since about the mid-2010s. The Žižekian argument may be read as an extension of the Jamesonian one which sees in postmodernism "the frantic economic urgency of producing fresh waves of ever more novel-seeming goods (from clothing to airplanes), at ever greater rates of turnover" (1991, 4), a cultural expression of the kind of social acceleration which Žižek identifies. My suggestion that *Ready Player One* counteracts Žižek's point should also be read as a repeat invocation of my larger point that speculative historism appears at the end point of the postmodern, and at the beginning of something new.

The link between the possibilities created by the OASIS's VR and the hopeful futures of the world is crucial to a second version of the claim to radicalness, where the shared recuperation of nostalgia and escapism come together. The key element in this final development is the novel's last scene. Having finally won the egg, Wade is addressed by James Halliday's avatar, the Mighty Anorak. "The game is over," he announces, and in a sparkle of lightning, Wade's avatar, Parzival, is transformed into Anorak, while Halliday's avatar becomes an image of Halliday himself. Wade is given a twelve-figure bank account and absolute control of the OASIS in this highly symbolic transfer of both power and identity. More crucially, he gets exclusive access to the "Big Red Button" which can "shut down the OASIS forever" (363). Wade, in simple terms, holds the fate of the world in his hands: everything, perhaps literally, now hinges on Wade's evaluation of what the OASIS means.

Halliday offers an interpretation of the OASIS at that moment. He confesses to Wade that he "created the OASIS because I never felt at home in the real world," but that "as terrifying and painful as reality can be, it's also the only place where you can find true happiness. Because reality it is *real*" (364, original emphasis). This trite conclusion is embedded in and counteracted by the novel in such a fashion that we are meant to recognize it as wrong. Instead of an "important perspective to gamers like Wade" as Justin Nordstrom has it (2016, 253), we should recognize it as severely limited when read against the novel's thrust. Halliday resurrects a narrative of escape that argues the VR of 2044 is defective. "Don't hide in here forever," his avatar advises Wade. In as much as the novel ends with a scene between Wade and Art3mis, offline, planning their future, the novel appears to understand their relationship as a source of "true happiness," the reason not to hide, and so Halliday may appear to speak for the novel's own sense of the OASIS. But I think the novel in fact puts several options on the table. First, Halliday's avatar is essentially deploying a pre-recorded message, rather than engaging Wade as Wade. That message is attuned to neither the struggle which has just taken place in the OASIS, nor the violence offline. In fact, whatever element of Wade and Art3mis's romance must be consumed offline, their online romantic relationship is what drives much of the interpersonal plot, and it is not easily denigrated by arguing that "happiness" can only be achieved offline. Halliday's avatar does not react to these issues because it cannot; and it cannot because it is looking at the OASIS from a vantage point much before the redemption of the OASIS's VR.

Second, Halliday's opinions on this matter should not be taken for gospel because Halliday is a thoroughly unreliable observer. After all, he was remarkably mistaken in his evaluation of what the OASIS would do in the first place. Polonius-like, he gives Wade paternal but pointless advice, based on knowledge that does not hold for the younger generation. What the appearance of Halliday's avatar signals is the way the events of the novel have shifted the discourse: whereas, for Halliday, the OASIS remains a place of negatively connotated escapism, one which stems largely from his own feelings of loneliness, for everyone else it is much more than that. For Halliday, the OASIS fails to give him the thing he desires most—narrowly, his business partner's wife, and more broadly, human connection, perhaps love—and so becomes a failure. The fundamental, political critique of the OASIS came not from Halliday, but from Morrow, whose point was not that the OASIS did not work for him, but that it did not work for society. Halliday's appreciation of the OASIS's defects lacks the kind of systemic reading which Morrow brings into play.

If we are not to take Halliday's presentation of the Big Red Button as the novel's suggestion that Wade should end the OASIS forever, then what is its purpose? In enabling Wade to abolish the OASIS, but leaving open what he ultimately does, the novel offers its most radical vision of emancipation, of a moment where everything is possible and nothing certain. Wade may yet build that spaceship of his and leave Earth to its fate, or he may become a despotic overlord in the OASIS. He may use his power for good, or get rid of it altogether. He may cure the defects of the world outside the VR, or he may fall into a solipsistic celebration of his new-found love and new-found wealth. He may even leave everything exactly as it is; but this is just one option among many. For Halliday, the purpose of Halliday's Hunt is not "to guide the reproduction of the social structure" (Condis 2016, 6), that is, to find a way of perpetuating the OASIS's existence in the shape in which he left it. This claim is counteracted by the simple choice given Wade at the end—a radical choice—to either delete the entire OASIS or not, by the mere push of a button. Halliday's decision to leave the choice of what to do with the OASIS to the winner of the Hunt is an abdication of Halliday's responsibility for the OASIS. It is also a means of placing Halliday in the entire logic of the narrative, a highlighting precisely of Halliday's inability to see the social structure, which is not amenable to his deeply personalized complaints against VR. Halliday becomes the avatar of more regressive versions of nostalgia and escapism than those which the novel, through its narrative, has revalidated.

Whatever intentions Halliday may have had with the Hunt, and the choice given the winner in either deleting the OASIS fully or simply retaining it (for the moment) at the status quo, the novel would appear to fully authorize a reading of this moment which does not focus too much on its ideological complicity. To read this ending as regressive militates against the entirety of the novel's narrative, which sees resistance against the logic of corporate overlordship as central. It suggests that despite its own declension narrative for the world outside, the OASIS is less unalloyed trouble than Halliday makes out. The novel, that is, disputes the very grounds on which Halliday makes deleting the OASIS an option. If we accept the notion that the novel ultimately resists negative readings of nostalgia and escapism, then this is only logical: the OASIS, even if it is wholly a tool for public escapism, is still a utopian place, and deleting it is not in any way an advance.

This is not, however, the only way in which I think we must deem *Ready Player One*'s conception of freedom radical: it is, like its nostalgia and its escapism, multilayered, both offline and online, both physically limited and not, opening the possibility of a better world on all levels. Its version of freedom is radical because it is at once personal, individual, very much in the tradition of humanistic liberalism, as well as social and even Socialist, seeing the greatest good for the entirety of humanity as its potential goal. The novel finally disavows the co-optation of public spaces, indeed of public life period, by corporate interests, while at the same time it strengthens a sense of communal action. While the image of the common resistance against the logic of corporate overlordship is quite obvious, even blatant, in the final battle between the now-allied gunters and IOI, the personal dimension may be less overt. But it is just as central because of the struggle between what the OASIS provides its users and what that means for them, offline and on. The capacity to hide behind an avatar, after all, is the central escapist motif; and its recuperation part and parcel of the novel's argument about the relative potentials of offline and online worlds.

The central question here is the question of what the offline avatars in the OASIS stand for, why they are the way they are, and how they relate to the real world. In a chat discussion, Art3mis and Wade discuss precisely this question: Wade's claim that "we exist as nothing but raw personality here," suggesting that the OASIS merely foregrounds offline character traits, is countered by Art3mis. Here as elsewhere the voice of logic driving Wade's awakening to the realities of his life on- and offline retorts that no, the "OASIS lets you be whoever you want to be. That's why everyone is addicted to it" (171). Her shrewdness explodes Wade's own somewhat less than woke take on life. "You're like me. You live inside an illusion" (186), she says. We should note that even Art3mis is not interested in closing the OASIS down, finally, despite her alertness to the problematic way in which the OASIS functions: rather, what she is after is to instill a sense of the reality of VR life into Wade. This is the point of the novel: not to play off VR versus offline reality, but rather to identify the ways in which either is useful, may offer means of resisting hegemonic power structures, may lead to a better world to come. Or rather, not in which either may, but in which it is necessary to operate in both to succeed in offering hope for a better world. Rather than playing off the one against the other, it suggests how we may reconcile digital technology and "real" life. The novel returns to this strand of the argument late, when Aech picks up Wade near the IOI headquarters as he exfiltrates it. Aech, it turns out, is a young Black woman, rather than a white male (319). Her mother had started using a white male avatar working in an online data-processing center, "because of the marked difference it made in how she was treated and the opportunities she was given." Her mother thought "the OASIS was the best thing that had ever happened to both women and people of color" (320). Between these two points—that the OASIS lets you live an illusion, and that the OASIS lets everybody else live your illusion, too—*Ready Player One* constitutes a critical conception of how VR works. Wade discovers that his connection with Aech does not depend on skin color or gender: rather, he finds he had connected to Aech "on a purely mental level," so that any "fears I had about the resiliency of our friendship in the real world" (312) vanish easily as the two fall into their old ways of talking. The point here is less the somewhat trite suggestion that behind the avatars of the OASIS always lurk actual people than to suggest the way the novel sees offline and online as inescapably interwoven. What the novel suggests then, finally, is that its own argument that there is a conflict between offline and online lives, and an irredeemable conflict between a declining offline reality and an online reality that is its cause, is far more complicated than that. The struggle for greater freedom—personal and public—must be won both offline and online, but either may help the other, much in the way Aech and Wade's online friendship marks their offline one.

Conclusion: No Limits to Popular Fiction

When Alain Badiou says that "there is no such thing as popular art" (2013a, 79–80), he proposes a complicated argument which suggests that taxonomical and formal distinctions between what are ostensibly "serious" and "popular" art forms are fundamentally mistaken, in as much as all popular forms originated in serious ones. What distinguishes them is that the one is art, and the other is not. For Badiou, that is not to say that what he calls entertainment cannot be interesting, but merely that it cannot be innovatory. What such texts have "of value is always a product of the history of truths, of the history of forms created in the element of art in the strict sense" (82). I want to take my departure from Badiou in as much as the major critical fault line between popular genre fiction and serious, literary fiction encodes genre fiction as resistant to interpretation and literary fiction as open to it (see also Lanzendörfer 2015, 2018; cf. Rosen 2018). Or, inversely put, it encodes genre fiction as lacking resistance, as lacking the push back against simple reading, whereas literary fiction is, by definition, resistant. "Art" has been transmuted into anything capable of sustaining critical attention, which is only a means of retaining essentially the same set of texts and concerns in critical practice that earlier might have simply been called "better." What Badiou's challenge thus helps open is the question of what happens when the fundamental difference between high art and low is taken to be immaterial. I have offered what amounts to a redemptive reading of genre fiction for two reasons. First, to offer a more complex test case for my suggestion that we need a utopian hermeneutics than the arguably more overtly political and more especially overtly literary novels discussed above. Second, to suggest more broadly the need to read genre fiction *well*, critically, indeed symptomatically, to engage with it on a level that is no different theoretically from our engagement with literary fiction, to pay "attention to its scholarly merits" (Nordstrom 2016, 239). The ultimate point of such an exercise would be, of course, to destabilize the categories of genre fiction and non-genre fiction, to argue against the need to think in these terms, or perhaps better to suggest that genre is itself inevitably literary (Lanzendörfer 2018, 183–92). *Ready Player One* provides a good test case for this precisely because it is, in many ways, limited; and it is these limits with which I want to begin this conclusion, before addressing again why we should nevertheless read it.

To read *Ready Player One* as a politically progressive and utopian narrative, and one which is in some way literary, is fraught—not just because the novel appears to miss signal criteria of literariness. It is unartfully written, with long passages of narrative exposition that fail to meet artistic criteria such as "show, don't tell" which have long been instilled in both professional writers and professional readers as signs of what Mark McGurl has dubbed the "craft" of literary writing (2009, 23). It has a simple plot and a straightforward happy ending, with apparently unlimited wish-fulfillment especially for its protagonist. Nor is it necessary to read this happy ending as particularly progressive, as I have done. The question which *Ready Player One* poses is essentially Fredric Jameson's:

> how is it possible for a cultural text which fulfils a demonstrably ideological function [. . .] to embody a properly Utopian impulse, or to resonate a universal value inconsistent with the narrower limits of class privilege which inform its more immediate ideological vocation? (1983, 279)

The novel's politics, the apparent belief that granting a single individual sole power over the world economy is a great solution to the problems of the world and slightly regressive argument for adopting white maleness online as a solution of sorts to sexism & racism, is awkward. It certainly permits itself to be read in a more critical vein than I have adopted here. It overtly privileges a personal rather than a systemic solution to the problems its world has. We may imagine Wade to use his new-found billions to help feed the world, of course, as he says he will do—but that simply begs the question it appears to answer. Halliday's decision to permit his inheritance to fall to the winner of an open contest may itself appear faintly like a 1980s call back. What is more capitalist, indeed more neoliberal, than the notion that to the winner belong the spoils, without regard for society? After all, there is no such thing as society. In this regard, despite the novel's attempts to deflect such a reading, we may be within our rights to suggest that Halliday is a successful "product" of

1980s neoliberalism, having imbibed all the right lessons—that winning is its own morality. *Ready Player One*'s solution to the problems that plague its present and which are, obviously, only extrapolations from our own, is quite clearly not systemic. It rests essentially on the more-or-less chance recovery of the billions of profit made by the inventor of a machine which the novel itself deems responsible for the very state of the novel's present. It never overtly challenges Halliday's moral right to these billions any more than it questions the nature of the quest which Halliday constructs; it does not suggest that Wade's triumph *will* really change anything, even as it suggests the *possibility* of change. Neither does it suggest that Wade's winning the contest cooperatively makes it in any way problematic that he now owns these highly dubious profits from Halliday's venture—this is what McGurl means when he notes the pervasiveness of the "fantasy of meritocracy" of the "litRPG" genre (2021, 81). And all this without even going into the nitty-gritty of the details with which Cline fills his world, such as the fact that IOI, apparently with the government's blessing, can take people who fail to pay its bills into inescapable indentured servitude. A more straightforward critical reading would likely foreground the way the novel is complicit in narratives of individual agency, of the need for heteronormative coupling, the dominance of (white) males, and other hegemonic practices, linked, as Megan Condis points out, to the novel's embedding in a "gaming subculture [imagined] as almost exclusively white and male" (2016, 9). I have no quibble with such readings: they are valid concerns for a novel whose own status as a commodity geared towards a certain audience is part and parcel of its appeal.

But my argument has been all along that to read for utopia means to suggest ways of teasing out underlying utopian moments even in narratives that appear to resist them. In a world, that is, where things fall apart—ours as much as Wade's—we can expect a little hopeful slouching towards Bethlehem, and await the birth of monster, but also of Messiah. Or, to mangle Yeats less, the halting movements, the fits and starts and dead ends of *Ready Player One* should not detract from its hopeful utopian speculation and readings which foreground it. That its solutions appear at best a mixed blessing is a valid point to make, but so is it to stress the ways in which it is affirmatively utopian in its outlook. And what is more, its adoption of a popular speculative narrative form enables it to be utopian in a way that more realist narratives might not be able to. Condis is correct to say that "[b]y favoring popular cultural texts over those traditionally prized by academia, Halliday's canon embodies the 'from the bottom up' system for determining cultural values" (2016, 7) that has become central to much media studies and appears to increasingly be recognized as important for contemporary literary studies, too. *Ready Player One* defends its own form as valid, and as a carrier of cultural value, and suggests the importance of setting itself beside more high-cultural writing of the contemporary. It demands that both it and the gaming world it represents so powerfully be taken seriously as utopian (see Nordstrom 2016). There are, the novel insists, no natural limits to genre fiction's capacity to express cultural concerns. The very nature of *Ready Player One*'s dual vision of where radical change may happen, necessarily offline and online, suggests the way genre fiction way more easily registers utopian potentials that are otherwise more readily questioned. Contemporary narratives of encroaching and engulfing digitization, from Gary Shteyngart's *Super Sad True Love Story* to Thomas Pynchon's *Bleeding Edge* to Jennifer Egan's *A Visit from the Goon Squad* are usually pessimistic about the possibilities inherent in it. *Ready Player One*, by contrast, is enabled not least by its appreciation of popular culture to see the potential for hopeful futures inherent in technology.

Reading *Ready Player One* brings us back to the question of (popular) genre fiction's political potential, already briefly raised in Chapter 3's reading of *Taft 2012*, and offers a striking answer: read in the same way, popular genre fiction is no less amenable to being understood as suggesting possible avenues for utopian thought. In this, little stands to be gained in separating the things *Ready Player One* does from the things, say, *Equilateral* does: they both offer imaginative approaches to contemporary questions, in this case through their shared interest in remediating history speculatively. The point here is not that any actual act of reading a novel marked as popular or generic will be read as an intervention into existing patterns of thought, that it will be read politically by unprofessional readers. Rather, the point is that the same holds true for ostensibly literary writing. We are without a guarantee of reception, which throws us back to the act of scholarly interpretation.

Chapter 5

Marvelous Histories, Possible Futures: Junot Díaz's *The Brief Wondrous Life of Oscar Wao*

This chapter argues that Junot Díaz's 2007 novel *The Brief Wondrous Life of Oscar Wao* must also be read as speculative historism seeking to reactivate history as a source for a utopian imagination of the future. It serves two purposes. It is a slightly different test case for my suggestion that we need a utopian hermeneutics, one which will tease out the perspective of hope from material which appears less concerned with systemic alternatives, but draws hope into a more personal register. It also draws in again on the question of the place of the form of speculative historism in the contemporary literary field, and advances my argument about the form's audiences towards its conclusion in the next chapter.

The Brief Wondrous Life of Oscar Wao narrates intertwined personal and family histories, chiefly those of the Cabral and de León families, of whom Oscar de León, the eponymous Oscar Wao, is the central figure. Oscar's mother, Belicia Cabral, fled the Dominican Republic during the rule of the dictator Trujillo, and the scars of the Trujillato mark many of the characters in the novel. The novel follows Oscar's school life and college career in the United States; Belicia's in the Dominican Republic, with extensive historical reference to the Trujillo regime; Oscar's sister Lola, who copes with the difficult home life created by Belicia in the United States in her own way; and Lola's sometime boyfriend and Oscar's finally friend and roommate in college, Yunior. Yunior also serves as the novel's narrator most of the time, and his life is the other major strand which the novel pursues throughout—indeed, as we will see, perhaps the most important one, the canvas on which the narrative of the Cabral family paints the possibility of a better life in the future. Covering about fifty years of history, the novel's heart is Oscar's life story, his quest for a woman's love, his desire to become a writer of fantasy fiction, and his effect on Yunior. It is Yunior's voice and his choice of references that chiefly shape the novel. Yunior has his own Dominican background, but unlike Oscar, he begins the novel as the epitome of what he and his friends believe is Dominican masculinity. An indifferent student whose chief interest is in pursuing girls, Yunior is an unlikely friend for Oscar, who is a "GhettoNerd" (11) who aims to become, in his own words, "the Dominican Tolkien" (192). Part of the novel is the narrative of Yunior and Oscar's development of a friendship that ultimately sees Yunior adopt the registers of Oscar's favorite genre fictions in order to narrate his combined history of the Trujillato and the Cabral family. Yunior's own journey goes from being "a guy who could bench 340 pounds, who used to call Demarest [his and Oscar's dorm] Homo Hall like it was nothing. Who never met a little white artist freak he didn't want to smack around" (170) to the narrator-writer of Oscar's story in Oscar's own creative registers: himself, perhaps, the "Dominican Tolkien," and at the end of the novel, "a new man, you see, a new man, a new man" (326). The novel is Yunior's bildungsroman, but with the twist that we find out very little about Yunior narratively, and have to understand his growth through the differences he presents between himself in the narrative and his narrator's persona.

Yunior's narrative insists first on the crucial importance of history, on family history as a means of understanding the world at large, including its possible futures. Second, on the necessity of rendering this history in terms of speculative fiction, comics, and other genre forms—in the terms of "nerd culture," as Christopher Pizzino has it, or "comic book realism," in Daniel Bautista's words (2010), and what I will call "genre-being" below: "Díaz treats nerd culture not simply as a natural topic for the nerd novelist, but as valid for thinking about history as such" (Pizzino 2020, 102). Speculative fiction, in other words, mobilizes historical thought in *Wao*, renders it understandable and accurately registers the real historical structures and events underlying *Wao*'s narrative. Third and finally, *Wao* broaches the possibility that speculative fiction can mobilize history effectively because history itself is fantastical. Genre writing does not merely metaphorically name the inconceivable horrors of the Trujillato; rather, it accurately describes them. But we cannot reduce its historical vision to the specific situation of the Dominican Republic. As Víctor Figueroa has it, the novel moves

> away from conventional realism [. . .] to present the novel's characters—particularly Trujillo—as incarnations (nodes or points of encounter) of structures of power so pervasive that their effects and influence cannot be exclusively explained in terms of the decisions of any one single man. (2013, 96)

The novel imagines genre writing to describe accurately the nature of hemispheric history, to draw out truths about the way the Americas' colonial past continues to inform our contemporary moment. The novel does not want actual readers to understand Trujillo as an actual supernatural force, but rather to understand that the register in which to talk about these things must be non-realistic in order to obtain purchase on its logics and its force.

Wao "has produced wildly different and sometimes wildly contradictory critical interpretations" (Graulund 2014, 37). Bautista (2010) and Monica Hanna (2010) both stress the importance of comics books, with Hanna emphasizing the importance of the Marvel series *The Fantastic Four.* I have stressed the importance to the novel of Tolkien's Middle-earth universe (Lanzendörfer 2013), and so has Schulenburg (2016). Other readers have focused on the novel's code-switching use of different languages and idioms (Lauret 2016), its use of science fiction (Miller 2011; del Pilar Blanco 2013; Sanchez-Taylor 2014), discussion and representation of homosexuality (Rosario-Vélez 2018), gender and fantasy (Fritz 2019), gossip (Rodríguez Navas 2017), readerships and authorship (Mahler 2010; Machado Sáez 2011; Graulund 2014; Vargas 2014; McCracken 2016), and narrative devices (Jones 2018). They have argued about the novel's sense of history (Hanna 2010; R. Saldívar 2011), the future (Perez 2012), and about its relation to the diaspora (Hanna 2010; Pifano 2014)—this list is by far not exhaustive. To read *Wao* through the lens of utopian hermeneutics offers us a new way of seeing what *Wao* does. It offers a postcolonial history of the world, rendered in a speculative form and mediated through references to speculative fiction, presented through family history and ultimately espousing the possibility of imagining a better future thanks to rethinking the world in terms of speculative historism. The particular vision of the future which *Wao* constructs is differently radical than that of the texts I have discussed above. Yet it helps to understand the novel as utopian regardless of its lack of an inherent, overt sociopolitical agenda. *Wao*'s hopeful vision insists finally on the possibility of breaking a vicious circle of violence and oppression, inaugurated in the colonial experience in the New World, by coming to terms with the reach of this history through the grand sweep of fantasy fictions. *Wao* offers two registers of hope and a question to the literary system.

The first register is systemic. Here, the novel's historical imagination becomes readable as a trajectory towards a hopeful future, one which begins in the novel's opening sentences about the colonial encounter in the New World. It runs through the entire book to end at the novel's conclusion and its hopeful immediate future, where Lola's daughter

Isis is conjectured by Yunior to be finally able to break the curse on her family and the post-encounter (New?) world. In its grandest sweep, the novel suggests that whatever acknowledged troubles this colonial encounter has produced, it is not a doom forever, but can be done away with, if only through a speculative encounter with its history. The second register is more low-key, centering on Yunior and his journey from an unabashed public advocate of toxic "Dominican" maleness and at best ambivalent and closeted genre aficionado to full blown genre nerd and, importantly, "new man" (326). What is involved in this is a larger recalibration of Dominicanness, diaspora identity, and the larger role of cultural production. The novel juxtaposes an ostensibly real Dominican identity, an un-Dominican affinity for genre fiction and popular culture in general, and an allegedly autochthonous Caribbean imaginary, including supernatural action, and poses the question of how to best relate those. Its answer favors what must in the novel's colonial context be read as a hegemonic, imperial cultural form, the comics, fantasy, and science fiction that Yunior's narration adopts as the right register to speak about what is also Dominican reality.

Yunior's successful mediation of history through speculative genres contrasts here with Oscar's own reading of Caribbean history *as* genre, as "being" sci-fi, rather than as readable through sci-fi. Sci-fi, in other words, supplants the inherent marvelousness of history with a second-order speculativeness. Genre obscures Oscar's reading of the world at the same time as, for Yunior, it renders visible what would otherwise be impossible to see. But it is this difference in situating genre against marvelous history that ultimately proves key to the two friends' comings of age. Oscar's desire to become the "Dominican Tolkien," his attempt to be a genre writer in the Dominican Republic, is a failure, his book is lost, his life forfeit. Yunior's choice to write not a fantasy novel, but a zafa, a counterspell against the curse that lingers on the history of the New World, rendered understandable through reference to but never confused with fantasy itself, is, by contrast, what helps Yunior get on the right track. The novel ends on a hopeful note for Yunior, but it also ultimately questions straightforward conceptions of identity, suggesting that what is entailed in being "really Dominican" is being attuned to one's history, a possibility open only after one's encounter with the hegemonic genres. *Wao* participates in the still-prevalent focus of ethnic writing on questions of identity, and within this dominant concern opens hopeful vistas for the future. These vistas include precisely a way out of identity, a category whose complicity in the perpetuation of structures of inequality has been frequently noted. *Wao* does become more politically utopian at a step removed, in expanding and extrapolating from the consequences of its narrative—much in the vein of how the novel's own narrator, Yunior, draws his lessons from the narrative he narrates.

Even as reading *Wao* through speculative historism returns a new interpretation of the novel, however, *Wao* also advances the discussion of the meaning of speculative historism in the contemporary. The unraveling of Dominican identity in the novel asks a surprisingly complicated but pertinent question: who is supposed to read *The Brief Wondrous Life of Oscar Wao*? This question turns essentially on its formal qualities: its code-switching between English and untranslated Spanish; its broad range of references not just to genre but also to postcolonial theorists, canonical literary fiction, table-top board gaming, role playing, and academic culture; and its winning of a Pulitzer Prize as only the most prestigious of many awards, all of them awarded to ostensibly "literary" texts, and now given to a text that appears to insist on the centrality of genre to itself. What readerships appear to be mobilized by the novel, how are they addressed, and what does such an address mean? Such questions let us speak meaningfully to the contemporary reach of speculative historism: they let us begin to end this book by starting to identify how significant speculative historism really is.

"Ain't just ancient history": Speculative History and the Imagination of the Contemporary

The Brief Wondrous Life of Oscar Wao starts with a prologue that informs our reading of the novel. Everything that it does echoes through the novel proper, from its use of a speculative ontology to its genre references, from the use of footnotes to interlink fantastic and "real" history to the introduction of the narrator Yunior's voice and presence as more than a mere observer. It produces ontological uncertainty, a simultaneous insistence on the supernatural as operative in history and a cautious refusal to set out precisely how it works. This will be the novel's mode: it never quite insists on the truth of the supernatural, but it insistently brings up its possibility; it never quite denies the existence of the supernatural, but it continually frames it so that it might be metaphor. Between the reframing of history as supernatural and of the supernatural as metaphor, *Wao* creates its sense of how history might be resuscitated for the contemporary moment.

The prologue begins in the realm of both history and myth:

> They say it came first from Africa, carried in the screams of the enslaved; that it was the death bane of the Tainos, uttered just as one world

> perished and another began; that it was a demon drawn into Creation through the nightmare door cracked open in the Antilles. (1)

The quasi-mythical "they say" is juxtaposed to the very real history of Native American death and African enslavement in the Antilles, events already here graspable chiefly through recourse to the supernatural, the language of demons, the horror-filmish suggestion of the "nightmare door." The novel's "it" in this case is "*Fukú americanus*" (original italics). Fukú denotes "a curse or a doom of some kind," in this case "the Curse and the Doom of the New World"—midwifed by Columbus but operative to this day. Even though Santo Domingo—on the island of Hispaniola, where Columbus first set foot on American soil—is, as the narrator informs us, held by Oscar to be the "Ground Zero of the New World," fukú's power ranges far afield. Characteristically, the novel immediately counteracts itself. Following on from the "They say" of the first sentence, the second paragraph offers a mere "it is believed"—here, that the arrival of the Europeans (rather than the "enslaved" presumed Africans of just a few lines before) "unleashed" fukú, and in extension of the earlier idea that Santo Domingo still is under its sway, the novel now insists that it has been unleashed "on the world," and that "we are all of us its children, whether we know it or not" (1–2).

The opening of *Wao* does not quite claim the existence of fukú as reality, but crucially, it also does not permit either itself or its audience to disbelieve in its existence. Fukú exists, though what it exists as, whether it is merely a metaphor or a genuinely accurate description of the postcolonial situation, ongoing to this day, remains to be seen. "But the fukú ain't just ancient history," the narrator announces, linking it, over the following pages, to the dictatorship of Rafael Leónidas Trujillo Molina, the Dominican Republic's dictator from 1930 to 1961. Trujillo, the novel suggests, was "a hypeman of sorts, a high priest, you could say," but here, as before, the novel hedges: "No one knows whether Trujillo was the Curse's servant or its master, its agent or its principal" (2–3). Nothing but fukú, the novel suggests, could explain Trujillo's impressive survival or the fates suffered by his opponents. From John F. Kennedy's assassination to the defeat in Vietnam, the prologue draws upon the supernatural as an explanation for history.

If this fukú is not (only) metaphor, something else clearly is. In footnoted explanations for "those of you who missed your mandatory two seconds of Dominican history" (2n1), Yunior not merely tells history, but reads it by reference to popular culture. Trujillo thus becomes "our Sauron, our Arawn, our Darkseid, our Once and Future Dictator," referencing the chief antagonist of J.R.R. Tolkien's *The Lord of the Rings*, a character in Lloyd Alexander's *Chronicles of Prydain*, the DC Comics antagonist who features heavily in *Superman* comics, and finally T.H. White's classic fantasy novel *The Once and Future King*. The mixture of mythology, fantasy both "high" and "low," and comics produces Trujillo for a broad range of readers but it also highlights how the novel strives less to name exactly than to approximate a reality that is already difficult to grasp. There is, after all, not a whole lot of overlap between Sauron and Darkseid, except that they are overtly powerful, quasi-supernatural (though the category, within their own universes, does not really apply), and antagonists. The point here is not analogy, but the development of a wider frame of reference, one in which the boundaries between the descriptive-metaphorical qualities of speculative fiction and the novel's very own speculative conceit are set on as wide as possible a basis: one in which each individual reference only serves to paint part of a larger picture.

Finally, the introduction gives us the central device by which the novel transports its version of history from here on out: the chatty, meandering, and very frequently genre-allusive footnotes. As footnotes, of course, they already raise a claim to authority of a specific, academic, kind. The history transported in the footnotes crucially underlies the narrative that the novel produces. Like much of the rest of the text, they are frequently contradictory, often ambivalent. But they are always interested in laying out a historical narrative, no matter its fragmentation, that supports the main text's focus on the family story of the Cabral and de León families by setting it in a larger context. Given that this larger context is already bound up in the still-larger system of colonial history the novel initially establishes, the footnotes do indispensable work in connecting the novel's different levels of history, from the grand sweep of its opening in the colonial encounter to the New Jersey diaspora lives of the de León family. They play a crucial role as marginalia that are by no means marginal, a formal manifestation of *Wao*'s argument that it is the marginal perspectives (genre, diaspora, small Caribbean countries, the view from the encounter, rather than from the imperial power) that permit us to see in new ways the historical structures underlying the present. But like the connection between genre and imperial power, the connection between the ostensibly marginal footnotes and the authorial power invested in them makes more complicated what might appear straightforward. Díaz's own interpretation of what the footnotes do and how they relate to the main text is quite wrong. His claim that "the footnotes, which are in the lower frequencies, challenge the main text, which is the higher narrative," and that they are "like the voice of the jester, contesting the proclamations of the king" (qtd. in López-Calvo

2009, 78) is belied by the way the footnotes pick up on and expand the main narrative most of the time, and certainly the way in which any reader must be hard pressed to detect the shift in "frequency" which Díaz claims (see also McCracken 2016, 51). Ellen McCracken is certainly right to suggest that main text and footnotes join "US and Latin-American culture as natural elements of a whole" (55). The same goes for the different levels of history the novel discusses, and their different registers, the supernatural and the speculatively metaphorical.

The introductory section spends a lot of time on an efficacious supernatural reality—fukú—which drives the narrative: the book we will read, the narrator insists, is both his "fukú story" and his "zafa," his "very own counterspell," an effort to "prevent disaster from coiling around you" (7). We must be leery of Yunior's protestations that he does not know if fukú exists or not, given the labor he will spend in order to defend himself against it. This first aspect of the introduction is complemented by the metaphoric use of genre fiction that is insistently not the same thing. Yunior offers an explicit corrective to that, quoting Oscar as asking, "What more sci-fi than the Santo Domingo? What more fantasy than the Antilles?," but contrasting this to his own designation of his story as a "fukú story." "I'm not entirely sure Oscar would have liked this designation," he notes, but insists, "What more fukú" (6) than the Caribbean? Yunior's early acceptance of the actual supernatural backdrop to his story importantly provides us with a genesis of the very book we are reading: a choice made in the full knowledge of everything that we will read in this novel, and thus already privileged over Oscar's developing version.

The prologue is not a mere "long digression about fukú" (Bautista 2010, 41), then; rather, it sets out precisely the way in which the novel will think history and the engagement with it. As Monica Hanna points out, "Yunior's story focuses on an entire family's lived experiences of history," but "the story of the family might not at first glance seem very 'historical'" (2010, 504). She argues that it is the way these lives "tie in to the public life of the nation" that gives them their historical force. It is the way the introductory section outlines the necessary historical connections that ground the narrative—fukú's arrival in the New World, its constitutiveness for the New World experience, its connection to Trujillo—that finally makes the lives of the de León family "meaningful" in a historical sense. In the de Leóns' lives, the historical forces which are manifested in Trujillo become intelligible. As numerous commentators have observed, Yunior is a narrator well attuned to his capacity to frame his story in a way that achieves its goals best. In an oft-cited later footnote, Yunior is quite open about the fictionality of at least some of his narrative. Here, Belicia Cabral, still in the Dominican Republic of Trujillo's rule, goes on a vacation with her lover. Yunior invents the destination ("In my first draft, Samaná was actually Jarabocoa," he writes (132n17)). There is "something supernatural" (Miller 2011, 100) about Yunior's capacity to know and relate details of family history, internal dialogue, near-death thoughts, and so on, that highlights the way the narrative is always framed by Yunior's own agenda: as T.S. Miller insists, "Yunior mediates every single word in his novel" (103). Yunior's initial insistence on the supernatural, global framework offered by his version of fukú is a framing device that makes explicable the supernatural occurrences in the family history that follows. But it also makes these supernatural occurrences at all times only part of a greater, grander global history, a dialectical cross-reading that structurally requires us to read what follows as not merely "about Dominica [sic] and its history" (Eaglestone 2013, 66) but in fact vested in a longue durée spanning the entirety of the postcolonial experience.

The seven-page introduction is crucial to the novel's insistence throughout on the deep links between its different registers, supernatural and speculative metaphorical, in its use of footnotes, and its different levels of historical imagination. It is on this ground that we can speak about what else the novel does with history. Two key episodes link the novel's sense of fantastical history to the larger problem of how to think about, and write about, a postcolonial past and future for the New World. The first is Yunior's narrative of the fate of Abelard Cabral, Oscar's grandfather, given in the novel's third section on Belicia Cabral, Oscar and Lola's mother, set in the Dominican Republic in 1955–62. The second is Oscar's own writing of a narrative about the Dominican Republic, the episode on which the novel ends. Both center on lost books and allow us to place Yunior's own writing more properly.

Belicia's story is a series of love stories which situate the narrative of the Cabral family in proximity to the Trujillo regime: first, Belicia's school affair with the son of a high-placed colonel. Second, her post-school affair with the Gangster that takes an ominous turn when Belicia becomes pregnant and the novel informs us that the Gangster is married to Trujillo's sister. Belicia's story's most crucial contribution to the novel is its insistent linkage with the Trujillo regime in the exhaustive explanatory footnotes that continually frame the regime in the terms of speculative fiction. Trujillo's later successor Joaquín Balaguer is "one of El Jefe's most efficient ringwraiths" and a "demon" (90n9); Trujiillo's son Ramfis, a "frozen-hearted demon" (99n13); Johnny Abbes García, "one of Trujillo's beloved Morgul Lords" (110n14); Felix Wenceslao Bernardino, "one of Trujillo's most sinister agents, his Witchking of

Angmar" (120n16). Belying Díaz, the main text offers a very similar set of metaphors, calling "Johnny Abbes, Joaquín Balaguer, and Felix Bernardino" the "regime's three witchkings" (121), and comparing Trujillo's death to the "end of The Return of the King," the final part of the *Lord of the Rings*, where "Sauron's evil was taken away by 'a great wind' and neatly 'blown away'" (156). Yunior's use of Tolkien is complex, and far less correct than might appear to either the casual reader or the uninitiated: there is only one witchking in Tolkien, and he is the only Morgul Lord in Middle-earth. What reads as individual characterizations of Trujillo's henchmen does not serve to establish simple parallels. The Dominican Republic is not easily and simply "sci-fi," but rather only metaphorizable, with all the limits metaphor entails. Díaz's novel progresses from individual metaphorical readings, as in Trujillo/Sauron in the introduction, to a more thoroughly allegorical system in which different elements from Tolkien's writings are combined to offer a more overarching reading of Dominican history. Fantasy's desire to establish a hierarchy of evil, manifest in Tolkien, breaks down when it confronts the reality of the Dominican Republic. This is evident through Yunior's metaphorical decontextualization of Tolkien, which becomes an even more complicated device in the course of the novel. The dividing line between the realistic tenor (the nature of the Trujillo regime) and the marvelous vehicle (the various creatures and their relationships in Tolkien, as well as fukú and its effects) becomes increasingly tenuous.

This extended but problematic riff on Tolkien does not, then, offer a straightforward way of reading Dominican history through fantasy metaphors, but rather establishes their usefulness and their limits, opening Dominican history to supernatural readings against which we must read the "actual" fantastic episodes that the novel soon throws up. From a general avowal of the existence of fukú in the introduction, we turn to what appears to be a largely realistic ontology for a considerable time in which fukú has no active role, and then to the effort, picking up from the introduction, of rendering Dominican history in increasingly ill-fitting metaphors drawn from fantasy. When fukú, immediately afterwards, makes its return, the repeated insistence on the translatability of Dominican history into the register of the fantastic becomes readable as laying the groundwork for accepting a more fully fantastical reading of what happens to Belicia to force her to leave the Dominican Republic for the New Jersey diaspora.

In the novel's first genuinely fantastic episode, Belicia, trying to find her lover, is driven down a road. By the roadside, "our girl could have sworn that a man sitting in a rocking chair in front of one of the hovels *had no face* and waved at her" (135). Certainty about the reality of what she has seen eludes Belicia, the narrator, and the reader. As it continues, the novel weaves an increasingly tighter web of speculative episodes. Seeking strength to fight for her niece's survival, Belicia's aunt La Inca feels that "a hand reached out for her and she remembered who she was [. . .]. You must save her, her husband's spirit said, or no one else will" (144). Neither narrator nor characters show any doubt about the factuality of La Inca's spirit-message. Belicia, beaten and almost broken by the henchmen of her lover's wife, soon finds herself the protagonist in an episode that is superficially fantastic but rendered too deeply in terms of the marvelous to leave the reader in too much uncertainty. "All hope was gone," but in "a miracle" Belicia finds in "her Cabral magis" strength enough to survive—and experiences "the strangest part of our tale" (148–49), the encounter with the supernatural being called the Mongoose. "Whether what follows was a figment of Beli's wracked imagination or something else altogether I cannot say," Yunior cautions, and then goes on to describe Beli's encounter with "an amiable mongoose" (149) that speaks to her and, by singing, leads her out of the cane field in which she has been left. An unambiguous footnote, however, makes Yunior's initial profession of uncertainty much less convincing:

> The Mongoose, one of the great unstable particles of the Universe [. . .] [a]ccompanied humanity out of Africa and [. . .] jumped ship to [. . .] the Caribbean [. . .] an enemy of kingly chariots, chains, and hierarchies. Believed to be an ally of Man. Many watchers suspect that the Mongoose arrived to our world from another, but to date no evidence of such a migration has been unearthed. (151)

Yunior's initial uncertainty vanishes in his crystal-clear enunciation of what the Mongoose is: "[i]t's all true, plataneros. Through the numinous power of prayer, La Inca saved the girl's life, laid an A-plus zafa on the family fukú" (155).

Belicia's backstory—she is eventually sent by La Inca to the U.S., to find safety in exile—is more than just Oscar's family history: it is also, halfway through the novel, crucially invested in rendering personal history (necessarily connected to the larger system of hemispheric and global history that is ushered in by the introduction) as driven by forces well out of the individual's reach, forces that require mediation in order to be understood. Is the Mongoose real? For certain senses—speculative senses—certainly it is. Is it an actual supernatural entity? For that, the novel produces too overt a connection between Yunior's self-identification as a "watcher" (4, 149, 329), the U.S. Marines of the

Dominican "watcher" slang (19–20n5), Jack Kirby's comics character the Watcher (92n10, 321), and this description of the Mongoose. The ontology of "supernatural" becomes decentered here: when a single word can describe a historically located phenomenon, a metaphorical usage for a narrative persona, and an ostensibly actual supernatural event, there is little to be done but to take all of these possibilities on board at once. To separate them out would do a disservice to the complicated interweaving of meanings, but also to the possibilities of seeing all of these levels of meaning differently, to accept them as providing a "different sensorium," a "different relationship between words and people" (Rancière 2011, 14), and a different relationship between words and history.

The importance of Belicia's story for the novel's historical imagination is thus difficult to overstate. Fifteen of the novel's thirty-three footnotes are crammed into this section, offering most of the information Yunior ever divulges on the fantasy nature of the Dominican Republic and linking the novel's repertoire of speculative genre allusions with an increasingly fantastic reality in the Dominican Republic through the vehicle of the Cabral family. The most fundamental expression of this linkage between family history and global history comes after Belicia's disappearance when she resists being forced into an abortion: La Inca, her aunt, Yunior reports, "knew in her ironclad heart that the girl was funtoosh, that the Doom of the Cabrals had managed to infiltrate her circle at last" (143–44). The capitalized Doom, of course, harks back to the Curse and Doom of the New World: the Cabrals' fate, here, is connected immediately to the original source of everything that is bad about the contemporary—the colonial encounter.

What to do about this? The answer, as the novel has it, is to write, but to write a particular kind of text: a text which does not foreground the supernatural at the expense of the non-supernatural, and which does not insist on rendering the Dominican Republic solely in the terms of non-Dominican genre fiction. This, I take it, is the gist of the novel's insistence on two lost or unfinished books: Abelard Cabral's exposé on the supernatural nature of the Trujillo regime, and Oscar's revelatory narrative of his stay in the Dominican Republic.

Of these, Abelard's comes narratively first. In fact, Yunior begins his family history of the de Leóns in 1944, with Oscar's grandfather, Abelard Cabral, and immediately complicates the idea of the very narrative he produces: "When the family talks about it at all—which is like never—they always begin in the same place: with Abelard and the Bad Thing he said about Trujillo" (211). Abelard is a successful doctor, a careful and passive man in dangerous Dominican society, and, for some time, successful at avoiding notice. As Yunior has it, "Abelard and the Failed Cattle Thief might have glided past each other in the Halls of History" (216) if Abelard had not begun to leave his wife and daughter out when meeting Trujillo, fearful of what Yunior narrates as Trujillo's tendency to seek out young woman to rape them. But Abelard cannot finally keep them away: in the "Caribbean Mordor" (226), such absences do not go unnoticed long, and when Abelard receives an invitation to a party in which his wife and daughter are explicitly named, he sees the writing on the wall. He refuses to bring them. He is arrested on the nominal charge of having slandered Trujillo and is tortured and abused. While in prison, he is visited by his wife, who it turns out is pregnant with his second daughter—Belicia.

In the quest to explain what has happened to the Cabral family here, Yunior initially throws up his hands: "Zafa or Fukú," he asks, wondering how to understand Belicia's conception: "You tell me" (242). Likewise, in explaining the rest of the events, Yunior insists that he cannot answer: did Abelard make a tasteless joke, or was he framed? Was it "accident, a conspiracy, or a fukú" (243)? Yunior initially suggests that we might as well decide for ourselves, noting that even the Cabral family would not talk about this anymore, "a silence that stands monument to the generations, that sphinxes all attempts at narrative reconstruction" (243). Even Oscar, when he seeks to reconstruct events later on, may have failed to deduce what really happened.

The options which Yunior puts on the table first, an "accident, a conspiracy, or a fukú," are also the ones which Oscar can be expected to have pursued—the "full story" which Yunior is not certain he discovered by the end of his life. But then Yunior shifts to another story: the possibility that Abelard was killed because he was writing "an exposé of the supernatural roots of the Trujillo regime!" (245). Trujillo, Yunior avers, may have been the subject of a book which held that he "was, if not in fact, then in principle, a creature from another world" (245). This story will remain inaccessible: "the grimoire in question (so the story goes) was conveniently destroyed after Abelard was arrested. No copies survive. Not his wife or his children knew about its existence, either. Only one of the servants who helped him collect the folktales on the sly, etc., etc." (245). Yunior plays hard to pin down, suggesting that the story may be "nothing more than a figment of our Island's hypertrophied voodoo imagination." But immediately afterwards he throws doubt on his doubts, noting that all of Abelard's books had been taken, that even after Abelard's arrest, Trujillo had not in fact made a move on Abelard's daughter, that "[n]ot one single example of his handwriting remains." He concludes, "But hey, it's only a story, with no solid evidence, the kind of shit only a nerd could love" (246). Importantly, though, it is a story that stands in a direct line from all the metaphorical reference to supernatural fiction and all the reported supernatural events that Yunior has spent two-thirds of his book presenting. Yunior's hedging loses much of its force when juxtaposed with his insistent destabilization of a realistic ontology.

The story of Abelard's book is how Yunior's narrative understands the nature of the supernatural history of the New World: supernatural if not in fact, then in principle. It is not fully grasped by any (even magical) realism, but significantly also not by the "mere" genre texts which Oscar reads and writes. When Oscar initially goes back to Santo Domingo, Yunior notes, "[h]e was imagining himself in love with an Island girl" (272). The plan for his "crowning achievement"—a "quartet of science fiction fantasies," "J.R.R. Tolkien meets E.E. 'Doc' Smith" (269)—is set aside as Oscar "goes native" (276). Oscar falls in love with a former prostitute, Ybón, whom he pursues quite against the wishes of his family, until he meets Ybón's boyfriend, a violent leftover of the Balaguer regime and current police captain. Oscar is taken by two policemen to a cane field, and beaten—like his mother before him—near death. (Whilst recuperating, he, too, has a vision of the Mongoose.) Broken, he returns to New Jersey for a while, but ultimately resolves to return to the Dominican Republic and seek out his fate. The proximate cause of this is Ybón, whom he cannot leave; but Oscar reads this, too, in terms of a personal curse: "It's the Ancient Powers, Oscar said grimly. They won't leave me alone" (315). Told to leave by Ybón, he resists, and instead spends a month writing and researching before the captain's henchmen turn up again, drag him out into the cane fields, and kill him.

The novel's final chapter reveals the limits to telling the truth about the Dominican Republic from the Dominican Republic. Yunior receives, eight months after Oscar's death, a package containing two manuscripts: parts of Oscar's sci-fi-fantasy opus, and a letter to Lola asking her to watch out for a more important package: "the new book he was writing." As Yunior has it in Oscar's voice, "This contains everything I've written on this journey. Everything I think you will need. You'll understand when you read my conclusions. (It's the cure to what ails us, he scribbled in the margins. The Cosmo DNA.)" (333). But that package never arrives. In lieu of the revelations Oscar promises, the letter to Lola carries news of a very personal kind: that he had actually slept with Ybón, that he had experienced the "little intimacies" of love. "If only I'd known! The beauty! The beauty!" (335).

There is a connection here between the two lost books of the Cabral and de León families. Whatever Oscar has researched may very well have been related to the story Abelard wanted to tell. Not, perhaps, in Abelard's way, as a story revealing the truth about a now long-dead dictator; but perhaps as a story about the supernatural in the de León family history, and thus, by extension, in the New World. Such a story, however, like Abelard's, cannot come out: it cannot become the narrative. It is significant to note that Oscar writes two books: a genre fiction novel which makes it out safely, if partially, and a researched manuscript of genuine power (or so he thinks) that does not. We should definitely note the way this contrasts with what Yunior has done, which is to employ genre fiction to mediate what he, too, understands to be a properly supernatural New World. Oscar has, we assume, done actual historical research, even if it is family history only: that is, whatever his exposé is about concretely, it is of the same kind as Abelard's. But historical writing that does not mediate the Dominican experience through the lens of genre fiction is doomed. It cannot even become. This is Yunior's chief historiographical lesson. Not just that he must mediate anyway, but that whatever needs saying about the supernatural nature of the New World is best mediated through an adoption of Oscar's genre love. Yunior, unlike Oscar, manages to bring together genre writing, supernatural history, and significantly a diasporic distance from the Dominican Republic. Yunior's history is more than just a family history, and it is more than a Dominican history. Yunior never quite adopts Oscar's late-in-life love for the Republic, but instead stays a distanced observer.

Despite these differences, it may be significant that the shift from third-person address in the final chapter, "he was writing" to "everything I've written," significantly confuses Oscar's and Yunior's voices. While there is no way of knowing the truth about whatever it was that Oscar has written, the larger claim—that "this" (the wrong demonstrative pronoun for a yet-to-arrive package, but not for the book we are reading at that point) contains "everything you will need"—is manifestly true for Yunior's vision of his life of Oscar Wao.

Where, then, is the hopeful future that I promise speculative historism looks for? In the next-to-last section of the novel, Yunior reveals where the purpose of his zafa lies: on Isis, Lola's young daughter, of whom he expects great things. Aware that he cannot keep the curse of the New World from her forever, Yunior hopes that she will, at a future date, turn to him, and then he will confront her with everything that her uncle, Oscar, has written, and let her find a way out:

> And maybe, just maybe, if she's as smart and as brave as I'm expecting she'll be, she'll take all we've done and all we've learned and add her own insights and she'll put an end to it.
>
> That is what, on my best days, I hope. What I dream. (330–31)

It is not the end of the novel. It is not a certain future. And yet, if there is a reason to zafa, this is where Yunior locates it: this is where everything that he has learned and taken down, his book included, comes to act on the future. This hope is tied to the historical imagination which Yunior has produced, hope which includes the possibility of an end. It is by no means straightforwardly utopian, but a hopeful narrative centered on the de Léon family. And, in as much as the characters in this novel are, as Monica Hanna suggests, themselves stand-ins of a sort for the progression of history, it thus also produces a more generally hopeful narrative for the greater historical dimension which it traces from the earliest colonial times.

Yunior finds a way of turning history into a narrative that promises relief from its oppressive force when framed wrongly. In his way, the forces that bear on the individual life become visible, even if this rendering visible entails a supernaturalization of forces which are in simpler terms merely larger than us. Yunior's story tells a history of the New World which insists on the idea that genre fiction can mediate something altogether too strange for "mere" history, but also resistant to being revealed without the necessary outside perspective that genre opens. Genre, that is, both for Yunior as the narrator and for the book itself (Díaz's novel), serves as a technology which renders sensible the forces underlying everyday life in the New World, whether in the Dominican Republic under a dictatorship or in the diaspora or anywhere else. That is the force of the idea that "we are all of us" in this together. Hanna is certainly right to point out that much "of the exploration of official Dominican history in the novel centers on the figure of the dictator" (2010, 502) Trujillo; but Trujillo, in turn, is explicitly linked to fukú and to the speculative metaphors which structure Yunior's telling of history. Trujillo and Dominican history come to be readable as exemplars, as central concerns for this novel but not the ultimate reach of its argument about the historical sources of the ills that Trujillo represents. *Wao* insists on construing fukú precisely as a New World curse. It insists on its own mediatedness, on the notion that truths can be told without everything needing to be true, on the historicity of all of its past events. It merely sets them into a different framework, one which does not counteract the factual history, but renders them in speculative terms to better grasp the logic behind them.

Wao's position in the world is structured by its use of pronouns, with the central question being who is spoken about when the novel says "they say," "we are," "our world," and so on. The possible referents are, if not endless, at least quite distinct: they could be references only to Yunior's diasporic community, his fellow Dominican Americans. If we must take the novel to speak to a wider history, in which all elements must be understood as figurations of the history of the colonial experience in the New World, there is also only one way of reading these pronouns. If the questions raised implicitly by *Wao*'s choice of addressing itself to largely unspecified reading audiences are, respectively, who are we, who are they, and what are we to one another, then my answer to the question of whose history is at the heart of *Wao* is also an answer to these questions. We are all of us addressed, as all subjects of the event of colonization. This is a complicated question of identity; and so, I would suggest, is the very use of genre that I have just read as central to the novel's creation of a hopeful future by re-envisioning the past in its terms. Genre fiction, after all, is not a Caribbean mode; and certainly, the specific system of references which Yunior employs is deeply embedded in a thoroughly hegemonic, imperial popular culture, whose adoption for the sake of telling the history of the New World cannot but be problematic. Popular culture grounds the narrative firmly in the United States, and suggests that the true history of the Dominican Republic can only ever be told away from the Dominican Republic. Like the issue of pronoun reference, genre raises identity questions.

"I wasn't as old-school as I am now": Local Identity, Global History, Genre-Being

Wao's genre form has been a touchstone in what amounts to a discussion about the novel's argument about identity: the question of whether its fantasy elements are appropriately described as "magical realism" or not. What is at stake here is the novel's relation to a tradition of Latin American writing in which the recourse to fantastical elements served to establish a form both original and rooted in authentic, often pre-colonial, cultural formations. It has been read as peculiarly suitable to the Latin American imagination ever since the Cuban writer Alejo Carpentier asked, "what is the entire history of America if not a chronicle of the marvelous real?" (1949, 88; cf. Santana-Acuña 2020). Carpentier's insistence on a uniquely Latin American reality, a "marvelous real that I defend and that is our own marvelous real encountered in its raw state, latent and omnipresent, in all that is Latin America" (1975, 104), is echoed by Gabriel García Márquez's insistence on being called, simply, a realist, notwithstanding foreign, frequently Western, critical categorization of his writing as the epitome of magical realism (Williams 1995, 5). Carpentier's and García Márquez's insistence on their own form of reality has led critics to see magical realism as "the literary language of the emergent postcolonial world" (Bhabha 1990, 6), to identify it with a specifically Latin American yearning for a postcolonial identity (Warnes 2009, 5), and to call it "a powerful form of indirect political resistance" (Bowers 2004, 41). In this sense, genre categorizations also serve to align *Wao* with a particular tradition of literary resistance: if it is magical realism, it immediately inscribes itself into *this* discourse, rather than opening its own, new ground.

Much ink has been spilled on the question of the novel's genre categorization (Hanna 2010; Miller 2011; Lanzendörfer 2013, among others). The novel's undoubted embeddedness in a number of literary forms serves to provide the formal grounds for its investigation of the questions of local identity, global history, and what I call genre-being. Quite a bit hinges on the question of form in this case simply because of the way these different discourses relate to hegemonic, postcolonial, and outsider positions. In juxtaposing magical realism, fantasy and science fiction, and the explanatory power of the supernatural throughout the novel, *Wao* asks specifically how best to relate Dominicanness, and what it can mean. This is a central question throughout the novel, and the answer is complicated. Oscar and Yunior relate to genre writing differently, bound up in different sociopolitical structures. The novel initially seems to parallel Oscar's "un-Dominican" (11) lack of success with women to his genre-nerdish behavior and reading practices, and to contrast those with Yunior's narrated self's disdain for genre and apparent success with women (which always plays out as conquest). As the novel progresses, its amassing of genre references serves to apparently rehabilitate Oscar's genre reading. And finally, Yunior's own turn to full-fledged "nerd" and "better man" in the aftermath of Oscar's death appears to speak quite clearly to the way genre reading is a means of finding a perhaps "truer," but certainly better self-identification than the toxic masculinity which Yunior has largely espoused before. Genre reading and genre reference appear to allow Yunior to identify the true history of the Dominican Republic and thereby offer a better sense of Dominican identity: the "who more scifi than us," as it were. Joy Sanchez-Taylor argues that "[d]ifferentiating between [science fiction] and magical realism allows Diaz to avoid becoming trapped in representations of Dominican history by linking his text to a genre outside of Dominican historical writings or traditions" (2014, 95). But this is actually complicated in a number of ways, of which the problem of drawing on imperial discourse to represent subaltern history is not the least. The novel has a vested interest in mediating identity questions: here, the same genre reading does not, in fact, serve Oscar to find a way out of the idea of maleness-as-having-sex that Yunior's part of the narrative challenges. After all, his "happy ending" is having sex with the prostitute Ybón, and dying for the privilege. Tellingly, it is Yunior—from the distance of the diaspora experience in New Jersey, without Oscar's desire to relocate himself to the Dominican Republic—who manages to come to terms with Dominican reality.

Dominican male identity throughout the novel means having lots of sex with many women. It is this superficial ideal that the novel challenges in Yunior's apparent turn away from his college persona to the writer of the text we are reading, a turn which also shifts his view of Dominican society more broadly. Much of *Wao* is given over to descriptions both of Dominican life in the diaspora and of its relation to "Dominicanness" as such, a deeply complicated relationship not made any easier by Yunior's narration. T.S. Miller argues that we might regard Yunior "as a homodiegetic narrator—i.e., one who takes part in the story's action—who nevertheless behaves for most of the book like a heterodiegetic narrator, and one who is self-consciously not quite omniscient" (2011, 106n5). I think it is necessary to separate two Yuniors: narrated Yunior, in the mid-1980s and mid-1990s, and narrator Yunior, writing in the 2000s, who are not the same. This point bears making simply because so much criticism does not fully notice it. Miller recognizes it sometimes, but at other times argues that Yunior's "inner nerd holds the pen that betrays again and again his enormous allegiance to Genre" (2011, 96), conflating Yunior's writing in genre with Yunior's earlier connection to genre, which is more ambivalent, and, even if existent, not something that narrator Yunior foregrounds about narrated Yunior. A similar and related point needs to be made for the toxic masculinity which narrated Yunior exudes for much of the novel, and which narrator Yunior criticizes heavily throughout.

Yunior's choice to foreground his hypermasculine side in the narrative of Oscar and Yunior's shared past is a necessary precondition for Yunior's arc of hopeful change. This is a change most aptly summarized in his admission early in their shared time that he "wasn't as old-school as I am now" (171), very elegantly nutshelling the difference between narrated Yunior and narrator Yunior and highlighting the importance of historical awareness for Yunior's growth. Narrator Yunior requires us to understand the fundamental difference of his earlier self from his current self as a means of establishing a narrative that permits us to read genre understanding as redemptive.

Yunior constructs a peculiar picture of himself, insisting, most of the time, on his own prototypical Dominican maleness. Yunior introduces this very early on, when Oscar is still in high school, and has his first awakening of a need to change from the nerdish persona he has developed to something more authentically Dominican. He "tried to polish up what remained of his Dominicanness, tried to be more like his cursing swaggering cousins, if only because he had started to suspect that in their Latin hypermaleness there might be an answer" (30). This passage opens the novel-length discussion of what José David Saldívar calls "Oscar's developing identity politics (who he really is)" (2016, 323), a question intimately related to the novel's central genre trope. An inveterate reader of genre fiction, Oscar, as Yunior tells it, is caught in a bind: "being a reader/fanboy (for lack of a better term) helped him get through the rough days of his youth, but it also made him stick out in the mean streets of Paterson even more than he already did" (22n6). Victimized by bullies, he retreats even more into his genre reading, hiding in a closet at home (easy to read as a queer reference, although Oscar does not give us much room to doubt his heterosexuality otherwise) to read, and to write. Oscar's nerdiness is explicitly juxtaposed by the narrator to narrated Yunior's own version of hypermasculinity. When Yunior, somewhat surprisingly, tells his then-girlfriend Lola that he will room with Oscar at Rutgers, to keep an eye on him after a suicide attempt, he insists on his own stature at that point, and his disdain (broadly shared by his circle) of the hall in which they will live: "Move in with him. In fucking Demarest. Home of all the weirdos and losers and freaks and fem-bots. Me, a guy could bench 340 pounds, who used to call Demarest Homo Hall like it was nothing" (170).

Yunior is not an innocent doe when it comes to genre knowledge. Right on the heels of his recalled disdain for Demarest and its inhabitants, he recalls his reaction to a sign which Oscar posts to their dorm room door: "*Speak, friend, and enter*. In fucking Elvish! (Please don't ask me how I knew this. Please.)" (172). The point here is less whether or not Yunior ever read Tolkien or a comic before, but rather the self-presentation which he chooses, his self-identification, his choice of identity. "At all times," Miller suggests, "Yunior's narratorial persona belies the picture of himself he paints as a scorner of sci-fi" (2011, 93–94). But that is not discriminating enough. It is certainly the case that the novel offers us occasional reason to doubt Yunior's depiction of his narrated self as a full-blown macho Dominican, as "one of those Dominican cats everybody's always going on about," as the novel has it, "home-run hitter or a fly bachatero," a "playboy with a million hots on his jock" (11)—this being Yunior's own listing of what Oscar is not. Narrator Yunior can let narrated Yunior's mask slip in the retelling, but narrated Yunior's identity—the way he presents himself to his immediate surroundings, and the way he publicly acts—is hardly ever in doubt. He is "the biggest player of them all" (186), forever chasing women, cheating on them, finding new ones, never once until the very end letting doubt infiltrate that to be like him is to be Dominican.

This form of masculinity is closely tied to sex in the novel. Christopher González notes that "*The Brief Wondrous Life of Oscar Wao* is a novel that, at least in part, concerns a Dominican man's fear of dying a virgin" (2015, 40). At college, now with Yunior as his roommate, Oscars asks, "I have heard from a reliable source that no Dominican male has ever died a virgin." Taken a little aback, Yunior answers, "O, it's against the laws of nature for a dominicano to die without fucking at least once" (174). Oscar's pursuit of women throughout centers on the hope for a sexual conquest, rather than a genuinely equal relationship: Oscar's intended story is not a love story, but a simple exercise of his prerogative and duty as a Dominican man. As González points out, "the conflation of a Dominican man's sense of identity with the sexual act" (2015, 39) is a theme for much of Díaz's fiction. In *Wao*, this conflation is produced with a double edge: what holds (perhaps) for Oscar does not hold for Yunior, whose narrator self sets itself off strongly against the narrated self of his time with Oscar.

Yunior "cannot stop *narrating* his tumultuous affairs and sexual conquests" (González 2015, 55, my emphasis), and he cannot stop bringing up others' disdain for Oscar on the grounds of his alleged lacking masculinity. When Yunior and Oscar have a falling out about Yunior's "Oscar Redemption Program," and Yunior stops protecting Oscar in front of the other Dominican "players" in their acquaintance, Oscar gets treated badly, largely, again, on the grounds of his lack of sexual experience: "you ever eat toto?" Knowing the answer, he gets told, "Tú no eres nada de dominicano" (180). Dominicanness, again, is an exclusively male identity in the novel: it is men striving for the most female conquests, men dominating women, men lording their conquests over one another. Narrated Yunior is the prototypical diasporic example of this. He cheats, lies, gets dumped, and so on, seeking the affirmation of his peers rather than the building of a relationship. This is what dooms his budding relationship with Lola as well. But Yunior is only an example. *Wao* insists on the thorough permeation of this notion of Dominican identity in the diaspora and the national homeland both. The novel depicts Trujillo as the ultimate expression of a general truth about Dominican manhood. When Yunior suggests that "Trujillo might have been a dictator, but he was a *Dominican* dictator" (216, my emphasis)—the "Number-One Bellaco [horny male] in the Country"—the point is precisely to ensure that this specific aspect of Trujillo's regime, its utter misogyny, is understood as something that is not otherworldly, as the way Dominican males create their maleness in general. There is a through line from Trujillo to Yunior and Oscar that is less than flattering. These forms of toxic masculinity remain stable in a Dominican diaspora—and not just there, given the captain's reaction to Oscar's relationship with his girlfriend. But, as Yunior's story indicates, they are not inescapable.

Yunior does escape them after Oscar's death. Now a teacher at a New Jersey community college, with a wife whom he significantly "adores," rather than uses, he does not "run around after girls anymore. Not much anyway." Instead, taking a cue from Oscar, he has taken to "write a lot. From can't see at morning to can't see at night. Learned that from Oscar. I'm a new man, you see, a new man, a new man" (326). This is the closest approximation in the novel of narrator Yunior—the return of an admission in the introduction that "[t]hese days I am nerdy like that" (6). We can surmise that "a lot" of the writing he gets done is his life of Oscar. There is at the very least a coincidence between Yunior's adoption of genre as a mediating trope for Dominican history and his turning away from toxic masculinity; and a formal and explicit correspondence between his becoming a "better man" and the overt nerdery of his writing. Whatever care narrated Yunior has invested in the past to avoid being identified publicly as genre-savvy himself, narrator Yunior not only avows genre-being readily—more readily, more publicly, more insistently and forcefully, and with more purpose, than Oscar ever does—but also, of course, outs his former self as genre-savvy on occasion. But here, such notes merely serve to solidify the impression that it is as much owning up to genre's capacity to inform one's idea of the world as it is the mere knowledge of them, "mere" nerdery juxtaposed against the deep understanding which Yunior has developed, and which Oscar does not. It is genre avowal, then, that identifies Yunior's future as a better man, not mere genre knowledge: genre-being, a wholehearted, knowing embrace of what genre can do. And this recognition is related to Yunior's identification of genre's power to describe New World reality, and the truth about Dominican life. Thus it is genre-being that offers access to a form of being Dominican which is further away from how Yunior depicts actual Dominicans, but much closer to what the novel's understanding of a truer version of Dominican identity entails.

The novel encodes two modes of identity at least, then: "Dominicanness," the heteronormative, violently toxic masculinity of Trujillo, narrated Yunior, and most of the young men we encounter in the New Jersey diaspora; and the "genre nerd," which is a freer conception of identity, not immediately tied to the nation, but also understood to be less desirable for much of the novel. The twist in this narrative is that genre ultimately permits Yunior—though not Oscar—to access a truer conception of Dominican identity, one which is tied to the nature of the historical narrative which he finally produces. But what fails in Oscar's case? It is not clear that Oscar ever fully gets over the toxic masculinity version of Dominicanness, despite his being genre-savvy. As Elena Machado Sáez notes, Oscar's "final initiation and devirginization" is a "pretty lie" (2011, 527), a domestication of Oscar's genre queerness in lieu of an engagement with it. The novel does not concede the propriety of Oscar's final act, does not suggest that Oscar's rendering of his life as having ended in "beauty!" (335) is correct. Oscar never quite sheds his foundational belief in the idea that (Dominican) masculinity is tied to having had sex. For Oscar, unlike Yunior, nerdishness amounts to escape, a way to find a space for himself, somewhat unsubtly metaphorized in the closet in which he is caught reading science fiction by his mother. Superseded by a "new generation of nerds" (269), he decides to actually go to Santo Domingo "for the first time in years," "imagining himself in love with an Island girl" before he even arrives (272). It is not that Oscar gives up on the idea of being a sci-fi/fantasy writer, but in the Dominican Republic, he fully surrenders to the logic of masculinity that the novel has been at pains to set off against nerdery. Oscar's stay ends, appropriately in this regard, with his final letter stating that he has, as the phrasing of his earlier tauntings by Yunior's friends had it, "eaten toto." Picking up the earlier taunt and its immediate correlation to his masculine identity as a Dominican, Oscar's insistence and Yunior's situating of this letter at the very tail end of the novel hint at the potential take-away: ¡Pero claro que sí es dominicano!

Oscar never completes his sci-fi magnum opus, his apparently revelatory last book remains unread, and what the novel asks us to take for a satisfactory end—his consummated love affair with a woman already in a relationship—sounds like a deeply Dominican story. Oscar's identity as a genre nerd takes a backseat in the final months of his life, at the very least narratively, in Yunior's reading of what we are to take away from the brief and wondrous life of Oscar Wao.

The point of this, of course, is to juxtapose the way the novel sets two trajectories against one another. "Yunior's relationship to Oscar," Machado Sáez notes, "is not one of solidarity but of competing diasporic identities" (2011, 525), suggesting that Yunior—Dominican-born—and Oscar—U.S.-born—offer different understandings of what the diaspora might mean, with Oscar requiring to be "domesticated according to the code of nationalist belonging" (526). For Machado Sáez, Oscar's attainment of heterosexual coupling is, in fact, a surrender to a logic oppressing Oscar's queerness, a surrender to a "heteronormative rationale" (523). I argue that it is a radical questioning of the possibility of understanding Dominican life from within Dominican life, an insistence that the diaspora reveals, through its embeddedness in a cultural sphere more attuned to speculative forms, a better version of locating Dominican identity, thanks to its clearer conception of hemispheric history. Yunior's bildungsroman, which sees him understand the key role that genre-being must play in any meaningful reconceptualization of Dominican identity, and Oscar's life-long pursuit of sexual love, at whose successful conclusion he dies, metaphorize the distinction. Oscar's life is "meaningless" in the way the epigraph to the novel hints: it lacks consequences and growth, except perhaps in Oscar's influence on Yunior. Oscar's return to Santo Domingo, coincident with his loss of his nerdish credentials, suggests the close connection between the unreconstructed forms of island masculinity and the impossibility of reaching—or at least, being able to communicate—the insights which Yunior creates in the diaspora. For Yunior, in turn, his own coming into genre-being coincides with a decision to remain in the United States, at a distance from Santo Domingo.

The novel, then, builds both of its hopeful moments—Yunior's hope for Isis, based on the potential that his zafa-book offers, and his own narrative of self-improvement—on the question of genre, and the need to achieve genre-being. Form permits us to navigate the way in which the diaspora allows for a clearer perception of what Dominican identity really is, or at the very least should be. It is the diaspora's granting access to the genre fictions which allow Yunior to mediate Dominican history that is crucial here. If Díaz's earlier short fiction, as Silvio Torres-Saillant points out, had invited "us to consider whether coming to the United States from the Caribbean may be deemed invariably good" (2016, 117), *Wao* must be read to answer this question: only in the United States is the mediation of identity that Yunior undertakes possible. It is here that Yunior's and Oscar's different origin stories are relevant again. Yunior, the immigrant, realizes what Oscar, the native, does not about America: that it offers the distance necessary, formally encoded through the distancing effect, the *Verfremdung* of speculative fiction. Yet it is not unproblematic to locate the possibility of a better sense of colonial power structures and their lasting effects as attainable only within the hegemonic cultural structures of the former colonial powers. Such an argument questions the reading of magical realism in a resistance tradition in Latin American literature (though cf. Santana-Acuña 2020). Monica Hanna, for example, explicitly reads magical realism as the other of "European realism," which is also U.S. realism: this "model of magical realism allows Yunior to recover experiences that might not fit within the bounds of traditional European models of realism. Seemingly supernatural forces have real effects and power in these stories and histories" (2010, 510). Hanna's point holds just as well, and in the context of the novel, much better, for fantasy, science fiction, and so on—non-resistant, and certainly not ethnically marked, genre fiction. Hanna is quasi-invested in calling Díaz's fiction magical realism; after all, she quotes García Márquez as saying that "[t]he interpretation of our reality through patterns not our own, serves only to make us ever more unknown, ever less free, ever more solitary" (511). Here, magical realism can serve to produce a resistance history in a way that speculative historism cannot. But if genre fiction, which is not particularly famous for being resistant, can take up the same function in *Wao*, what are we to make of the power relations that the novel describes? What are we to make of the question of how one relates Dominican identity, when one can only really relate it from the hegemonic culture of the diaspora?

Perhaps the chief difficulty which readings such as Hanna's must contend with is the nature of the speculative fiction that *Wao* references, which are almost exclusively Western, but certainly (in dated terminology) first world. The relationship which *Wao* builds thus goes beyond the merely generic: it is not just a question of speculative fiction's generic possibilities in investigating the postcolonial condition of the Caribbean that is at stake but also one of cultural hegemony. *Wao* appears to recognize this trouble in its early signposting. Its opening epigraphs, one from Marvel Comics' *The Fantastic Four* and the other from "The Schooner Flight," by Trinidadian poet Derek Walcott, set against one another not just the tonal registers of high-literary poetry versus pulp comic fiction. They also take note of a (more) explicitly autochthonous version of Caribbean writing. Walcott was himself immensely attuned to the "challenge of coming to terms with West Indian history" (Baugh 2006, 8), a challenge bound up in the perception that there is a dearth of historical achievement, even of historical action, in the Caribbean. As Edward Baugh notes, Walcott's answer to this was not to deny this as much as to transform it, from "a stigma of non-achievement and hopelessness to an inviting challenge and opportunity, a blank page on which there is everything to be written" (2006, 8). We encounter this notion in the "páginas en blanca" of Caribbean history a number of times in *Wao*, where they reference the tradition even as they also serve as reminders of how broad the possibilities of blank pages are. *Wao*, however, insists that blank pages need to be filled usefully. Here, the possibility that Oscar has discovered something of importance in the Dominican Republic, the chance that Abelard has dug up a true report of Trujillo's supernaturalness, has far less import than Yunior's book, which communicates a version of Dominican identity and New World history that identifies concrete versions of hopeful possibilities.

There is a corollary question raised by my argument just now: who are the readers of the very book we are all reading? Who are the "you" that Yunior is so frequently addressing? I want to discuss this crucial bit in the last section of this chapter, since it brings together the two previous arguments meaningfully, and attaches them to the larger question of speculative historism's shifting place in the literary marketplace.

So:

Who Reads *Oscar Wao*?

The Brief Wondrous Life of Oscar Wao constantly addresses itself to its readers, sets off groups from one another, plays with pronoun references from the opening's "They say," "we are all of us its children," "no matter what you believe, fukú believes in you" (1), to addresses such as "remember: Dominicans are Caribbean" (149). Here, the question of who exactly is included and excluded takes on a force heightened by the novel's choices of registers otherwise: Díaz's use of untranslated and unitalicized Spanish words and phrases, on the one hand, and genre references on the other. These serve as implicit addresses to sets of readers, readers whose understanding of either set of non-mainstream literary English registers is tied to the question of who the novel is for. Were we to assume that an understanding of the genre references is necessary to an understanding of the novel, the intended audience of the novel would immediately include a set of genre readers that are something more like Oscar and narrator Yunior than they are the typical readers of Pulitzer Prize-winning fiction. Conversely, if we assume that a full understanding of all Spanish phrases is key, or indeed if we argue with Efrain Barradas that "only a reader who is familiar with Dominican Spanish and with the history of that country can understand" (qtd. in Torres-Saillant 2016, 119) the novel, we assume a radically different intended audience. Or we assume a set of overlapping but non-congruous audiences equally appealed to, but both excluded from significant parts of the novel. The question arises too from external issues, the most important of which is its winning of a Pulitzer Prize, a clear indication that the novel is, whatever else it is, a literary novel, in the sense that Mark McGurl uses the term, a "genre in its own right" (2009, 44) which stands in opposition to genre fiction.

The question of "who reads" the novel is not an empirical sociological question. I am not interested in discovering anything about actual readers, but rather interested in the different reading situations which the novel calls up. This is a question which is closely tied to the question of how genre mobilizes hopeful versions of history and identity. For whom is the narrative that genre fiction reactivates historical awareness significant? What is the interaction between the respective registers of Spanish and genre, between references that are local and those that are strongly "Western"? Despite the obvious offers made to readers of genre, diaspora readers, Dominican readers, and other groups that appear to have a meaningful outside position in the literary field, the novel is geared primarily to the kind of liberal, white, and literary audience for whom either the Spanish or the genre references might not necessarily be fully understandable. This suggests something about the place of the speculative historism that is at work in the novel, and to prepare the grounds for the last chapter, where I will raise a similar question for *The Underground Railroad*, a novel which offers a radically different answer. The comparison will allow us to see what the respective cultural valence of speculative historism in ca. 2007 and ca. 2017 was.

I have argued above that genre-being becomes an important alternative, a better way of being Dominican, to Yunior in the course of the novel. *Wao* engages with Dominicanness; but the question is, for whom, and how? To read *Wao* as a "corrective to [. . .] definitions of authentic representation that critics brought to [Díaz's short stories]" (Machado Sáez 2011, 523) is useful. The problem here is what specifically the novel calls up as Dominican, a problem related to the question of whom this Dominicanness is presented to. As Silvio Torres-Saillant puts it, a "Dominican reader of the novel might at first take issue with the adverse representation of the 'community' in the text" (2016, 141). Torres-Saillant then attempts to recuperate Yunior's narration as so over the top that it cannot be taken seriously, but this is to miss the low-key change in personality of Yunior's utopian moment. If we are to suppose that Yunior's implicit complaint about Dominican male behavior is not meant wholly seriously, his own turn away from it becomes less important as a motive—less important than the novel itself takes it. It also asks how we are to read Lola's disgusted comment that "she would never return to that terrible country. On one of our last nights as novios she said, Ten million Trujillos is all we are" (324). With so many assurances that Dominican life is not to be desired, it is difficult to construct a redemptive narrative of Dominican identity outside Yunior's genre-being.

Yunior's bildungsroman is a recuperation of genre reading: his hopeful turn into a "new man you see, a new man, a new man" (326) is irreducible from his other change, that into a genre nerd. Such a turn does not translate well unless intended for a Dominican diasporan audience, however. If we read *Wao* to speak *about* the Dominican diaspora only, rather than *to* it, if we read its narrative, in other words, to provide this betterment narrative of Yunior's only to an audience of non-Dominican readers, the novel's politics becomes radically problematic. If Díaz aimed, as he said in an interview, to "screw with traditional Dominican masculinity" (qtd. in López-Calvo 2009, 77), but produces at the same time "stereotyping and essentialism" (76), the novel is in an awkward limbo. And yet this appears precisely what it is actually doing. Díaz, as Ignacio López-Calvo points out, spends a lot of time informing readers about Dominican slang and mythology, information which is expected to be available to any Dominican reader. It is difficult to read Díaz other than as a "native informant" (78), producing Dominicanness for an audience unfamiliar with it. It is this same audience which now has to contend with what we must take to be a speaker who is, by his own identity, authorized to speak about Dominicans, telling his audience of non-Dominican readers something that coming from anybody but a Dominican would smack of racism. Elena Machado Sáez is on point when she calls the novel "responsive to the values of an academic readership by addressing the example of diasporic discourse" (2011, 523). But we should note that the particular discourse we are presented as an academic readership is of a "resistant diasporic subject" (525) who construes himself as "better" than those whom he designates with "Dominicanness."

The novel's depiction of Dominicans suggests that it is not meant for Dominican or Dominican American readers. In this light, too, we should read the question of its genre readers. For some commentators, genre is simply the other of the Dominican background of the novel. Thus Diana Pifano argues that the genre "references at play are specific to modern North American culture and are most easily recognized by Anglophone readers. While other readers, namely Dominican and other Hispanic readers, possess no such knowledge." Pifano corroborates this claim by pointing to the novel's translations, which exhaustively explain the genre references. Conversely, she suggests, the same "Anglophone reader" "lacks a basic knowledge of Dominican history" (2014, §12). For Pifano there are two positions with an insider–outsider relationship: Dominicans who can decode Díaz's Spanish and cultural references to the Republic, and (shorthanded) Americans who understand genre. But this is clearly too simple a juxtaposition, given the breadth of genre references the novel handles. The novel seems to invite genre readers in: to offer them a literary exculpation of their reading choices. Such a reading suggests that the genre references are individually meaningful, that genre readers are invited in by their ability to decode them properly and thereby obtain a better understanding of what the narrative says. Yet, as Rune Graulund notes, the novel encodes such a wealth of registers that even readers versed in some of them might not identify others. Readers of fantasy novels might catch the Tolkien references, but it is "by no means certain that this same reader will be able to identify Frank Miller and Alan Moore [. . .] as authors of graphic novels, let alone the finer nuances that differentiate the two" (2014, 33). There is no "Anglophone reader" who easily recognizes all of these references. And, as I have noted, there are quite a few instances where Yunior's use of genre references as metaphors for the Dominican Republic in fact collapses—something perhaps more likely to turn off genre readers with a vested interest in their texts than pull them in.

The point of the genre references, then, is not so much to broaden the section of people who read *Wao*. Almost certainly, the novel does not intend all of its readers to get all of its references. The full set of references can only possibly be reduced to something like a lowest common denominator—Trujillo is an immensely powerful, even supernaturally powerful, antagonist. This point can be gleaned, however, without understanding all of them, and the readers who can be expected to understand the reference to fantasy as readily as that to DC Comics may be few; indeed, it is quite possible that the point may be understood without getting any of these references at all.

In a harsh review, Henry Wessells argues that these references serve as "so many bars of a freak-show cage" (qtd. in Bautista 2010, 44). The sensationalist spectator is the non-genre reader, the consumer of literary fiction who is the central addressee of Díaz's fiction—and also very much the sensationalist spectator of Dominicanness for whom Yunior, there as here a "native informant," acts in similarly flashy and stereotypical fashion. This reader, the "you" of so many of Yunior's addresses, may be persuaded that genre serves a useful function in Díaz's speculative historist text, but is not required to actually have knowledge of "the genres" in order to draw correct inferences from the references.

Right in the middle of *Wao*, Yunior addresses the novel's readers once again: "You ever seen that Sargent portrait, Madame X? Of course you have" (181). Easily assuming our familiarity in much the same way as he does elsewhere with the genres, here Yunior also acknowledges that he knows we know, or rather, he insists that we would know if we were the ideal reader he is addressing. Now, this may seem a bit far-fetched: this is only one reference among many. But unlike the other references, this one actually makes sense. Very little about the novel makes sense if we assume it is written for a Dominican American audience. Little of it makes sense if we assume it is written for a genre-reading audience.

Lots of it makes sense if we assume it is written for the *New Yorker* crowd: upper middle class, white, Anglo-American, culturally embedded in a space where some genre metaphors may be available, but desperately in need of help with all things Dominican. And unsurprisingly, this is also where Díaz was, immediately, well received: as Silvio Torres-Saillant points out, Díaz's initial reception "saluted the author's entry onto the American literary scene as a remarkable new presence in contemporary fiction" (2016, 116).

We may come closer to appreciating what the novel is doing when we locate it in the literary marketplace, as what Ellen McCracken has called "postmodern ethnic commodity" (2016, 14), and against its own affirmative inscription in literary and literary critical discourse throughout. From its early mention of McOndo to its passing references to key Caribbean thinkers from Édouard Glissant to Fernando Ortiz, to Yunior's knowledgeable reference to "one of those nightmare eight-a.m. MLA panels" (299), the novel is suffused with writing tailor-made for an academic audience. Or, as Günter Leypoldt has argued, the novel embodies "strong values," a belief that there is "something larger" at work than mere entertainment, allowing "the taste-making groups with the greatest capability to shape public standards [. . .] 'to recognize itself'" (2018). Díaz's novel does what it does without challenging the audience it is intended for, the very taste-making groups which provided the novel with its biggest pitch, the winning of the Pulitzer Prize. Winning the Pulitzer Prize, as McCracken has noted, certainly opened a wide variety of different readerships to the novel—simply by its signposting that it "must be worth reading": the Pulitzer names a particular kind of literary artifact, the consecrated, high-literary text, and broadens its reception to the "mass marketplaces" (2016, 17). The question of who reads *Wao* is tied to the question of when—before or after the Prize—they read, but also, in the wake of the Prize, somewhat untied from its inherent address. In this regard, T.S. Miller's apparent attempt at literary gatekeeping—"we should no more dub *Oscar Wao* a work of magic realism than we should nominate it for a Nebula" (2011, 93)—in *Science Fiction Studies* is telling. Why should we not nominate it for a Nebula, one of the highest prizes in the science fiction community? Because "no one could mistake *Oscar Wao* for a science fiction novel" (92). But as we shall see in the final chapter, such certainties about reception have short shelf-lives. After all, somebody "mistook" *The Underground Railroad*, which is far less invested in speculative fiction or speculative ontology than *Wao*, for science fiction: the Arthur C. Clarke Award committee. What we can say is that nobody *did* mistake *Wao* for a science fiction novel, and so its reception remains tied to its status as a high-cultural text, within which we must make sense of its genre references. We are less likely to see the text's dealing with identity as a problem. After all, as Mark McGurl has pointed out, "high cultural pluralism" has for decades been a dominant strand of so-called "literary fiction" (2009, 59). Yet it remains important to recognize that *Wao* formally addresses itself to a very narrow segment of readers, readers in need of having everything Dominican explained to them even as they are inundated with enough genre references to not have to grasp every single one of them. For such an audience, the idea that the novel produces anything very resistant at all is complicated.

Indeed, I would venture to suggest tentatively that little about the novel makes sense if we were to assume that Díaz is actually writing back against anything. Monica Hanna suggests that the "very form of the text being shaped by Yunior is meant to counteract a history of glorious nationalism" (2010, 504), to which the appropriate question in the context of the novel's production of its own reception is: what history? *Wao* can hardly be a "resistance history" (500), a counter-narrative to the "national history presented by the regime" (504). The superficial plausibility of this argument runs afoul of the narrative's own logic, which narrates Dominican history in the full awareness that it reaches an audience which has "missed your mandatory two seconds of Dominican history" (7). As Hanna points out, this instance clearly marks an audience: "as the novel is written in English [. . .] and relies heavily on United States popular cultural tropes, this interpolated 'you' is likely to be a United States reader" (2010, 502). But this is precisely where the problem of resistance crops up most forcefully: Yunior, the narrator, may be writing something resistant, a story that resists what Yunior knows is a false history of the New World, and in particular of the Dominican Republic. *Wao*, the novel, by contrast, is embedded in a cultural context in which to write "resistance history" requires the question, "resistance to what?" Whose perception of Dominican history gets shaken, who gets to discover the seedy underbelly of their historical awareness, in Díaz's rewriting, if no one has any grounding in Dominican history in the first place? Conversely, the concrete form which this alleged resistance history takes may be even less available to the diasporic readership which commentators envisage for the novel, given the way the novel describes Oscar's treatment at the hands of his compatriots, all of whom, after all, hold Oscar's genre reading in disdain. *These people*, we might ask, are supposed to take on board a resistance history written in genre?

The point here is to think about what its address to this audience tells us about speculative historism ca. 2007. What is entailed in not winning a science fiction award and in Miller's literary gatekeeping is to situate speculative historism firmly within the high-cultural literary sphere, to suggest that its genre work can be accommodated without the need to rethink the categories that structure our engagement with literature, but also without outreach. *Wao* does not seek to bridge the gap between readers of high-cultural pluralist, multiethnic fiction and readers of genre. It uses genre to mediate New World history for a highly specific audience. Leypoldt argues that the novel's genre elements produce a "grit aesthetic," which "can revitalize conventional literary practice if its use of materials formerly stigmatized as inartistic or low produces a powerful sense of new direction among its taste-making practitioners" (2018). But I wonder what all this means for the readers of genre as such; and more particularly, what this means for the vision that the novel produces for hopeful futures writ larger. Díaz's novel, for all its virtuosity and its interest in understanding genre as recuperative, is translating genre for a specific, narrow audience, an audience which it artificially transcends through its prize winning, but which nonetheless remains foundational to its work: it speaks *about* genre and identity to the white middle-class literary fiction reader. If it produces only a narrow vision of a hopeful future, this is a vision that its intended audience may more readily subscribe to than it would like to admit. And it does not actually bridge the gap between literary readers and genre readers, as its winning of the Pulitzer Prize, but not a Nebula, indicates.

In the same year, 2008, that *Wao* won the Pulitzer, Michael Chabon's *The Yiddish Policemen's Union* won the Nebula Award and Locus Award for science fiction, the Hugo Award for science fiction and fantasy, as well as the Sidewise Award for Alternate History. Chabon's previous novel, the comics-centered *The Amazing Adventures of Kavalier & Clay*, had won the Pulitzer Prize in 2001. I would submit that this tells us something about the state of speculative historism in 2008 that echoes my argument about *Wao*, showcasing the heavy compartmentalization at work. Like *Wao*, *The Yiddish Policemen's Union* is invested in both history and speculative fiction, centering around the potential appearance of an actual Messiah and the political machinations that revolve around the possibilities opened in the Zionist imaginary by this appearance. Given Chabon's previous winning of the Pulitzer, it is also, always already, literary. But in 2008, this is still an either–or proposition, an inability to recognize the form of speculative historism as a necessary, and necessarily political, challenge to the very idea of genre differentiation. I will show in the next chapter how this has changed in the decade since the publication of both of these novels, but also that there is a complicated interaction at work here between the novelistic address of a text, its reception, and the underlying sociopolitical and literary structures at work.

Conclusion: Writing Hope

Wao is invested in its speculative form, a historical vision, and the creation of hopeful moments in their conjunction. The fact that the novel does not at first glance appear to offer hopeful futures, certainly does not foreground them, suggests the purchase of utopian hermeneutics. Even a text as complicatedly bound up in ideas of cyclical history and fateful dooms offers room for hopeful readings. The novel offers this only through the device of speculative fiction, through its simultaneous use of genre as metaphor and genuinely fantastical events. These are not to be read as suggesting an actual fantastical world history, as raising any extra-fictional claims. But it does suggest that in order to make visible the forces that act upon the individual in history, rendering these forces in terms of the supernatural is a helpful narrative conceit.

José David Saldívar suggests an important juxtaposition at play in *Wao* between an actual "attempt to represent radical alternatives" and the "imperative to imagine alternatives" (2011b, 211). Saldívar's belief that this is encoded in Oscar's desire to become the "Dominican Tolkien" is probably a misreading. Oscar does not manage to imagine any kind of genuine alternative at all, opting for three already existent modes of relating to the world: genre writing, the "supernatural exposé," and the hypermasculine Dominicanness that he pursues throughout the novel. But Saldívar's point is still valid for the novel. *Wao* produces a hopeful prospect in Yunior's depiction of Isis, Lola's daughter, as someone who might possibly end the vicious circle in which her family is caught, a narrative that is also, given the novel's conflation of this family history with New World history, a more broadly hopeful vision for a better hemispheric future. But this future remains "only" a possibility. The novel also produces a hopeful narrative for Yunior, one which is more than just a possibility, but it is not a "radical alternative" in the systemic sense in which Saldívar employs the term: it may not even be an alternative, period, given the sheer amount of resistance to genre-being which Yunior narrates and, one assumes, faces within his community.

Oscar's final words, "The beauty! The beauty!" (335), obviously reference Joseph Conrad's *Heart of Darkness* and thus inscribe themselves peculiarly in a history of writing about colonialism. They can be read both "optimistically, as an affirmation of the difference that [. . .] small moments of connection can represent in human relations, or pessimistically, as a retreat into a domain of private domestic bliss at the expense of larger collective issues" (Figueroa 2013, 106). It is certainly possible to read Oscar's final letter as itself a hopeful message: it "proposes the possibility of change instead of an 'eternal return'" (Hanna 2010, 516). If so, however, it is a change for the worse: a change away from the diasporic possibility of finding in genre fiction a medium that permits a distanced, careful appraisal of where to locate Dominican identity and history, and how to react to it. Oscar's final letter shows no development on Oscar's part. Rather, it is itself a return to an earlier moment where the challenge put to him, of being no Dominican on account of not having had sex, is one which Oscar can now fairly challenge. Is this hope? For the novel it is not: it is the final nod towards the overarching idea that Oscar fails at what Yunior achieves, to understand how to shape the narrative about himself. Indeed, as readers reading for genre, we are forced to contend with an even more structural problem, namely how to read Oscar's final voyage in terms of genre. Genre, after all, provides a means for Yunior's growth: recognizing its ability to name the historical structures underlying his contemporary moment, it enables Yunior to come to terms with what Oscar's life means. What does genre mean for Oscar, though? In part, the problem here is that the novel constitutes Oscar's genre use as (negatively) escapist. For Yunior, genre-being is a means of structuring and making meaningful the entanglements of history and his own contemporary situation, a realization that the supernatural possibilities inherent in the notion of fukú are impossible to translate except through registers which already allow for, indeed require, the supernatural to exist. His hedging about the concrete extent of the supernatural nature of the Caribbean is in part counteracted by the choice of metaphors. The act of rendering it in genre metaphors is in this sense an act of translation. It permits readers to grasp that for all Yunior's hemming and hawing and reporting of hearsay, it is difficult to escape the conclusion that Dominican reality—and so, in fact, all history—is best grasped as genuinely marvelous, fantastical, speculative, beyond the reach of "mere" (historical) realism. But this is still different from Oscar's grasp of things, which never quite gets the implications of this truth. Oscar never makes the necessary move from direct equivalence—the Antilles are science fictional—to representational truth—the Antilles are best represented through science fiction. The consequences for him are dire. Oscar's struggle to be the "Dominican Tolkien" (192) is doomed from the start, simply because while Tolkien's work can be used to mediate reality in *Wao*, it is already superseded by it. Going to the Dominican Republic to become the "Dominican Tolkien," as Oscar does, merely serves to illuminate Tolkien's shortcomings: the marvelous, speculative reality of the world will always exceed the imagination of fantasy, or certainly any single text. This is what the introduction already insists on when it suggests that Trujillo is *in fact* "a personaje so outlandish, so perverse, so dreadful that not even a sci-fi writer could have made his ass up" (2). Oscar's end takes on the guise of a chivalrous romance—he has "romantic ideas about the world" (Hanna 2010, 515)—something out of a fantasy epic, a sacrifice worthy of *The Silmarillion*, rather than a clear-eyed view of his situation. What more fantasy than to sacrifice yourself for love?

Wao is an art commodity aimed at a particular kind of readership, and should be read against that readership. But texts are more than just commodities: they are also efforts to symbolically resolve the inherent contradictions of the times we live in. My final thought then for this chapter is to suggest a way of parsing what T.S. Miller has called "Yunior's inability to dismiss, accept, or account for the fantastic" (2011, 101) in his narrative, a way of suggesting that this inability registers something larger. Yunior does the most he can with what he has to work with at his particular moment: a moment at which the upheavals which structure our own time lie in the future, and are at best dimly noticeable already. At this moment, Yunior's willingness to entertain the possibility that there is a fantastic out there—not willing to avow it to the extent that it does become more than a matter of interpretation—is the most that can be done.

Chapter 6

Slavery and Speculation: Colson Whitehead's *The Underground Railroad* and Ben Winters's *Underground Airlines*

Colson Whitehead's 2016 novel *The Underground Railroad* has a simple speculative conceit: what if the Underground Railroad was an actual railroad, tunneling beneath the slave-holding South, and carrying escaping slaves away? A winner of the National Book Award, the Pulitzer Prize, a selection of Oprah Winfrey's Book Club 2.0, but also, strikingly, the Arthur C. Clarke Award for Science Fiction in 2017, Whitehead's novel spans the critical gamut of appreciation. *The Underground Railroad* inscribes itself into a number of different contemporary discourses. It is concerned with race relations and the meaning of slavery for the "Black experience" more generally (I am using both scare quotes and the term "Black experience" here advisedly, and the rest of the chapter will show why). Formally, this ties it to the notion that ethnicity is a major determinant for the kind of "speculative realism" that Ramón Saldívar discusses. More broadly, the issue of how to read politically, what the value of literary fiction is, and the question of how to mobilize history for the contemporary are prominent.

I set *The Underground Railroad* against a novel that mediates the same kind of sociopolitical developments, is not much "worse" than Whitehead's novel, but not only did not garner the same kind of critical attention, but was criticized for some of what it does, and for some of the way it was talked about. Ben Winters's *Underground Airlines* (2016) is a different kind of alternative history, set in a present United States that never fully abandoned slavery, and explores the consequences of this development in what amounts to a thriller plot. Winters's novel features a Black former slave protagonist—Winters himself is white. *Underground Airlines* and *The Underground Railroad* allow us to see the fault lines of the argument I have been presenting, and the greater context of literary reception and production. They mutually inform each other's reading, contrasting a more strongly structural take on the persistence of slavery's causes and consequences in Winters's novel with the more strongly individualistic—but ultimately, necessarily ambivalent—take which Whitehead's novel finally offers. Both of them present challenges to the notion which I have pursued throughout, that speculative historism is a means of recovering history for its utopian potentials in the contemporary situation, yet they both still remain amenable to utopian hermeneutics, indeed suggest the need for such a hermeneutics.

Both follow the long tradition of the neo-slave narrative. The neo-slave narrative "evolved from a change in social and cultural conditions in the late sixties," and "later deployments of the form have engaged in dialogue with the social issues of its moment of origins" (Rushdy 1999, 5). It developed in the larger political and social context of the Civil Rights Movement and its attendant recovery of a Black historiographic consciousness. As a literary form it grew from a desire to "salvage the literary form of the slave narrative from what was generally thought of as its appropriation" (6) by white writers such as William Styron and Daniel Panger, whose *The Confessions of Nat Turner* (1967) and *Ol' Prophet Nat* (1967) both adopted the outward guise of a slave's autobiographical writing. Black neo-slave narratives were written explicitly against the appropriation of the Black voice and of Black experience by white writers, against the backdrop of a period of heightened sensitivity to racial concerns. Ashraf Rushdy defines the neo-slave narrative as "contemporary novels that assume the form, adopt the conventions, and take on the first-person voice of the the [sic] antebellum slave narrative" (1999, 3). While fully commensurate with his corpus, such a definition appears overly restrictive. In Bernard Bell's broader definition, neo-slave narratives are "modern narratives of escape from bondage to freedom" (1989, 289). Perhaps the best way of framing the shared interest of neo-slave narratives is to see them all as part of a "broader range of fiction that revisits slavery without necessarily rewriting the genre of the nineteenth-century fugitive slave narrative" (Dubey 2010, 333). Both *The Underground Railroad* and *Underground Airlines* originate in a tradition of literary reference to and representation of slavery as a means of exploring what it means to be Black in the United States—and which, already, was willing to breach the boundaries of straightforward realism.

This background is suggestive for the relation between the two novels and their respective relation to the present. Three issues are key to me here. The first is broadly political: it is to note the emergence of the form roughly coincident with, but not antecedent to, a moment of significant political upheaval, the passing of the Civil Rights Act in 1968. As Madhu Dubey notes, "it seems logical to assume that the genre of the neo-slave narrative emerged in response to historical amnesia about slavery" (2010, 333), but in fact it emerged at a point when slavery had already returned to the political and cultural spotlight, as had the issue of its representation. The neo-slave narrative, as Rushdy points out, appears culturally belated, speaking to an "earlier cultural conversation" (1999, 17). Rather than appearing in the middle of the Civil Rights era, and mobilizing a new historical awareness for the political purposes of that era, it engages the specific cultural politics surrounding the adoption of a Black voice in Styron's *Confessions of Nat Turner*. Neo-slave narratives "return to and reassess the cultural moment behind the production of a literary text" (18). The original set of neo-slave narratives engaged the question of cultural formations, rather than racial politics as such. We may see suggestive connections here to Whitehead's and Winters's novels. Published at the end of the Obama presidency, rather than at its beginning, after "we were eight years in power" (Coates 2017), the two novels engage a version of African American history after this political moment, reflecting on it. The moment is that of a significant political event (the election of President Obama in 2008) with consequences for our understanding of race relations in the United States including the repeated invocation of the arrival of the "post-racial era." It appears to set into sharper relief the forms of oppression under which African Americans still live—in other words, a similar moment to 1968, where the positive change of the Civil Rights Act likewise set into relief the way it did no more than alleviate structural imbalances of power and persistent racial animosity. The novels' interest in a speculative historicization of slavery's lasting impact on the contemporary United States lies, much like the neo-slave narrative's genesis, after what must have appeared as a significant advance with equally significant limits, and needs to be explained in this context.

The second issue is to delineate the particular speculative forms of postmodern neo-slave narrative from the way history and speculative fiction operate in the two novels. Neo-slave narratives such as Ishmael Reed's *Flight to Canada* (1976), postmodern historiographic metafictions, "tended to target historiography as such" (Konstantinou 2017, 16), suggesting the limits to historical writings' truth claims. They did not aim to recuperate history, but rather conversely empowered fiction writing: they should be read, with Linda Hutcheon, as "an expansion" of "the scope and value of fiction," putting its own mediation of history on a similar epistemological footing as historical writing. In Hutcheon's words, historiographic metafiction "acknowledges that history is not the transparent record of any sure 'truth'" (1988, 129). To undermine history's claim to truth is also to question the regimes which control the writing of history, the hegemonic structures that tend to limit the expression of minority voices. Historiographic metafiction in this regard also inscribes itself into a larger discourse about the meaning of writing as such for minorities; but historiographic metafiction does not grasp what the novels I discuss here do.

Third and finally, we should note the significant shifts—and strange stagnations—which *The Underground Railroad*'s terrific success highlights in the literary field. As Rushdy points out, despite its appearance as an act of recovery, *The Confessions of Nat Turner* was in fact a "master text," a text usefully described as dominating slave narratives. This master text's dominance is marked, Rushdy suggests, by the "publishing strategies and marketing events surrounding the publication" of Styron's novel. Rushdy notes:

> When the paperback edition did appear, it boasted on its cover the "Pulitzer Prize Winner of the Year" and "An All-Time Best Seller," a novel that was not only a "triumph," in the words of the New York Times reviewer, but also the "most profound fictional treatment of slavery in our literature," according to the quoted excerpt from C. Vann Woodward's New Republic review. (1999, 18)

I will have more to say about this in the third section of this chapter, but for now let me note that Whitehead's novel boasts on (one version of) its cover "Winner of the National Book Award," "Winner of the Pulitzer Prize for Fiction 2017," and "Winner of the Arthur C. Clarke Award," and is described not only as "wildly inventive," in the words of an *Observer* reviewer, but also "Terrific," according to no less a figure than Barack Obama (this is on virtually all cover versions). If Styron's novel was, according to Rushdy, "actively promoted to achieve canonical status as a master text in the field of cultural production" (1999, 18), we need to note the way the question of the "master text" takes on a radically different valence in *The Underground Railroad*. The cultural validation of Whitehead's writing looks different from the one accorded Styron, if only because Whitehead is himself Black. This is perhaps the most difficult and awkward claim of this chapter, and I wish to postpone it just a little.

I offer an argument about writing a historical novel about slavery in the contemporary moment, and about the nexus of processes of validation and valuation and the methods and modes of fictional writing. We may see both *The Underground Railroad* and *Underground Airlines* as departures from a more common mode of engagement with the past. As Philipp Löffler has argued, "the idea that people write about history not to establish true accounts of particular historical events but to express the particularity of an individual life or an individual culture" (2015, 5) has been at the center of American historical fiction since the end of the Cold War. Toni Morrison's neo-slave narratives, for example, from *Beloved* (1989) to *A Mercy* (2008), are less interested in an overarching, structural historical truth than they are interested in "meditations about the individual self in history" (Löffler 2015, 96). They are interested in connecting the personal to the historical, the historical character and her "experience of history," which readers are enjoined to understand as at once personal and "valid and reliable" (91). They do not produce "true accounts of particular historical events" but rather "express the particularity of an individual life or an individual culture" (5)—so that, in a novel such as *A Mercy* the "single subject position" prevails, and an "emotional vision [. . .] is rendered the arbiter of historical meaning" (28).

By contrast, Whitehead's protagonist Cora serves less as someone experiencing history than as an observer of history. In South Carolina, for example, it is not Cora who suffers through the forced sterilization of "[c]olored women who have already birthed more than two children, in the name of population control. Imbeciles and the otherwise mentally unfit, for obvious reasons. Habitual criminals" (113). For Cora, sterilization is a choice—one she never picks. She is spared the structural violence meted out by the white society in which she temporarily lives. Cora works as a "type," as a living exhibit in the Museum of Natural Wonders, on a plantation diorama. Here, watched, she can watch back, watch the "white monsters on the other side of the exhibit" (116). Notably, in her strolls through the museum, Cora's access to history is very much the same as the visitors', non-experiential and distant. "She knew," the narrator informs us, "the white men bragged about the efficiency of the massacres" of the Indians. "The land she tilled and worked had been Indian land" (117). "She knew" encodes precisely the opposite of what Löffler suggests is Morrison's poetics of history: a fact-based, impersonal truth, rather than a personal experiential, and therefore also presentist, interpretation of historical meaning. We may see something similar at work in the two following chapters. Cora, first sitting in an attic in North Carolina and then in the back of a wagon in her journey through Tennessee, stands by as history transpires, watching the depredations of the white inhabitants on Black people in North Carolina, and then the post-apocalyptic landscape of Tennessee from the (relative) safety and (real) distances afforded her. What these instances share is that Cora witnesses rather than experiences history. She does not authorize history through its effects on her, and the narrative is not about her in history; but rather it is about history as such.

Usually, Whitehead's novel does not operate according to the logic of the post-Cold War historical fiction Löffler discusses. Occasionally, it still does—it still reverts to the emotional reading modes Löffler sees Morrison as adopting—and thus complicates a simple narrative of transition. In as much as Löffler's argument is at least also a periodizing argument, so is it to hint at a periodizing argument to suggest that things have changed, or are changing, even if in fits and starts. It makes sense to read Whitehead against Morrison also with regard to his place in the literary market versus hers, and what the difference means for contemporary literature. These issues are bound up in the reading strategies variously mobilized by the stance towards history which Whitehead's novel takes. The kind of "emotional vision" centered on a character's experience which the novel occasionally exhibits suggests a reading approach with greater emotional investment, while the distanced observations that the novel also provides through Cora suggest, in turn, a more critical, distanced reading. Even talking about narrative alone, Morrison appears a potent foil. The choice of a female protagonist draws a straight line from Morrison's fiction as much as the choice of a non-realistic form does. In each case, Whitehead's novel departs from the Morrison model significantly, producing a text that avoids the difficulty and theoretical acumen of Morrison's novels in favor of an accessible, and ultimately usable, immediately hopeful text.

My argument in what follows will proceed in three steps. First, I will offer a reading of *The Underground Railroad*. I will read *The Underground Railroad* as a hopeful narrative, a reading at once banal and challenging. Here, I will discuss the novel's historical vision, which is avowedly affirmative of the possibility of attaining access to history, even if that access requires speculative mediation, and I will offer a first pointer to the difficulty of placing *The Underground Railroad* in the contemporary literary field. Second, I will offer a contrastive reading of *Underground Airlines*, again beginning with a close reading that then traces the question of the meaning of the debate around the novel, and delineates the chief differences in their respective arguments about both race as a contemporary problem and the hopeful solutions to the problem. From these two points, I will develop a larger argument about the places of these texts in the contemporary literary field, which, I will argue, is an inescapably necessary act in order to understand the valences of their respective versions of hopeful futures.

The Underground Railroad, the Neo-slave Narrative, and Hope

The Underground Railroad is a "modern narrative of escape[] from bondage to freedom" (1989, 289) in Bernard Bell's phrasing, which already implies its generally hopeful outlook. The novel offers some complexity: an interlocking of character motivations and plot drivers that smoothly tie into one another. For all that, it remains a straightforward text, which is precisely why we need to talk in more detail about it. It narrates the story of Cora, a third-generation slave on the Randall plantation deep in Georgia, sometime after the invention of railroads and before the Civil War. The novel begins, very traditionally, with a middle passage, in this case of Cora's grandmother Ajarry, and initially stays within the traditionally realistic mode of the slave narrative as it narrates the experiences in slavery first of Ajarry and then of Mabel, Cora's mother. Mabel, who disappeared some years before the plot of the novel proper starts, is widely held to be the only slave who ever successfully escaped the Randall plantation, despite being hunted by Ridgeway, a notorious slave-catcher. It is Mabel's disappearance that is the most profoundly personal haunting that Cora experiences, struck as she is by the way Mabel left her not merely alone but thoroughly caught in the system of slavery. Cora's despair over Mabel's act of abandonment is not, however, drive enough to let her attempt her own escape until the barely tolerable mode of existence on the Randall farm collapses. After it had been run, split in half, by the two Randall brothers, the death of Cora's comparatively kind master brings the plantation together under Terrance, who immediately sets out to ensure that even minor freedoms for his slaves are removed. With that, Cora decides to accept her fellow slave Caesar's offer: try to escape, using Caesar's knowledge of the existence in Georgia of a branch line of the Underground Railroad.

The railroad itself is the first speculative conceit of the novel: an actual network of railway tunnels and stations running from the Deep South to the free North. The historical Underground Railroad was "a diverse, flexible, and interlocking system with thousands of activists [. . .] with a minimum of central direction and a maximum of grassroots involvement, and with only one strategic goal: to provide aid to any fugitive slave who asked for it" (Bordewich 2005, 5). It aided fugitive slaves in their escape to the North, and most usually to Canada. Almost as importantly, it functioned as a movement, which gave Black Americans both an "experience in politics and organizational management" (6) as well as a means of practical resistance. The notion of a community of individual actors, and of an essentially humanitarian and decentral engagement, is replaced in *The Underground Railroad*, and the consequences of this are meaningful.

From the moment of their departure from Georgia, the Underground Railroad serves as a structural device, permitting the novel to investigate alternative historical versions of the United States, and race relations in particular. From Georgia, Caesar and Cora make their way to South Carolina, which has set up a quasi-benevolent white supremacist government, an apparently enlightened way of keeping Black men and women in menial work and little education. South Carolina is an alternative historical space: technologically and politically, it appears to be set in a 1920s analogue, with a Fordist factory system, high rises and elevators, sterilization programs for "inferior" Black women, and other markers that this is not simply a reimagined antebellum South. Having stayed here for several months, Cora is finally driven to flee by the arrival of the slave-catcher Ridgeway, losing contact with Caesar in the process. The Underground Railroad takes her further north, to North Carolina, which is a sharply different experience. Here, white slave-owners have decided to abandon Black slavery for European indentured servitude, and to outlaw the presence of any Black people in the state, on pain of death. Cora takes refuge with the former station manager of the Railroad, living in his attic until she is discovered by Ridgeway: put in chains, she is dragged along by Ridgeway to Tennessee. Here, the narrative conflates racial conflict and disease in the vision of a post-apocalyptic wasteland. Cora is freed by a band of free Black people and other fugitive slaves and placed on the Railroad again, this time making her way to Indiana. In Indiana, she becomes part of the utopian experiment at the Valentine farm, a farm for free Black people and fugitives, which for a good while seems like a potential home. But the Farm's project collapses, as much from the external pressure of its white neighbors as from the internal strife among its members, and in the violent destruction of the community, Cora is once more seized by Ridgeway. She is forced to show him the Indiana terminal she arrived at, but, in their descent to the station, manages to trip Ridgeway, and to injure him, likely mortally, in a fall down the stairs. Cora escapes on the unfinished line, and ultimately passes out of the bowels of the Earth somewhere further north. She is finally picked up by the Black driver of a wagon, in a train going west.

There is much to unpack here narratively, thanks in part to the novel's structure. Each of its five major chapters, titled after the state it is set in, offers a radically different vision of the United States, from the realistic setting of the opening's Georgia through the variously alternative histories of the three Southern states to the again-realistic, but still alternative-historical Indiana. What is more, each of these chapters, with the exception of the ongoing plot of Cora's flight and Ridgeway's pursuit, remains largely disconnected from the others. The railroad's effect is to take her out of the narrow confines of her situation in each state (the limits of a single town in South Carolina, the narrow space of an attic in North Carolina, the back of a wagon in Tennessee, the limited farmlands of the Valentine community in Indiana) and into a new one, almost without transition. The journeys through the blackness of the railroad's tunnels function similarly to filmic fade-outs and fade-ins, as shifts of sceneries without transition, utterly new locales every time. This is the novel's avowed purpose, as Lumbly, the manager of the Georgia station, insists early on. Narratively tasked with the expository dialogue that explains the railroad, the novel gives him this argument:

> "Every state is different," Lumbly was saying. "Each one a state of possibility, with its own customs and way of doing things. Moving through them, you'll see the breadth of the country before you reach your final stop."
>
> [. . .]
>
> "If you want to see what this nation is all about, I always say, you have to ride the rails. Look outside as you speed through, and you'll find the true face of America." (68–69)

We should start by unraveling this quote, because it is central to the novel's sense of its work. The notion of different states of possibility is recalled several times in the course of the narrative; it returns repeatedly in Cora's memory. When she crosses, as Ridgeway's prisoner, into Tennessee, she remembers Lumbly's lines, and holds that the "tunnels had protected her" (205)—a subjective belief hardly corroborated by the novel. When she manages to slip from Ridgeway's grasp in the Indiana station, passing her hand along the rough sides of the final tunnel leading north, she muses:

> Her fingers danced over valleys, rivers, the peaks of mountains, the contours of a new nation hidden beneath the old. *Look outside as you speed through, and you'll find the true face of America.* She could not see it but she felt it, moved through its heart. (304, original emphasis)

The novel's insistent recall here—in italics, no less, so as to ensure it is not missed—at the end of the novel all but demands that we take its claim seriously: that in its alternative historical versions of the U.S. past, "states of possibility" are encoded. If so, they are encoded for the novel's readers, rather than for its characters: it is impossible to read

Lumbly's strangely touristic line, "you'll see the breadth of the country before you reach your final stop," as being meaningful advice to Cora and Caesar, who surely would rather simply cross it quickly. It is the reader who is expected to take in the "breadth of the country," and to see Cora's journey north as a panorama of America's possible and actual pasts—a Rancièrian seeing. This final recurrence signals at least one expected readerly relation to the novel, one which both is open to the "new nation" that must be built from the historical narrative communicated by *The Underground Railroad*, and insists on "feeling." Even in as much as the novel means this here in the sense of a sensory impression, the overtones of the emotional response are strong, especially given the way the novel ungrammatically brings up "its heart" here. *The Underground Railroad* meanders between demanding to be read with the kind of emotional investment called for by these formulations and the more distanced way in which it represents its history elsewhere, including the very complex North Carolina episode. Cora's underground journey recalls Rancière's notion that the writer of history is "the archeologist or geologist who gets the mute witnesses of common history to speak" (2011, 15). If the novel literalizes this tracing of history in stone in Cora's own thoughts, this merely reinforces for now the ambivalence of the passage. Cora's "feeling" of history directly translates Whitehead's writer's position onto the page—Whitehead as the geologist who unearths the meaning of the novel itself—somewhere between emotional feeling and scientific detachment.

Lumbly's comment also points us towards what Anna Kornbluh calls the novel's "spatial emphasis" (2017, 406), and more specifically to the way the novel constructs place, and understands location. Lumbly's comment is true and banal, insightful into the novel's mechanics and wrong about what it actually narrates. If all the states Cora visits are "states of possibility," nothing of this is experienced by "looking outside": for Cora, the railroad's outside is the dark tunnels, with nothing to see at all. As a device, the novel's Underground Railroad serves to take Cora from location to location without the experience of shifting scenery. Despite smallish nods to connectedness, especially between the South Carolina and North Carolina episodes, the "states" remain distinct. Whatever blight has touched Tennessee has no consequence for Indiana; whatever progress has been made in South Carolina does not touch anywhere else. Setting foot in each of these scenarios, Cora can take them in and leave them, and so can readers; modes of life, moments in (African) American history, can be left behind as easily as going on a train journey. But at the same time, in situating all of these states of possibility in the same time frame, *The Underground Railroad* also suggests that there is no real leaving behind of any of them: history lingers, and keeps pursuing us in much the same way as Ridgeway, the slave-catcher, keeps pursuing Cora.

Cora, in all this, represents most clearly the novel's ambivalence between modes of representing history. The first chapter, set on the Georgia plantation on which she is still a slave, reads fairly straightforwardly in the tradition of anti-slavery literature and neo-slave narratives, almost melodramatically simple, a dutiful narrative of the ills of slavery. Cora's grandmother Ajarry is enslaved, put on a ship for the middle passage, sold at a slave auction in Charleston, South Carolina, and finally arrives at the Randall plantation. We learn about Cora's mother Mabel and the small plot of land she occupies for herself in lieu of real freedom; about the politics of the plantation, the more-or-less good slaveholder James Randall, who owns half of the plantation, including Cora, and Terrance, his almost tritely evil brother. We read about the random beatings and casual violences of life as slave, and the gendered violence of rape which Cora suffers. And when Cora and Caesar finally decide to run away on the Underground Railroad, it is after the death of James and the transfer of the northern half of the plantation—where there was at least some personal freedom—to Terrance.

Such a retelling of the Georgia chapter may seem callous. I do not mean to suggest that what the novel tells us about slavery is meaningless or should not be remembered or written about; only to note *The Underground Railroad*'s opening chapter has very little new to say, or a new voice to do it in (though cf. Kelly 2018). Throughout this first chapter, Cora is our conduit into the experience of slavery, perhaps nowhere better narrativized than in the short scene in which she tries to stop Terrance from beating a fellow slave: "A feeling settled over Cora," the novel notes—suggesting, immediately, the importance of an empathetic response—and she grabs Terrance's walking stick. But she cannot hold on: "Then the cane was out of her hand. It came down on her head. It crashed down again and this time the silver teeth ripped across her eyes and blood splattered on her shirt" (33–34). For the duration of the Georgia chapter, this is the narrative perspective: direct, involved, and almost too close. The novel thus opens very much in the manner of its forebears in the neo-slave narrative tradition. The truth of slavery in history is embodied, personalized and individualized in Cora herself. But this perspective soon shifts.

The first such shift may be detected in South Carolina, the first stop on the Underground Railroad. Cora's initial impression of South Carolina is suitably hopeful: the limited freedom of the "much more enlightened" (91) leader of Southern secession appeals to both Cora and Caesar, freshly escaped, so much so that Cora finally proposes that "[m]aybe we should stay for good" (105). South Carolina does appear more than a step up from slavery: although by a "technicality" the property of the U.S. government, slaves in South Carolina "get food, jobs, and housing. Come and go as they please, marry who they wish, raise children who will never be taken away" (92–93). Cora herself is taught how to read and write; Caesar obtains a job in a factory. South Carolina suggests *The Underground Railroad*'s debts to the postmodern neo-slave narrative, like Reed's *Flight to Canada*, in its relentless anachronism: it appears to be a version of the 1920s in the United States. At the center of town stands the fourteen-story Griffin Building, which sports an elevator (itself a call back, perhaps, to Whitehead's first novel, *The Intuitionist* (1999)); Caesar's job is in a factory that has its own conveyor belt and a Fordist system for organizing labor. There are limits to South Carolina's benevolence. It sports a sterilization program for Black women held to be inferior, and there is a program of medical experimentation going on whose subjects are "unfit" Black people. But these issues do not ultimately get to matter. Cora never explicitly chooses to leave South Carolina on her own terms: rather, it is Ridgeway's arrival that finally requires Cora's flight. Even in flight, Cora still bemoans her belief that "two lowly slaves deserved the bounty of South Carolina" (145). The novel leaves the question of Cora's capacity to make a moral choice in abeyance.

Anna Kornbluh suggests that it is "the novel's unflinching third-person narration, so oblique to the testimonials and multifocal first persons of the literary tradition the text otherwise engages" that produces what she calls "purchase on the general state of things" (2017, 406)—that is to say, which allows the novel to speak not the states of the past, but rather the states of the present. I do not think that that is wrong. It misses, however, that we nonetheless get a shift from Cora's personal experiences in the Georgia section and onto depersonalized witnessing in the next few chapters; and it also does not account for the question of focalization, which still routes largely, and in the longer chapters solely, through Cora. The most crucial aspect of this new role in the South Carolina section is Cora's new job. Initially serving as a maid, she is later recruited to be a "type," a living display at the Museum of Natural Wonders. The narrator reports Mr. Fields the curator's conception of the museum:

> the focus was on American history—for a young nation, there was so much to educate the public about. The untamed flora and fauna of the North American continent, the minerals and other splendors of the

> world beneath their feet. Some people never left the counties where they were born, he said. Like a railroad, the museum permitted them to see the rest of the country beyond their small experience, from Florida to Maine to the western frontier. And to see its people. "People like you," Mr. Fields said. (109)

The novel's explicit connection here between museum and railroad (both present the "length and breadth of the country") is also a connection between the museum and the novel itself, between the acts of seeing that occur in a museum and those that occur in a novel (see also Dubey 2020). The suggestion that the museum serves as a metaphor for the novel takes on an added dimension in the reply Mr. Fields delivers to Cora when she notes that cotton plantations did not have spinning wheels outdoors, like the display does. Fields replies that "while authenticity was their watchword, the dimensions of the room forced certain concessions" (110). It is possible to hear here an argument about the novel's own form: its own departure from the realism of a historical novel also forces certain concessions from the idea of authenticity, although in *The Underground Railroad*, this merely serves to highlight the limits of the idea of authenticity in the first place.

Cora serves on three displays in the museum: the "Scenes from Darkest Africa," the "Life on a Slave Ship," and "Typical Day on the Plantation." It should be noted that these idealized displays mean little to Cora—with the exception of the plantation—and she can only have "numerous suspicions" (110) about them; the point here, again, is to confront readers with history, and their reactions to it. The novel builds on the readerly recognition that the displays in which Cora acts the role of the Black woman are historically wrong: that is, it builds on readers' knowledge of slavery. But it does not require it. In presenting us the story of Cora's grandmother's own abduction, middle passage, and sale into slavery, *The Underground Railroad* already offers a counter to white people's attempt to produce a version of history, a history fit for a "young nation." This history finds its end point in a display that has a Native American receive what appears to be a contract from a group of white negotiators. Asked about the display, Mr. Fields tells his types, "We like to tell a story in each one, to illuminate the American experience. Everyone knows the truth of the historic encounter, but to see it before you—". The novel then has Cora repeat this as a question to a mannequin in the "Life on a Slave Ship" display: "Is this the truth of our historic encounter?" (116). That it quite obviously is not the truth, that the museum can stage a false version of history, and that it does so in terms of realistic depiction, suggests the novel's own sense of history. There can *be* a truth of a historic encounter, but this needs to be communicated in a different fashion, such as through *The Underground Railroad*. The novel never actually reneges on the possibility of truth: in juxtaposing Cora's sense of what is correct to the museum's, the novel insists on there being a truth, and that access to it can be had, even if the museum is not the place to seek it.

Cora draws from the various displays in the museum a measured and level-headed—and distanced—conclusion. "The whites came to this land for a fresh start and to escape the tyranny of their masters [. . .]. But the ideals they held up for themselves, they denied others" (117). In the Tea Party display, she sees that "[p]eople wore different kinds of chains across their lifetimes, but it wasn't hard to interpret rebellion, even when the rebels wore costumes to deny blame" (115). She draws from the Native American display the lesson that to "take away someone's babies" is to "steal their future" (117), the most overt rejection of South Carolina's sterilization laws. Importantly, it is not personal experience but mediation that allows her to make up her mind. We may contrast her way of reading the displays—critically, and with care to note what does not fit—with Fields's suggestion that what the museum does is to follow something that you already "know"—the "truth of the historic encounter"—with an act of seeing it, seeing it acted out. There is no desire in the museum to re-orient seeing to perceive a different truth; this is Cora's specific talent. It still remains inefficacious, does not fundamentally appear to challenge anything. Cora leaves South Carolina in a hurry without the novel's taking a stance towards what kind of progress or not South Carolina represents in the overall scheme of things, without commenting overtly on anything that goes on.

From South Carolina, Cora is taken north on the Underground Railroad. In North Carolina, Cora will remain an observer of things: she will, owing to the danger of being caught, sit in the station manager's attic, only to be discovered and put into Ridgeway's hands. It is important to recognize this repetitive insistence here on Cora's distance from the events that the novel wants to show, such as the lynchings on the village green; but it is equally necessary to recognize the shift which the North Carolina episode brings to the novel's sense of how race functions, and what the structural basis for slavery is. Up to now, *The Underground Railroad* has already challenged the idea that experiential narratives are key to the mediation of slavery for the contemporary. But it has not offered a challenge to the idea that the best narrative of slavery is one which highlights the individual's suffering in it, which reads it through a racial lens informed by the contemporary, post-slavery but by no means post-racial moment; a reading that overtly links contemporary race relations to historical slavery. In the North Carolina episode, the novel offers—though temporarily, and without full conviction—a different reading: one which foregrounds the structural, capitalist origins of slavery and the consequent embeddedness of race relations in a greater, impersonal problematic.

North Carolina's new state has been hinted at by the novel a number of times before, but now Cora sees it with her own eyes for the first time. As she is brought into town by North Carolina's station master, she passes hundreds of Black bodies swinging from the trees lining the road. "In what sort of hell had the train let her off?" (153), she wonders. As it turns out, the "state of possibility" in North Carolina is one in which Black slavery has, just as in South Carolina, been abandoned, but for far different reasons. Cora soon obtains the full story from Martin, the station manager. North Carolina has decided to "solve the colored question" (163). As Martin—and by extension the novel—recognizes, this is a question firmly rooted in economic logic: "[a]s with everything in the south, it started with cotton," a "ruthless engine" with an irresistible logic. "More slaves led to more cotton, which led to more money to buy more land to farm more cotton" (161)—a fully capitalized enterprise, in other words, in which the logic of profit comes to dominate even in the face of a rising problem, the increasing slave population which it becomes ever harder to control. It is this question that North Carolina solves, led by a planter named Oney Garrison. Garrison "grew up by the profits of cotton, and its necessary evil, n****rs," and his simple solution is to have "more of the former and less of the latter. Why were they spending so much time worrying about slave uprisings and northern influence in Congress when the real issue was who was going to pick all this goddamned cotton?" (163, my asterisks, here and below).

Recognizing the influx of European immigrants to the North, North Carolina begins advertising for the labor this represents, and soon enough a steady stream of white migrants arrives to replace, in indentured servitude, the Black slave population of the state. The benefits of this, as Martin reports, are numerous: not only will North Carolina not have to fear slave rebellion anymore, but it will also, in due course, when the Irish and German immigrants have "paid back travel, tools, and lodging" (164), have a sizeable population of voters ready to increase the state's weight in Congress. In one sociopolitical shift, North Carolina appears to have successfully solved all its problems, at the price of banning forever all Black people from the state, on pain of death.

What is interesting about this is the way in which the novel frames the replacement of one socioeconomic structure—slavery—by another—indentured servitude. It is Cora who first broaches the difficult question of the relationship between race and class in this story: "'Never seen a white person pick cotton,' Cora said" (164). Martin quickly disabuses her of the notion that servitude is necessarily a racialized structure, and the terms of his argument are noteworthy: "True, you couldn't treat an Irishman like an African, white n****r or no" (164). What Martin's description-reprise of the argument in the planters' discussion offers is a deeply systemic view of the conflation between race and class, between the economic realities of a cost-benefit analysis and the construction of appropriate social structures to reproduce race and class. It more than coincidentally echoes Immanuel Wallerstein's pithy summary of the way racism and economic, capitalist logics are intertwined. No matter what the concrete boundaries of social groups are, and whether they are racial or national or religious, "there are always some who are 'n****rs'. If there are no Blacks or too few to play the role, one can invent 'White n****rs'" (1991, 34). As Wallerstein points out, such "racism constant in form and in venom, but somewhat flexible in boundary lines" solves the problem of regulating "the lowest paid, least rewarding economic roles, according to current needs" (34), as well as ensuring the reproduction of particular social communities and ensuring a constant basis for the justification of inequality.

The echoes of Wallerstein's three-part argument should be evident in the way *The Underground Railroad* envisages North Carolina's decision in favor of white indentured servitude. It finds, or so the North Carolina planters believe, the most cost-effective class of workers, weighing not just the material costs of food and lodging but also the threat of slave uprisings and a violent response to them. At the same time, Southern society ascertains that it socializes its new white members, notwithstanding their socioeconomic inferiority, in the "appropriate roles" for Southern society. After all, it assumes that these indentured servants, once free of their obligations, would find Southern society congenial to themselves: "they would be allies of the southern system that had nurtured them" (164). And finally, it also envisages these newcomers as no threat to the established order in a more general sense, seeing the new white European immigrants as liable to be in lasting economic inequality despite the promise of a possible political equality.

Martin's narrative, already rendered impersonal through the narrator's transposition of it, concludes, "In effect, they abolished slavery. On the contrary, Oney Garrison said in response. We abolished n****rs" (165). The unnamed interlocutor who evaluates the North Carolina move as having "abolished slavery" has a point, of course: in immediate political terms, this is what they have done. But Garrison's response is more interesting. On the one hand, his denial suggests immediately the recognition that beyond surface appearances, beyond the shift from Black to white and from involuntary to voluntary bondage, nothing meaningful has changed. Slavery has not been abolished, it has merely been renamed. But at the same time, his insistence that "n****rs" have been abolished suggests the persistence of racial categories as the key determinants in who is or is not a "n****r." After all, we can, with Wallerstein and the novel both, understand that what the North Carolina decision has done is produce its Irish and others as "white n****rs," and realize that you cannot have slavery without also having some kind of outcaste. What has been abolished, Garrison suggests, is Black people—and this is clearly also what the novel implies in everything else, from the violent persecution of Black people Cora witnesses from her attic hideout to her own fate later in the novel. Unlike Wallerstein, Garrison still separates the racial identity of the slave from her economic role. He acknowledges that slavery persists, in a different form, but also that the attitude towards Black people has not changed, even though Garrison himself had previously advanced what were essentially economic arguments about the role of Black slavery—who was to pick all the goddamned cotton.

Yet these positions are not incommensurable: there is a necessary time-lag between what happens economically and how society will produce a cultural consensus around those shifts. We should no more take for granted Garrison's extrapolation—that the white indentured servants will be less an outcaste than their Black predecessors—than we should take for granted that the still-racial violence meted out against Black people is the necessary end point of the development. That, in other words, no matter Black people's role in society, they will always remain racially marked. This does not appear to be the ultimate point of the novel, unless one wants to adopt the position from which Garrison speaks, and which does not seem to be anymore condoned than any alternative. I would also quibble with Anna Kornbluh's suggestion that *The Underground Railroad* "insistently connects labor and struggle" (2017, 406), which Adam Kelly echoes (2018). For Kornbluh, it is the novel's central conceit itself that does so, building on the rhetorical question which Cora is given in answer to the question of who built the Underground Railroad: "Who builds anything in this country?" Here, the sheer presence of a physical Underground Railroad highlights the foundational role of Black labor in the United States. The novel's narrative slightly militates against this reading. The Underground Railroad's materiality, after all, serves barely any narrative purpose: at no stage is it narratively required, or central to what happens. It is a device for shortening voyages that historically could be made, if more slowly.

Recognizing the role of Black labor in its reconstruction serves a more general purpose of recognizing the centrality of Black labor power for the United States as such, if indirectly. Second, however, Kornbluh's argument leaves the Underground Railroad as a quasi-substrate for reading the novel in a way that requires us to ignore the many ways in which the novel does *not* connect labor and struggle.

In the North Carolina episode, right in the middle of the novel, we have a turn towards something like historical explanation. The Georgia section developed a fairly straightforward story, in which especially Cora's grandmother's journey does not offer anything like a rationale for the middle passage, and which largely subscribes to the notion that narration of the consequences and reality of slavery is at the heart of the literary engagement with slavery. The South Carolina episode, as we have seen, already broadens this perspective, making Cora into more of an observer of social realities than the object of description, displacing the experiential narrative of history—in which no truth is possible—with one in which truth is insisted upon. The North Carolina section expands on this, not just by making Cora even more of an observer but also by suggesting the way the history of slavery is bound up less in the violent logic of racism and more in the even more violent logic of capitalism. Kelly's diagnosis is that *The Underground Railroad* understands that "[f]reedom after neoliberalism [. . .] begins to look possible only as freedom after capitalism" (2018, 29), and the point here must be that "freedom" is a category linked to more than racial struggle. We may see a progression here as well. From Georgia, where we never get any kind of logic at all, to South Carolina, and its paternalistic white society that sees itself within its rights to decide which Black people will get to procreate, to North Carolina, which grounds its decision to abandon Black slavery on a simple cost analysis, *The Underground Railroad* stretches out a canvas of possible historicizations of slavery. It continues in a similar vein in the Tennessee and Indiana chapters, proposing different ways of reading race relations and the consequences for emancipation, if not in as increasingly progressive a fashion as it does in the first three sections.

Cora finally is caught in North Carolina, but before she can suffer the fate of the other Black people she has seen captured and lynched on the village green, she is picked up by Ridgeway, the slave-catcher. After some little time on the move in Tennessee, Ridgeway is surprised by a group of Black people who free Cora just before she is raped by one of Ridgeway's henchmen. They take Cora north on the Underground Railroad again to Indiana.

In Indiana, Cora is offered a choice: she can catch a connection north, towards Canada, or she can stay on the farm of John Valentine, a free Black man passing for white whose farm is both an "office" of the Underground Railroad and a place for fugitives to stay and contribute to a meaningful community. The farm asks a question: what is the place of a community of Black people in the midst of white hegemony? As Cora muses, recalling the night of her escape from the slave-catcher, "Ridgeway had called Cora and her mother a flaw in the American scheme. If two women were a flaw, what was a community?" (265). Briefly, it bears pointing out the vestiges of the North Carolina episode here: Ridgeway is calling Cora and her mother flaws not as Black women, or as slaves, but rather as *escaped* slaves, as those who aim to escape the logic of the slave-capitalist system. The novel's initial glimpse of the farm suggests its deep rootedness in utopian writing. "The entire farm was something beyond her imagination," a "miracle" (252), its one hundred souls a "fantastic figure" (246). *The Underground Railroad* naturally evokes the language of speculative fiction to describe both the general reaction to the farm and Cora's in particular. With its motto, "Stay, and contribute," a "request, and a cure" (253), Valentine farm takes on the character of an outside to the system, a safe space to which free Black people and fugitives come from all over the United States.

It is this that makes the novel's Indiana chapter perhaps the most morally complicated, and at the same time most traditionally utopian. The Valentine farm represents a utopian experiment in the tradition of Helicon Home or of Fruitlands, the farm experiment set up in Massachusetts in 1843 by Amos Bronson Alcott and Charles Lane, which lasted for just seven months—literalizing the idea of a good place in a way that is especially powerful given that it also offers a direct rejoinder to the plantation. The superficial similarity of Black toil over the land highlights the economic embeddedness of slavery, suggesting the way these forms of labor relate to exploitation, and implicitly picks up also on the common anti-abolitionist refrain about how the North's industrial workplaces differed little from Southern slavery. As Kelly points out, the narrative also insists heavily on embedding the utopian farm in the realities of the capitalist system of local trade and finance that it cannot escape (2018, 22). The farm also recalls the plot of land that Cora's mother and grandmother had claimed as their own on the Randall plantation. Valentine farm stands as an alternative model of both communal living and economic organization, a suggestion which sets into starker relief the ultimate fate of the farm. For, as the novel apprises us, somewhat later in the Indiana chapter, there are both "philosophical disputes" about the venture as well as "the very real matter of the white settlers' mounting resentment of the negro outpost" (265). Cora's unquestioning desire to stay on Valentine farm with its "seductive plenty" (266) thus takes on ominous overtones.

Like so many other utopian ventures, the Valentine farm project collapses. And while it does so in part under the pressure of exterior forces, neighbors unwilling to put up with the presence of Black men and women, the chief instigator of the project's demise is, possibly, another Black man, Mingo. Mingo, a former slave himself, believes the farm has gone too far. A gradualist, he aspires to limit its intake of more fugitives in order not to alienate the white settlers. Against him, a public speaker and free Northern Black man named Lander argues that Black people must stand up for one another unconditionally. They debate this at a public meeting on the farm; and as they do so, a posse of white people, ostensibly searching for fugitive slaves, assaults the farm, kills many, and ends the project for good. The novel appears to deny the possibility of utopian hope not just in the collapse of the farm and the death of so many of its people, but also in the reappearance of Ridgeway, who catches Cora once more. The repeated appearance of Ridgeway initially suggests that the system will not be denied. But things, finally, change. Ridgeway drags Cora to the Indiana nexus of the Underground Railroad: the discovery of an ingress into the railroad, somewhat implausibly never having happened before, would lay open the entire system to destruction. But as the two descend into the station, Cora trips Ridgeway; he falls down the stairs and is injured, likely mortally. Cora escapes on a handcar set on the rails, and rushes north through the tunnels. She abandons the car on the way and gropes her way to an exit, finally pushing through some brambles into the open.

The Underground Railroad ends, after having juxtaposed spaces of possibility and individualized psychograms with a wide-open non-space: the North, from which Cora departs to an even more open, vaguely stereotypical American space of hope, the West. The novel had set this out as a trajectory in the South Carolina museum, where Cora passes a display:

> Two determined explorers posed on a ridge and gazed at the mountains of the west, the mysterious country with its perils and discoveries before them. Who knew what lay out there? They were masters of their own lives, lighting out fearlessly into their futures. (115)

After Cora stumbles from the final tunnel of the railroad, and sits down exhausted by the side of a road, she is passed by a wagon train. The Black driver of one of those wagons picks her up, gives her food and water, and tells her the wagons are going west, perhaps as far as California. While still in Tennessee, Cora had mused briefly that if she "made it north she would have disappeared into a life outside" the "terms" of either the slavers' or the abolitionists' discourses (222). Cora, that is, represents the fantasy of escaping, rather than changing, the system, of being bound by neither oppression nor resistance, to simply be oneself.

Recall Ursula K. LeGuin's note that "[t]he direction of escape is toward freedom" (2017, 83), which highlights that any escape is already a hopeful act. It is not the achievement of escape only that is hopeful; the "grace of striving" (Kornbluh 2017, 406) is the novel's utopian heart. Even if Cora's previous experiences of escape have always reduced her to bondage again, the mere act of repeating her escape gives room for hope. Structurally the novel lays a heavy burden on Cora. Without positive knowledge of Ridgeway's death, we may imagine him to return soon enough, and any knowledge of the logic of fugitive slave law would suggest that Cora's escape cannot be final. But I would stress again that this is a matter of reading and interpretation. A suspicious reading would probably more strongly foreground the problem that Cora's "final" escape appears formally little different from the previous ones, and offers little immediate reason to be accepted as necessarily successful. It is both unlikely as well as structurally militated against by the novel's logic. Such a reading might also stress the sheer problem of what critical purchase a neo-slave narrative has in the twenty-first century, especially when it is so fully bound up in its own commercialization. It might note how complicit it is with an entertainment industry whose value for the cause it appears to champion is at least doubtful, a novel that in form and narrative content appears tailor-made for winning Oprah's endorsement and an Amazon TV adaptation, both of which it actually did get. In as much as such a reading leaves it little different from genre fictions like *Ready Player One*, it also presents itself as a slightly different test case for the utopian hermeneutics that I have been championing. It is not a negative judgment of the novel's value to suggest that it was written for a popular reading audience and with the possibility of television adaptation in mind. Rather, it is to point to the confluence of cultural modes again, the growing impossibility to delineate at all, let alone neatly, between popular fiction and literary, and to highlight their mutual fertilization.

There is also a tension between what I have dubbed the novel's structural and individual visions of slavery's history and contemporary significance. In placing *The Underground Railroad* in a trajectory from the neo-slave narrative onward, one inescapably also appears to ask about the novel's relation to its own contemporary moment, to ask about the relationship between its form and its time. It is almost too obvious to point out with Lee Konstantinou that as "a novel about slavery,

The Underground Railroad arguably has a special place in US literature and culture" (2017, 15). Indeed, it does so not just in being about slavery, but in being about slavery in the particular way that it is about slavery, as a historical novel of slavery formally representing slavery through the personal narrative (if in the third person) of an escaping slave. This form prefers to read history as accessible only in the most immediately embodied forms, and does not often read the regime of slavery structurally. *The Underground Railroad* appears to formally inscribe itself in a discourse which understands slavery as a historical but personalized evil. Only it does not do so fully: at several points in the narrative, it offers conflicting understandings of slavery as more interestingly bound up in economic structures, rather than simply racist ideology (or, more properly, it suggests that inevitable bounded-upness of racist and economic ideology). But I would insist that it does not do so sustainedly. While "the labor of struggle, the work to survive against the work of the nation, is not historical fiction in the past but searingly ongoing reality in the present" (Kornbluh 2017, 406), the novel never actually completely centralizes this conflation of labor and labor's conditions and the (racialized) struggle Cora focalizes. The consequence is a text that clearly signals its understanding of the position Kornbluh sketches out, even as it also partakes of the more personalized and individualized experiential narrative of slavery in the neo-slave narrative tradition. Later in this chapter, I will seek to outline an argument for how this is significant; for now, I would simply like to end with the observation that *The Underground Railroad* sits uneasily astride a number of discourses about the historical reality of slavery and by extension the contemporary reality of racism.

"Freedom is a matter of logistics": Ben Winters's *Underground Airlines*

The obvious reason to talk about Ben Winters's 2016 novel *Underground Airlines* is its topical similarity to Whitehead's novel and that its title plays on the same Underground Railroad that inspires Whitehead, and so it situates itself within the larger ambit of texts that address the continuing meaning of slavery in the contemporary moment. While this is a crucial part of what the novel does, a less obvious reason to talk about it is to juxtapose what it does, and how it does it, to *The Underground Railroad*. *Underground Airlines* takes a more strongly structural view of what slavery means for American history, and more overtly suggests the interlinkages between "labor and struggle"—

between labor struggle and racial struggle. This section will seek to develop a reading of *Underground Airlines* that foregrounds the specifics of its claims about race, slavery, and their meaning for the contemporary moment. It will also set the ground for the next section, where I will establish the importance of debate around those two novels, which allows us to take in the prevalence of questions of literary quality, racial identity, and genre and literary fiction.

Winters's novel is narrated by a freed former slave whom we get to know most often as Victor. The novel is set in an alternative present in which, following the assassination of Abraham Lincoln before his first inauguration, a set of compromises has kept slavery alive until the present, at least in the set of states known only as the "Hard Four." Victor works as a freelance agent for the U.S. Marshals Service, hunting fugitive slaves, under the supervision of a control chip in his neck that prevents him from escaping. His new assignment is to find a slave named Jackdaw, a "Person Bound to Labor" recently escaped from the Alabama cotton plantation of Garments of the Greater South, Inc. Victor falls in with a white woman, Martha, and her son, Lionel. Martha is looking to find and free Lionel's father, who is also held somewhere in the Deep South. As Victor discovers more about the nature of the Jackdaw case, he and Martha embark on a mission into the Hard Four to uncover information about sinister goings-on at Garments of the Greater South that go far beyond slavery. As Victor is told, Jackdaw had "Evidence. Powerful evidence that will bring down the very foundations of slavery" (188). Victor eventually discovers that the company is working to create clones, tailor-made to labor in the cotton fields, the t-shirt sewing plants, and other slave-based economies in the South. "They're growing slaves" (311), as Victor has it. Victor gets the information to a network of abolitionists called Underground Airlines, and then, himself freed from the bondage of his control chip, sets out to free Martha's beloved.

Much of the novel is structured like a noir thriller—hardboiled, first-person narration included. But while the mystery of Jackdaw's escape and the information that he was carrying drives the plot, the revelations the novel offers about its speculative reality are more relevant to my discussion here. Throughout the novel, Victor offers information on the history of the United States in the wake of Lincoln's early assassination, such as the crucial point that after Lincoln's death, a new compromise has prevented secession and enshrined slavery, and on contemporary American politics, beginning on the opening, two-page spread which offers a map of the United States. Here, the four remaining slave states—Louisiana, Mississippi, Alabama, and the new state of "Carolina"—are marked, as are a "Republic of Texas (Disputed)" and a "Special Economic Zone" in the Gulf of Mexico. All of them become relevant for the narrative, and all of them are deeply intertwined with the history of slavery.

At the heart of this alternative history is the construction of an economic system. From the very beginning, Victor passes on information that helps us understand how slavery works, and does not, in the twenty-first century. "Clean hands" laws in the free states bar "places of public accommodation from serving anything" produced in slave states (9); foreign countries have agreed to the "European Consensus" blocking trade with the U.S. (12); the result is a "fucked-up, piecemeal economy":

> all that proud but self-defeating unwillingness to do business with the Hard Four; all the blood and treasure wasted in the Texas War; all the industries, from cars to coal to computers, that had bloomed and then wilted in the face of international boycotts and sanctions (while, funnily enough, the slave states prosper, protected by the economic insulation of permanently deflated labor costs). (80)

The Texas War itself was fought over "American oil under all that sand" beginning in 1964. It ended in 1975 (it is the novel's mirror of Vietnam), with a contested Republic of Texas and the "Special Economic Zone" in the Gulf of Mexico that protects American oil reserves and becomes, as the novel reveals later, the most harrowing of slavery's experiences, a law-free zone where Black slaves are sent to die.

In *Underground Airlines*, slavery is an economic problem: both a problem *for* the economy, apparently only succeeding in depressing American industry, and a problem *of* the economy, best understood in economic terms, rather than through individual experience. Slavery is fought over politically only because it is of economic benefit to the states that have it, and remains a problem because of its legal codification in the Constitution. That is not to say that we do not discover much about what lives slaves lead, nor to say that outside of the Hard Four proper, racism is not a problem, or that Black lives matter as much as white lives. But the novel is more interested in why they are like that. As Victor notes, speaking of Chicago's Black neighborhood, Freedman Town,

> Freedman Town serves a good purpose—not for the people who live there, Lord knows; people stuck there by poverty, by prejudice, by laws that keep them from moving or working. Freedman Town's purpose was to the rest of the world. The world that sits, like Martha, with dark glasses on, staring from a distance, scared but safe. Create a pen like that, give people no choice but to live like animals, and then people get to point at them and say *Will you look at those animals? That's what*

> *kind of people those people are.* And that idea drifts up and out of Freedman Town like chimney smoke, black gets to mean poor and poor to mean dangerous and all the words get murked together and become one dark idea, a cloud of smoke, the smokestack fumes drifting like filthy air across the rest of the nation. (140, original emphasis)

Underground Airlines is not interested in validating the experience of living in Freedman Town: it is interested in diagnosing the processes which produce the kind of life which is lived in Freedman Town. Instances of this narrative perspective abound, including Victor's own history. His own past as a slave in a slaughterhouse, which comes back to him in a series of dreams, is largely structured around the progression of jobs which he takes on there, before his final flight, and includes his reminiscences of the presence of Chinese investors, very much linking his own personal story to the larger systems at work beyond.

Underground Airlines' view of the legacy of slavery is informed by a broader historical awareness, which also amounts to a sense that a meaningful engagement with the present requires historicization. Historically grounded, it suggests that an engagement with the present requires an awareness of historical change. *Underground Airlines* fully takes on board the way in which historical developments modify existing technologies of exploitation and racialized violence; its modernist-managerial vision of slavery's continuation is all the more chilling for it. *Underground Airlines* is what Fredric Jameson would call "properly historical" (2003, 712): it speaks about slavery with a view towards what a recent history of slavery has called the "metastatic transformation and growth of slavery's giant body" (Baptist 2016, xxvi). It depicts slavery as changing with the economic (technological, social, political) twists and turns of history.

We can probably best see the novel's take on this in its chapter set in the Deep South. Victor, caught out as a federal agent by the Underground Airlines' Father Barton, is pressured to go south to retrieve the data which Jackdaw had been meant to bring. Victor and Martha go to the facility of Garments of the Greater South from which Jackdaw fled, Martha impersonating a salesperson for a management consulting firm, and Victor, her assistant. They manage to meet a mid-level manager, Matthew Newell, in his office, and are given a tour. Beginning by the facility's "twenty-four-hour-a-day operation," Newell continues, speaking to Victor, "None of your cousins got a thing to complain about down here." When Victor appears dubious, Newell goes on:

> I mean it, son. This is not the slavery of fifty or even ten years ago. People think about slavery, and they still think—still!—about the whips and the

> dogs and the spiky neck chains, all of that nasty business. But this is *now*. This is the twenty-first century. (258, original emphasis)

Newell goes on to prize the "Jeffersonian" design before proudly announcing that "we do not use Tasers here. Once in a blue moon, maybe, is it thought to be necessary. Because this here is an incentive-based facility, okay?" (259). The neoliberal language of incentives combines with the insistence on a surface humanity in Newell's account that refuses to acknowledge the underlying structure of slavery, notably even in a discussion between people that already accept slavery. Martha's pretend-salesperson, after all, is no critic of slavery, but someone out herself to profit from it. Slavery has been incorporated into the general logic of twenty-first-century capitalism: Martha, seeking to distract Newell while Victor searches his office, launches her sales-pitch by saying, "What is it that y'all are selling here? [. . .] What you are selling is *time*." Martha goes on to distill the heart of contemporary (and all) capitalism, the effort to derive ever-greater surplus value from labor: "it's their *time* that you all are selling," meaning the "Persons Bound to Labor" in the factory, "every darn *minute* of it, *that* is the product" (261, original emphases). Martha's pretend salesperson gets to the heart of the post-postmodern workplace:

> Let's say he works one hour. How many minutes are in that hour? [. . .] Maybe it's fifty. Maybe thirty. Maybe a hundred! It all depends on what's going on in that man's head, what's going on with that man's body. What we sell at Peach Tree, what we do is, we sell minutes. With our system of incentives and corrections, we add minutes to the hours that your PBLs are putting in, and you know what that does? [. . .] It makes money, Mr. Newell! (262)

The problem for Garments of the Greater South that Martha sketches is essentially this:

> in the system of slavery [. . .] frankly and openly, labour power itself is sold. [. . .] [I]n the slave system, the advantage of labour power above the average, and the disadvantage of labour power below the average, affects the slave-owner; in the wage-labour system it affects the labourer himself, because his labour power is, in the one case, sold by himself, in the other, by a third person. (Marx and Engels 1993, 542)

If what you pay for is labor power, rather than labor-time, you can simply reduce a wage-laborer's wages; but you cannot reduce the subsistence of a slave, since it is already only subsistence; so what you need to do is increase his output, increase the time spent on production. Martha—speaking to the system—has understood this basic principle, and successfully applies it to the managerial practices of twenty-first-century slave-holding.

Underground Airlines thinks slavery economically throughout. Readers of *The Underground Railroad* might be forgiven for asking what all the slavery in that novel is *for*. Readers of *Underground Airlines* are brought face to face with the realization that it serves as the foundation of an economic system, and an economic system, to boot, that looks much like our own. This impinges on the interrelation between speculative historist form and the production of hopeful futures. *Underground Airlines*' properly historical contemporary slavery, being systemic, requires systemic approaches and solutions. It also understands how the derring-do of expeditions to save individual slaves (like the one that saves Cora in Indiana, and Victor and Martha's quest to free her beloved) must be supported by more than just the actual infrastructure of escape. "Forget the glory of the predawn raid. Smashing in the face of the system and pulling free the enslaved was mostly a matter of paperwork. [. . .] Freedom is a matter of logistics" (98). We may not be inclined to question the particular kind of hope Cora has, paper-less and unsupported, in the West, and we should probably take her freedom in the West as a meaningful ray of hope regardless. But we should also not miss how *Underground Airlines*' vision of emancipation confronts us with the limits of narratives of individual fates.

Which should bring us to the novel's central speculative conceit, "growing slaves," as Victor has it. In Garments of the Greater South's cloning facilities, race becomes an utterly immaterial factor. As Bridge, Victor's immediate boss, notes, "If the population held in bondage, if they were—not technically . . . people any longer. Certain constitutional issues, certain political issues . . . would be resolved." Victor immediately realizes the purpose of cloning slaves: "people with no bloodline, people with no past and no future, people with no claim to freedom" (312, original ellipses). Without any kind of ethnic heritage, makeable and modifiable according to whim, these new slaves' ethnic heritage becomes immaterial: they are a caste, rather than a race, which does not mean that they do not have a skin color, but negates its fundamental importance. Victor realizes this, and the novel understands it as a historical logic: "They'd been improving the machinery of slavery for two centuries, inventing new tortures to make people work harder and longer" (312). This is the culmination: not just the dehumanization of slaves, over and over, but the dehumanization of slaves once and for all. It is this perspective—the historical trajectory which the novel sketches out, and which it insists on as the proper way of framing slavery's impact—that informs its understanding of what history is.

In fact, we might go so far as to suggest that it confronts us with the limits of a historical narrative that depends for its truth claims on individual experience. Later on in the chapter in which Victor and Martha infiltrate the Garments of the Greater South factory, Victor successfully subdues Newell by force, who, in panic, tells him, "'I never—I never did anything to hurt any Negro,' he said. 'I never did.' Sincerely he said it. Believing it." Victor replies, "'I know. [. . .] You never did any harm to any Negro person'" (269–71). Victor's emphasis establishes a fundamental truth about the writing of fictional history. Victor both acknowledges the probability of the truth of the man's conviction that he has never harmed a Black person in his life and the immateriality of that truth. For the manager, not harming an individual Black person is the moral grounds on which he can hold himself blameless, and through which he aims to escape punishment. More than just setting out *Underground Airlines*' own structural view of the violences of slavery, it also offers a serious challenge for historical fiction that insists on approaching history through individual experience. It is impossible to accost the manager on those grounds: after all, his personal experience, his "experience of history," as it were, is that he "never did anything to hurt" a Black person. *Underground Airlines* lays bare the problem when such an approach to history is accorded not just the victims of structural deprivations, but also the perpetrators. The only historical truth, after all, is a felt truth—an experienced truth—and in the double meaning of "felt truth" lies the problem: Newell's truth about his own (historical) role is not fundamentally different from the truth which any of his "Persons Bound to Labor" would be able to offer, even though their moral positions are shockingly different. *Underground Airlines*' antidote to this is to read slavery structurally, to look for the remedy not in the individual truths of lived lives, but in the fundamental truth of the system's working.

This holds in most of the other dimensions of slavery it addresses. Throughout, the persistently foregrounded business of slavery is tied to politics. Victor follows the nomination hearings to the chair of the Federal Securities and Exchange Commission, to which Donatella Batlisch has been named. Batlisch appears to be a proponent of punishing "investment companies that trade in plantation profit" (22). Again watching the nominee speak at a hearing, Victor muses, "Let's say she did get confirmed. Maybe she does what she says—maybe she brings new vigor to the prosecution of financial firms that trade in blood money. [. . .] Nothing would change" (151). The novel renders the politics of slavery here as involving not individual agency and action so much as public prosecution and the execution of laws, as a structural, complex, and long-term struggle. Batlisch does not get confirmed: as Victor is told shortly before he departs for Alabama and his mission to discover the secret of Jackdaw's escape, she has been shot and killed by an unknown assailant. This matters less, however, given the novel's insistence that all she had ever planned to do was follow the laws—given the novel's insistence, that is, on thinking slavery structurally and almost willfully obscurely. We can feel with Cora; we can hardly feel with the struggle to impose a vigorous legal prosecution on a bank. Yet *Underground Airlines* insists not just on foregrounding this aspect of its political situation repeatedly, it also insists on the weight accorded it. People in *Underground Airlines* are invested in politics: they genuinely believe that this is a moment of possible change, even if Victor disagrees.

It is this disagreement with the idea that change is possible that drives the utopian moment of the novel. Victor, detached and cynical, spends much of the novel commenting on the political moments of hope he witnesses. Reading the paper at breakfast early on, he encounters an editorial question tied to the Batlisch confirmation hearings: "Is this a moment when things begin to change? 'No,' I said to the paper. 'It's not.' I took another bite" (23). Witnessing the hearings on TV, as noted, he comments, "Nothing would change" (151). And, having finally been put into the picture by Father Barton, and confronted with Barton's belief that he could and would change the world, he notes, "I didn't believe it for a second. I could see the future. I knew what would happen, and what would happen was nothing" (193). Yet by the end of the novel Victor comes to appreciate the limits of his own cynicism. Having retrieved the information that he was sent to get, he is confronted with the surprising revelation that one of Father Barton's compatriots, Cook, is also an agent for the U.S. Marshals Service. Victor faces a reckoning: the evidence which Barton has sought, with all its potential, suddenly becomes real to Victor, too. Realizing that Cook's superiors, like his own, want only to destroy the evidence that he has uncovered, he finds himself "mourning that alternative future" that Barton had sketched, "longing for a victory I had never really contemplated." What he calls the "hopeful, lunatic words" of Barton, the idea that the revelations he has could "shake the foundations" (304), becomes a sudden imperative, so much so that he is not even willing to trade the information that he has found for his own freedom later on. Rather, he effectively gambles his release from bondage to the U.S. Marshals Service on the success of a move to obtain control of this information by force. In another instance of the novel's sense of hope, Victor does, in the end, achieve both goals.

He manages to obtain a confession from his superior as the Marshals Service's own stakes in not revealing the information about the attempt to clone slaves, and successfully escapes the constant surveillance of the Service, becoming, for the first time, a free man. The novel concludes on a final, profoundly hopeful note: as Victor and Martha set out to free her beloved from the Special Economic Zone oilrig to which he has been sent, Victor concludes the novel, "Everything can happen. Everything is possible" (322).

Underground Airlines thus finally repudiates the necessity of Victor's mantra that "[n]othing would change" (151): without affirming positive change as a necessary consequence of the novel's events, it denies the certainty of non-change and stresses the possibility and the need for hope. More to the point, however, *Underground Airlines* offers a sense of systemic hope, as it were: the aim of Father Barton and his group being limited not to the aid of the individual slave, but to secure Jackdaw's information for greater purposes. The discovery of the cloning facilities in Alabama might "shake the very foundations, bring down not just this plantation but all the plantations" (178). This is the major difference in the endings of *The Underground Railroad* and *Underground Airlines*: while both of them end with their protagonists emancipated, only *Underground Airlines* transposes this individual manumission into a higher register. Victor and Martha's continued quest to free Martha's beloved already contrasts with Cora's departure west, which leaves the systemic inequities untouched, and, indeed, in most ways no longer a concern for Cora herself. *Underground Airlines* argues that it is necessary to keep up the struggle, to stay faithful to the Idea of emancipation, but also not to lose sight of the way in which any work to end the inequities of slavery systemically takes precedence over the individual. Hope resides in the idea of changing the system more than in individual manumission. *The Underground Railroad*, by contrast, insists on foregrounding hope as finally embodied—explicitly collapsing hopeful systems such as the utopian farm experiment in Indiana. I would still hold with the possibility, and within the context of a utopian hermeneutics with the need, to read this as a way of insisting to continue the struggle, but it is nonetheless awkward. To center Cora's escape as the hopeful moment of the story hinges, in part, on the idea of the West as an amorphously hopeful space. But the West is a peculiarly white space. As Jason Pierce points out, "the notion of the West as an ideal location for white Americans" (2016, 124) in the antebellum period meant that both white settlers and the national government sought to reduce free Black migration. The myth of the West is a white myth. As Pierce has it, "the West came to be identified with such a grandiose vision as the white man's West, for the region had always been as much an idea, a belief, as a physical place" (11). The West is a space of white hope, then, and to send Cora off into it at the conclusion of the novel is at best a complicated vision. We may certainly imagine reading this as a racially utopian intervention of sorts, which writes Black people back into a white space that has not figured them strongly. But that is an ill fit for the rest of the narrative (which has seen Cora acquiesce to roles, rather than shape them for herself). Rather, *The Underground Railroad* does, in fact, figure the West as a space of hope somewhat unreservedly: it taps into the prevalent discourse of the West for a particular audience, one which already reads it as that space of hope: white, well-read liberals. We cannot understand, I think, the way *The Underground Railroad* works without understanding its location in the literary field, its playing to a variety of audiences. Doing so will also help us, however, understand the place of speculative historism in that, inevitable and crucial, marketplace of literary works.

Speculative Historism in the Literary Marketplace: On Genre, Value, Race, and Class

The Underground Railroad and *Underground Airlines* let us speak to the interrelations between form and history, between what might with Badiou be called Event and Idea. There is at least a suggestiveness to the way the publication of *Underground Airlines* and *The Underground Railroad* appears to mirror the inception of the neo-slave narrative. The confluence of genre writing, historical consciousness, the presence of racial controversy, and the processes of valorization which the two novels are subjected to are instructive in reading the contemporary moment not in literature but rather through an engagement with literature's system. They lead us to situate speculative historism better: to understand its force and limits, but also to recognize its import in a larger system of interrelated parts.

The Underground Railroad and *Underground Airlines* reveal something about the way we read now, about the reception of literature, about processes of consecration (see Leypoldt 2014), and finally about the need for the kind of utopian hermeneutics which I have been championing. It may be surprising when I say I take *The Underground Railroad* to be the key novel of the contemporary moment, the best exponent of the way in which the contemporary literary system operates. I think we may see this especially well in the difference from *Underground Airlines*, a difference in their importance driven by formal choices and thematic concerns, finally ratified by consecrating authorities. This section expands my reading of the two novels from interpretation to what Günter Leypoldt calls the "contemporary cultural marketplace" (2016, 379). *The Underground Railroad* is part of a triangulation of a path between different kinds of readers in order to find, formally and narratively, common ground for responding to issues which it identifies as important—to shorthand, race and class in the contemporary moment. Its critical validation, its winning of a vast, indeed unprecedented array of prizes and other recognitions, here ultimately lets us discuss the meaning of its narrative choices. It is this placing of *The Underground Railroad* in a greater context of reception and production, of value judgments and different genre economies, that lets us go from the *what* and the *how* of the novel to the more problematic question of *why* it does what it does. It also lets us perceive better why *Underground Airlines*' more structural vision of slavery has fared comparatively more poorly, up to and including the identitarian backlash against Winters's appropriation of a Black voice.

We really can only arrive at this argument with *The Underground Railroad*. It is *The Underground Railroad*'s success that signals speculative historism's arrival as a form in (more) popular consciousness, but which also sets into relief the possibilities of the mode in the contemporary. The perspective of the cultural marketplace goes to the heart of the question of why we are seeing the books we are seeing, certainly, but *The Underground Railroad* speaks to the form's possibilities and limitations in a broader sense, forcing us to ask the question of where we locate the form in the contemporary literary imagination. I will give a complicated answer to that, one that highlights *The Underground Railroad*'s complex dialectical work: to register and at the same time produce a language for a realignment of contemporary cultural alliances across race and class boundaries.

For "realignment," I draw on Stephen Shapiro, who derives it from Raymond Williams's notion of "alignment" as well as Antonio Gramsci's of "realignment" and Michael Denning's description of cultural politics in the 1930s to suggest that in the contemporary moment, "the formerly devalued medium of television" fuses "elements and groups" which serve as a new "cultural front" (2017, 154). "Realignment is the process through which one class disengages from its prior alliance [. . .] and attempts to join or create another" (2016, 181). Shapiro suggests that a variety of distinct but structurally similar groups highlight a "process of convergence at a time of crisis." He argues that different processes, positions, and relations—from the "identitarian multitudes," #BlackLivesMatter, LGBT rights activism to environmental concerns, worries about student debt and precarity and big data, to forms and medial opportunities from social networks to prestige TV, register and mobilize a "new coalition of the dispossessed." These "cultural statements," Shapiro argues, "combine to convey a language that is mutually resonant and enabling—be it of the affective heart or the desire to be an agent of change—for disparate groups" (155). Realignment here suggests for Shapiro the process by which the middle class becomes attuned to the dispossessed's concerns and increasingly comes to see itself as more usefully allied to what amounts to the contemporary working class, rather than its previous allies among the upper class.

We should understand the so-called literary novel as already bounded off by class, as constituting a spectrum of fiction geared towards everything from "lower-middle-class" to implicitly higher-but-still-middle-class readerships (see McGurl 2009 for an implicit argument on this point). The entire edifice of "the novel" is perhaps inescapably "middle class" (see Boulukos 2009)—and for sure, "the novel" as a marker of genre excludes genre fiction, which may be in novels but is never "the novel" (see also Lanzendörfer 2020). The novel may be late to the game of realignment—but as the epitomical genre of the middle class, we should not be surprised to see it registering, in much the same way as quality TV does, shifts in contemporary group alignments. *The Underground Railroad* registers a tentative attempt at realignment between a liberally minded middle class of readers that is, predominantly, white; a similar, but slightly broader readership that is not necessarily class based, but is ethnically Black—somewhat ham-fistedly, "Oprah's readership"—and a (at least theoretically) lower-class genre readership, all of which we may suppose to have little overlap in their usual reading habits. None of these readerships needs to exist empirically, and they do not, at any rate, have to be actually monolithic: what is key to me here is the way understanding *The Underground Railroad* as addressing itself to such readerships gives us a handle to understand why it does the things it does, and what this doing means. There is a congruence between this version of what literature's readerships look like and the categorizations which Mark McGurl sees at work in the writing programs. As McGurl notes, MFA programs reward heavily insisting on the poles of experience, creativity, and craft, but exclude genre fiction (with its own links to creativity as a matter of practice, but not a matter of recognition). We will see all of this at play and at stake in this section: the insistence on experience as authorizing writing about Black life and history, the assumption that craft and creativity signal literariness, and the role of genre.

The Underground Railroad and by extension *Underground Airlines* are bound up in the larger question of narratives about, or perhaps for, the "Black experience." I use these scare quotes here because the prospect of talking about the Black experience is, well, scary, not just because I am not Black myself, but because the term, in all its volatility, appears to grasp something necessary about contemporary African American fiction. If experience authorizes the writing of history, something similar is at work in the way the public reaction to *Underground Airlines* centers on the writer's ethnic identity and the question of what the act of writing about slavery means when a white man does it. In June 2016, the *New York Times* reviewed Winters's then-forthcoming book. The review, after briefly summarizing the novel's plot, quickly turns to the question of what writing about "racial injustice" means when done by a white man: "creatively and professionally risky," as the *Times* averred. It quoted Winters as saying, "We tend to think of racism and slavery as something that's appropriate only for black artists to engage with, and there's something troubling and perverse about that" (Alter 2016). Two other lines drew the biggest public backlash: a quote from *Time*'s literary critic Lev Grossman ("This is a white writer going after questions of what it's like to be black in America. It's a fearless thing to do"), and Winters's own acknowledgement that what drew him to the project was the murder of Trayvon Martin, the Black teenager shot by a white Floridian under the state's stand-your-ground laws. Criticism of both of these stances was swift online: Winters was accused of "gross exploitation" of the Martin case, and the *New York Times* was taken to task for its apparent belief that writing a Black voice was a fearless thing to do for a white man—or would in any way impinge on his career.

At the heart of the debate over Winters's book was not skin color, but the ability to empathize, if not relate immediately to the topic at hand by virtue of one's personal life story. Or, as Gavia Baker-Whitelaw has it, the problem of a white man writing about "topics others have already covered with more personal expertise" (2016). I take no stance, especially as a white male German academic, in this debate. But we can think about the difficulties of the assumptions made in this debate. "Personal expertise" here cannot mean that writing about slavery requires the experience of slavery. What it means is that writing about slavery is always already linked to the contemporary experience of Black lives in the United States, and that these lives cannot merely be "understood," but are "defined by the particularities of our lives and our lifeworlds" without "larger truths" (Löffler 2015, 65) that would be accessible to just anybody. There is little ground for disputing the notion that you cannot know what it is like to be Black in the United States unless you are Black in the United States. (The reach of "personal expertise" has a limit, however, that is revealed by *The Underground*

Railroad where a Black *man* writes a Black *woman* protagonist, including a scene in which she is raped, without so much as anyone—that I could find—batting an eyelid.) The point seems to be less that experience is required as much as that experience is made—that writing about slavery is the making of the experience of slavery in any post slavery society, given that any experience of slavery must be in a distantly mediated form. In this light, the backlash against *Underground Airlines* becomes clearer: it is not just the exploitation and appropriation of Black life that Winters is charged with, but the creation of a particular version of Black life, ways of seeing the world, in other words, an offer to readers which they may subscribe to, and thereby an attempt to forge alliances. These actions are deeply political very much in the Rancièrian sense, in that they aim to make visible certain things about the world, but they also highlight their conditionality: nobody can be forced to see.

I do not mean to take a stance towards the normative question of whether Winters "should" have written, or "could possibly" have written, meaningfully about a Black life, or Whitehead about a woman: these are, I think, the wrong questions to ask about these novels. What we can see is the way literary production and reception are marked by systems that easily elude the "mere" reader, but which we can trace through an attention to the novels' position in the literary field. Whether you and I acknowledge the work of forging new alliances or deny it on ethnic, generic, or institutional grounds is neither here nor there—it is the larger context of reception which reveals a text's success in this regard. But it is important to recognize that such inhabited positions are also positionings: that is to say, they can be produced—and if they are a consequence of the formal and narrative choices of novels, as they must be, those choices are meaningful, ways of placing a novel in a crowded field. We need to unravel the question of *The Underground Railroad*'s position, the meaning of what we know about its position. This position is marked by the novel's astounding critical and public success: winning both the Pulitzer Prize and the National Book Award, being chosen for Oprah Winfrey's Book Club 2.0, and most importantly, winning the Arthur C. Clarke Award for Science Fiction. We explain this perfect storm, this congruence between the ostensibly high-literary and mostly middle-brow, literary and genre fiction, between Pulitzer, Oprah, and Arthur C. Clarke, best by understanding it as a recognition of *The Underground Railroad*'s success in triangulating a cross-class, cross-ethnic readership, a success very much due to its narrative and formal choices.

These awards and recognitions mark, among other things, different "elements and groups," which is to say "readerships." The reason why no previous novel has won all of these awards is that their value judgments are, in fact, widely disparate; perhaps no novel *should* win all of them. Much recent work has sought to illuminate the way the literary marketplace works, from James English's notion of the "economy of prestige" (2005) to work by Günter Leypoldt on the literary market more broadly. What these scholars share is, in Leypoldt's terms, the belief that "the contemporary cultural marketplace allows sacralized and everyday economies to coexist" (2016, 379). Not only is there room for "literary" and "genre" texts, for reading complex texts for edification and simple texts for entertainment, but the same "literary" texts may easily be received differently in different contexts—and be marketed as working like that. Leypoldt's most illuminating example is Toni Morrison. Morrison, too, is a Pulitzer Prize winner, an author of highly complex prose and formally challenging fiction. Yet she, too, became an Oprah Book Club selection, even though Oprah's readers found her difficult to read. This last bit is somewhat important: Oprah's readership, unlike the Pulitzer Prize committee, is not generally expected to value the specific kind of literary complexity which Morrison's high-cultural pluralist fiction (the term is McGurl's) routinely produces. This is not a judgment. There is no value-free way of prizing "complex" literary fiction over less complex fiction: complexity is a formal requirement for literary fiction (see also McGurl 2009). But it is to note that there are different regimes of readership, which emphasize, quite value-free, different modes of reading. Leypoldt has dubbed one of those "therapeutic" after Eva Illouz—"in which readerly wellness goes hand in hand with self-realization and moral growth" (2016, 383)—and we may perhaps call the other "literary"—suggesting the realization that there is a reading of literary fiction on its own terms, appreciative of what Leypoldt calls such fiction's "formal difficulty" and "poetic uncertainty" (2014, 74). In the case of Morrison, this challenge is perhaps best exemplified by the episode which Leypoldt also notes: faced with Oprah's selection of her seventh novel, *Paradise* (1997), a notoriously complex text, readers found themselves at a loss, so much so that Oprah moved her show to Morrison's Princeton classroom to get the Nobel Laureate's help in deciphering the novel. Oprah's selection of Morrison was not based on Morrison's high-literary credentials, but rather on her status as an icon of African American emancipation: on the belief that "her novels authentically express both the African American condition and a politics of black emancipation" (Leypoldt 2016, 382). We should note the echo of "experience" in the idea of authenticity. Morrison's writing is Oprah-worthy *despite* its formal resistance to therapeutic reading, and *because* of Morrison's status as an African American icon, but Oprah's readers will forever be excluded from the "real" meanings of Morrison's work in a way that the more literarily attuned Pulitzer Prize committee, and readers taking their cue from it, would not be.

Much of this merely seems to restate that it is possible for texts to exist in a number of relationships to their audiences, a reading in which *The Underground Railroad*'s many prizes merely affirm that this is a great novel in many registers. But there is a complex dimension to this, especially to me, given my arguments about utopianism, which is always also political. After all, it is not just personal uses of literature that literariness encodes. As Morrison herself argued, "the political power of literature unfolds precisely when the text resists conceptual clarity" (in Leypoldt 2016, 382). There is a clear parallel in the arguments about Oprah's readership and about pluralist historical fictions: in both cases, experience authorizes writing, whether as part of personalized lifeworlds or as history proper. In both cases, too, properly political modes of reading are evacuated of meaning: everything becomes personal, perhaps including the meaning of politics in the context of African American fiction. The notion of politics which Morrison uses is very much based on an experiential footing as well: it is an identitarian politics, rather than a structural one.

In this, Morrison appears to be in tune with other, similarly well-regarded observers. Ta-Nehisi Coates suggests that "[t]he tradition of black writing is necessarily dyspeptic, necessarily resistant" (2017, 11)—necessarily political, to link this more forcefully to Morrison. Coates renders Black life in terms which are very much reminiscent of "Oprah" reading. Diagnosing a "rage that lives in all African Americans, a collective feeling of disgrace that borders on self-hatred" (30), he turns to a quasi-political prescription, if in negative form: "Liberalism, with its pat logic and focus on structural incequities, offers no balm for this sort of raw pain" (31). In suggesting that Black writing is "necessarily resistant," the mere act of writing becomes elevated into a politics; in the notion that a "balm" for "pain" is preferable to the solution of "structural inequalities," Coates suggests, however, that such politics is always also fundamentally different from the peculiarly "liberal" politics of other writing. Coates thus lets me try to tie together all of these points. Tentatively, there is a particular logic to the idea of the political in African American fiction that does not immediately coincide with the idea of politics writ larger. The problem is that there is a non-coincidence between what Coates takes to be the politics of the wider liberal world—a politics which is also, I think, the politics of the wider literary world—and the politics of African American fiction. What I have read above as a problem of *The Underground Railroad*—that it reduces its politics to the individualized hope for Cora's better life in the future—is very much the kind of politics which is geared towards an African American, an Oprah, reading audience. It is to speak to African American audiences who hold literature's power of resistance up—understanding that resistance is the embodied politics in the vein of Morrison—but at the same time seek the affective responses, the "balm" that goes beyond the cold analysis of systemic inequities.

I have turned to the writing of Ta-Nehisi Coates not just because he echoes much of what we can also glean from Morrison, but also because of his position. A Pulitzer Prize winner himself, Coates is still the most audible African American voice in the contemporary literary sphere. Whether or not he may be fairly said to speak for African Americans generally, and realizing that he may or may not have any particularly privileged insight into African American life, people privilege his insight. *The Underground Railroad* affirmatively inscribes itself into a particular discourse, which understands all Black writing is "necessarily resistant," without the need for a particularized "literary" resistance through formal and stylistic complexity, and thus opens itself up to a wide audience. Whitehead's novel is, its critical success notwithstanding, not very "good," for literary versions of what "good" means. To bounce off of Morrison again: in the particular, concrete model of resistance to "conceptual clarity," *The Underground Railroad* offers very little: instead, it insists on being as concrete, and as clear, as it can possibly be—"deliberate and occasionally heavy-handed" (Dubey 2020, 111).

What does, in all that, the Arthur C. Clarke Award mean? It claims that *The Underground Railroad* is science fiction, is genre fiction. Genre, as John Frow has it, "indicates the formulaic and the conventional" (2009, 1). The Arthur C. Clarke Award appears at odds with the Pulitzer and the National Book Award, both of which suggest themselves as awards for a completely different kind of writing; but the remarkable thing about *The Underground Railroad* is that it is a deeply conventional novel. Conventional should be understood here very much in opposition to the formal difficulty and resistance which McGurl and Morrison identify as key to literary fiction, and by extension to the nature of its literary politics. The one thing "original" and "challenging" about *The Underground Railroad* is the way it is conventional in so many different registers, the way it insistently smooths out narrative difficulty, insists on closure and explanation (see also Dubey 2020). Recall the overt return of the metaphoric reading of the Underground Railroad offered by Lumbly. Or notice how characters also are consistently offered closure. Cora leaves South Carolina without Caesar, but we find out about his fate from Ridgeway and a point of view chapter. The North Carolina station master's wife, Ridgeway, and the doctor whom Cora speaks to in South Carolina also get such chapters. Egregiously, her mother Mabel's disappearance haunts both Cora and Ridgeway, for whom she is the only failure in his slave-catching record, as well as the reader—for 300 pages or so, until the novel tells us her fate in a point-of-view chapter. Mabel, it turns out, died a day out from the Randall plantation of a snake bite in the swamp.

All of this—more might be added—is challenging in so far as it has a problematic relationship to the notion of literariness as I have sketched it out above, and more specifically even to the idea that art's political power rests on its capacity to resist simplicity. Neither in metaphoricity, narrative drive, formally, nor stylistically does it seem fair to call *The Underground Railroad* resistant. But nothing about this impinges on its capacity to be political and hopeful: in fact, the novel's chief recognition is that it can rely on the idea that African American writing is per se resistant and political, in order to address itself to an audience which might otherwise be turned off, as Oprah's audience was by *Paradise*. Whitehead's discovery, we might say, is that Morrison is wrong: the political power of African American writing unfolds very much more strongly on the terms of Oprah's audience, and misses the point when it becomes, as *Paradise* was, undecipherable.

This argument must appear valuative itself, to suggest that *The Underground Railroad* is undeserving of its prizes. But the point is not that *The Underground Railroad* is a bad book but rather that it is formally not the "literary" novel of Morrison. And it recognizes that there are gains to be made by its removal of what appear to be unnecessary markers of literariness in the contemporary. The difference as I see it between Morrison's writing and Whitehead's is that Morrison's positioning as a writer capable of reception in both the everyday economy and readership of Oprah and the sacralized ones of prestige prizes and academic discourse is done *to* her—for reasons which are closely related to her position as icon, as Leypoldt avers—while Whitehead's is explicitly, formally, thematically, narratively, self-made. Whitehead's novel formally embeds itself in a "lower" register than Morrison's texts do. Furthermore, *The Underground Railroad* remains open to readerships less liable to insist on the need for experientiality, which is to say in this case, for white middle-class liberal audiences of the kind disparaged by Coates. *The Underground Railroad* seeks this mediation. This, I contend, is what the winning of so many different prizes and awards finally recognizes as successful: this actually is a book for readers with a broad range of political, social, ethnic, and class positions, all of whom are expressly addressed by aspects of the novel. The prizes which the novel has garnered, that is to say, are one way of judging its success at triangulating the realignment it identifies as necessary, but which, following Stephen Shapiro's argument, may also be increasingly relevant as a fact of contemporary social relations. Barack Obama's cover blurb quote for *The Underground Railroad* sounds blithe: "Terrific." But Barack Obama functions in a variety of roles here, not the least of which is a negative one: he is not a literary gatekeeper, as Toni Morrison would be. He is an African American idol without the baggage of a particular literary style; he is a liberal, without offending the Coatesian dichotomy between lived Black life and the structural prescriptions of liberalism as such; and through this duality of positions, his anemic, contentless "Terrific" becomes as openly readable as the book itself.

The answer to the question I slipped in a while ago then, why we are seeing the books we are seeing, is crucially doubled. On the one hand, if we take it to ask why the books that are being written are being written, we may take our cue from the discussion of *Underground Airlines* and note that they respond to socioculturally urgent questions, inscribe themselves into contemporary discourses and seek to intervene in them: they are meant politically. On the other hand, we may take this question to address itself to their specific form, and here the answer is that genre serves dialectically as a marker of changed class and ethnic literary alliances and the means to fabricate them. On the third hand (bear with me), we may take the question to ask more literally why we are *seeing* them, why they are prominent in the literary field, and this question is best answered by suggesting that the confluence of specific themes and concrete form are apparently sufficient to generate, at least in the specific instance of *The Underground Railroad*, an ideal text, capable of reaching a wide range of different audiences. Finally, on the fourth hand (these conclusions require two people to hold), the notion that we are "seeing" these various things happen brings us back, for a final time, to Rancière, and allows me to propose that it is *The Underground Railroad*'s very visibility that suggests a genuine political potential for speculative historism as a form, not because the novel is the best example of what the form can do, but because it has managed to bring the form into the limelight. None of these points ultimately could be made without recurring to the question of where in the literary field *Underground Airlines* and *The Underground Railroad* are situated—only now can we fairly adjudicate the work that these texts do. I have clearly privileged the vision which *Underground Airlines* has, as far as its speculative historism and its capacity to express hopeful futures are concerned. But we cannot miss the fact that the precise way in which it offers a far more sustainedly useful critique of existing socioeconomic conditions, via an alternative history of slavery, is severely bounded by its formal constitution, its "pat logic," to pick up Coates's criticism. Literature need not mobilize alliances for change, to be sure. But *Underground Airlines* does not even register the chance for a realignment, suggesting instead, certainly to a number of Black observers and commentators, the elevation of a class discourse over the need to know something about the Black experience in the contemporary United States. Such a vision does not fully register the way in which the contemporary moment appears capable of shifting the boundaries between discourses of class and race, readily encompassing both to shape new alliances. *The Underground Railroad*, by contrast, manages precisely this: it carefully, and cautiously, triangulates a narrative in which formally as well as thematically, new alliances between readerships ostensibly separated by class and race become possible. Prizes recognize the success of this endeavor. Far more than just capable of registering different social lives of novels—parallel lives without real meaning—they offer us a glimpse at the very deepest meanings of *The Underground Railroad*, suggesting in no uncertain terms the success of its formal and thematic triangulations.

Conclusion: Speculation, Race, and the Future of Fiction

This chapter has attempted to sketch the way speculative historism works in two texts explicitly marked as intervening in a racial and ethnic discourse, two texts which require analysis in different ways and come to be differently readable as hopeful and utopian, and whose versions of speculative historism are signally different. These two novels indicate the breadth of the reach of the speculative historist form. Their visions of future life are unformed, and their chief aim is to mediate better forms of life for African Americans. In this, they are different both from the set of novels I began with, all of which understand utopia to manifest in (different versions of) economic and political terms, or in concrete programs such as Socialism. Neither *The Underground Railroad* nor *Underground Airlines* thus follows exactly in the mold of previous texts. Nor, like *Wao*, do they necessarily take the global, or at least hemispheric view. Unlike *Wao*'s ethnically marked, but ultimately insistently holistic view of history's capacity to inform hopeful futures, both novels take a more limited view of things, a more restrictive utopianism.

I end on a contrasting reading of a novel that has achieved the greatest possible success in the literary sphere, a novel that, while not as banally generic as *Ready Player One* or *Taft 2012*, nonetheless offers an instructive counterpoint to *The Underground Railroad* in form, reception, and utopian idea. This novel is Whitehead's previous novel, *Zone One*. *Zone One* is a far "better" book, in terms of its literary registers, more complex, less willing to explain, abjuring closure in favor of an open-ended commitment to questioning the all-encompassing power of contemporary consumer capitalism. *Zone One* is precise at diagnosing the contemporary's class and race problems, and makes its diagnosis into "better" literature; *The Underground Railroad* is more successful in forging a necessary cross-class, cross-ethnic literary alliance. We need to be careful about claiming that such a literary effect has any social effects, but the point here is not, anyway, that *The Underground Railroad* necessarily stands at the beginning of a future races-bridging literary class alliance, but rather that it registers the wider need for such an alliance. It offers a purely literary suggestion of how to build one by insisting on the complementarity of literary traditions such as the neo-slave narrative and the draw of genre fiction.

Yet even such a slightly tentative argument has some strong corollaries, the most radical of which, in terms of literary studies, may be that writing such as Toni Morrison's is going the way of the dodo. That is not to say, of course, that Morrison will not be read; rather, it is to say that the kind of writing which was successful and presumably efficacious in the immediate past will cease to be as prominent as it has been. Morrison's writing, which is still as formally resistant and complex as it has ever been, does not register the kinds of tidal shifts in the constitution of readerships, and more especially their willingness to be addressed by different registers of fiction, that Whitehead's *The Underground Railroad* does. But neither does *Zone One*, which did not win any prizes whatsoever. It is blunt to suggest that it did not do so specifically because it did not triangulate its position between the kinds of affective and experiential narratives of African American life, a liberal-structural consciousness of the conditions for such life, and the broader base of readers offered by genre fiction—by speculative fiction. *Zone One* is not in fact deeply concerned with race as experience, but rather with race as an issue irredeemably tied to the violence of capitalism (see Lanzendörfer 2018). It almost willfully denies its own readability in terms of experientiality, refuses closure, and resists the easier solaces of genre fiction. It resists adoption as genre fiction—no Arthur C. Clarke Award for it, in other words, since it is too fully reliant on "literary" registers. The immediate difference between *Zone One* and *The Underground Railroad*, in all of these dimensions, but also between *The Underground Railroad* and Whitehead's previous novels, notably perhaps *Apex Hides the Hurt* (2006) and *The Intuitionist* (1999) with regard to these texts' visions of what the "Black experience" is, suggests the way Whitehead himself manipulates the positioning of his fiction. It demonstrates how the shift to genre fiction alone does not serve to produce fiction that is as broadly received as *The Underground Railroad*. Given that part of my argument has been that genre serves to mobilize history in the contemporary, this appears a crucial point, not for the matter of form as such, which is largely unperturbed by the question of reception, but for the question of the efficaciousness of the form, which we can now finally broach.

Part of this, I think, depends on the way form and genre interact in *Zone One*, compared with *The Underground Railroad*. *Zone One*'s generic referent is the zombie novel, but the zombie novel is not a genre that either aspires to or is generally thought to have literariness. At the same time, *Zone One* depends at every moment on readers' knowledge of the actual history of zombie fiction to be fully grasped. That knowledge is only in part culturally dissipated. It is a frame of reference which is not available to many readers of Whitehead. It militates against reception in the context of a broadly popular, but generically cautious reading group such as Oprah's, but also that of the Pulitzer Prize or National Book Award. Conversely, Whitehead's intensely literary style and thematic distance from the standard of zombie fictions makes the novel difficult to place in the context of genre fiction's own prestige economies. *Zone One*'s powerful analysis of contemporary race relations, therefore, does not win awards. It does not mobilize a sufficiently broad coalition *or* a sufficiently narrow one to do so.

I stole my phrasing of a sentence just now from Lee Konstantinou, who has argued that *The Underground Railroad* "depends at every moment on the reader's knowledge of the actual history of the Underground Railroad" (2017, 18). Given my belief that the actualization of the metaphor of *The Underground Railroad* is a somewhat pointless gimmick, I obviously disagree. It strikes me that while *Zone One* genuinely requires a background in zombie fiction, *The Underground Railroad* explicitly requires a background in nothing—largely because its one assumption about readerly knowledge, the fact that the actual Underground Railroad was not an underground railroad, has no narrative consequences. We should more properly suggest that *The Underground Railroad* offers a different mode of reading to readers who have knowledge of its literary precursors, knowledge which makes it possible to read ironically much of what it does narratively, but that it insists on absolutely no preconditions for reading it. If it mobilizes an informed readership through the possibility of irony, fair enough—but this is only one, crucially not the only, way of reading it. *The Underground Railroad*'s very point, the chief feature of its triangulation, is that it can be read without precondition, providing the necessities of interpretation to its various audiences. Any precondition would serve to vitiate its quest for a broad readership.

I have called *The Underground Railroad* the key novel of the contemporary, and I want to reiterate this claim. The work that it does appears crucially invigorating. What occurs in the formal move to genre can also be called, after all, a democratization. When *The Underground Railroad* reduces its interpretive openness by relentless closure, limits its meanings, it also makes those meanings that remain more widely available. The political power of its happy ending lies in its capacity to unite the different reading modes the novel calls upon, and it manages to successfully hold them together with a message of hope: almost as if to say that whichever way you read *The Underground Railroad*, you will get to the same, hopeful place. Nothing reveals the importance of speculative historism more than *The Underground Railroad*'s successful mediation of it: the novel reveals the way in which the move to genre in speculative historism is capable of doing actual work, work which is unavailable to texts which stay true to an inherited literary form whose time may be getting to be past.

Conclusion

Speculative Historism and Contemporary Hope

This book champions utopian hermeneutics, a way of reading for utopia in an age where utopian thinking is necessary. This is also an age of literary criticism where we find ourselves over and over engaged with disputes about modes of reading. I offer utopian hermeneutics not as the ultimate critical intervention, the reading mode to end all reading modes, but rather as itself a hopeful possibility, the possibility that through reading for hope, we may more easily encounter hope, we may more easily become hopeful ourselves.

I also argued that we encounter such hope specifically in a new mode of literary engagement, speculative historism. My largest claim in the preceding chapter has been that *The Underground Railroad*'s success shows the overall importance of speculative historism as such a mode in the contemporary. In suggesting that the novel is the key novel of the contemporary moment, I also suggested that speculative historism is the key mode, perhaps the key genre, of that moment, the best to describe how we relate to the past and the future. As Theodore Martin has recently argued, the "historical drag of genre," the questions of "what changes in a genre over time, and what stays the same" (2016, 2), appears to correlate strongly with our notion of the contemporary. Martin reads the contemporary as a "*strategy of mediation*":

> The contemporary compels us to think, above all, about the politics of how we think about the present. The contours and currents of our current moment—its temporal boundaries, its historical significance, its deeper social logics—are inseparable from the historically determined and politically motivated ways we choose to divide the present from the past. (5, original emphasis)

Speculative historism constructs a particular version of the contemporary, a version which insists that this moment is different from that moment only a few years past when history and utopia were at an end, a moment no longer postmodern; a moment in which it is important to relate to history in a particular way, a new way of dividing, in Martin's words, the "present from the past," exactly by insisting on their connection. The fuzzy moment of the emergence of speculative historism is also the moment of the emergence of the contemporary. I say fuzzy here because I do not think we can easily name a sharply delineated before and after. My texts range from about 2006 to 2016, short enough a time in the first place, but 2006 did not inaugurate either speculative historism or the "contemporary." Rather, we can see one contemporary as marked by the emergence of speculative historism, as not bounded off except in the fuzzy growth of the form's corpus, and perhaps signaled as fully arriving only in the critical achievement of *The Underground Railroad*. We would be in a new contemporary now, a contemporary markedly different from eras before, but impossible to cleanly delineate.

The contemporary of speculative historism obtains its purchase as the contemporary specifically through refusing to identify itself as meaningfully separate from the past. For speculative historism, the idea of pursuing a place outside of history is anathema. But it is not just a different version of historical fiction. In its insistence on invoking genre fiction, speculative historism also draws on an inherent historicity: genres, as Martin points out, "lead distinctly double lives, with one foot in the past and the other in the present" (6). Martin considers a range of genres in his argument, from noir to the western; for the texts I have discussed here, genre means speculative genres from fantasy to science fiction and horror. The consequence for my modification of Martin's argument is that these genres automatically insist on understanding any relationship with history as already more than "just" the question of what "differentiates the present from the past as well as what ties the two together" (7). Speculative fiction of any kind is always interested in the wider relationships between past, present, and possible futures. The genre work which speculative historism does in the contemporary then is to situate the contemporary historically into the future, to tie together all three dimensions, the past, the present, and the possible, through the complex relation between the very historicity of genre itself and the particular historical narratives which the texts unfold.

The most grandiose claim would be to proclaim speculative historism the beginning of a new "artistic configuration, a series of works that constitute the procedure of truth typical of the field" (Lecercle 2010, 174): to suggest that speculative historism is itself evental. Such a claim is as yet impossible to make, but it echoes my argument from Whitehead's *The Underground Railroad*. For what is the creation of a new, shared audience of readers under a single, somewhat narrower but still ultimately political claim—the utopian ideal of better futures in a more (racially) just society—than the process of creating new subjects, subjects willing to understand themselves as bound to the realization of this idea? As Slavoj Žižek notes, "the rise of a new art form is an event" (2014a, 3); and perhaps the idea of the "art form" can be a compromise between the different terms I have been flinging about, somewhat recklessly: genre, mode, form. Speculative historism is not already an event—not least because events are always retrospective. But to read speculative historism as an "evental genre" (Wegner 2011, xvii) with the possibility to become an event, appears to be not wholly far-fetched at all. As Phillip Wegner points out, science fiction has already become an event in certain moments (52). I would want to bring attention to these moments, since they suggest the way the idea of the event in literature may be fruitfully drawn on. We do not do undue violence to the heart of Badiou's philosophy when we decide that for our purposes, it offers useful avenues to describe the crucial role of genre shifts in the perception of possible futures. Perhaps the key difference from what Wegner identifies for science fiction is the two genres' relation to the events that constitute them narratively, namely, that "events do not occur" in science fiction, and that "the reader is offered the blocking out of an event and the narration of its consequences on subject(s) and the world at large" (52). In Ursula K. LeGuin's *The Dispossessed*, the revolution that produced Anarres is already past, and what the novel is concerned with is precisely its consequences. In the fictions which I have discussed, that does not hold true as much: their relationship to events is more complicated, invoking narrative occurrences as metaphors for historical events. Thus, we find in *The Accursed* that the Crosswicks Curse stands as both an actual event in the text proper as well as a metaphorization of a greater Event, which is the turn of the twentieth century's Socialist movement. Like the quasi-event in *Equilateral*, like the insistence in *U.S.!* on the importance of holding on to the Socialist idea which Upton Sinclair represents, here the Event is both in and of the novel.

Wegner recognizes that his choice of texts is by no means simply necessary: science fiction and speculative historism may be evental genres, but not all texts are equally as effective at producing narratives of Events. The choice of texts we undertake—the choice of texts that I have undertaken here—"is a political decision, a throwing of the dice on the wager that in reading this way we might begin to identify some of the texts [. . .] that might be most useful in helping us to think" (2011, 52). Any study which insists on the need to closely read its texts must necessarily be selective, and must necessarily, in being selective, have principles for selection. Wegner's are as good as any; I have used the metaphor of the parabolic arc to describe my selection. Being selective also entails, however, there being something to select from, and in this case, this involves something about the validity of understanding speculative historism as a form beyond the few texts discussed herein. I have already noted one text, Michael Chabon's *The Yiddish Policemen's Union* (2007). Other books which work similarly would be Lydia Millet's *Oh Pure and Radiant Heart* (2005), Austin Grossman's *Crooked* (2015), Nathan Hill's *The Nix* (2016), Matt Ruff's *Lovecraft Country* (2016), George Saunders's *Lincoln in the Bardo* (2017), or Silvia Moreno-Garcia's *Mexican Gothic* (2020). These examples serve to highlight the expansive nature of speculative historism, encompassing both established literary fiction writers like Millet and up-and-coming talent like Hill as well as genre mainstays such as Moreno-Garcia or Ruff and less well-known writers such as Grossman.

Speculative historism explicitly redraws the lines between genres. The amalgamated form of literary–genre fiction that is speculative historism draws upon the resources of speculative fiction for very clear political goals; whatever else it is, the entire effort is also a politicization of literary fiction. It points us to the vagaries of generic designations as such, something few of the texts in this study illustrate as well as does Joyce Carol Oates's *The Accursed*. Oates already appears liminally literary as a writer. Extremely prolific, her texts have always straddled the boundaries. As Mark McGurl has noted, Oates's writing "presents no neat separation between genre fiction, middle-brow fiction, and high literary fiction" (2009, 323). For Oates, this gambit has been (critically) unsuccessful, though of course Oates is a successful writer: her writing, while not derided, has also not found itself in the same consecrated spaces that would have been open to a writer less enamored of genre writing. In Günter Leypoldt's words—not meant for Oates, but applicable—"[w]riters who live too close to the genre-fiction badlands remain largely invisible to the sphere of literary prestige" (2018). Read from the position of speculative historism, however, her writing can in some ways be understood as being just a little ahead of its time. This, after all, is what might be readable into the fact that *The Accursed* was initially drafted in the 1980s, but now, published thirty years on, is suddenly locatable among a number of texts which do not just do the same thing, but are increasingly, publicly, successful for doing so. *The Underground Railroad*, in this sense, retroactively uplifts Oates's previous work, just as it appears to point out the possible futures of the mode.

I think this, too, is the basis on which to rewrite, for the moment, Leypoldt's suggestion that the "literary turn to genre" is going to face "ageing effects in the very near future." He argues that "the gentrification of grit [i.e., in this case, genre fiction] happens only when the appropriation of stigmatized materials appeals to central consecrating institutions" (2018)—such as the Pulitzer Prize committee, as perhaps in the case of Junot Díaz. But at the same time, consecrating institutions are only sometimes consecrating institutions for literary fiction. In the case of Whitehead's *The Underground Railroad*, what initially begged explanation was not the literary consecration of genre by the Pulitzer Prize committee, but rather the genre consecration of an indifferently generic novel by the Arthur C. Clarke Award. In this regard, the opposition between a (literary) avant-garde and a (non-literary) "grit" capable of supplying temporarily necessary refreshment to the literary field misses the larger context in which these texts operate. It also strikes me that even if we grant the argument that there is a finite amount of time in which a literary avant-garde draws upon any source of revitalization before it moves on, this has little impact on the question of whether genre is going to stay relevant to literary fiction, only on whether the genre turn will continue to be the mode by which literary fiction renews itself. Almost tautologically, it will not. But what will find renewal in the future, from some other source, will be that literary fiction which is already genre-amalgamated. The avant-garde might move on, but genre and literary fiction may well continue their alliance: Literature, after all, is a way to register sociopolitical and socioeconomic realities, and speculative historism is perhaps the strongest contemporary mode at doing that, registering the way in which there is a renewed sense of the possibility of a different future. Wegner notes that one of the things which LeGuin's narratives insist on is that once an "event—a new word, a new deed—has been introduced, it remains irrevocably part of our world" (2011, 59). Speculative historism appears to me to be here to stay, at least until the conditions for its arising dissipate.

Any book which insists on the act of reading already has a subtle utopian impulse of its own. It insists that reading can change, if not the world, then something about how we relate to the world—how we see it. I have been stressing that this is the point of utopian hermeneutics: to both look for the utopian impulses of and in texts, and to be itself utopian. As Jacques Rancière has it, "interpretations are themselves real changes, when they transform the forms of visibility a common world may take" (2011, 30). For what this study has done, this has two points of purchase. First, the interpretations of history which the novels I have discussed offer are themselves real changes to the way we perceive the common world. Second, my interpretations of these texts are real changes, giving clearer voice to the utopian imaginations of these texts and placing them firmly in a moment in which such utopian imaginations are both ever more needful and finally possible again. Indeed, as Ramón Saldívar points out, "[w]hether fantasy can effect political change or not is ultimately beside the point" (2011, 595): what matters is, to speak one final time with a nod to Badiou, that it remains faithful to the ideas which animate a desire for a better, more hopeful, world. The central importance of speculative historism as a form lies in its capacity both to return emancipatory power to history and to offer to the present the hopeful future that the idea of emancipation entails.

"With a political event, a possibility emerges that escapes the prevailing power's control over possibles" (Badiou 2013a, 11). I want to suggest that literary events are equally as open, and if they do not produce immediately tangible results in power relations, at least they manufacture glimpses of real-world possibilities. Literature can *become* event, and literature may prepare us for the kinds of real-world Events that genuinely shift the political realities. "Being prepared for an event consists in being in a state of mind where one is aware that the order of the world or the prevailing powers don't have absolute control of the possibilities" (13); Badiou comes relatively close here to Ernst Bloch's *Hoffnung*, which is as much a lived reality as a way of reading the world. And having made this connection, we may perhaps also with Bloch reframe the notion of the "end" as such, from where we started. As Ze'ev Levy points out, Bloch wished to "describe the history of the world, or more exactly, human history, as a totality that ought to be conceived and explicated by its end." End, here, however, does not mean a conclusion, but rather the opposite: the purpose, and the opening of unlimited "new possibilities" (1990, 4). The fictions I have discussed above turn away from the end of history to the *end* of history. They raise the question of the work that writing (any kind) of historical fiction does, to which goal history is both striving and being mobilized. Such a reading of the end of history allows us to see speculative historism as both a minor shift in emphasis in contemporary historical fiction as well as a grand change: a minor shift, formally perhaps, from the metafictional historical writing of postmodernism, but a giant leap away from its apolitical pastiches.

Genly Ai, the Ekumen envoy to the Gethenians in Ursula K. LeGuin's *The Left Hand of Darkness* (1969), begins his narrative with an observation on the nature of capital-T Truth, and I will end by stealing it for my purposes: "Truth is a matter of the imagination" (1); so is history; so is the future. The novels I have been talking about here argue that it takes imagination, it takes fantasy to arrive at truths. Realism does not produce truths, such an argument would go, realism reproduces what is taken for truth. There is no truth other than what you can imagine, and a limiting of one's imagination is also a limiting of what truth can be seen. Speculative historism does this work. It asks us to open our imaginations to alternative versions of history: this is the purchase of its speculative side. And speculative historism asks us to take our contemporary moment seriously historically, and to understand us as subjects to events long past with purchase on our shared futures.

Bibliography

Primary Sources

Auslander, Shalom (2012). *Hope: A Tragedy*. London: Picador.
Bachelder, Chris (2006). *U.S.!* London: Bloomsbury.
Cline, Ernest (2011). *Ready Player One*. London: Arrow.
Díaz, Junot (2007). *The Brief Wondrous Life of Oscar Wao*. New York: Riverhead.
Heller, Jason (2012). *Taft 2012*. Philadelphia: Quirk.
Kalfus, Ken (2013). *Equilateral. A Novel*. New York: Bloomsbury.
Oates, Joyce Carol (2013). *The Accursed*. New York: Ecco.
Whitehead, Colson (2016). *The Underground Railroad*. New York: Doubleday.
Winters, Ben H. (2016). *Underground Airlines*. New York: Mulholland.

Secondary Sources

Alexander, Jeffrey (2009). "'Globalization' as Collective Representation: The New Dream of a Cosmopolitan Civil Sphere." *Globalization and Utopia: Critical Essays*. Ed. Patrick Hayden and Chamsy el-Ojeili. London and New York: Palgrave Macmillan. 28–39.
Alter, Alexandra (2016). "In His New Novel, Ben Winters Dares to Mix Slavery and Sci-Fi." *The New York Times*, July 4. Web.
Anderson, Amanda, Rita Felski, and Toril Moi (2019). *Character: Three Inquiries in Literary Studies*. Chicago: University of Chicago Press.
Anker, Elizabeth S. and Rita Felski, eds. (2017). *Critique and Postcritique*. Durham: Duke University Press.
Appadurai, Arjun (1996). *Modernity at Large: Cultural Dimensions of Globalization*. Minneapolis: University of Minnesota Press.
Appiah, Kwame A. (2006). *Cosmopolitanism: Ethics in a World of Strangers*. New York: W.W. Norton.
Apter, Emily, and Bruno Bosteels (2014). "Introduction." Alain Badiou. *The Age of the Poets: And Other Writings on Twentieth-Century Poetry*

and Prose. Ed. and transl. Bruno Bosteels. Intro. Emily Apter and Bruno Bosteels. London: Verso. viii–xxxv.

Ashcroft, Bill (2016). *Utopianism in Postcolonial Literatures*. London and New York: Routledge.

Auerbach, Erich (1953). *Mimesis: The Representation of Reality in Western Literature*. Transl. Willard R. Trask. Princeton: Princeton University Press.

Badiou, Alain (2014). *The Age of the Poets: And Other Writings on Twentieth-Century Poetry and Prose*. Ed. and transl. Bruno Bosteels. Intro. Emily Apter and Bruno Bosteels. London: Verso.

—— (2013a). *Philosophy and the Event*. With Fabien Tarby. Transl. Louise Burchill. Cambridge: Polity Press.

—— (2013b). *Plato's Republic: A Dialogue in 16 Chapters*. Transl. Susan Spitzer. New York: Columbia University Press.

—— (2012). *The Rebirth of History: Times of Riots and Uprisings*. Transl. Gregory Eliot. London: Verso.

—— (2005). *Handbook of Inaesthetics*. Transl. Alberto Toscano. Stanford: Stanford University Press.

Baker-Whitelaw, Gavia (2016). "Controversy is Brewing around *Underground Airlines*, a New Novel that Mixes Slavery and Sci-Fi." Dailydot.com. Web.

Baptist, Edward E. (2016). *The Half Has Never Been Told: Slavery and the Making of American Capitalism*. New York: Basic Books.

Baudrillard, Jean (1994). *Simulacra and Simulation*. Ann Arbor: University of Michigan Press.

Baugh, Edward (2006). *Derek Walcott*. Cambridge: Cambridge University Press.

Bauman, Zygmunt (2017). *Retrotopia*. Cambridge: Polity Press.

Bautista, Daniel (2010). "Comic Book Realism: Form and Genre in Junot Díaz's 'The Brief Wondrous Life of Oscar Wao.'" *Journal of the Fantastic in the Arts* 21 (1), 41–53.

Bell, Bernard (1989). *The Afro-American Novel and Its Tradition*. Boston: University of Massachusetts Press.

Best, Stephen, and Sharon Marcus (2009). "Surface Reading: An Introduction." *Representations* 108, 1–21.

Beville, Maria (2009). *Gothic-Postmodernism: Voicing the Terrors of Postmodernity*. Amsterdam and New York: Rodopi.

Bhabha, Homi (1990). *Nation and Narration*. London: Routledge.

Bieger, Laura, Ramón Saldívar, and Johannes Völz (2013). "The Imaginary and Its Worlds: An Introduction." *The Imaginary and Its Worlds: American Studies after the Transnational Turn*. Ed. Laura Bieger, Ramón Saldívar, and Johannes Völz. Hanover: Dartmouth College Press. vii–xxviii.

Bloch, Ernst (1995). *The Principle of Hope*. 3 vols. Transl. Neville Plaice, Stephen Plaice, and Paul Knight. Cambridge: MIT Press.

—— (1988). *The Utopian Function of Art and Literature: Selected Essays*. Transl. Jack Zipes and Frank Mecklenburg. Cambridge: MIT Press.

Bonnett, Alastair (2015). *The Geography of Nostalgia: Global and Local Perspectives on Modernity and Loss*. London: Routledge.

Bordewich, Fergus M. (2005). *Bound for Canaan: The Epic Story of the Underground Railroad, America's First Civil Rights Movement*. New York: HarperCollins.

Bould, Mark, and Rone Shavers, eds. (2007). *Afrofuturism*. Special Issue of *Science Fiction Studies* 34 (2).

Boulukos, George (2009). "How the Novel Became Middle-Class: A History of Histories of the Novel." *Novel* 42 (2), 245–52.

Bowers, Maggie Ann (2004). *Magic(al) Realism*. New York: Routledge.

Boxall, Peter (2013). *Twenty-First Century Fiction: A Critical Introduction*. New York: Cambridge University Press.

Boym, Svetlana (2001). *The Future of Nostalgia*. New York: Basic Books.

Breisach, Ernst (2003). *On the Future of History: The Postmodernist Challenge and Its Aftermath*. Chicago: University of Chicago Press.

Brooks, Neil, and Josh Toth, eds. (2007). *The Mourning After: Attending the Wake of Postmodernism*. Amsterdam and New York: Rodopi.

Brown, Nicholas (2019). *Autonomy: The Social Ontology of Art under Capitalism*. Durham: Duke University Press.

—— (2013). "Close Reading and the Market." *Literary Materialisms*. Ed. Mathias Nilges and Emilio Sauri. Basingstoke: Palgrave Macmillan. 145–68.

—— (2005). *Utopian Generations: The Political Horizon of Twentieth-Century Literature*. Princeton: Princeton University Press.

Carpentier, Alejo (1975). "The Baroque and the Marvelous Real." *Magical Realism: Theory, History, Community*. Ed. Lois Parkinson Zamora and Wendy B. Faris. Durham and New York: Duke University Press. 89–108.

—— (1949). "On the Marvelous Real in America." *Magical Realism: Theory, History, Community*. Ed. Lois Parkinson Zamora and Wendy B. Faris. Durham and New York: Duke University Press. 75–88.

Carroll, Hamilton, and Annie McClanahan, eds. (2015). *Fictions of Speculation*. Special Issue of *Journal of American Studies* 49 (4).

Coates, Ta-Nehisi (2017). *We Were Eight Years in Power: An American Tragedy*. New York: One World.

—— (2015). *Between the World and Me*. New York: Spiegel and Grau.

Cohen, Samuel (2012). "Fables of American Collectivity Circa 2005: Chris Bachelder's *U.S.!*, Lydia Millet's *Oh Pure and Radiant Heart*, and George Saunders's *The Brief and Frightening Reign of Phil*." *Conceptions of Collectivity in Contemporary American Literature*. Ed. Clemens Spahr and Philipp Löffler. Special Issue of *Amerikastudien/American Studies* 57 (2), 207–20.

—— (2009). *After the End of History: U.S. Fiction in the 1990s*. Iowa City: University of Iowa Press.

Cologne-Brookes, Gavin (2014). "The Strange Case of Joyce Carol Oates." *A Companion to American Gothic*. Ed. Charles L. Crow. Malden and Oxford: Wiley Blackwell. 303–14.

—— (2005). *Dark Eyes on America: The Novels of Joyce Carol Oates.* Baton Rouge: Louisiana State University Press.

Condis, Megan Amber (2016). "Playing the Game of Literature: *Ready Player One*, the Ludic Novel, and the Geeky 'Canon' of White Masculinity." *Journal of Modern Literature* 39 (2), 1–19.

Cooper, John Milton (2009). *Woodrow Wilson: A Biography*. New York: Vintage.

Cooper, L. Andrew (2010). *Gothic Realities: The Impact of Horror Fiction on Modern Culture*. Jefferson, NC: McFarland

Creighton, Joanne V. (1992). *Joyce Carol Oates: Novels of the Middle Years*. New York: Twayne Publishers.

Daly, Brenda (1996). *Lavish Self-Divisions: The Novels of Joyce Carol Oates*. Jackson: University Press of Mississippi.

Dath, Dietmar, and Barbara Kirchner (2012). *Der Implex. Sozialer Fortschritt: Geschichte und Idee*. Frankfurt: Suhrkamp.

del Pilar Blanco, María (2013). "Reading the Novum World: The Literary Geography of Science Fiction in Junot Díaz's *The Brief Wondrous Life of Oscar Wao*." *Surveying the American Tropics: A Literary Geography from New York to Rio*. Ed. Maria Cristina Fumagalli, Peter Hulme, Owen Robinson, and Lesley Wylie. Liverpool: Liverpool University Press. 49–74.

Denning, Michael (1996). *The Cultural Front: The Laboring of American Culture*. London: Verso.

Di Leo, Jeffrey R., ed. (2014). *Criticism after Critique: Aesthetics, Literature, and the Political*. New York: Palgrave Macmillan.

Dubey, Madhu (2020). "Museumizing Slavery: Living History in Colson Whitehead's *The Underground Railroad*." *American Literary History* 32 (1), 111–39.

—— (2010). "Neo-slave Narratives." *A Companion to African American Literature*. Ed. Gene Andrew Jarrett. Malden: Wiley-Blackwell. 332–46.

Eaglestone, Robert (2013). *Contemporary Fiction: A Very Short Introduction*. Oxford: Oxford University Press.

Eagleton, Terry (2015). *Hope Without Optimism*. New Haven: Yale University Press.

English, James F. (2005). *The Economy of Prestige: Prizes, Awards, and the Circulation of Cultural Value*. Cambridge: Harvard University Press.

Eyers, Tom (2017). *Speculative Formalism: Literature, Theory, and the Critical Present*. Evanston, IL: Northwestern University Press.

Felski, Rita (2022). *Hooked: Art and Attachment*. Chicago: University of Chicago Press.

—— (2015). *The Limits of Critique*. Chicago: University of Chicago Press.

—— (2011). "'Context Stinks!'" *New Literary History* 42 (4), 573–91.

Figueroa, Víctor (2013). "Disseminating 'El Chivo': Junot Díaz's Response to Mario Vargas Llosa in *The Brief Wondrous Life of Oscar Wao*." *Chasqui: revista de literatura latinoamericana* 42 (1), 95–108.

Fisher, Mark (2009). *Capitalist Realism. Is There No Alternative?* Winchester and Washington: Zero Books.

Fisher, Mark, and Jodi Dean (2014). "We Can't Afford to be Realists. A Conversation with Mark Fisher." *Reading Capitalist Realism*. Ed Alison Shonkwiler and Leigh Claire La Berge. Iowa City: University of Iowa Press. 26–38.

Fritz, Robert K. (2019). "Gender and Genre Fiction in the Brief Wondrous Life of Oscar Wao." *Chasqui* 48 (1), 206–23.

Frow, John (2009). *Genre*. The New Critical Idiom. New York: Routledge.

Fukuyama, Francis (1992). *The End of History and the Last Man*. New York: Free Press.

Gallagher, Catherine (2011). "What Would Napoleon Do?: Historical, Fictional, and Counterfactual Characters." *New Literary History* 42 (2), Spring 2011, 315–36.

Ghosal, Nilanjana (2020). "Gothicizing American History: Religion, Race, and Politics in Joyce Carol Oates' *The Accursed*." *IUP Journal of English Studies* 15 (2), 14–24.

González, Christopher (2015). *Reading Junot Díaz*. Pittsburgh: University of Pittsburgh Press.

Graulund, Rune (2014). "Generous Exclusion: Register and Readership in Junot Díaz's 'The Brief Wondrous Life of Oscar Wao.'" *MELUS* 39 (3), 31–48.

Gula, Mark (2012). "What's Going On: Resurrecting the American Political Novel in Chris Bachelder's *U.S.!*" *Midwestern Quarterly* 54 (1), 23–37.

Hanna, Monica (2010). "'Reassembling the Fragments': Battling Historiographies, Caribbean Discourse, and Nerd Genres in Junot Díaz's *The Brief Wondrous Life of Oscar Wao*." *Callaloo* 33 (2), 498–520.

Hanna, Monica, Jennifer Harford Vargas, and José David Saldívar, eds. (2016). *Junot Díaz and the Decolonial Imagination*. Durham: Duke University Press.

Harman, Graham (2012). *Weird Realism: Lovecraft and Philosophy*. Winchester and Washington: Zero Books.

Harvey, David (2011). *The Enigma of Capital and the Crises of Capitalism*. London: Profile Books.

Hayden, Patrick (2009). "Globalization, Reflexive Utopianism, and the Cosmopolitan Social Imaginary." *Globalization and Utopia: Critical Essays*. Ed. Patrick Hayden and Chamsy el-Ojeili. London and New York: Palgrave Macmillan. 51–67.

Hayden, Patrick, and Chamsy el-Ojeili, eds. (2009). *Globalization and Utopia: Critical Essays*. London and New York: Palgrave Macmillan.

Higgins, David M., and Hugh C. O'Connell, eds. (2019). *Speculative Finance/Speculative Fiction*. Special Issue of *CR: The New Centennial Review* 19 (1).

Hobbes, Calvin (1985). "The Dynamics of Interbeing and Monological Imperatives in *Dick and Jane*: A Study in Psychic Transrelational Gender Modes." *Antinomies of Contemporary Theory*. Ed. William Watterson. Arkham, MA: Miskatonic University Press.

Hoberek, Andrew (2017)."Post-Recession Realism." *Neoliberalism and Contemporary Literary Culture*. Ed. Mitchum Huehls and Rachel Greenwald Smith. Baltimore: Johns Hopkins University Press. 237–52.

Huehls, Mitchum (2018). "Historical Fiction and the End of History." *American Literature in Transition, 2000–2010*. Ed. Rachel Greenwald Smith. Cambridge: Cambridge University Press. 138–51.

Hutcheon, Linda (1988). *A Poetics of Postmodernism: History, Theory, Fiction*. London: Routledge.

Jacoby, Russell (2005). *Picture Imperfect: Utopian Thought for an Anti-Utopian Age*. New York: Columbia University Press.

—— (2000). *The End of Utopia: Politics and Culture in an Age of Apathy*. New York: Basic Books.

Jameson, Fredric (2019). *Allegory and Ideology*. London: Verso.

—— (2015a). "The Aesthetics of Singularity." *New Left Review* 92, 101–32.

—— (2015b). "In Hyperspace." Review of Wittenberg, David. *Time Travel: The Popular Philosophy of Narrative*. New York: Fordham, 2013. *London Review of Books* 37 (17), 17–22. Web.

—— (2013). *The Antinomies of Realism*. London: Verso.

—— (2009). *Valences of the Dialectic*. London: Verso.

—— (2005). *Archaeologies of the Future: The Desire Called Utopia and Other Science Fictions*. London: Verso.

—— (2003). "The End of Temporality." *Critical Inquiry* 29 (4), 695–718.

—— (1998). *The Cultural Turn. Selected Writing on the Postmodern, 1983–1998*. London: Verso.

—— (1995). *The Geopolitical Aesthetic. Cinema and Space in the World System*. Bloomington: Indiana University Press.

—— (1991). *Postmodernism, Or: The Cultural Logic of Late Capitalism*. Durham and New York: Duke University Press.

—— (1983). *The Political Unconscious: Narrative as a Socially Symbolic Act*. London and New York: Routledge.

—— (1979). "Reification and Utopia in Mass Culture." *Social Text* 1, 130–48.

Jones, Angela, ed. (2013). *A Critical Inquiry into Queer Utopias*. Basingstoke: Palgrave Macmillan.

Jones, Ellen (2018). "'The página is still blanca': Reading the Blanks in Junot Díaz's *The Brief Wondrous Life of Oscar Wao*." *Hispanic Research Journal* 19 (3), 281–95.

Kelly, Adam (2018). "Freedom to Struggle: The Ironies of Colson Whitehead." *Open Library of the Humanities* 4 (2), 1–35.

King, Stephen (2013). "Bride of Hades: Joyce Carol Oates's *The Accursed*." *New York Times*. Web.

Konstantinou, Lee (2017). "Critique Has Its Uses." *Focus: Postcritique*. Ed. Matthew Mullins. Special Issue of *American Book Review* 38 (5), 15–18.

—— (2014). "Another Novel is Possible: Muckraking in Chris Bachelder's *U.S.!* and Robert Newman's *The Fountain at the Center of the World*."

Blast, Corrupt, Dismantle, Erase: Contemporary North American Dystopian Literature. Ed. Brett J. Grubisic, Gisèle M. Baxter, and Tara Lee. Waterloo: Wilfried Laurier University Press. 453–74.

—— (2013). "Periodizing the Present." *Contemporary Literature* 54 (2), 411–23.

Kornbluh, Anna (2017). "We Have Never Been Critical: Toward the Novel as Critique." *Novel: A Forum on Fiction* 50 (3), 397–408.

Lane, K. Maria D. (2010). *Geographies of Mars: Seeing and Knowing the Red Planet*. Chicago: University of Chicago Press

Lanzendörfer, Tim (2020). "The Novel Network and the Work of Genre." *The Novel as Network: Form, Idea, Commodity*. Ed. Tim Lanzendörfer and Corinna Norrick-Rühl. Cham: Palgrave Macmillan. 69–86.

—— (2019). "Toward the American World-Novel: The Aesthetics and Politics of Transnationalism and Cosmopolitanism in Aleksandar Hemon's *Nowhere Man* (2002), Teju Cole's *Open City* (2011), and Peter Mountfords's *A Young Man's Guide to Late Capitalism* (2011)." *The American Novel in the Twenty-First Century*. Ed. Michael Basseler and Ansgar Nünning. Trier: WVT. 135–52.

—— (2018). *Books of the Dead: The Zombie in Contemporary Literature*. Jackson: University Press of Mississippi.

—— (2015). *The Contemporary Novel and the Poetics of Genre*. Lanham, MD: Lexington Books.

—— (2013). "The Marvellous History of the Dominican Republic in Junot Diaz's 'The Brief Wondrous Life of Oscar Wao.'" *MELUS* 38 (2), 127–42.

Lanzendörfer, Tim, and Mathias Nilges (2019). "Literary Studies after Postcritique: An Introduction." *Literary Studies after Postcritique*. Ed. Tim Lanzendörfer and Mathias Nilges. Special Issue of *Amerikastudien/ American Studies* 64 (4).

Lauret, Maria (2016). "'Your Own Goddamn Idiom': Junot Díaz's Translingualism in *The Brief Wondrous Life of Oscar Wao*." *Studies in the Novel* 48 (4), 494–512.

Lavender, Isiah III, and Lisa Yaszek, eds. (2020). *Literary Afrofuturism in the Twenty-First Century*. Columbus: Ohio State University Press.

Lecercle, Jean-Jacques (2010). *Badiou and Deleuze Read Literature*. Edinburgh: Edinburgh University Press.

LeGuin, Ursula K. (2017). *No Time to Spare: Thinking about What Matters*. Boston and New York: Houghton Mifflin Harcourt.

—— (1969). *The Left Hand of Darkness*. New York: Ace.

Lesjak, Carolyn (2014). "Reading Dialectically." *Literary Materialisms*. Ed. Mathias Nilges and Emilio Sauri. Basingstoke: Palgrave Macmillan. 17–48.

Levine, Caroline (2015). *Forms: Whole, Rhythm, Hierarchy, Network*. Princeton: Princeton University Press.

Levitas, Ruth (2013). *Utopia as Method: The Imaginary Reconstitution of Society*. Basingstoke: Palgrave Macmillan.

—— (2010). *The Concept of Utopia*. Berlin: Peter Lang.

Levy, Ze'ev (1990). "Utopia and Reality in the Philosophy of Ernst Bloch." *Utopian Studies* 1 (2), 3–12.

Leypoldt, Günter (2018). "Social Dimensions of the Turn to Genre: Junot Díaz's *Oscar Wao* and Kazuo Ishiguor's *The Buried Giant*." *Post45*. Web.

—— (2016). "Degrees of Public Relevance: Walter Scott and Toni Morrison." *Modern Language Quarterly* 77 (3), 369–93.

—— (2014). "Singularity and the Literary Market." *New Literary History* 45, 71–88.

Löffler, Philipp (2015). *Pluralist Desires: Contemporary Historical Fiction and the End of the Cold War*. Rochester: Camden House.

López-Calvo, Ignacio (2009). "A Postmodern Plátano's Trujillo: Junot Díaz's *The Brief Wondrous Life of Oscar Wao*, More Macondo than McOndo." *Antípodas: Journal of Hispanic and Galician Studies* 20, 75–90.

Lukács, Georg (1983). *The Historical Novel*. Lincoln: University of Nebraska Press.

Lyotard, Jean-François (1984). *The Postmodern Condition: A Report on Knowledge*. Transl. Geoff Bennington and Brian Massumi. Manchester: Manchester University Press.

McCracken, Ellen (2016). *Paratexts and Performance in the Novels of Junot Díaz and Sandra Cisneros*. Basingstoke: Palgrave Macmillan.

McGurl, Mark (2021). *Everything and Less: The Novel in the Age of Amazon*. London: Verso.

—— (2009). *The Program Era: Postwar Fiction and the Rise of Creative Writing*. Cambridge: Harvard University Press.

Machado Sáez, Elena (2011). "Dictating Desire, Dictating Diaspora. Junot Díaz's *The Brief Wondrous Life of Oscar Wao* as Foundational Romance." *Contemporary Literature* 52 (3), 522–55.

McLennan, Rachael (2020). "'We Cannot Create': The Limits of History in Joyce Carol Oates's *The Accursed*." *21st Century US Historical Fiction: Contemporary Responses to the Past*. Ed. Ruth Maxey. Cham: Palgrave Macmillan. 95–110.

Mahler, Anne Garland (2010). "The Writer as Superhero: Fighting the Colonial Curse in Junot Díaz's *The Brief Wondrous Life of Oscar Wao*." *Journal of Latin American Cultural Studies* 19 (2), 119–40.

Manske, Eva (1992). "The Nightmare of Reality: Gothic Fantasies and Psychological Realism in the Fiction of Joyce Carol Oates." *Neo-realism in Contemporary American Fiction*. Ed. Kristiaan Versluys. Amsterdam: Rodopi. 131–43.

Martin, Theodore (2016). *Contemporary Drift: Genre, Historicism, and the Problem of the Present*. Baltimore: Johns Hopkins University Press.

Marx, Karl, and Friedrich Engels (1993). *Capital, Vol. 1*. Collected Works, Vol. 35. London: Lawrence & Wishart.

Miéville, China (2002). "Editorial Introduction." *Symposium: Marxism and Fantasy*. Special Issue of *Historical Materialism* 10 (4), 39–49.

Miller, T.S. (2011). "Preternatural Narration and the Lens of Genre Fiction in Junot Díaz's *The Brief Wondrous Life of Oscar Wao*." *Science Fiction Studies* 38 (1), 92–114.

Moi, Toril (2017). *Revolution of the Ordinary: Literary Studies after Wittgenstein*. Chicago: University of Chicago Press.

Morris, Christopher, ed. (1999). *Conversations with E.L. Doctorow*. Jackson: University Press of Mississippi.

Muñoz, José Esteban (2009). *Cruising Utopia: The Then and There of Queer Futurity*. New York: New York University Press.

Nealon, Jeffrey (2012). *Post-Postmodernism: Or, The Cultural Logic of Just-in-Time Capitalism*. Stanford: Stanford University Press.

Nilges, Mathias (2021). *How to Read a Moment: The American Novel and the Crisis of the Present*. Evanston, IL: Northwestern University Press.

Nilges, Mathias, and Tim Lanzendörfer, eds. (2023). *Futures of Literary Studies*. Special Issue of *Textual Practice* 37 (2).

Nordstrom, Justin (2016). "'A Pleasant Place for the World to Hide': Exploring Themes of Utopian Play in *Ready Player One*." *Interdisciplinary Literary Studies* 18 (2), 238–56.

Oates, Joyce Carol (2007a). "Afterword (2007) to *The Mysteries of Winterthurn*." Web. Accessed 03.02.2015.

—— (2007b). *The Journal of Joyce Carol Oates, 1973–1982*. New York: HarperCollins.

—— (1988). "Preface to *The Mysteries of Winterthurn*." *Woman(Writer): Occasions and Opportunities*. New York: E.P. Dutton.

—— (1985). "Afterword (1985) to *The Mysteries of Winterthurn*." Web.

—— (1980). "Author's Note." *Bellefleur*. New York: E.P. Dutton.

Parrish, Timothy (2008). *From the Civil War to the Apocalypse: Postmodern History and American Fiction*. Amherst: University of Massachusetts Press.

Perez, Richard (2012). "Flashes of Transgression: The Fukú, Negative Aesthetics, and the Future in *The Brief Wondrous Life of Oscar Wao*." *Moments of Magical Realism in US Ethnic Literatures*. Ed. Lyn di Iorio Sandín and Richard Perez. Basingstoke: Palgrave Macmillan. 91–108.

Pierce, Jason E. (2016). *Making the White Man's West: Whiteness and the Creation of the American West*. Boulder: University of Colorado Press.

Pifano, Diana (2014). "Reinterpreting the Diaspora and the Political Violence of the Trujillo Regime: The Fantastic as a Tool for Cultural Mediation in *The Brief Wondrous Life of Oscar Wao*." *Belphégor: Littératures populaires et culture médiatique* 12 (1). Web.

Pizzino, Christopher (2020). "Can a Novel Contain a Comic? Graphic Nerd Ecology in Contemporary U.S. Fiction." *The Novel as Network: Forms, Ideas, Commodities*. Ed. Tim Lanzendörfer and Corinna Norrick-Rühl. Cham: Palgrave Macmillan. 87–110.

Poster, Mark (2001). *The Information Subject: Essays*. Commented by Stanley Aronowitz. Amsterdam: G+B Arts International.

Rancière, Jacques (2011). *The Politics of Literature*. Transl. Julie Rose. Cambridge: Polity Press.

—— (2010). *Dissensus: On Politics and Aesthetics*. Ed. and transl. Steve Corcoran. London: Continuum.

—— (2006). *The Politics of Aesthetics: The Distribution of the Sensible*. Ed. and transl. Gabriel Rockhill. London: Continuum.

Reinhard, Kenneth (2013). "Introduction: Badiou's Sublime Translation of the *Republic*." Alain Badiou. *Plato's Republic: A Dialogue in 16 Chapters*. Transl. Susan Spitzer. New York: Columbia University Press. vii–xxiii.

Ricœur, Paul (1986). *Lectures on Ideology and Utopia*. New York: Columbia University Press.

Robbins, Bruce (2022). *Criticism and Politics: A Polemical Introduction*. Stanford: Stanford University Press.

Rodríguez Navas, Ana (2017). "Words as Weapons: Gossip in Junot Díaz's *The Brief Wondrous Life of Oscar Wao*." *MELUS* 42 (3), 55–83.

Rosario-Vélez, Jorge (2018). "Virginidad masculina, homofobia y la nueva mujer dominicana en the brief wondrous life of Oscar Wao de Junot Díaz." *Chasqui: revista de literatura latinoamericana* 47 (2), 204–17.

Rosen, Jeremy (2018). "Literary Fiction and the Genres of Genre Fiction." *Post45*. Web.

Rushdy, Ashraf (1999). *Neo-slave Narratives: Studies in the Social Logic of a Literary Form*. New York and Oxford: Oxford University Press.

Saldívar, José David (2016). "Junot Díaz's Search for Decolonial Aesthetics and Love." *Junot Díaz and the Decolonial Imagination*. Ed. Monica Hanna, Jennifer Harford Vargas, and José David Saldívar. Durham: Duke University Press. 321–50.

—— (2011a). "Conjectures on 'Americanity' and Junot Díaz's 'Fukú Americanus' in *The Brief Wondrous Life of Oscar Wao*." *The Global South* 5 (1), 120–36.

—— (2011b). *Transamericanity: Subaltern Modernities, Global Coloniality, and the Cultures of Greater Mexico*. Durham: Duke University Press.

Saldívar, Ramón (2013). "The Second Elevation of the Novel: Race, Form, and the Postrace Aesthetic in Contemporary Narrative." *Narrative* 21 (1), 1–18.

—— (2011). "Historical Fantasy, Speculative Realism, and Postrace Aesthetics in Contemporary American Fiction." *American Literary History* 23 (3), 574–99.

Sanchez-Taylor, Joy (2014). "'I was a Ghetto Nerd Supreme': Science Fiction, Fantasy and Latina/o Futurity in Junot Díaz's *The Brief Wondrous Life of Oscar Wao*." *Journal of the Fantastic in the Arts* 25 (1), 93–106.

Santana-Acuña, Álvaro (2020). *Ascent to Glory: How* One Hundred Years of Solitude *Was Written and Became a Global Classic*. New York: Columbia University Press.

Schulenburg, Chris (2016). "Nerd Nation: *La breve my maravillosa vida de* Óscar *Wao* and Life in Tolkien's Universe." *MLN* 131 (2), 503–16.

Shapiro, Stephen (2017). "The Culture of Realignment: *Enlightened* and 'I can't breathe.'" *Navigating the Transnational in Modern American Literature and Culture*. Ed. Tara Stubbs and Doug Haynes. London: Routledge. 144–61.

—— (2016). "Realignment and Televisual Intellect: The Telepraxis of Class Alliances in Contemporary Subscription Television Drama." *Class Divisions in Serial Television*. Ed. Sieglinde Lemke and Wibke Schniedermann. Basingstoke: Palgrave Macmillan. 177–205.

Shapiro, Stephen, and Neil Lazarus (2018). "Translatability, Combined Unevenness, and World Literature in Antonio Gramsci." *Mediations* 32 (1), 1–36.

Shonkwiler, Alison (2017). *The Financial Imaginary: Economic Mystification and the Limits of Realist Fiction*. Minneapolis: University of Minnesota Press.

Shonkwiler, Alison, and Leigh Claire La Berge, eds. (2014). *Reading Capitalist Realism*. Iowa City: University of Iowa Press.

Sim, Stuart (1999). *Derrida and the End of History*. New York: Icon Books.

Sinclair, Upton (2003). *The Jungle*. New York: W.W. Norton.

Spooner, Catherine (2007). *Contemporary Gothic*. London: Reaktion Books.

Su, John J. (2005). *Ethics and Nostalgia in the Contemporary Novel*. Cambridge: Cambridge University Press.

Suvin, Darko (2010). *Defined by a Hollow: Essays on Utopia, Science Fiction, and Political Epistemology*. Bern: Peter Lang.

—— (2000). "Considering the Sense of 'Fantasy' or 'Fantastic Fiction.'" *Extrapolation* 41 (3), 209–47.

—— (1977). *Metamorphoses of Science Fiction: On the Poetics and History of a Literary Genre*. New Haven: Yale University Press.

Tally, Robert T., Jr. (2022). *For a Ruthless Critique of All that Exists: Literature in an Age of Capitalist Realism*. Winchester: Zero Books.

—— (2013). *Utopia in the Age of Globalization*. New York: Palgrave Macmillan.

Thompson, Peter, ed. (2013). *The Privatization of Hope: Ernst Bloch and the Future of Utopia*. Durham and London: Duke University Press.

Torres-Saillant, Silvio (2016). "Artistry, Ancestry, and Americanness in the Works of Junot Díaz." *Junot Díaz and the Decolonial Imagination*. Ed. Monica Hanna, Jennifer Harford Vargas, and José David Saldívar. Durham: Duke University Press. 115–46.

Vargas, Jennifer Harford (2014). "Dictating a Zafa: The Power of Narrative Form in Junot Díaz's *The Brief Wondrous Life of Oscar Wao*." *MELUS* 39 (3), 8–30.

Vertovec, Steven (2009). *Transnationalism*. New York: Routledge.

Wallerstein, Immanuel (2004). *World-Systems Analysis: An Introduction*. Durham and London: Duke University Press.

—— (1998). *Utopistics: Or Historical Choices of the Twenty-First Century*. New York: New Press.

—— (1991). "The Ideological Tensions of Capitalism: Universalism versus Racism and Sexism." *Race, Nation, Class: Ambiguous Identities*. Ed. Etienne Balibar and Immanuel Wallerstein. London: Verso. 29–36.
Walpole, Horace (1769). *The Castle of Otranto*. London: J. Murray.
Warnes, Christopher (2009). *Magical Realism and the Postcolonial Novel: Between Faith and Irreverence*. London: Palgrave.
Watanabe, Nancy Ann (1998). *Love Eclipsed: Joyce Carol Oates's Faustian Moral Vision*. Lanham: University Press of America.
Wegner, Phillip (2020). *Invoking Hope: Theory and Utopia in Dark Times*. Minneapolis: University of Minnesota Press.
—— (2011). *Shockwaves of Possibility: Essays on Science Fiction, Globalization, and Utopia*. Oxford: Peter Lang.
—— (2009). *Life Between Two Deaths, 1989–2001: U.S. Culture in the Long Nineties*. Durham: Duke University Press.
Williams, Evan Calder (2011). *Combined and Uneven Apocalypse: Luciferian Marxism*. Winchester: Zero Books.
Williams, Raymond L. (1995). *The Postmodern Novel in Latin America: Politics, Culture, and the Crisis of Truth*. New York: St. Martin's Press.
Womack, Ytasha L. (2013). *Afrofuturism: The World of Black Sci-Fi and Fantasy*. Chicago: Chicago Review Press
Zamalin, Alex (2019). *A Black Utopia: The History of an Idea from Black Nationalism to Afrofuturism*. New York: Columbia University Press.
Zipes, Jack (1988). "Introduction: Toward a Realization of Anticipatory Illumination." Ernst Bloch. *The Utopian Function of Art and Literature: Selected Essays*. Transl. Jack Zipes and Frank Mecklenburg. Cambridge: MIT Press. xi–xliii.
Žižek, Slavoj (2018). *The Courage of Hopelessness: Chronicles of a Year of Living Dangerously*. London: Allen Lane.
—— (2014a). *Event*. London: Penguin.
—— (2014b). *Trouble in Paradise: From the End of History to the End of Capitalism*. London: Allen Lane.

Index